"El Diablo . . . Rodrigo . . ." She had thought that she was dreaming at first but realized now that the kiss had been real. She smiled sleepily, bringing her hand up to touch her lips.

"Do not worry, señorita. I will not harm you."

"I know." She was all too achingly aware of the warmth emanating from his gaze, the longing that his kiss had evoked deep within her. No longer could she deny the truth of what she felt for this bandit. Angelica was suddenly aware of her body as she had never been before. Meeting Rodrigo's eyes she felt a tingle in the pit of her stomach, knew the urge to reach out and bring him back to kiss her again.

"Señorita . . ."

"Angelica. Say it. My name is Angelica." She wanted to hear her name on his lips. Wanted that and more. She had never before been curious about what went on between a man and a woman but now she was. She had never felt desire until he kissed her but now she knew his kiss was a prelude to something much more wonderful . . .

Angel of Passion

KATHRYN HOCKETT

ZEBRA BOOKS
KENSINGTON PUBLISHING CORP.

ZEBRA BOOKS

are published by

Kensington Publishing Corp.
475 Park Avenue South
New York, NY 10016

First printing: January, 1989

Printed in the United States of America

This book is lovingly dedicated to the newest member of the family—Aric Wesley Hockett—grandson and nephew.

A thank-you to Ervin O. Kramer for taking us up the coast to the mission at Santa Barbara. It was there this story began.

And once again to Lydia Paglio, editor, mentor, and friend, whose expertise has worked magic. I value your opinion and know beyond a doubt that my writing is better because of you. You have been a wonderful teacher. Better yet you care, and it shows. Thank you, my friend. Here's to the future!

Author's Note

The history of Spanish California dates back to 1493, just after the discovery of America. However, European settlement did not take place until 1769. During the interim period the mission system grew, dotting the area from north to south with the splendid architecture of the Franciscans. Entire villages complete with church, shops, schools, and thriving farmlands tilled by the converted Indians, became landmarks of Spanish rule. Orchards, vineyards, and flower gardens flourished in a land that some had once called "barren" Indian territory.

The occupation, conquest, and settlement of California, the "golden state," was a cooperative enterprise on the part of State and Church. It was a peaceful conquest, carried out in a Christian manner, though military and political reasons prompted it. Over a period of almost three centuries Spanish explorers blazed an awesome spiderweb of trails across the West and opened a wilderness nearly five times the size of Spain. Spain, however, let California slip through its grasp and with it a most valuable treasure, both in gold ore and land.

Mexico nearly made the same mistake when it obtained California along with its independence in 1821. There were no courts, no schools, and little or no available communication with Mexico City. Under loose Mexican rule the missions began to crumble slowly into ruin and vast landholdings were seized and sold. Few churches survived though some courageous friars hung on. Indian converts were turned loose to survive on their own with near-tragic results. One era had come to an end, another had begun.

When the Americans arrived in the mid-nineteenth century they found a small and scattered population which had at its core the wealthy and aristocratic *caballeros,* some barbaric, some elegant. It was a society of great riches or desolate poverty, similar to that of the Old South, a land of *ranchos* whose territory swept for miles amidst a riot of color in spring. Having no middle class, the poor standard of living led to the emergence of bandits, who robbed from the rich to survive.

Despite the social conditions, however, the Americans were charmed by the beauty of California. President James K. Polk saw promise for this territory, even though it was far from the borders of the United States. It was assumed that California could be infiltrated as Texas had been; thus Americans were sent in droves to settle there.

The Mexican Californians welcomed the Americans at first, until the Mexican-American War embroiled them in its clutches. Angered by John C. Fremont's actions, the Californios took up arms against the invaders and Southern California became a battleground. The once colorful land became bathed in blood.

It is against this backdrop that a young beautiful woman, leaving the confines of her life behind convent walls, meets the only man she will ever love, a bandit. Devil and angel, Mexican and gringo, bandit and postulant, their love will face the ultimate test.

Part One:

The Captive Angel

California Territory—1845

"Be not forgetful to entertain strangers: for thereby some have entertained angels unawares."

—New Testament, Hebrews, XIII, 2

Chapter One

Dark clouds hovered high above the hillside abbey, releasing rain on the wooded hills and jagged mountains below. The air smelled of nature's rebirth, of grasses, flowers, and leaves. The young woman breathed the fragrance in deeply as she leaned over the stone window-sill. Raindrops spattered her spectacles as she looked about at the splendid scenery. There was a promise of spring and the joy and happiness the season would bring. To Angelica Howe, however, it meant her time of decision had drawn very near, that moment when she would be taking her vows as a novice, to live a life of seclusion behind the abbey's walls.

"Dear Lord, please guide me in making the right decision," she whispered aloud, raising her eyes as if she might look into *His* face.

The sudden doubts sprang from the good-natured teasing of her companions and fellow postulants, comments which caused Angelica to look deep within her heart. Was she taking these most holy vows because she sought to serve God or because of her brother's prodding? Was it her shyness that led her to want to live a sheltered life behind cloistered walls? Was it devotion and love that led her on, or fear? Fear of this often hostile land of

California where violence and lawlessness had been responsible for her parents' deaths.

"Ah, Angelica, I thought I would find you here." Mother Bernadette's low, soothing voice startled Angelica out of her musings as she turned around to stare into her kindly superior's face, a face lined faintly with wrinkles. Roadmaps of wisdom, Mother Bernadette called them.

"I was watching the rain and thinking . . ."

"Thinking so diligently that you forgot you were to meet me in the library?" Though her tone of voice was scolding, the round face did not lose any trace of Mother Bernadette's smile. "Ah, Angelica, Angelica, what am I to do with you? How often must I tell you that discipline is essential to your calling? With a head full of dreams you cannot fully serve God. There is more to being a bride of Christ than saying your prayers."

The Mother Superior's deep-set gray eyes studied the young face. Angelica's blue eyes were hidden by thick spectacles but lovely nonetheless, and the straight nose, high cheekbones, and gently curving mouth made up a nearly perfect face. The only imperfection was the overly high forehead which blended with pale-blonde hair. Anxiety creased that forehead now.

"I was not daydreaming, Mother Bernadette. I was doing as you bid me, giving all my thoughts to looking within my heart. I've tried to cast away all my doubts but there are still some lurking in a little corner of my mind. They nag at me, telling me I am not truly ready to take my vows. Perhaps I am a foolish dreamer. I do spend more time than I should on my own private cloud. Although I've tried and tried, every now and then when I hear a bird sing or smell a rose I find myself transported beyond my lessons. Still, I cannot help but think that God understands. It was He who made the birds and gave the flowers their fragrance and He who gave me an imagination capable of dreaming."

"Then you have your answer, by your own words, my child. You are *not* ready to take your vows. As long as there is even a flicker of doubt you must wait." Hurriedly she reached out to touch the young girl's arm. "But there are other ways to serve God. I have seen the smiles you have brought to the little children. They love you, Angelica. You are a most able teacher. You do not have to be a holy sister to give your heart and time to them."

"I love the children, all children." Her full pink lips broke into a smile. "They make me think of angels, untouched by greed or malice until they are taught hatred and other sins by adults."

"Angels? I might well imagine there are those among them who are more devil. Manuel for instance. I can still feel the lizard he put in my shoe. And Ramón with his constant pranks. I have not the patience with such things as do you." The bell sounded for matins and Mother Bernadette motioned for Angelica to walk beside her toward the small chapel, talking quietly as they made their way. "Which brings me to the point of this conversation. I must speak quickly while there is time. Today at noon a small caravan is traveling to Santa Barbara, to the mission. It is our order's intent to teach the small children, Indian children there. If you would want I am prepared to request that you be allowed to accompany them. It will give you time to consider this matter of your vows away from the abbey's walls so that you can come to an unbiased decision."

"Go to Santa Barbara?" The thought of traveling outside the safety of the abbey walls filled her with a brief moment of panic. Was it then her need for security that led her towards the Church? Indians had ruthlessly murdered her mother and father. Could she bear to live among them? She knew she had to conquer her terror or remain always a prisoner of her fear. If she could conquer these feelings which quivered through her now and if she still chose to

13

take her vows, she would be free of all doubts. Only then could she truly serve God. "Yes, I would like to go. I must go, Mother Bernadette. But please, you must get word to my brother. He wrote that he was coming here to see me."

"He is already here, waiting in the courtyard."

"Edward. Here?" There was no more time for talk. As the door of the chapel opened she took her place on the cold, damp floor to kneel before the altar. Her mind was in turmoil, anxious to see her brother, who had taken care of her since their parents' deaths. Though Edward did not always display his affection freely she knew he loved her. It had been his staunch suggestion that she come to the abbey, his hope that she would find security behind its walls. For two long years they had been parted, but now she was going to see him again and that thought quickened the beating of her heart as she mouthed her prayers.

She had always tried to please Edward. Older than Angelica by three years, strong, intelligent, and daringly brave, he had always been a hero to her. At sixteen he had been forced to use all his wiles and what little money had been left to them to keep a roof over their heads and food in their mouths. If it made him a bit edgy and easily prone to anger she could not help but understand. Edward had had little time for childhood. All too quickly he had found it necessary to become a man. Now he was here, and soon she would see him.

When Angelica thought she could no longer stand the waiting, when her knees were stiff from kneeling on the damp floor, another bell rang out heralding breakfast. At last she could speak and poured forth her questions to Mother Bernadette.

"How long is he going to stay? Is he well? Does he look much the same?"

"Only a few hours, yes, and he has grown a fine mustache, to answer your questions in order." Once again

Mother Bernadette smiled. How could she help it when this young woman charmed her so. Angelica reminded her of a young colt, untamed and innocent, yet possessing more strength than the young woman realized. "Your brother is one among the caravan who is taking the sisters to Santa Barbara. You see, my child, if you decide to go, you will be in his company."

"Then my answer is doubly yes! But please, where is he now? I must go to him. It's been so long. . . ."

"After breakfast. Remember what I said about discipline."

Breakfast was the usual porridge and herb tea, though Angelica would hardly have tasted it, even if it had been a feast of delights. The refectory buzzed with the voices of the sisters who welcomed this time to break their silence. But Angelica kept silent. Eating as quickly as she could, she put down her bowl with a wistful eye towards the door. At last she received the Mother Superior's nod of approval and made her way with as much dignity as she could, through the doorway and down the steep, winding stairs, tripping on the skirt of her habit.

Stepping through the courtyard archway she saw the tall, familiar, oh-so beloved form of her brother standing with his back to her, his large hands placed on his slender hips. The pale blond hair so similar to her own left no doubt that it was Edward who stood there. Even so, she gave a start of surprise as he turned around. More than the mustache had changed his appearance. The once straight nose had been broken, his face scarred, the once smiling face now downcast in a frown. Even so, she ran to him, throwing her arms about him as she called out his name.

"So we meet again, little sister." Pulling away from her embrace he cupped her face in his hands, looking deep into her eyes. "You've grown beautiful, despite those windows that you wear at your eyes. Sometimes you remind me so much of Mother." As quickly as a smile

15

formed at his lips, it vanished. "But no more talk of how lovely you look. Now that you are a nun it is a less than fitting conversation."

"I'm not a holy sister. Not yet." Angelica hated so to displease him. Edward had been very anxious for her to take her vows. Would he understand her hesitation? Somehow she'd make him understand. "Mother Bernadette counseled me to wait to take my vows until I knew beyond a shadow of a doubt that I had no reservations."

"She what?" He squinted in anger. "That interfering old windbag!"

"Edward! That is no way to talk. She deserves your respect. She is . . ."

"Yeah . . . well . . ." He dug his booted toe in the dirt, an action she remembered since childhood. Edward never said he was sorry about anything, so she didn't expect it now. Still, his attitude puzzled her. He was not displaying the warmth she had expected. They'd been apart for a long time but all he seemed to be concerned with was that she hadn't taken her vows. Did he consider her a stone around his neck? Had he thought that once she entered the confines of the abbey he would be rid of the responsibility to look after her? No, she couldn't think that of him. Something else was troubling him, that was all.

"In the meantime, I'm going with the caravan . . ."

"You sure as hell are not! I won't have you traipsing about the countryside putting yourself in danger. If not the Indians then the bandits pose a threat. Not to mention the fact a war seems to be brewing."

"I'll be safe with you, I always have been. You've always taken care of me. I'm not afraid." Hesitantly she smiled.

"Well, you should be! You can't understand, you don't know . . ." He broke off as if fearing he might reveal too much and again Angelica was surprised by his reaction. "I won't allow you to go!"

Her answer was gentle but firm as a strong reassurance

16

that she had made the right choice came over her. "It is not for you to say, Edward. It's in God's hands now. When you brought me here you transferred your authority to Him."

"Angie!"

The determined expression written so clearly on her face silenced any further discussion of the matter, though Angelica suffered in full measure the potent glare of fury her brother cast her from time to time. At last he took his leave of her with a mumbled curse, throwing a last comment over his shoulder.

"Whatever happens it will be upon your head and not mine. I wash my hands of your welfare from this very moment. Do you understand, Angie! Whatever happens you will have no call to blame me."

Angelica watched as he ran up the stairs feeling a brief shiver of anxiety and apprehension travel up her spine. Whatever happened she would have to agree that it was her decision to leave the abbey, her desire to go to Santa Barbara.

Chapter Two

Streaks of coral and red appeared on the horizon, reflecting over the hills and valleys. The wide acreage looked to Rodrigo O'Hara's eyes like the gentle curves of a beautiful woman. He had no time, however, to let his gaze appreciate the beauty, for a menacing cloud of dust announced a rider coming his way. God grant that it be the messenger he had been waiting for.

Rising from his seat beside a large cactus, Rodrigo stretched his well-muscled frame and quickly mounted his horse. He set out to meet the other man, reaching towards the leather gunbelt slung low on his hips to assure himself that if the rider proved to be a foe he would be well prepared. When he reached the rider he was not disappointed. The tall, slim figure, dark hair, and bushy black mustache was very familiar and proved to be the man he had been expecting.

"What news have you for me, Margaro?"

"The news I have, amigo, will make you smile. The guns that we are so badly in need of are coming our way," Margaro answered in his gravel-voiced baritone. Even under the gravest of circumstances he always seemed to have a smile beneath his mustache. But he was reliable and gave Rodrigo his strength, his wisdom, and his loyalty. As he looked at him Rodrigo thought that he couldn't have made a better choice for his right-hand man.

"The guns? Do you know this to be a fact?"

"Sí. I have a most reliable source of information." Margaro pointed at his chest. "Me!"

"How many guns? How will they be transported? How many men will there be on guard?" The set of Rodrigo's jaw showed his impatience. He was anxious for all the details, but Margaro, the more complacent of the two, nodded his head and motioned towards a large grove of trees up ahead. "Yes, you are right. There is no need to speak of such matters right now. Come, we will seek the shelter the trees can offer and then we will speak in detail about this."

"Ah, now you see things my way." Margaro grinned and pounded Rodrigo on the back. "I am glad we are amigos, that we are bound together by such strong a bond of friendship."

Together the two men rode off, engaging themselves in a playful test of horsemanship as they raced each other towards the small oasis. As usual Rodrigo won, but Margaro conceded with his good-natured humor.

"You can outride me, outshoot me, outrope me, but I can still outdrink and sometimes outtalk you. As I will prove when we get back to camp." Sitting down beside a large rock, beneath the shade of a sparsely leafed tree, Margaro seemed happy to rest his tired body at last. "I forgive you if you also get all the women. But why not? You are a handsome devil. No doubt the señoritas are mesmerized by those glittering blue eyes of yours, eh?"

"They are eyes like any others. A gift of my half-Irish heritage, that is all, as is this thatch of red-brown hair." Taking off his hat, Rodrigo ran his fingers through the thick, dark waves, remembering how often it had been the object of conversation.

"Ah, a touch of red to hint at your volatile temper. Is it

any wonder there are those who say you are dangerous. Ruthless towards your enemies. But those of us who know you have learned the truth, that you would give up your life to help those in dire need of your friendship. Saving you from that rat-infected prison was no doubt the wisest thing I have ever done, for me and for our people." Taking off his neckerchief he mopped his brow. "If only I had a tequila."

"That will come soon enough. But first you must tell me what you have learned. Speak quickly, Margaro, lest I grow impatient." Lighting a match to the black cigarillo clamped between his straight white teeth, Rodrigo puffed slowly and thoughtfully as Margaro revealed the tale.

Enjoying a good joke and priding himself on his clever disguises, he had donned the garb of a blind beggar to infiltrate a gringo cafe. Holding forth a cup, he had pretended that he had no interest in anything except the coins which were thrown at him from time to time. He had purposely made himself so foolishly bothersome that the Americans had not suspected that he was listening. At last they had ignored him, speaking, their plans in whispery voices, but loud enough that he could hear.

"I heard a gringo with the palest of yellow hair bragging about how clever he is. He has many guns which he is going to hide in a supply wagon carrying medicine and food to a group of Indian children."

At the thought, Rodrigo's mouth narrowed into a bitter line, his blue eyes angry. "So, like all gringos he would use others' misery to aid himself." He felt a kinship with the Indians, for just like the Mexicans they had always been exploited by these lighter skinned men who sought to strip the country bare.

Images burned in his mind, memories of his own abuse at the hands of those who looked down their noses at a boy of mixed heritage. Both Spanish and Irish blood ran in his veins. His loyalties had been divided once but no longer.

21

The gringos' hostility to him had changed that. He was Spanish. His mother's people had been here long before the gringos had pushed west. This land belonged to him and to his people. They would not be pushed into the ocean! He would do whatever must be done to ensure his people's tranquility. If that made him a *bandito*, then so be it. Let the gringos call him what they might. He could not steal that which rightly belonged to him.

"This gringo thought himself to be most clever. He knows that even the most feared bandit has reverence for God. He knows how we respect those who wear God's badge, the priests and the sisters. That is why he seeks to use them as a decoy, to hide his true intent."

"Then we are lost, for I will not risk God's wrath by attacking those of His own. I may be a fearsome bandit, but I am not a fool, Margaro! I need God on *my* side."

"And *He* will be, have no fear! From what I could gather the priests who will be traveling with the caravan will be the gringos' men. I suppose it will be the same with the holy sisters. Imposters! Imagine their surprise when we swoop down upon them!" Opening his mouth, Margaro laughed boisterously. Rodrigo soon joined him. It would be like taking candy from the hands of babes. The gringos would be so certain that they would not be attacked, they could be taken unawares.

"Then we will do it!" Reaching for his cigarillo, Rodrigo tossed it to the ground, grinding it with the heel of his boot. "And just as I have crushed this, amigo, so will I crush these gringos. On that you have the word of El Diablo!"

Chapter Three

The sun was like a torch, blistering the canvas-covered wagons with its heat, and for just a moment Angelica wondered at the wisdom of her haste to join the caravan. Still, one look at the smug expression on her brother's face caused her to hold her tongue. He thought she was a fragile flower and perhaps she was, but she would not admit it now! She was not at all anxious to hear his "I told you so!" Whatever discomfort she might suffer, she was determined not to complain. Even if she melted she would never beg to be taken back to the abbey.

Wearing a plain dark gray dress and not her postulant's garb, Angelica's gown was of homespun cotton, high-necked, and designed to be overly prim and pristine. A wide-brimmed straw hat covered her pale blond hair worn in a bun. Her kerchief proved useful in wiping the perspiration away, which as the caravan continued along became more annoying. She had never dreamed there were places in California that could be this hot!

"Heaven help us! If hell is even half this blistering I pity the sinners who must go there!" Sister Theresa, a short, stocky nun a year or two older than Angelica, voiced her opinion.

There were two of the abbey's sisters accompanying the

caravan, Sister Theresa and Sister Miriam, a woman about forty years old, as tall as Sister Theresa was short. Ten men from the town to the north of the abbey drove three of the wagons and acted as guardsmen in addition to her brother's men, who rode along behind the wagons. There were also three priests, though Angelica had been shocked to hear one of them swearing violently. Had she not seen with her own eyes his priestly apparel she would never have believed this man to be a priest. Angelica told herself, however, that it was not up to her to judge. She supposed that each and every human being had some faults, and perhaps swearing was an evil this man had to overcome.

Angelica had taken little with her, just a few bundles of clothing. In truth, she had few belongings, for Edward was perilously close to a miser. When she had gently complained, he had merely reminded her of her intent to take the veil and the matter had been dropped. Angelica supposed that her brother needed all of the money he possessed and never begrudged him his lavish wardrobe of bright-colored shirts and matching trousers. It was as he said—in his line of business it was important that he look successful. Otherwise he would look like a trader who had come upon hard times, or so he insisted.

The pitted road was rocky, and as she sat upon the hard seat of the second wagon in the cavalcade, Angelica was certain that her backside would never be the same again. The jolt of the wagon jiggled her bones and bruised her tender flesh. Anxiously she adjusted her spectacles and peered down the road, hoping for sight of a tree or cactus, anywhere that they might pause to get some respite from the heat. But there seemed to be no trees at all, just a few scrub bushes and a rock or two.

"I can read the truth on your face, Angie. You are miserable. I warned you." Edward Howe guided his horse beside the wagons wheels as he spoke. Wearing a bright-blue pair of breeches which hugged his long slim legs like

24

a second skin, a cotton shirt of the same hue, sewn with silver beads and braid, a light tan hat with a huge brim and finely crafted brown leather boots he was a handsome man, Angelica thought. The kind of man who would turn many a female's head. Only the holster from which protruded the handle of a revolver and the knife sheathed in the top of his boot gave any hint that this brightly bedecked peacock could also ward off danger. It made Angelica achingly aware of the vulnerability of this caravan.

"I'm not miserable, really Edward. I'm fine. Don't worry. Though I do fear for Sister Miriam. She looks as if she has wilted! How long before we reach our destination?"

"Two hours. Though we have traveled through the worst of it already. Up ahead the foliage is lusher, greener, and hopefully we might have some rain. Until then be sure to wear your bonnet, lest you sunburn your nose." It was the first show of concern he had expressed for her, and Angelica smiled, sensing he was not angry with her any longer.

"I will," she promised, reaching up to push it further down on her forehead. "Thanks for looking after me." She settled back on the seat, but as another half hour passed and every jar of the wagon pinched her spine, she realized that the journey was not in any way going to become easier. Dust from the pathway covered her face like a mask, except for the area around her eyes which her spectacles had protected, and she longed for the sight of water. Just a small cool pool where she could wash her face. Even so, she found some humor in the situation as Sister Theresa stifled a grin.

"You look like a raccoon," the sister ventured, "except that your mask is light instead of black. Tell me, am I just as covered with grime?"

Angelica answered that she was, taking the kerchief

25

from around her neck, sprinkling water from a canteen on it and reaching out to wipe Sister Theresa's face and then her own.

"Listen, I think I hear the sound of birds!" That was a thought which cheered her, yet Angelica heard another sound as well. The muffled sound of horses' hooves came from the distance, setting her nerves suddenly on edge, reminding her of another time she had heard such a sound. "Indians!" she shrieked before she could hide her terror.

"Not Indians but much worse," a man poised nearby her answered. *Bandits!* Pointing towards the horizon, he gave proof to his words as a swarm that had once looked like ants now took shape and form.

"Bandits?" To Angelica's mind it seemed far better to deal with desperados than savages, but as events ensued she was proven to be wrong. The galloping, mustached men they faced right now seemed capable of anything. Watching from the wagon she saw several of her brother's men felled, heard the shots ring out that took their lives, and cringed in horror. Sister Theresa had spoken of hell; now Angelica was certain that that was just where they were. Surely that fearfully awaited place could hold no greater terror. Screams and gunfire echoed through the air as the men of the wagon train were quickly overcome. Angelica was ordered to get down from the wagon and join the others in a circle.

It seemed hundreds of guns were pointed at her, yet as she counted she assessed the number to be thirty-five. Behind each one was a face which looked unnervingly angry. Every bandit looked capable of pulling the trigger without giving it a second thought and Angelica trembled uncontrollably. How she managed to speak she would never know, but somehow speak she did.

"What kind of men are you to attack a supply wagon with needed goods for those in danger of dying? We have nothing but medical supplies and food!" Angelica's words

26

were met by laughter, which rumbled forth like thunder.

"Food? Supplies?" A paunchy bandit nodded his head and several of the caravan's captors attacked one of the wagons, ripping at the boards, splintering the wood until they found just what they were after. "It is guns that we seek. We have enough food." The incriminating crate was pushed out by two of the brawnier Mexicans.

"Guns?" Angelica was confused. Her brother had made no mention of weapons. She watched in stunned silence as crate after crate was uncovered.

"Margaro! Do you suppose there are more guns where these came from?" she heard another bandit ask. "Perhaps we should see."

"I think we should assume that there are, amigo."

Both men busied themselves in their search for rifles, uncovering an added bounty in the form of bars of gold. So intent were they that they did not see the black-garbed priest behind them with a large rock in his hands. Angelica held her breath, fearing a tragedy was about to ensue. It came more quickly than she realized as the bandit with the dark mustache whirled around, striking out at the priest, rendering him senseless.

"You dare to strike a man of God!" Sister Miriam voiced Angelica's thoughts.

"He is no more a priest than I am!" The truth of that accusation was soon revealed, for beneath the black robe and white collar, the man was dressed in buckskin pants and a muslin shirt. "It is but a clever device, a ruse to fool us. But we are not as foolish as you gringos suppose, eh." Tauntingly he walked round and round the middle-aged nun. "Nor do I think you are who you profess to be."

"I beg your pardon!" A flush of red stained the sister's cheeks. "How dare you! May God have mercy on your soul."

Twirling the ends of his dark mustache he smiled. "Shall I look beneath your gown so that I can see for

27

myself if you too are a fraud?" In answer, the frightened sister scurried away, to seek safety in one of the wagons. A rippling sound of laughter accompanied her flight. "Bah, that one has no sense of humor, eh?"

"Margaro!" The voice was so commanding, so filled with power that Angelica involuntarily sought out the owner with her eyes. She had not noticed this bandit before, a tall man with wide shoulders garbed completely in black except for his brown leather boots. Shining silver spurs jingled as he walked. Angelica drew back as he approached her. "Leave the woman alone. I will not have it said that El Diablo is a brute. I will not have you torment them." She knew instinctively that this was the bandit leader. He looked ominous and frightening, like a wild beast about to strike.

"*Sí! Sí!*, El Diablo. I was just having a bit of fun. Trying to teach them not to try and fool us again."

"I think they have learned their lesson well."

For the first time his eyes settled on Angelica, eyeing her with a grimace she supposed was a smile. His eyes. Those blue eyes seemed to bore into her soul. Hastily Angelica whispered a prayer. What would be their fate to be at the mercy of such a man? She was soon to find out, for after questioning several of the men the bandit's strong voice rang out again, sending shivers dancing up her spine. "There are more weapons and a great deal more gold where this came from. The bald man has confessed as much." The bandit grinned. "After a bit of gentle persuasion."

For the first time since the bandits had attacked, Angelica located her brother. He was alive, and for that she gave thanks, but he looked wounded and she fought her way through a baracade of bandits to come to his side. "Edward! Edward!" Lashing out at her captors she bent down to care for him, relieved to find he had only superficial wounds. When she looked up again the

28

bandit's eyes were on her, staring at her intently.

"You. Señorita. What is your name? What is your relationship to this man?" The muscles in his arms and thighs tightened as he stode forward.

"I am his sister. My name is Angelica Howe. Miss Angelica Howe to you." Though she met his gaze with a bravery she most certainly did not feel, her hands were trembling violently.

"Ah, an angel! Angelica. A most beautiful name. How amusing that you should find yourself held captive by El Diablo, the devil!" Unlike the others this man had little trace of an accent, Angelica noticed.

"I know what El Diablo means. I have been taught a little Spanish by the sisters at the abbey." She was determined to hide her fear. The last thing in the world she would do was grovel at this man's feet. Instinctively she knew her life and her brother's life depended on her courage.

Rodrigo ignored her comment, repeating her name. "Angelica Howe." She was a sight. Wide-brimmed straw hat cocked at an angle, her face covered with the road's grime, he was fascinated by her. She seemed, despite her fraility, to be a brave little thing. More than anything Rodrigo admired courage. "And do you wish to tell me that you are a holy sister as well?" His question was accompanied by the laughter of the others who were still certain the sisters were frauds.

"I . . . I . . . no!" Angelica found herself really looking at the bandit for the first time. He was the most handsome man she had ever set eyes on, even a finer-looking man than her brother was. His nose was straight, proud and well shaped, with high cheekbones in his tanned face. His jaw was strong with a determined set to it. Unlike all the other men who wore mustaches, he was clean-shaven, no doubt because of his vanity, she reasoned. A wish to show his face.

The garments he wore did little to hide his masculinity, the shirt open to reveal the dark hair across his broad chest, the pants tight against the flat belly and well-muscled thighs. Like the others he wore an ammunition belt which crisscrossed his torso, the handles and barrels of the guns gleaming a dazzling silver in the sun.

"Margaro! Manuel! Chewy!" Turning his back to her, seemingly dismissing her, the bandit leader called his men together. "And just what should we do with these kind people?" he asked. A grin tugged at the corners of his mouth. "Shall we let them go?"

Angelica breathed a sigh of relief. Perhaps these men were not as brutal as she had supposed. Maybe they would let them continue on their way without any real harm done. All they would have lost was the guns and gold. The food, supplies, and their baggage still belonged to them. Her calm was soon shattered however, as she heard the bandits talking and realized the bandit leader had only been joking. There was talk of hostages, a conversation which made both sisters chatter and twitter in fear, certain that they would be ill used if left in the hands of such dangerous men.

Angelica clasped her hands together so tightly that she winced, waiting to find out their fate. At last the man called El Diablo strode over to where she stood, folding his hands across his chest as he addressed the frightened group. "Ah, it is with regret that I must tell you that my men are not as kind-hearted as I. They insist on obtaining more of your fine guns and gold. We have voted to take hostages." He cocked a well-arched brow in answer to the twittering that ensued. "There must be payment for our inconvenience. We expect your leader to bring more rifles and another box of gold bricks. We will take five hostages. When we get what we desire they will be released. *Comprende?*"

"Hostages?" Angelica breathed.

"You cannot say that is not to be a very fair trade, eh?" His eyes roamed over Angelica once again and even such a cursory glance brought blood to her cheeks. "Who will stay and who will go, it is for you to decide." In a benevolent gesture he made a sweep with his hand, indicating the members of the wagon train. As was to be expected, all remained silent. None among them wished to be held captive by such violent men. "Then I will have to decide." He motioned towards Sister Theresa. "That one!" And towards the bald man, "And him."

"No! No, please!" Succumbing to her panic Sister Theresa tried frantically to get away, only to be subdued by two of the bandits standing close to her.

"And the pale-haired man. That should assure that we do indeed receive our guns." Nodding towards Edward Howe, he then proceeded to name two more hostages, a young beardless boy and a bearded gray-haired man.

"No! You can't!" Without really being aware of what she did, Angelica found herself rising to her feet and walking towards the bandit leader. Despite the chilling fear she felt to the very core of her she mumbled, "Take me instead. Instead of my brother and Sister Theresa." The courage she exhibited amazed her, yet she forced herself to maintain at least a shred of dignity despite her violently shaking and quaking legs. Somehow she managed to come to the bandit's side without stumbling.

"So, there is at least one brave soul among you." El Diablo's eyes swept over her from head to toe, and Angelica lowered her eyes, thankful for the spectacles which hid her quivering eyelids. "I salute you, señorita." He turned his gaze on Edward, fully expecting him to protest. Surely no real man would allow a woman to take his place, but no protest was forthcoming. "Then so be it. We will agree upon four hostages instead of five. The woman will be just as valuable as her brother." The thought never entered Rodrigo's head that the pale-haired

31

man would not keep his word. The life of his sister hung in the balance and he was certain the man would be most prompt in meeting the terms. "Chewy, load up the señorita's baggage. I will not have it said that we do not make every effort to make our *guests* comfortable, eh?"

Mounting his horse, motioning to Margaro to assist Angelica in finding a horse for herself, he was soon out of sight, thundering down the road. As he slowly disappeared from view Angelica suddenly realized what she had done. She had just made herself the prisoner of the most notorious bandit in California.

Chapter Four

The camp lay sprawled along the edge of a valley, hidden from sight by a rock formation that from the distance seemed to be a mountain. Following her captors down the small winding road, she arrived at last at the camp, amazed to see that there were little children running about. Somehow she had assumed that the bandits would be living in an environment of only men.

Desert scrub, cactus, and weeds grew abundant along the edge of the small adobe and wood buildings. These huts proved to be humble but clean, or so Angelica supposed by the outer walls.

The courtyard was alive with the chatter of women as they worked hard to prepare the evening meal, guitar music and the laughter of men as they put aside their tools and gathered about the campfire for their supper. All that noise very quickly was silenced as the bandits rode into the camp, bringing with them their captives.

Rodrigo's eyes scanned the people he had vowed to defend, people used to hardship. Many of them had been rescued from enforced servitude, their only crime being poverty. In carving this small haven, he had given them a home and hope for the future.

"Señoritas, take care of the woman!"

At his command several women with brightly colored skirts hurried forward. Angelica's only thought was to thank God for the women. They gave her a slight feeling of safety. Dismounting, she followed the women to the cooking pots where chili simmered over tiny fires and ears of corn roasted among the coals. Despite what had happened she was hungry. Famished in fact. The slapping sound of the women forming dough into tortillas was a reminder of that. The tantalizing aroma made her mouth water as she breathed in the smells of the food. Sitting on a large rock by the fire Angelica soon devoured the food that was offered to her. Only then did she look again at the *bandido* leader. He had taken off his flat-brimmed sombrero, and she was surprised to see that his hair was a much lighter brown than that of the other men. It flashed just a hint of red in the light of the setting sun. She thought undoubtedly there were many other things about this man that she would find surprising.

"He cannot help but draw a young señorita's eye!" The shrill tone of voice startled her. Walking towards Angelica was an old Indian woman. Bent with age, shuffling as she walked, she had a certain air of dignity about her.

"He is frightening!"

"Yet it is not fear that makes you freely gaze at him. It is his male beauty, his power, his strength."

"Will he harm me?" Angelica could not help but voice her apprehension.

"That all depends upon you!" The dark eyes assessed her. "I do not think so. Not unless you prove to be a danger to the rest of us. Rodrigo, for all his anger, is a man of his word."

"Rodrigo? So that *is* his name." She cocked her eyebrows in question. "Why is he so filled with hatred?"

"The years spent in a gringo jail for a crime he did not do, the death of his mother and father. I have watched just what cruelty and injustice can do to a man." The old

34

woman seemed to regret telling Angelica any such tattlings, for she shuffled off as quickly as she had come. Still, her words had set Angelica to wondering. What had he been like once, before he became a bandit? As she watched him a sudden gust of wind whipped at his hair, and she was horrified at her longing to smooth it back from his forehead. That she would even think such a thing shocked her to the depths of her soul. He was a bandit, and until today she had visions of becoming a nun. How could she even contemplate touching a man who was everything she had been taught to abhor. Her eyes quickly searched out the corral, wishing she had the nerve to steal a horse and ride away.

But no, she thought. Leaving might well cause harm to fall upon the others, and she could not do that. She had volunteered to come, had given her word, and she must abide by that. Besides, she would have to be crazy even to think of doing such a thing. There was nothing but scrub brush and dirt surrounding the bandit hideaway. She could easily become lost and might perish before she was found. No one could make it back to the abbey without knowing the way. And yet she knew that one thing was certain, she could not stay for long. Her attraction to the man named El Diablo made leaving imperative. Heaven hope her brother arrived with the gold and the guns very quickly.

The flames of the campfire pulsated in rhythm to the guitars being strummed, or so it seemed to Rodrigo. He watched as the smoke from the fires twisted up towards the sky, breathing in the pungent odor of the dried mesquite that crackled and glowed. Anything to keep his gaze away from the gringo woman. Why were his eyes drawn to her over and over again? The small little sparrow should hold no attraction for him. Why then did he have the strangest thoughts weaving through his mind?

"She is just a woman. Like many others!" he muttered aloud, startling Margaro who sat beside him.

"She is not much to look at, perhaps, but *carumba*, what a brave one." He looked at Rodrigo reflectively. "And perhaps were she to take off those round, wire-rimmed pieces of glass from about her eyes she might be very pretty. I got a look at her eyes. They are blue. And her hair looks like a ray of sunshine. Were she to unwind it from behind her head I would bet it reaches to far below her shoulders." He stood up. "Shall I see?"

"Stay right where you are. I will not have you anywhere near her. I know how you are with the women. This one is not to be touched. Not by you, not by Pedro."

"Not even by you?"

"Especially not by me! I gave my word that no one would be harmed."

"A little kiss, an embrace beneath the moon is not dangerous. That would not harm her."

"Margaro! No more talk about it!" Usually one to share Margaro's good-natured teasing, Rodrigo proved to be sensitive about this subject. A tug of war waged between his conscience and his common sense on the matter of the gringo woman. He admired her. Not a man among the gringos had done what she had done. They were cowards, but this one, this one had been very brave. How could he help but admire that. And yet if her brother did not make good on his word he would be forced to give the order that she must die. *Cristo glorioso* that it would come to that! But he would not be surprised if the pale-haired man double-crossed him. There was something in his eyes that spoke of a coward, of greed and of selfishness. Somehow Rodrigo did not want to think of that now. It was too grim a reminder of what might very well have to be done.

The sound of laughter drifted on the wind to his ears, and looking up he saw the newcomer in their midst encircled by the camp's children, tugging at her in curiosity. He well expected her to send them away but instead she motioned them to sit beside her. She soon had the little ones laughing, and he supposed she was telling them a story.

His blue eyes stared at the gringo woman stoically. Having washed her face and hands and without her bonnet she looked much prettier, and he wondered if Margaro was right. With her golden hair flying about her shoulders she would make a— But no, he must not allow himself to think about that. She was nothing but a plain little sparrow who would soon fly away when she was traded for rifles and gold.

In agitation he threw a rock into the fire, watching as the coals sparked. This woman was a gringo and he had little doubt that she thought of him as lower than dirt. Like all of her kind she would consider a man of Mexican blood to be far beneath her. The gringos rarely considered that the Spaniards had brought their culture to these lands long before *their* forefathers landed upon these shores.

As if realizing that she was the object of scrutiny, the young woman turned her head his way. Their eyes met and held for just a moment, before she quickly averted her eyes. In that short amount of time he could read her apprehension. Rodrigo wondered if it was fear for her life or her virtue that he had read in her gaze. Well, she had no need to fear his intentions. He was a man of honor, and, besides, a bespectacled, plain little sparrow did not interest him. Or did she? He argued with the voice inside his head which said that she did. Her grace, her dignity, the proud way she held her head kept drawing his eye across the fire.

Ha! Were I to even touch her hand she would break down in a flood of hysterical weeping, he thought. No. On second thought he decided that she would not. She had not cried when the wagon train had been ambushed. Truly this gringo woman was surprising, and he could not help but respect her.

"So, you bring a gringa woman into our camp." Rodrigo knew that voice all too well. That husky, throaty voice. Bonita Mendoza stood behind him, the smell of her heavy perfume wafting to his nostrils.

Quickly Margaro rose to his feet and walked away, showing his aversion to the woman. Whenever Margaro and Bonita were anywhere near each other tempers always flared. Rodrigo had a mind to follow Margaro but the touch of her hand on his shoulder stopped him. "Why has she been brought here?"

"She is a hostage, Bonita! I use her and the others to trade for guns and gold."

He turned to appraise the raven-haired beauty with the wine-red lips and long flowing hair, the woman he had once loved. Now he knew it had been the love of a foolish boy for an experienced older woman. Though Bonita was only five years older than he, she had learned very early in life the ways of using her body to get what she wanted. Too late he had learned that the unspeakable delights she offered had a high price. She was a grasping and ambitious woman who had tried to own him. Now at last he had put her out of his life.

"And do you tell me you have no desire to find her in your bed?" The beautiful, generously endowed Bonita had the habit of perceiving every woman as her rival and that irritated him.

"I do tell you that. The gringa woman is our hostage. And yet were I to decide otherwise it would be *my* business! Remember that."

Swaying her hips as she moved forward she said, "You have no need of her when I am here." Wrapping her arms about him, she sought his mouth, but Rodrigo pulled away roughly.

"No, Bonita. I will not be entrapped by your wiles again. What we had has long since died."

38

"No. I think not, *querido*." Her eyes searched his face, then lowered to his body, caressing every part of him with her gaze. Moistening her bright pink lips with her tongue, she smiled. "You will come to love me again."

"Love?" She had no knowledge of what such a word really meant. She was carnivorous like a wolf or a mountain cat. "Were I to allow it, you would destroy me. Slowly but with a certainty." Without realizing it his eyes strayed to the gringa woman, comparing the two in his mind. Why was that? Why did she draw his eyes? What was it about the woman that intrigued him? Could it be that he sensed a fire beneath her cold hauteur? What would happen if that fire was sparked?

Leaving Bonita, seeking solitude, he pondered such thoughts. A woman like Bonita was not capable of love, only of coupling with a man. But he wanted more. Much more! All his life Rodrigo had felt that something was lacking in his life. He wanted a woman who would be his soul mate. It seemed to be an impossible dream, and yet something about this gringa intrigued him. She sparked an undefinable emotion. Lust? No. Admiration. Respect. It was said that still waters ran deep, and he wanted to explore the matter. He was intrigued to find out all he could about this woman before the time came when she would be set free.

Chapter Five

Sunlight, warm and golden, filtered through the cracks of the adobe hut pricking Angelica's eyelids gently until she opened her eyes. "I must be up quickly for morning prayers . . ." she mumbled, clutching at the blanket, ready to rise from her bed. Instead, she found out much to her shock that she was already on the floor, lying on a hard, straw pallet. Wide-eyed with sudden apprehension she slowly looked about her, only to find her fiercest fears realized. So it had not been a dream then after all. She *was* in the bandits' camp.

Once again her eyes swept the room, taking in the brightly colored wooden bowls and pottery, the multi-colored woven rugs that were strewn haphazardly across the floor. Most definitely *not* the abbey. Bolting up to a sitting position, she tried to remain calm.

A leather belt hung on a pole beside the doorway, a large, wide-brimmed sombrero hung on a peg on the wall, and an assortment of men's garments were piled haphazardly in the corner. The bandit's possessions. El Diablo! Even his name caused her to shiver. She was his hostage, his prisoner. Even now she could hear his thundering baritone voice issuing orders right outside her door. He was frightening. Arrogant. Ruthless, no doubt. Over-

41

bearing. Dangerous? Most certainly. What was going to happen to her? To the others? To discover the answer, she listened attentively to the murmur of the voices outside.

"How long will you give the gringo, Rodrigo?"

"Ten days and not a moment more. It should not take long to return to the North and load up the rifles. Ten days."

"And if the pale-haired gringo does not return by then?"

Angelica could not hear the muffled answer, and yet she sensed intuitively what the answer would be. Death for her and the others. Pressing her fingertips together she uttered a frantic prayer, trying to remain calm and courageous yet having a difficult time of it. She'd heard chilling tales of the punishments that awaited those who thwarted the bandits. Would it be by rope, knife, gun, or the fiery sun that she would die? Closing her eyes, she tried to remain calm. Edward would come. He would bring the ransom the bandits demanded. How could she even think otherwise? Hadn't Edward always been a most dutiful brother? He would return, she and the others would be freed, and one day she would look back upon this moment as little more than a terrifying memory.

Anxiously her hands fumbled at the folds of her skirt as she fought to resign herself to her fate. The idea of escape had entered her mind more than once during the night but she had severely scolded herself for such a selfish, idiotic idea. She could not desert the others and leave them to face the angry bandits alone. There was more at stake than her own fears and discomfort. Perhaps she could be a settling influence on the bandits to ensure at least a measure of peace and tranquility. Then too there was the matter of honor. She had given her word that she would be their hostage, had volunteered, as a matter of fact. No, she could not leave. Whether she liked it or not she was here to stay, at least for a while. And yet the way El Diablo had looked at her caused her to shiver, not from fear exactly but from an emotion she dared not even think about.

As if her thoughts had conjured him, he stood right outside the doorway, his tall, well-muscled form casting a shadow across the dirt floor of the adobe hut. Angelica held her breath awaiting the confrontation she knew was to come. Oh, what could she say to him? How could she maintain her poise under the scrutiny of his cold, blue-eyed gaze? Biting her lower lip she searched for another way out of the hut so that she could avert the inevitable but saw there was none. Like it or not she was trapped and could only watch apprehensively as he stepped inside.

"Ah, señorita. You are already awake. Am I then to assume that you slept well?" The corners of his full, well-chiseled mouth turned up in a smile as he greeted her.

"As well as could be expected under the circumstances." Slowly, with as much dignity as she could display, Angelica rose to her feet, looking up at this El Diablo who towered over her by more than a foot. Somehow he seemed taller this morning, she thought, fumbling with her glasses so that she could meet him eye to eye. Taller and infinitely more intimidating somehow.

"Circumstances I most humbly regret. But while you are here it will be my desire to see that you are as comfortable as possible." This time his smile was a dazzling one, showing the perfection of his straight, pearl-white teeth. What a fascinating mouth he had, she thought, staring back at him until the amusement in his blue eyes caused her to look away.

I *am* attracted to him, she thought with alarm. I know it and he senses it. There was no use in lying to herself. From the very first moment she had first looked at him she had been intrigued by him. "Hopefully my stay and that of the others will not be very long!" Her voice was icy cold as she tried valiantly to hide her inner turmoil. She had led a quiet, peaceful life, a sheltered life perhaps, but a life to which she was fully accustomed. Now this bandit had turned her world topsy-turvy and she was not prepared, nor experienced in dealing with her traitorous heart.

43

"*Sí*, hopefully your brother will return in haste and bring me that which I most greatly desire."

His gaze seemed to burn her as a tense, awkward silence fell between them. What was he thinking, she wondered, feeling the warmth of a blush stain her face. Why was he appraising her as if she were a different species?

"Don't look at me like that." Before she could think, the words were out. Oh, what a sight she must make this morning, a comical one no doubt, with her sunburned nose, disheveled hair, and torn dress. Why, he seemed to be laughing at her.

"I apologize if I am staring, señorita. I was merely thinking that you might nearly be pretty if—" Rodrigo hastily put such thoughts from his mind. It would do him no good to have such musings about this woman, and yet she was disarmingly attractive at the moment. The sad thing about it was that she didn't even realize how pretty she would be if she took those damn spectacles off. But that did not concern him. She was a prisoner for the moment and no more. And yet he could not help but wonder how she would look with her hair unbound, falling freely about her shoulders. She might very well be beautiful, he thought, if she wore a colorful, feminine dress instead of the dull, drab clothing she affected.

"I don't care to be pretty!" Her manner belied her words. Reaching up, she toyed with her hair, trying to fashion it into the semblance of its original bun. Any other words she might have said to him became a muddle in her brain. What could she say? Nothing in her past had prepared her for a man quite like this one. He was far beyond the scope of her experience as she had been limited in her acquaintances with men. Her brother, townsmen, and men of the cloth. Just what did one say to a bandit? Particularly one so handsome? "What matters to me are things of the soul." It was the first thing that came to her mind.

"The soul?" For just a moment his eyes looked sad,

44

disillusioned, as if he sincerely regretted the things he had done. "I have no soul, señorita. The devil has no need for one."

Angelica sensed his pain. Despite all that had happened she felt sorry for him. She sensed a gentler man beneath the haughty, hard exterior of the bandit. Hadn't the old woman told her he had been the victim of injustice? What was the story of his life? Suddenly she wanted very much to know.

"We all have souls. Each and every one of us and . . ." She might have said more but for the entrance of another man, the tall bandit she remembered from last night.

"Rodrigo! Come quickly. There are three armed men approaching the camp."

"I'm coming, Margaro."

Without even a backward glance the bandit leader was gone and Margaro with him. Angelica was alone once more and busied herself in tidying the room. She had learned last night that this was El Diablo's hut and that knowledge made her somehow feel closer to him. He had been generous in giving her his own quarters. At times he even seemed to be a gentleman.

But he *is* a bandit! She chided herself for such foolish fantasy. No matter how handsome, how charming he might be, he was an outlaw. She must not let herself forget that. This El Diablo had a price upon his head. No matter how polite he had acted, how much he might have been wronged, facts were facts. She knew nothing about him, how many people he might have robbed or killed. A man such as he would have to answer for his wrongs before his earthly judge and before God. All she knew was that he was the arrogant and proud acknowledged leader of this group of people. And yet there had been something about this bandit leader that decried the fact that he was a brutal man. There was a sensitivity about him that Angelica had glimpsed a moment ago.

She had a nagging need to know more about him and

satisfied herself by looking about the room. He seemed to have an appreciation of art, for though it was but a humble adobe he had decorated it with colorful sand paintings, wooden carvings, and multicolored woven rugs. Had all these objects been stolen? Or did they speak of another time, a phase of his life that was ended? It was a question she ran over and over in her mind.

The room contained the usual masculine things—an extra pair of boots, spurs, two sombreros, a pouch of tobacco for fashioning the cigarillos the bandits all seemed to smoke, a knife with a broken blade, but it was the pile of books, so neatly stacked that caught her eye. Books for a bandit? She had heard it said that such people could not read. Rodrigo's possessions? In curiosity she opened one and found a name inside. Rodrigo Delgado O'Hara. Was that El Diablo's name? Whoever he was, his name was neatly scrawled inside the cover of every one of the seven books.

"Rodrigo Delgado O'Hara." Angelica whispered, remembering that the old woman had mentioned that Rodrigo was El Diablo's first name. It was just one more piece of the puzzle. Angelica was more determined than ever to find out all that she could about the man who held her life in his hands.

Pushing aside the tightly woven cloth covering the hut's entranceway, Angelica viewed the members of the camp from a distance. Dogs barked, goats bleated, chickens cackled in rhythm to the chatter of voices as the entire hideaway came alive after a night's repose. There was a flutter of activity, like the buzzing about of bees in a beehive. Women left their huts to begin the morning's chores, walking in a lively gait towards the spring to get the precious water needed for cleaning and cooking. The air was soon resounding with the noise of rattling dishes and pans, clinking spoons, and the sound of water pouring as the morning meal was prepared.

"Are you hungry, señorita?" A lovely young woman with dark brown hair passed by the hut, motioning for Angelica to join her at the morning fires. "My name is Luisa," she offered.

"Angelica." Angelica was reminded of the kindness of the woman last night. She had given her water for bathing, had helped her to mend her dress, offered herbal potions for her sun-parched skin as they had exchanged smiles. She had seemed sympathetic to her situation. Joining her now at the communal fire she watched as Luisa bustled about. A pretty woman, Angelica thought, with a sweet yet aristocratic manner. Puzzling.

The aroma of brewing coffee bubbling in clay pots filled the camp and Angelica took hold of the tin cup offered to her. The hot coffee was strong and flavored with spices. It seemed that spices were used abundantly here. "Delicious. *Gracias.*" The brew gave her a burst of energy as Angelica kneaded dough for the *sopapillas* which were to be the morning's fare. It seemed to be a peaceful camp. Angelica reflected that perhaps the time spent here would not be too distressing.

Her eyes were drawn to several outbuildings in a walled compound. From this storehouse women carried baskets of corn. At least there appeared to be food aplenty. Looking searchingly at some of the men who went about their tasks, she reflected that even they did not look quite as fierce and frightening this morning as they had last night. One of the men even smiled at her as he sat high atop a corral fence.

"Do not encourage that one, señorita." Luisa's warning came with a smile. "Lest he talk you to death. Enrique has oh too many tales to tell and we have grown weary of hearing them."

"I thank you for the warning, though I would imagine I will have a great deal of time to listen," Angelica answered with a sigh as she put two of the corn pancakes on the hot

47

earthen griddle. "Luisa . . ." The girl turned her head and Angelica asked the question that had been plaguing her since the moment she spied the books. "What is the bandit leader's name? Is it Rodrigo O'Hara?"

"Yes. And I am Luisa O'Hara. His sister."

"His sister?" The eyes, Angelica thought. Both Luisa and Rodrigo had eyes the color of sapphires. She should have realized at once that they were of the same blood. The shape of the nose, the red glint in the dark-brown hair, the high cheekbones decried the girl was his kin.

"It makes me very proud to be sister to such a brave man." The young girl squinted her eyes, obviously wondering at Angelica's curiosity.

"I saw some books inside and . . . and I wondered to whom they belonged. Now I know they are your brother's."

"Rodrigo is a very learned man . . ." The sound of gunfire disturbed their tranquil conversation. Angelica stiffened, remembering the terror she had experienced the day before.

"What is it? What's happening?" Could it be Edward? Was it possible that he had brought a rescue party to free the hostages? The very thought caused her to catch her breath as she searched the horizon for the origin of the loud, popping sound.

Puffs of dust stirred in the air like a menacing cloud as both women watched the serape-clad riders approach. "Rodrigo. Margaro. Manuel. Ramón." Riding back towards the camp were four of the bandits.

"But what . . .?" To Angelica's horror she saw that they were leading a fifth rider who was slumped over in the saddle, clinging to his horse's neck with hands smeared by blood. The green flannel shirt and red hair made him recognizable. Jesse Harrison," she whispered under her breath. He was one of her brother's men. Willingly or not, the bandits had taken another hostage.

Chapter Six

Rodrigo watched as the captive slid from his horse to the hard ground and signaled the Indian woman to tend him. "Foolish gringos. They came like lambs to a wolves' den trying to be heros, thinking to take us unawares and free the others. This one is lucky. The other two are food for the vultures."

Rodrigo hated violence, hated needless killing, yet there were times when there was nothing else to be done. He had to protect his people, his camp. The three gringos had come upon the hideaway with guns drawn, intending mischief, and though he had warned them, had told them to drop their weapons and settle the matter without gunfire, they had started the shooting. In the crossfire two had been killed instantly. This man had been more fortunate. Perhaps, Rodrigo thought, it would be *two* deaths on his conscience and not three. That was his hope.

"Is he dead?" The blond-haired woman's eyes reproached him as she ran forward.

"Not yet, but he is bleeding very badly." Rodrigo turned his back on her cold, disdainful eyes remembering another look that had passed between them this morning. Strange that he should care what this young woman thought of him. He wanted to explain to her about what had

49

happened, make her see that sometimes the only alternative was to kill or be killed, but instead he kept his silence, trying to ignore her barbed stare. "What are his chances, Najalayogua?"

The old woman probed the injured man with long slim hands that were skilled in healing, clucking her tongue all the while. "Mmmm. The wounds are deep. He has lost much blood. We must move him at once to a place of quiet." She babbled her instructions to two of the bandits who carried the red-haired newcomer to the hut beside Rodrigo's. "Careful. Careful. Ayee, we do not want to do any further harm." Nodding in Luisa's direction, she bade the girl follow her, but when Angelica moved towards the wounded man she shook her head. "No! I will tend him."

"But you must let me help. I know him." Angelica pushed through the crowd of onlookers only to have Rodrigo block her way.

"All the more reason for you to stay away. He needs healing potions not your tears." The tone of his voice was gruffer than he intended it to be.

"He may need more than a healer. He may need a priest!" Her glistening eyes condemned him. "Have you and the others not already done enough harm, spilled enough blood? You said you had no soul. Now I know you have no heart as well." Any sympathy Angelica might have felt for this bandit was pushed away at the sight of Jesse's wounds. And what of the others? By the bandit's words they were dead. Was Edward among them? Had they killed her brother then, after all?

"What need have I for a heart? To be strong is my only desire. I want to be feared."

"And loathed!" Angelica clenched her jaw, remembering Mother Bernadette's teachings over the years. Forgive your enemies, pray for those who would abuse you. Now she found it was much easier said than done, though she tried. Closing her eyes, she willed herself to

50

remain calm. "Was my brother one of the dead?"

"No, señorita." He wanted to tell her what had happened, try to make her see that he had done only what was necessary. He wanted to exonerate himself in her eyes, but instead he kept silent. Fool, he thought, she would never understand. She is a gringa and you are a man of half-Mexican heritage and therefore to blame. Her biased sense of justice would prejudice her against him no matter what he said.

"My brother was not . . ." Her sigh of relief was audible. She felt a twinge of guilt in not feeling more sorrow for the others. Hastily she said a prayer for them in an effort to atone for her first selfish thought. "May God have mercy on their souls," she said aloud. "They must be given decent burial and a priest must . . ."

"The wind will blow dirt over what remains of their bodies. That is all the ceremony they will receive. As to a priest, there are none in my camp and I cannot take the chance of bringing one here, lest he too remain a hostage." It was the decision he had to make to protect the living.

"No burial? No priest?" Angelica shuddered at the thought. "What kind of a man are you?" She had been so perilously close to falling under his spell, had even acquitted him in her mind of the deeds he had done. She had searched to find a reason for his anger, his misdeeds, had told herself that in spite of everything he was a civilized man. Now the folly of her thoughts was made all too apparent.

"What kind of man am I? A leader who does not let *anything* stop him from doing all that is necessary to attain his goals. Sentiment does not move me, señorita, as you will soon see."

"I understand." Dear God, he was ruthless. Angelica took a tentative step back, wanting to flee but knowing she was entrapped.

"I'm glad that you do. Now, I must take my leave. If you

will excuse me." He had to get away from her, from the wide, searching eyes which seemed to hold more condemnation with every word he spoke.

Angelica watched him walk away with a feeling of indefinable sadness and regret. What was it that turned men into brutal, heartless animals? She thought how apparent it was that Satan and not God ruled this land of violence. Was her faith strong enough to conquer God's erring angel? Was her coming to this camp a test of her steadfastness? Of her fortitude?

"So Jesse Harrison is now a captive too." A low, growling voice caused Angelica to whirl around to see Jeremiah Adams behind her. "Before this is over they'll kill us all. Filthy bastards." Taking off his hat he wiped his hand over his hairless head. "If I had a gun I'd shoot them."

"And be just as bad as they are." Angelica shook her head. "No, we must stay calm and not give them any reason for violence. Edward will be here soon and then we will be free."

Laughter was his answer, unnerving, sniggering. "Of course he'll come and bring with him all of God's holy angels. Oh, how naive you are. Edward will save his own hide. We won't be seeing him again. If we want to stay alive we have to get our hands on guns. Shoot our way out of here." Holding up his thumb and forefinger, he mimicked the firing of a revolver. "Bang. Bang. Bang. No more bandits." He winked at her conspiratorially. "'Course now I think you could be a whole heap of help. Bandit seems to have taken a shine to you. You just wiggle that well-curved bottom of yours in his direction and he'll be putty in your hands."

Angelica drew in her breath, shocked at his crudity. "My dear sir . . ."

"You keep him distracted and me and Will Cooper will get us some guns. I'm not about to let any half-Mexican

52

bastard murder me. No siree." He edged up closer to Angelica. The odor of his breath was unpleasant as he whispered his plan. "Flirt with him. Get him all friendly like. Occupy his attention, that's all I ask. Find out where the munitions are kept, and if they're locked up get the key."

"I couldn't. I don't want . . ."

"If he gives you any trouble crack his skull, but not before you find out what we need to know. Understand?" Seeing one of the bandits approaching, he stepped back. "Glad to know you're in good health, Miss Angelica. I worried about you last night. I was afraid your honor might be sullied."

"No . . . no, I'm just fine, Mister Adams. There is no harm done. Nor will there be." Angelica was determined not to have anything at all to do with his plan. It would mean more violence, more bloodshed. There were over thirty-five bandits and only five of *them*, a woman, a boy, a gray-haired old man, a wounded companion, and Jeremiah Adams. The odds were against them no matter how he might boast and swagger.

"Glad to hear that." He feigned a smile in the bandit's direction, only to be met by an icy stare. "Morning. Fine day, isn't it? I'm as hungry as a desert fox. Got any grub?"

"If you want to eat you must work for your fare, señor." Margaro lifted one thick black brow, his brown eyes staring at Jeremiah Adams suspiciously. He was not at all fooled by the bald man's attempt at comaraderie. "I suggest you stop jabbering with the señorita and help the others mend the fence. Then you can talk of eating." At the other man's hesitancy he waved his hand impatiently. *"Vamos!"* He grinned as Jeremiah Adams stalked away.

"How . . . how is the man . . . the wounded man?" Having seen him enter then leave the hut that housed Jesse Harrison, she had to ask.

"Najalayogua stopped the blood and put moss on his

53

wounds. At this moment she and Luisa are carefully watching him." He watched her thoughtfully, appraisingly, as if at that moment he formed his opinion of her. "I think he will survive. Perhaps then your prayers will be answered, no?"

"May I . . . may I see him? I promise I will not make a scene. El Diablo said . . . but . . ." She thought he looked far less formidable than the bandit leader. There seemed to be a glint of suppressed laughter in his dark eyes. If one did not compare him to Rodrigo he too seemed handsome, his nose a bit wider, flatter than his leader's, a reflection of Indian heritage perhaps. His face was rounder, his hair much darker.

"You want to see him, señorita?" He shrugged his shoulders. "I don't see why not. Rodrigo can be overly stubborn sometimes." He scanned the camp, and seeing that Rodrigo was not around agreed. "But hurry. Like the bare-headed gringo you too must earn your keep. Nor would I have Rodrigo chide me for going against his command." The edges of his mustache trembled as he smiled and Angelica sensed at that moment that she had found a friend among the bandits.

"Thank you. I will be but a moment."

The interior of the hut was very dark, swathed in shadows that were caused by one flickering candle. Even so, she could see how deathly pale Jesse Harrison's face was. Pale and grimaced with pain.

"Jesse? Jesse? Can you hear me?" As if sensing her presence, hearing her, he groaned and stirred in his dreamless slumber.

"Najalayogua gave him a potion, señorita. It will make him talk out of his head. *Loco.*" Luisa hovered like an ever-watchful guardian over the red-haired man, wiping the perspiration from his brow, watching him with a worshipful gaze that spoke of her attraction to him. Her attentiveness, though welcomed, worried Angelica. Such attraction could only cause trouble. She had noticed that El Diablo watched over his sister with eyes like a hawk. If Jesse survived, which she prayed that he would, he could not help but be tempted by Luisa's beauty.

"Jesse? Jesse?"

He responded to his name, the thick red lashes fluttering as he mumbled beneath his breath. The words were unintelligible at first, then sounded like a plea. "Shot us . . . Pete . . . Dan. Have to free them . . . hostages."

Angelica could barely hear, yet she knew what he was muttering. He was naming the men who had been killed. Pete Sanders and Dan Henderson, her brother's hired hands. She moved closer to him, to keep Luisa from hearing her. "You tried to save us. It was very noble." Reaching out she stroked his brow. "Edward? Is he safe? When is he coming with the rifles? Jesse? Jesse? If you can hear me, please tell me."

He opened his eyes suddenly and she could see the dilated pupils of the hazel depths. "Edward?" He shook his head. "No. No, he is *not* coming. Not coming. That is why . . . we rode . . ." His voice had been so low that Angelica had barely heard him. He closed his eyelids again, obviously having exhausted his strength by talking, but he had said enough to chill Angelica's heart. He had dashed all her hopes. All she could hope was that Luisa had not heard him too because if what he said was true then she and the others would be left at the mercy of the bandits.

Chapter Seven

The sun was unmercifully hot, causing the inhabitants of the camp to seek the shade, yet one man ignored the discomfort as he strode up and down before the communal area like a restless, prowling wolf. Back and forth, up and down, Rodrigo wore a path in the dirt.

"Rodrigo, my friend, why do you not siesta? Your walking about makes me nervous, amigo." Rising from his perch on the ground Margaro approached his friend. "I have seldom seen you like this. What ails you?"

"The matter of the hostages. They have proved to be more of a danger than I had foreseen, Margaro. Perhaps I was wrong to have brought them here. If not for them we would not have had the shoot-out with the three gringos. I cannot help but wonder if there will be others. More bullets, more killing." Pausing in his stride he kicked at a rock, sending it bouncing along the ground.

"Killing gringos has never bothered you before. Can it be the golden-haired señorita who makes you have second thoughts? Is the brave El Diablo afraid of her scorn?"

"I am afraid of no one, least of all a woman! But I grow weary of blood and violence." Walking to a large water barrel he took a drink out of the dipper. "I keep wondering if I was a fool to trust the pale-haired gringo. What if he does *not* bring the guns and the gold?"

"Then the hostages will pay the price." Margaro followed Rodrigo's example, drinking from the long-handled tin cup. Throwing back his head he let the water trickle over his face and neck. "Ah . . . that feels good."

"And so we will kill them just like that. Like swatting a swarm of bothersome flies. No guns, no gold and . . ." He moved his index finger across his neck from left to right.

"I do not think it will come to that. I do not think the gringo will forfeit the life of his sister. *You* would not. Were it Luisa being held you would ransom your very life to see that she was safe."

"Yes, *I* would, but the matter of the three men who blundered near the camp makes me wonder. I heard the wounded gringo talking in his sleep. Luisa heard him too. From what we could understand there will be no ransom. That was why the foolish *americanos* tried to shoot their way into camp. To free the captives." Fumbling with his tobacco pouch, he fashioned a cigarillo and stuck it in his mouth. Striking a match with his thumbnail, he lit the cigar and took a thoughtful puff. "It has not been my practice to kill women, Margaro."

"And so we come to the reason for your unease. The woman. The saintly-faced señorita. She has gotten under your skin just as I thought she would."

"She asked me what kind of a man I am. The question started me wondering. I am not the man I was, Margaro. Once I collected things of beauty, now I destroy them. She told me that I have no heart, and she is right. That is what troubles me." He put his hand to his chest. "Now I am empty here."

"Empty? Bah! No one has a bigger heart for his people. If not for you we would all be rotting in some gringo's jail or slaving away for some rich *caballero*. And what of Luisa? By your every deed you prove your devotion to her." Margaro threw up his hands in frustration. "I will

58

not listen to any more of your chiding yourself. There is no other man that I so greatly admire. You are brave, strong, ruthless only to those who deserve it."

"And does that include the woman? What harm has she done to me? And yet I hold her life in my hands as I do the others." Picking up a stick he twisted it in his hands, at last breaking it in two. "And if the rifles do not come, how then shall I kill her? Tell me, Margaro. What am I to do?"

"The rifles *will* come, and the gold. The gringo is no fool. When he sees there is no other way he will bring what we ask of him to the meeting place we arranged. Then you will turn the woman loose into her brother's waiting arms and banish her from your mind." He grinned suddenly. "That is unless you decide to keep her as your own. I would were I in your place. I think the señorita is passably pretty. Like a flower just waiting to bloom."

"I have no need for a flower. I would only crush its petals." He gazed out thoughtfully at the horizon as he finished smoking his cigarillo. Then, without a word, he made his way to the toolshed. Margaro followed him, watching as he took hold of a shovel.

"What are you doing? It is a time for rest not for work."

"I am going to dig two graves, amigo."

"Two graves?" Margaro raised his eyebrows in surprise as the reason came to him. "The gringos. The two that were shot today. But why? The scavengers will take care of them."

"They are men, not animals. As such they deserve a proper burial. The woman was right in what she said."

"The woman . . ." Margaro threw back his head and laughed. "Ah, Rodrigo. Despite your denials, she *has* charmed you. But there is no wrong in that." He pulled at his mustache. "In fact, I am delighted. It will give Bonita some well-deserved competition."

Rodrigo was vehement in his denial. "I have no interest in the woman. I merely do what needs to be done to

preserve my honor, my favor in the eyes of God."
Thrusting another shovel into his companion's hands he
barked out an order. "Stop braying like a burro and follow
me. I would like to finish our task before the setting of the
sun."

Following the small path which twisted downward,
Rodrigo led the way with Margaro following close
behind. The two men were unaware of the eyes that
watched them, or of the smile that curled the lips of
Jeremiah Adams's mouth as he saw the bandit's absence as
the perfect chance for escape.

Moving slowly, cautiously Adams moved towards the
paunchy, sleeping bandit. Riveting his eyes on the rise and
fall of the slumbering man's chest, he crept carefully closer
to him. A buzzing fly landed on his quarry's nose and he
held his breath waiting for the bandit to awaken. Instead, a
pudgy hand reached up lazily to brush the offending insect
away, tugged the sombrero down over his face, and
continued his siesta.

"That's right, sleep," Jeremiah whispered beneath his
breath, sighing in relief. Getting down on his hands and
knees, glancing behind once or twice to make certain his
actions were not being watched, he crawled closer,
stretching out his arm until his fingers closed around the
cold steel of a gun. Hastily he pulled his treasure back and
hid it in the folds of his shirt with a smug smile. It had
been so easy. Standing up he stealthfully retraced his steps,
putting a full measure of distance between himself and the
man whose weapon he had *borrowed*.

"What are you doing?" A low, feminine voice startled
him as Angelica pushed through the doorway of the adobe
hut. "Put that gun back. Your recklessness will be the
death of us all."

"Or our salvation." Before she could say another word
Jeremiah gave her a shove that sent her back inside and
sprawling to the hard, earthen floor. "That bandit and his

friend have left the camp for one fool errand or the other. While they're gone I intend to take leave of their hospitality and I'm taking the others with me. Stay or leave, it doesn't matter."

"You can't leave Jesse behind. If we go they might very well take out their anger on him." Angelica struggled to sit up.

"I won't drag along a wounded man. Jesse will just have to take his chances. Gonna be hard enough getting away." Checking the gun for ammunition he seemed satisfied that there were enough bullets to get him out of the camp.

"And yet Jesse nearly lost his life trying to rescue us."

"An unfortunate truth and one which revealed to me the desperation of our plight. Now, are you coming or ain't you?" His scowl was menacing, though he reached out to help her to her feet. An odd gesture of courtesy, since he had been the cause of her fall in the first place.

"I'm coming!" Though Angelica had no intentions of leaving Jesse, she supposed that it was best to see just what Jeremiah had in mind. She followed him as he went from hut to hut, rounding up his fellow hostages. Tom Cowdrey, a young, dark-haired, freckle-faced boy seemed aprehensive and frightened at first when Jeremiah explained his plan, but at the older man's taunting was soon persuaded to make his way to the corral. Once there it would be his duty to secure four horses.

"Come hell or high water!"

"Come hell or high water." the boy replied, feigning a smile.

Angelica watched the lad go with a feeling of fear coiling in her belly. It sounded too pat, too easy. She had begun to wonder if perhaps they were being tested to see if they *would* try to escape. So far they had been given the run of the camp, had been allowed to roam about freely without being bound or locked up. What would happen if they were caught before they could get away? The answer was all too obvious. She couldn't help but wonder as she followed Jeremiah to another hut.

"Will! Get off your backside and come help us." The old gray-haired man was curled up on his pallet, mimicking his captors by taking a nap. At the intrusion he grumbled, opening his eyes. "Get up, I say." Jeremiah held up the gun proudly. "It's your turn, old-timer. A rifle if you can manage it."

Will came automatically to his feet, grinning at the bald man from ear to ear. "Stealing weapons is my specialty. I've already figured on gettin' me a rifle from one of these Mexes takin' a nap. If I get the chance. We'll pay them back for what they done."

"All you will do is get yourselves killed. These bandits aren't going to let you walk out of camp without a fight. You cannot believe that you are any match for them?" Frantically Angelica looked first at Will and then at Jeremiah, then back to Will again. "Think, gentlemen. Think."

Jeremiah twisted his lips in a grin that was menacing, threatening. "They would if I had El Diablo's sister Luisa. If I were to threaten to shoot her I would dare to say that we could and would get free. Checkmate, you might say."

"No!" Angelica liked the young woman and could not bear to see her harmed. "She has done nothing to you." That Jeremiah would carry out his threat she had no doubt. By all intents he was a dangerous and ruthless man. She'd even heard her brother say that.

Jeremiah grunted in anger at her argument. Pulling back the curtain just an inch, he peered out, searching for Luisa with a heated gaze. Hatred or lust? Angelica didn't know but she sincerely feared for the dark-haired woman who had befriended her. The bandit leader would severely punish any man who dared to touch her.

"Gonna be easy." Licking his lips with the tip of his tongue, Jeremiah surveyed the scene. Unaware of any danger, Luisa bustled about the communal fire preparing the food that would be partaken of after the siesta. Two women aided her but neither looked to be any threat to the two men. "Come on, Will!"

Angelica watched them with conflicting emotions, loath to interfere lest she aid in bringing about a tragedy. She wanted to warn Luisa but knew that it might very well bring about the death of her two fellow hostages. She didn't want that. Nor could she really blame them for wanting to escape. If what Jesse had mumbled was true she too should try to escape and flee for her life. Yet to leave Jesse behind seemed the utmost degree of selfishness.

What should she do? Go or stay? Fear warred with her sense of justice. What would Mother Bernadette say? That she must put her faith in God and seek His guidance. And yet what if God meant for her to make her own decision? She closed her eyes, whispering a hurried prayer, but quickly opened them again as she heard Luisa's muffled scream. Jeremiah had cornered his victim and now held the gun to her head.

The entire camp had come alive, like a disturbed hill of ants. All watched in horror as Jeremiah brandished his gun. "Move back! Move back, I say, goddamn it, or I'll blow her head off. I will!"

Fearing for Luisa's life, the bandits and their women did as he said, but one man with piercing dark eyes and a scar across his cheek uttered a vow of what he would do to the gringo were he to get his hands on him again. Throwing down his rifle, he darted a glare in Angelica's direction as if somehow she were the one to blame. The hatred glowing in his eyes was unnerving and somehow Angelica sensed that if she found herself in his clutches she would pay the price for what was happening now.

"You coming, Angie?" Will Cooper displayed far more concern for her welfare than Jeremiah had, tugging gently on her hand as she stood in agitated silence, trying to make

63

up her mind. "Come on. I haven't got a gun to protect us. I don't think I can go if you don't. Please."

Luisa's terrified eyes seemed to add to the plea, sensing just as Angelica did that she would find no mercy at her captor's hands. In that moment Angelica made her decision, to go with them as far as the boundaries of the camp to make certain that Luisa did not come to any harm. Once they were out of camp she would set the young Mexican girl free. Surely such a gesture of compassion could not be met with anything but mercy from Luisa's brother. Surely he would offer to Jesse and herself clemency and a respite from death. She would wait for Jesse's wounds to heal, and when they did she would ride from the camp with him.

"Are you coming or staying?" Jeremiah's voice was gruff.

"I'm coming." Looking over her shoulder nervously to see if they were being followed, Angelica trudged along after the two men and the woman, heading for the outskirts of the camp and the corral.

Tall weeds were abundant along the wooden fence and she paused once or twice, doubly cautious as she walked along. There could be snakes slithering about in the wild grass and she had no wish to encounter one now. Snakes were the one thing which made her shudder in horror and lose all sense of reason. As a young child she had suffered a snakebite and had very nearly lost her life. It was a memory she could not forget, yet one which she tried to put out of her mind now as she pushed at the corral gate.

"Tom? Where is Tom?" It seemed to be the only hitch in Jeremiah's plans and he uttered a violent oath as he looked around for the boy and the horses. "Damned fool kid, he was supposed to saddle us up horses. Goddamn it!" His hands trembled violently as he toyed with the gun aimed at Luisa's back. Looking from right to left he seemed suddenly apprehensive about Tom's whereabouts. "Either

Tom has forsaken us or something is wrong."

"We'll just have to manage on our own," Will Cooper answered. "Can't turn back now lest we assure our death warrants." Several slats of wood were missing and the gate creaked its need of repair as the old man tried to open it. Only by kicking it could he budge it.

"Hurry! Hurry, you old fool."

For just a moment Jeremiah's concentration was shattered as he cast his eyes in Will's direction, but it was just enough time for Luisa to break free and seek the shelter and protection of a huge rock positioned by the corral. Her eyes darted to a clump of shrubbery as if sensing someone there, and Angelica's own gaze swept that direction just as El Diablo made himself known. In his hand was a knife which he threw across the space between himself and Jeremiah. With a thump it landed in the wood next to Jeremiah's outspread legs, just an inch from his groin. Jeremiah watched it quiver, seemingly in fascination, then turned to meet El Diablo's eyes. "Don't kill me. You would have done the same."

"If you ever touch my sister again, gringo, you will find yourself a eunuch, this I promise you. I will make your death so torturous that you will beg to be spared." He nodded his head and Margaro stepped from behind a large tree aiming his rifle at the bald-headed man's heart. "I should tell my amigo to shoot you down this minute like the dog that you are, but I will not show such disrespect for the ladies. You see, I am not so evil or heartless as you may have thought, señorita." His blue eyes met Angelica's and held them for a timeless moment before he looked away. "Take them back to camp, Margaro. Keep them tied up and confined. I will not have a repetition of this foolish matter of breaking free."

"Tied up? Oh no." The very idea was too humiliating for Angelica to bear. "Please. I won't try to leave. You have my word."

65

El Diablo's face was expressionless. "I trusted you, señorita. You betrayed that trust by . . ."

"I wasn't . . . I didn't . . ." Oh, how could she explain. Even if she found the right words he would never believe that she was going to return. "So be it then." Though she felt like crying, she somehow managed to maintain her dignity as Margaro led them back to camp. Angelica could not help thinking that she truly was a prisoner now, in every sense of the word. A prisoner of El Diablo. The devil. Maybe she would find out that was just who he was.

Chapter Eight

El Diablo meant what he said. Angelica's wrists were tied together with ropes during those moments when there was no one standing guard over her. She was mortified and totally humiliated. She would never again sympathize with Rodrigo as she had before. She had committed no wrong and yet she was being treated so harshly.

Night had descended quickly and Angelica looked up at the dark sky with its spray of shining stars. Another time she might have thought how beautiful they were or relished the quiet and calm. Now all she could think about was how very much she wanted to awaken from this horrible dream, to find herself safely cloistered once again within the abbey.

As she watched and waited, apprehension and dread welled up within her. What was to be her fate? Just what did El Diablo have planned for her? She pondered the matter, all the while working frantically at her bonds trying to loosen them so that she could at least get somewhat comfortable. Her hands felt numb, her back ached from sitting so long in one position, and she cursed the bandit leader as the long minutes passed.

Voices from around the communal fire droned on for a long while as the stars moved across the sky. It seemed she had been forgotten, at least for the moment, or so she hoped. She saw a gray-haired bandit rise to his feet, yawn and stretch then enter his hut for the night. Another left, then another, staggering as they walked. It seemed quite a few had drunk too much tequila and this troubled her. Men were often more violent when they were drunk. She regarded El Diablo warily from across the fire and felt relieved to see that, unlike the others, he seemed sober. Even so, his glittering blue eyes seemed to impale her as she caught his eye and she hastily looked away. Why did he look so stern? Hadn't she already paid the price for her transgression? Angelica huddled herself into a tight crouch, as if to make herself invisible.

The fire flickered and died, burning itself to ashes, and only then did the bandit leader approach her. Looking down at her feet, Angelica avoided his gaze.

"Shall we go, señorita?"

"Go? Go where?"

"To the hut. I'm going to sleep there too so that I can watch over you."

"No!" The thought of being enclosed in that tiny dwelling with him was unsettling. Staring down at her now he looked tall, dark and ominous yet so very handsome. He radiated masculinity. Perhaps that was what frightened her the most.

"Your escapade today makes it necessary. I must make you an example. Discipline you, so that the idea of escape will never come to your mind again." Reaching out, he helped her to her feet. Angelica recoiled at his touch. "Very well, then I will let you manage on your own."

"I will, despite the fact that you bound me like a slave." Struggling to gain her balance, she stood up, swaying precariously on her feet. "All I want is for you to leave me alone." Her lips quivered, tears stung her eyes, yet she managed to regain her dignity and conquer her fear as she followed him to the hut.

To Rodrigo she looked proud, most definitely not cowered as she pushed through the entranceway. He swallowed, feeling a slight sense of shame. Perhaps he should not have given the order that she was to be tied. Now that his temper had cooled he realized that he had been overly harsh with the gringo woman. Was it because she brought out feelings in him he'd fought so long to suppress?

"I'm sorry if you have been made to feel uncomfortable." It was the closest to an apology that he would come. "But you have disappointed me, señorita." Striking a match, he lit a small lamp.

She wanted to tell him the truth, that she had not been an accomplice to Jeremiah's foolish daring, that her intent had been to protect his sister, but instead Angelica kept silent. He would not believe her anyway. Let him think what he might. At least *she* knew.

"And you have shown *me* just how ruthless you can be and how uncompromising." She dared not say more lest she dissolve in a flood of tears. What a fool she was, a fool who had tried to look beyond his frowns and surliness to see the man inside. She had held a hope that he might be other than what he was but she had been wrong. "I too am disappointed."

They stared at each other, two silent, shadowy figures in the dimly lit hut, all too achingly aware of the other. The very air pulsated with expectancy. Angelica could not help but wonder what he was going to say, what he was going to do. She sat like a stone figure, her eyes never once leaving him as he took a step forward. She was frightened but vowed not to show it. Men who were violent thrived on creating fear.

Rodrigo knew he had her at his mercy, but far from reveling in that fact he felt sudden compassion. A woman such as this should not be humbled no matter what she had done. So thinking he walked across the room and without saying a word untied her, working at the bonds with fumbling hands. Why was he nervous? She was just a woman after all. More pious than most but a woman. Was it bravery she displayed or stubbornness? He was not quite sure. Whatever it was, he admired her, it was as simple as that and yet a bit more complicated.

Women had paraded in and out of Rodrigo's life since he was fourteen. He drew women to him, that he knew. They had served an uncomplicated need, fulfilled his passion and he moved on to newer territory when he grew tired of a particular woman. It was a matter of the body and not the heart. That was the way he wanted it. All his love he had given to Luisa, protecting her, admiring her, letting her trespass into an area of his heart where others could not go. Now suddenly he felt this gringa, this woman he did not know, threatened to invade that sacred place too.

"It is a thing I will not allow!" Without realizing it, Rodrigo spoke his thoughts aloud.

"Will not allow what?" Angelica trembled as his fingers touched her wrists. What was he up to? First he spoke of punishment and now he was untying her.

"I will not allow you to go beyond that door." He hid his true feelings by speaking in an angry tone. "If you disobey me you will be very sorry. Though I have up to this time not harmed you, I cannot promise the same for my men." His mouth curved in a smile. "I find you too skinny, but Pedro, Carlos, and the others might not. They have been known to force their attentions on unwilling gringa women. Do I make myself clear?"

"Very." And what of you? she wondered, her pride stung by his comment that she was skinny. She should have been relieved that he did not find her attractive, that she would not have to worry about any amorous advances from him. In a way she was and yet in a way she was not. How strange that this man she hardly knew could so complicate her feelings.

70

"There will be several guards posted about the camp just in case you do not heed my words, señorita." He stood near the foot of her sleeping pallet, the flame of the flickering fire casting shadows on his face. His brows were drawn together, his mouth set in a grim line.

"I understand." Flexing her fingers, she sought to bring back the circulation to her hands, yet they remained cold. Clenching and unclenching her hands she took solace in the pain her nails brought. It took her mind off El Diablo's piercing eyes, eyes which seemed to probe into the depths of her soul. "I will promise to stay inside, as long . . . as long as you remain a gentleman." She regretted the words as soon as they were out and winced as he threw back his head and laughed.

"A gentleman. A bandit, a gentleman. I adore your sense of humor, señorita." His eyes eased up and down, over the curves of her hips, the tapering of her waist, the fullness of her breasts. He knew the sudden desire to show her just how far from a gentleman he was, but then just as quickly regretted his thoughts. This woman was different from the others he had met. This one was a *lady*.

"I . . . I only meant . . ." Her words trailed off and the light of the lantern emphasized her blush.

"Then we have what you gringos call a Mexican standoff. Would you not agree?" He stood so close to her that he could have kissed her had he taken another step. The very thought of it caused her lips to tingle, sent a shiver of excitement dancing up and down her spine. She felt strangely bereft when he turned his back and walked to the other side of the room. "You must be very tired after the tension of the day. I would be selfish not to allow you the blessedness of sleep." His voice was soft, and had she not been in such a precarious position she might have thought it soothing.

"I *am* tired. Thank you." Angelica settled herself on the straw mattress, kneeling as she closed her eyes. She was going to need all the strength God would grant her to get

71

through this situation.

"What are you doing?" He seemed unnerved to see her on her knees.

"Praying."

"Say a prayer for me as well. Will you do that, señorita?" She was such a pious woman, he thought. One might almost think she was a nun. And yet instead of cooling his attraction to her it seemed to fuel it. He seemed to sense that the comfort, the understanding that he so needed could be found in her arms.

"I *will* pray for you, Rodrigo." Angelica prayed for Jeremiah, Will, Jesse, and Tom as well, then lay down on her side, pillowing her head on her arm. She could see El Diablo's shadow as he undressed and watched in horrified fascination as he stripped off his shirt to reveal his broad shoulders, his well-muscled arms. She turned her head slightly and caught her breath as she saw the hair that covered his chest. Just the right amount to tell beyond a doubt of his masculinity. She stared, unable to look away as he blew out the lantern. Then the room was shrouded in darkness. She listened, waiting to see if he would come towards her again, but he did not. If he touched her she would scream. But who would hear her? Who would care? Did she expect one of the bandits to come to her rescue?

Rodrigo swore beneath his breath as he crouched on his haunches, remembering the gringa's soft line of curves. He could hear her sigh as she relaxed and he ground his jaw in frustration. There was danger here, he thought pensively. If he were not careful this hostage could turn out to be his Achilles' heel. If he were not careful it could possibly be this Angelica Howe who held *him* in bondage. He must be cautious and very, very careful. So thinking, he settled down to sleep, yet sleep was very long in coming. Very long.

Chapter Nine

The flames of the oil lamp illuminated the pale face of the man lying on the rough straw pallet. Luisa gently wiped the perspiration from his face as she watched over the red-haired gringo. Strange how he had made her feel protective of him right from the first. She'd never had any special feelings for any gringos before. Certainly not for the kind of men who had tried to abduct her to facilitate their escape from the camp. She cringed at the thought, realizing what would have been her fate had Rodrigo not happened by when he did. Gringos. She had never held anything but hatred for them, and yet suddenly this one had been thrust into her care.

Najalayogua had removed his shirt to tend his wounds, and now Luisa let her eyes wander over what she could see of his body. His skin was several shades lighter than hers, a ruddy hue that she had seen on gringos with red hair before. Lightly freckled on his well-muscled arms and on his face. A tuft of red hair covered his broad chest and trailed in a thin line down to his navel and she realized that just looking at him was definitely exciting. She had to take care not to let Rodrigo know of her feelings, she thought, lest he forbid her near the red-haired man. Still she could not keep from appreciating his male beauty. He was nearly as handsome a man as her brother.

As if sensing her searching eyes, the man stirred in his sleep, a soft groan escaping his mouth. He was weak from loss of blood, had lapsed into unconsciousness from time to time, but he was alive and for that she gave thanks to God.

"You are safe now, Señor Jesse. I will let no one harm you. Rest." He winced in pain, struggling as if with some phantom attacker, and Luisa hastened to his side to calm him. "Do not struggle so, señor. You will reopen your wounds."

"Don't care . . . got to get free." For just a moment his eyes opened and Luisa could see bewilderment in the green eyes staring back at her. "Who . . . who are you?"

"It does not matter, señor. Only that I will not let anyone harm you. Not while you are with me." She meant to keep that vow. This man had already suffered enough. She would not allow her brother nor any other man to kill him. Nor the gringa who had looked at her with sympathy tonight, who Luisa sensed would have helped her had not Rodrigo come along. Blood begat blood, killing caused more killing. She would try to make Rodrigo see that truth.

"You will help . . . me?"

"Yes."

In gratitude he reached out to touch her face. "Thank you." It was a light caress, soft as the kiss of a feather, and yet she was moved. Despite the circumstances of their meeting, the danger, and his condition, she felt giddy at his closeness, in much the same manner as when she had partaken of too much tequila on fiesta night.

"I will not leave you." Her words seemed to comfort him, for he closed his eyes.

All through the night, though she was tired and longed for sleep, she watched over him. The sound of neighing horses, chirping birds, and the squawk of chickens at last announced dawn. Soon the camp would awake to another day and Najalayogua would come to push her away. Luisa didn't want to leave. She reached out to touch the gringo's face, returning the caress he had given her. The stubble of his unshaven face was rough to her fingers but she did not draw her hand away. Not until she heard the harsh sound of intaken breath behind her.

"Luisa! What are you doing?" Rodrigo stood behind her, his eyes reflecting suspicion. It would not do for her to have fond feelings for this gringo man. Bad enough that he was drawn to the *americano* woman.

"I'm . . . I'm just feeling his face for any sign of a fever." Luisa quickly stepped away, averting her eyes from her brother's searching eyes.

"And does he have one?"

"No."

"Then you may go. I will look after him until Najalayogua comes." Seeing that the man's chest was uncovered, Rodrigo strode forward and quickly pulled the linen blanket over the half-nude body.

"I need to cleanse his wound. Do not trouble yourself with such things, my brother. It is woman's work." She cheerfully bent to the task, dampening a cloth in Najalayogua's cleansing potion, using any excuse not to leave.

"Woman's work? Bah. I've tended wounds a hundred times before. You do not fool me, Luisa. You have a softness for this one. I've seen it in your eyes and I urge you to remember that this gringo is our enemy." Folding his arms across his chest, he openly displayed disdain.

"Enemy? Why? Because you will it?"

"He tried to break his way into camp."

"To save his amigos and the señorita. The ones you so cruelly had brought here, Rodrigo, to satisfy your own greed." Luisa refused to be cowered. It was time she had her say. In this matter of the hostages, Rodrigo was wrong.

75

Very, very wrong. "I know were it Margaro, Ramón, or Miguel you would have done the same. Argue that, if you can."

He couldn't. What she said was true, but that didn't soothe his anger. "Think what you will, I will not have you looking cow-eyed at some gringo. It will be all the more painful for you if . . ."

"If you decide to kill him?" She came to his side and reached for his hand in supplication. "Don't, Rodrigo. No matter what happens, even if we do not get the guns and the gold. Do not do this thing."

"It may be out of my hands. I will have to abide by what the others think as well as my own judgment." That was the thought that had been torturing him last night, the reason why he had hardly slept a wink. Things were not going as he had planned.

"You are *jefe*. You can keep the hostages from being killed. You must, Rodrigo. If you are the man I've always looked up to, the brother I remember, then you will. No matter what the others may say."

"Luisa . . ."

"You say *I* am soft on the gringo but I sense that *you* are drawn to the señorita. Is that what is bothering you, Rodrigo? The true reason for your scowl? It is not me but yourself with whom you are angry. No? You like the pale-haired woman. Well, so do I. Yesterday, when the man had the gun pointed at my head she looked at me in a way that told me she wanted to help me. It was the only thing that helped me keep calm. She didn't want the gringos to hurt me."

"She thought only of herself and her own escape!" He tried to convince himself of that. It made everything so much easier.

"No. You are wrong. If you look into your heart you will know what I say is true. She should not be shackled like the others. You know it and I know it."

76

"I cannot let her escape." Clenching his jaw, he met her pleading eyes.

"Because of your pride, or because you hate to lose her?" Najalayogua entered the hut and Luisa knew she had no reason to prolong her stay. Still, as she walked to the doorway, she turned her head. "Well, Rodrigo? What is the answer?"

"She must be held until the matter of the rifles and the gold is settled. That is the reason." He could not admit the truth of the matter. Not to Luisa and not to himself. Yet his sister's words rang in his ears as she walked away.

"You can lie to me, Rodrigo. But not to your heart."

Chapter Ten

Five days passed and still the rifles and gold did not come. It was a frightening time for Angelica, wondering what had happened to Edward. Surely he would not have deserted her. She couldn't believe that of him. He loved her. She was his sister. And yet Jesse's mumblings echoed in her mind. "No, he is not coming," he had said.

Perhaps Edward did not know that the rescue mission was thwarted. That was it! He was waiting for them to return with the hostages before he made his move. As soon as he realized they were not coming he would send the ransom. That was the only thought that kept Angelica going as the minutes passed into hours and the hours into days.

Time passed by relatively quickly, a whirl of unending chores during the day to keep her mind and hands busy. At night, however, it was another matter. She was only too aware of the bandit leader sleeping only a few feet away from her. The husky sigh of his breathing, his every motion, was all too much a reminder that he was there. At times she nearly thought she could hear his hearbeat thundering across the room. His presence was unnerving, keeping her awake for long periods into the night until she at last gave in to her exhaustion.

She was a fool for not escaping when she could, she told herself now. Had she helped Jeremiah when he requested it perhaps they would be far away from here, away from the man who haunted her thoughts during the day and her dreams at night. And yet such musings of escape were after all only a fantasy. No matter what Jeremiah had said there was really no way to slip past the guards without Rodrigo's sister in tow, nor could Angelica have left Jesse to his fate. No matter how many times she let the thoughts replay in her mind she always came up with the same answer. Though Jeremiah wished to have visions of a wondrous escape, they were trapped, as if they were chickens in a coop. Prisoners until El Diablo said otherwise.

The early-morning air held just a hint of a mist from yesterday's rainstorm and Angelica relished the soothing moisture on her skin as she stood in the doorway of the hut. Rodrigo had now given in to her plea, leaving her hands untied. Perhaps he thought his warning about what the other bandits would do to her had been reason enough to keep her from trying to escape or perhaps his conscience bothered him. Even so, she felt his eyes on her as he watched her from across the camp. He was always watching her but Angelica was slowly getting used to that now. Let him keep her within sight. She would do nothing to displease him or to endanger the others but neither would she hang her head and reveal to him the sadness that was in her heart. Let the arrogant desperado wonder what she was thinking, for she would never reveal her inner feelings. How could she when she really didn't know herself?

Walking slowly towards the communal fire, Angelica looked out at the rugged mountains rising in the distance, shadowed against the bright pastels of the early-morning sky and felt calmed. God's world, His beauty. Surrounded as she was by His handiwork how could she wear a frown?

It was a beautiful world. She had to remember that and try to keep her spirits up. Despite El Diablo and the danger she was in, she would try to be happy. Contentment was a state of mind. Wasn't that what Mother Bernadette had always told her? She forced the corners of her mouth into a semblance of a smile, determined not to scowl.

It really is not so *very* bad, she thought now, glancing at the others as they went about their work. Several of the women had befriended her. Najalayogua had promised to show her some of her healing potions, Maria had accepted Angelica's offer of teaching her to read, Elisa had welcomed her with laughter and smiles. Luisa had been the most gracious of all. Right from the very first Angelica had felt a bond with the bandit's sister. She saw her coming towards her now and answered her smile.

"How is Jesse?" Angelica asked. She had been forbidden to see him and the other hostages as well. That rule had rankled her at first but she had resigned herself to El Diablo's command. His word was law in the camp. Everyone knew that, even Jeremiah, who was now being a model prisoner, obsequious to El Diablo's every request. "Is Jesse better?"

"Much better, señorita. This morning I gave him some goat's milk. It will bring back his strength." She laughed. "He can be stubborn, that one. I nearly had to pour it down his throat. He told me he doesn't like milk."

"Most men do not. My brother never drinks it anymore, though I tell him over and over again that it would be good for him. Men can be pigheaded and usually are." She didn't realize that she looked straight towards El Diablo when she said the words until Luisa giggled.

"You mean Rodrigo, don't you? *Sí*, he is pigheaded. Most definitely so. I have tried to make him see reason but my chattering doesn't seem to do much good."

"Except that he isn't tying my hands anymore. Do I have you to thank for that, Luisa?"

"No. It is his own decision. I only tried to make him admit to himself that in this matter he is at fault. Always I have admired Rodrigo, but in this matter I disagree. He was wrong to bring you here. I think he realizes that now. He is not a brutal man. Do not let what has happened make you hate him."

"I do not hate him. I cannot truly hate anyone. I . . . I . . . well, I just don't know what I feel. I've never met a man like your brother before. He was ruthless with the three men who tried to rescue us and yet the children . . ." Even now he was ruffling the hair of a young boy who followed him around as if he were a hero. Perhaps to the child's mind he was. She only knew that he treated all the children with a gentleness that touched her heart. Lion or lamb, hero or villain, which was this El Diablo? Would she ever really know?

"He loves the children. Each and every one. He is a good man at heart, a kind man, though he has learned to hide that side of himself. And yet were it not for him these little ones would be roaming about the streets, hungry and in search of shelter and food. Most of them have no parents."

"But I thought . . ." Angelica was astounded. She had thought the children belonged to the bandits and their women. "Luisa, tell me what happened to bring your brother to . . . to this kind of life. I saw books and paintings in his hut that lead me to believe that both you and your brother shared another kind of life once."

"Once Rodrigo was a wealthy *caballero*, living on the land our mother's father had given him. *Our* father died when we were just children and so he had learned since boyhood how to be a man. He took care of my mother and of me and proved himself to be most knowledgeable in running our *rancho*." Closing her eyes Luisa relished the memory of another time. "We were a very respected family, and Rodrigo was known for miles around because of his fairness to the Indians who worked his land. In all

82

ways he treated them well." Opening her eyes again she tossed her head. "Our hacienda was always filled with neighbors and those who were our friends. It was a happy time."

"Then how . . .?"

Luisa's face darkened. "Rodrigo was unjustly accused of a crime he had not done. It was for the purpose of stealing our land. One of our neighbors, a gringo," she spoke the word like a curse, "gave false testimony against my brother in the matter of a murder. Rodrigo was imprisoned. He was going to be hung. Margaro just happened to be in the cell next to him and the two became amigos. When Margaro escaped he couldn't leave Rodrigo behind and so rescued him from the jail. He brought him to his hideaway and introduced him to the others, and before long they were looking towards Rodrigo as their leader. They recognized his worth and . . ." She might have said more had not another woman come to stand beside them. This one was one of the *unfriendly* ones, a dark-eyed beauty who had made it obvious right from the first that she did not welcome Angelica into the camp. Her eyes were hostile now as she eyed Angelica up and down.

"Rodrigo is asking for you, Luisa," she said without even turning her head. "It seems your wounded amigo has been making trouble." Her expression seemed to say that she was glad as she met Angelica eye to eye. "Rodrigo has his hands full with the hostages, no?"

"What has Señor Jesse done?" Luisa asked, her eyes mirroring fear. Like her brother she sensed that Jesse was volatile, easy to ignite to anger. It worried her that the two men she loved might someday come to blows.

"He somehow managed to get Rodrigo's gun and tried to shoot him. Now he will pay for what he has done. Your brother is threatening to hang the gringo. He should have done that in the first place and saved himself all this trouble."

"No. He cannot!" Luisa echoed Angelica's words as she ran towards the hut. Angelica started to follow but Bonita stood in the way.

"Luisa has no need for a shadow. She can handle El Diablo very well."

"I'm certain that she can. I was merely going to offer my help." Angelica met the woman eye to eye, stunned by the obvious anger she saw in her expression. "The wounded man is someone I know very well."

"The wounded man? He is not the reason you are like a nervous little bird, flitting away at the first cry of danger. It is Rodrigo that draws you. Do you think that I don't know?"

"Rodrigo? Oh no, you are wrong." There was something about this woman that unnerved Angelica. Was it because she could somehow delve into her mind and read the truth Angelica thought to be so well hidden? "I was concerned for Jesse."

"Your thoughts were upon Rodrigo. Do not imagine that I do not know."

Combing one hand through her hair, Bonita gave Angelica the benefit of her perfect profile. She was beautiful, the kind of woman to turn a man's head with amorous thoughts.

"I have not been blind to the looks you give to him. Hot enough to start a fire. For all your prudish looks I know what is in your mind. You wish that he would bed you!"

"No!" Quickly, all too quickly, Angelica shook her head, denying the accusation. "No. He means nothing to me." She hastily looked away, afraid that the other woman might be able to read the lie in her eyes.

"Do you think me a fool not to see? Have I not eyes in my head? Do I not have a woman's knowledge of such things?" Taking a step closer Bonita chuckled, a low, throaty sound that sent shivers of apprehension up and down Angelica's spine. She could feel the woman's eyes on her, eyes that never left Angelica's face, burning with their venemous glare. "You want him, whether you will admit it or not. But it will not do you any good. Rodrigo is mine. Mine! Do you hear? No, little *innocent* dove, I am not fooled. But he will never even look twice at you."

"I . . . I don't want . . . I didn't . . ." The buxom, dark-haired woman had startled Angelica with her words. It was true that she was attracted to Rodrigo O'Hara, she had known it from the very first. What she had not realized was that anyone else could tell. "He . . . and I . . ."

Throwing back her head, Bonita bubbled forth her laughter, a devastatingly scornful sound. "Your heart is written on your face every time you look his way. Lie to yourself but not to me. How he must laugh to know that such a plain, timid, uninteresting creature should even think he might look upon her with favor. What a joke he must think it to be." Her laughter died as quickly as it had flared and the malice returned to her gaze. "But no matter how funny Rodrigo may find the situation, he will have no second thoughts about spilling your blood if the rifles and gold do not come. Think on that, señorita, when you long for him to make love to you. He does not care for you! You are a hostage and nothing more. If he does not get what he wants from your brother he will kill you this quick." To emphasize, she snapped her fingers, causing Angelica to jump. "You had better pray that the rifles and gold come. With every breath that you have in your skinny gringa body, you had better pray!"

Chapter Eleven

Three days had passed and still the rifles had *not* come. Nor had any riders. Angelica scanned the horizon, hoping to see horsemen through the haze of the dust, but at last the truth could not be ignored. Edward was not coming. No one was coming. That thought chilled her blood. What was going to happen to her now? To Tom, Will, Jeremiah? She could at least be thankful that they hadn't hung Jesse. Luisa had managed to calm her brother's anger. Her hands were icy as she gripped them together. Dear God, what were they going to do?

An endless ocean of sand and scrub brush as far as the eye could see stretched out beyond the camp. Rocks, dirt, cactus, and an occasional tree imprisoned her as securely as any prison wall. Beyond that wilderness somewhere was the abbey. How she wished she were there now with the nuns and Mother Bernadette. She feared it was a place she would never see again.

There had been grumblings in the camp for the past few days. Arguments between the bandits. Angelica had an intuitive feeling that these angry murmurings concerned the hostage situation. No doubt there were some of those in camp crying out for blood. One bandit in particular frightened her, the one with the scar across his face. His eyes were menacing, following her about whenever she was in his line of vision. She found out from Luisa that Juan Garcia was his name, a *bandido* whose wife and children had been murdered by a marauding band of Americans.

Last night in the middle of the night she had been awakened by the clamor of gun shots, shouting, and cursing. Several of the *bandidos* had been fighting with each other, obviously drunk. Terrified, Angelica had pushed aside the covering to the doorway of the adobe hut and peered outside. Silhouetted against the light of the moon two figures had huddled, pushing and shoving at each other as they quarreled violently. At that moment she would have given anything to understand Spanish. As it was, their heated words were just so much mumbling, and she was forced to turn away without knowing what was being said. Only the words *"gringo"* and *"immediato"* made any sense. The appearance of Rodrigo had sent them scurrying like desert lizards, making it obvious to Angelica that whatever was being planned was not for his ears. Was it any wonder that she had spent a sleepless night, fearing she might be set upon at any moment?

How am I going to convince El Diablo to let us go? she wondered. She had been meek of late, in the face of his stern countenance. Avoiding him whenever she could for fear that Bonita's chiding was the truth, that Rodrigo knew she was drawn to him. She had remained aloof, as cold to him as a winter frost, but now she wondered if she should confront him. Argue. Show some spirit. Beg for their lives if need be. She couldn't just sit idly by as the sands in the hourglass ran out on them, then calmly prepare herself to die. Surely being pious didn't mean being meek as a lamb. Lambs were the only animals which would follow their leader over a harrowing cliff to their deaths. Angelica wanted to live.

"I won't just wait to die, I won't . . ." she mumbled

beneath her breath over and over, trying to boost her courage. There had to be a way.

"Señorita Howe?" Luisa tapped her on the shoulder. "You were talking to yourself. Are you all right?" Worried blue eyes appraised her.

"As well as I can be." Her shattered nerves were perilously close to the breaking point. "It's just that I don't want to die! I am not ready to leave this world, Luisa. There's so much that remains for me to do. And . . . and the rifles . . . and the gold . . . have not . . . may not . . . come. What then? Will your brother send us to our deaths?"

"I cannot believe that he will! Rodrigo is an honorable man. Despite being a bandit, he is not a cold-blooded murderer. But some of the men . . ." Luisa looked away, afraid to meet Angelica's gaze.

"I have heard them. I know what they want. They want us dead, because my brother did not give in to their demands. They seek to make us scapegoats to save their pride. I know what is coming but I am not resigned to my fate." Taking Luisa by the shoulders, she forced her to look at her. "Would you be? Were you at this moment standing in my shoes how would you feel?"

"I . . . I . . ." Pulling away, Luisa covered her face with her trembling hands. "Señor Jesse and . . . and you, I cannot bear to think of you being killed . . . nor . . . nor the others. But Rodrigo does not have complete control over what happens. Please . . . try to understand."

Angelica could see Najalayogua watching them, appraising Angelica. Somehow she sensed that there were two members of the camp who did not want to see her die. Perhaps that was a start. But what of Rodrigo? And Margaro? Would they prove themselves to be her enemies in the final moments of this ordeal?

Looking about the camp she could see that the two men were absent and wondered what was going on. One by one

89

the *bandidos* were disappearing, heading off through the trees without a backward glance. Something was happening! Angelica knew she had to find out what and descended the same pathway she had seen the *bandidos* take.

Staying hidden as she arrived at the clearing, she could see the faces of the men reflected in the light of the glowing fire, their mouths set in lines of determination as they looked in Rodrigo's direction. "We have waited long enough, amigos, the time has run out. I say the gringos must die!" One man voiced all their thoughts.

"They must be put to death," emphasized the man with the scar. It seemed that after Rodrigo and Margaro this man had the most respect and power. Angelica supposed it was because the others were afraid of him. He seemed fearless, the kind of man who would face death with a smile. Now he was asking for the deaths of the hostages.

"We will wait until I say otherwise!" Rodrigo's voice was louder than the others, perhaps because he knew that this Juan Garcia thought he was Rodrigo's rival. There could only be one leader of any band.

"Wait?" Garcia's voice issued a challenge that was echoed by the grumbling of the others. Bounding to his feet, he looked ominous as he ran his fingers over his knife.

"Yes, we wait." Rising to his feet, Rodrigo, taller by two inches, cooly stared him down until Garcia returned to his seat beside the fire. "I have not yet become a cold-blooded murderer. We took a gamble and we lost. Are we not men enough to laugh it off. Or do you want to add killing a helpless woman and a gringo who is little more than a boy to your list of sins?"

"Rodrigo is right." Always steadfast in his loyalty, Margaro turned a defiant glare in the other *bandido's* direction as if to warn him to be silent. "I for one would not want to be the one to take their lives. Killing in a raid or in a battle is one thing, shedding blood while looking a victim in the eye is another."

Garcia was not to be silenced. His eyes darted sparks of fire in Margaro's direction. "Bah, killing gringos is not murder, it is justice. I will not rest until every one of them is chased from our land. Gringos!" He spit the name between clenched teeth. "They are rats and vermin on the land, pouring in in greater amounts every year. We should have killed every one of them who set foot on our land."

"And would that have included my father? He was by your definition a 'gringo' and yet there was not a better friend to the Mexican people. Should he have been murdered too, Garcia?" Anger trembled on Rodrigo's tongue as he spoke and Angelica could see how difficult it was for him to maintain his self-control.

"He was the exception. The other gringos are like poison. They are evil. We must kill them."

"Kill, kill, kill, that is all you know, Garcia. Would you have us called butchers? That is not what I want. I only seek retribution from those who have given me harm. The woman, the boy, the wounded man have not done me or my people any injury. They were merely pawns in this chess game we played with the gringos." He seemed to have made up his mind. "We will wait. For one more day. Then, if the rifles and gold have not come, I will leave the matter of the gringos up to a vote." He motioned his head in Margaro's direction. "Margaro, my friend, I think it is time for you to take on another disguise. Perhaps the look of a señorita, eh? There is a *cantina* in the town four miles from here, near the spot where we were to meet the messenger with the guns and the gold. Go there and see what you can find out."

"Margaro a señorita? Ugh . . ." One man, a short, jolly, fat *bandido* made a face. "Too ugly. He will give the Mexican woman a bad name."

"I will make a lovely señorita." Margaro pretended to take offense, mimicking a woman as he swayed his hips

91

and danced around.

Rodrigo was in no mood for jokes. Banging his fist on an old log, he motioned for silence. "Margaro will go and he will find out all that he can. When he returns, *if* there are to be no guns and no gold, then we will decide. Until then we will assume that the hostages will be ransomed."

Angelica breathed a sigh of relief. For the moment they were to be spared. Rodrigo was buying them time in hopes of convincing the others to show mercy. At that moment she had never cared for him more. He was not as bad as she had first supposed. In his way he was trying to be just, fair and merciful. There was still a chance that they would not have to die. Perhaps if she could send a letter to her brother with Margaro, pleading with him to bring the rifles and the gold . . . As Margaro walked to the clearing she approached him with that thought in her mind.

"Margaro . . .?"

"You heard?" He was angered by that fact. "Our council was not for your ears."

"But I did hear and I'm relieved, Margaro. I had thought . . . but it doesn't matter. At least I know there is still a chance and . . . and if I were to give you a letter, from me to my brother, maybe it will not be too late." Taking him aside she had soon convinced him of the wisdom of her plan, then went in search of paper and pen. God had not deserted them after all. Perhaps in His wisdom he could soften Edward's heart and turn a near tragedy into a homecoming.

Chapter Twelve

Long after the fires of the camp were extinguished Rodrigo Delgado O'Hara stared out into the night, fighting a war within his heart. He had been able to grant the pale-haired gringa a reprieve thus far, had given her at least one more day, but what then? What would be her fate if Margaro found out that there were to be no guns or gold? What would the council decide?

"Garcia!" he snorted in anger, lighting a cigarillo and taking a puff. He exhaled the smoke, watching it form rings as it floated upward. Garcia relished trouble, his own hatred blinding him to justice. He would be a difficult man to control, to outmaneuver, in this matter of the hostages. Garcia would demand payment in blood if the ransom was not met. But Rodrigo could not, would not stand idly by and watch a cold-blooded execution. If that meant he must stand against his own men then so be it. There were times when honor and decency had to be upheld above all. Only then could he live with himself.

Rodrigo was tense, like a stick of dynamite about to explode. Garcia was causing trouble in the camp, trouble that did not just center around the hostages. He was challenging Rodrigo with every smirk, every glance, every word, telling by his every movement that he thought himself to be a better *jefe*. He was brazen, overbold, cruel, and impulsive and viewed Rodrigo's caution and wisdom as weakness. He'd said as much. The matter of the hostages gave him an excuse to confront the others, to stir up unrest and strife. Rodrigo knew he must be wary and beat Garcia at his own game. So thinking, he took another puff of the cigarillo while walking slowly about the camp. It seemed to be peaceful. There were no telltale signs to warn of danger; still, he walked until he was exhausted, only then seeking the solace of the hut, pausing before the entranceway to grind the cigarillo beneath his boot. At last he sought his bed.

It was late, well past midnight, yet Rodrigo found he could not sleep. Time after time his eyes were drawn to the sleeping form of the woman prisoner reflected in the pale candlelight and he was stunned at the longing he felt to reach out to her. He found himself wondering how she would feel in his arms, imagining how her mouth would taste were he to kiss her. Thoughts that he knew he should push away but which nevertheless haunted him.

"The angel and the devil," he whispered. They were a totally mismatched pair, yet he was more attracted to her than he had ever been to any woman. He admired her bravery, her loyalty to the others, and most of all he relished her gentleness, her smile. Rodrigo had had very little of either lately. He needed a woman's love, not just in the physical sense, for there were many women who could satisfy his body's urgings, but a woman who would truly care. Somehow he judged Angelica Howe to be that kind of woman. She did not deserve to die!

Rising to his feet, he walked over to where she lay, finding a strange sense of peace and calm in just looking at her. She lay sound asleep on her side, her head resting on one outflung arm, her blond hair spread across her arm and shoulder like a cloth of golden threads. She was wearing one of her simple colorless gowns, pink calico

94

this time, the skirt tucked up around her ankles. Her feet were bare and he found them alluring, small feet with perfectly formed toes. She looked so young, as innocent as a child, and he found himself wanting to protect her as she lay so peacefully in sleep. What a strange contradiction that was, to want to guard one's prisoner from the danger he himself had brought her. Yet he did.

Angelica's glasses lay on a small table by the pallet and he looked at her face minus the spectacles. Yes, she was pretty. He had been afraid to admit it to himself before, doubted that she even knew the full potential of her blossoming beauty. Perhaps that was another thing that drew him to her so potently. Bonita used her full-blown charms to get what she wanted, played upon them until she seemed to grow ugly, but this one was like glimpsing a sunrise for the very first time.

"Lovely." His eyes moved almost tenderly over her face, from the long lashes that shadowed her wide blue eyes to the gently curving mouth that was now slightly open as she breathed. She looked so untainted by the world's evil. Had he ever been like that? Yes, though it seemed a lifetime ago. All too soon he had been forced to take on the responsibility of manhood, the head of the family, and then the leader of a band of homeless souls.

Rodrigo's mouth tightened as he remembered the pain he had felt at his mother's death, at the bitterness and hurt she had been made to suffer. "Mexican" they had called her, as if she were dirt that might soil their hands. He had hated the man who had scorned his mother, had wanted him dead a hundred times or more; yet he had not killed him, no matter what lies had been told. Of that crime he was innocent, though the injustice he had suffered, and the hatred, had led him to commit violent acts. Acts that made him totally unsuitable for the gringa. In her eyes and in his. And yet just once how he wished he might touch her, feel the softness of her lips.

His gaze slid slowly over her slim body, lingering on the rise and fall of her small, firm breasts, visually caressing the length of her long, slender legs. Unwillingly he felt desire stir and was stung by his suppressed passion. He wanted her. God protect her, only at this moment did he realize how much.

One kiss, he thought. Just to feel her lips touch mine is all I need. One kiss to remember her by. He gave in to that sweet temptation, leaning over to brush his mouth against hers. Her lips were soft and sweet, and for just a moment he let hungry desire claim him fully. This was how it should be between a man and a woman, this feeling that surged through him. Far from quenching his thirst for her, however, it only increased it, and fearing what he might let happen were he to stay so close to her, he pulled away. Still, his lips held a smile, a smile that Angelica saw as she opened her eyes.

"I'm sorry. Forgive me, señorita. I should not have taken such liberties." There was no mockery in his eyes, only a gentleness she had never seen before. "It is just that I wanted to satisfy my curiosity." Oh, that I could satisfy much more, he thought.

"El Diablo . . . Rodrigo." She had thought that she was dreaming at first but realized now that the kiss had been real. Once she might have been terrified but after hearing Rodrigo's words at the council, she felt calm. She had wanted him to kiss her. Right from the very first she had been drawn to this man. She smiled sleepily, raising her hand to touch her lips. Bonita had been wrong! He did care.

"Do not worry, señorita. I will not harm you."

"I know." She was all too achingly aware of the warmth emanating from his gaze, the longing that his kiss had evoked deep within her. Though it was a chaste kiss it had awakened her to the full depth of her feelings. No longer could she deny the truth of what she felt for this bandit.

She was unutterably moved by the vulnerability and longing she saw in his gaze. Angelica was suddenly aware of her body as she had never been before. Meeting Rodrigo's eyes she felt a tingle in the pit of her stomach, knew the urge to reach out and bring him back to kiss her again.

"Señorita . . ."

"Angelica. Say it. My name is *Angelica*." She wanted to hear her name on his lips. Wanted that and more. She had never before been curious about what went on between a man and a woman but now she was. She had never felt desire until he kissed her but now she knew his kiss was a prelude to something wonderful.

"Angelica." He could not take his eyes off her, though he knew he should walk away from the temptation she presented. She looked beautiful in the moonlight, so beautiful that he could not leave her, at least not for the moment. He wanted to tell her that he loved her but swallowed his words, fighting the longing to pull her into his arms and kiss her again. "Angelica . . ."

They were all too aware of each other, of every breath, every blink, every sigh. His eyes held hers, staring at her with his mouth set grimly in that arrogant way of his, yet she had seen that mouth soft and smiling, had felt the gentleness of his kiss. Oh please let him kiss me again, she thought. As if reading her mind, his head moved slowly towards her as he reached out to take her in his arms. Angelica felt her heart cry out to him as his mouth claimed hers. Instinctively she reached up to touch his face, tilting her head back so that she could look at him in the aftermath of what had happened.

He had tried to stay away from her. *Dios*, he had tried. She was not the kind of woman to be taken lightly. She was an honorable woman, and yet somehow he had lost all self-control. Now he realized that she was the dangerous one and not he. Never before had anyone brought forth such tender feelings, a warm glow that started a fire not only in his loins but also in his heart. Even so he pushed violently away, startling the silence with his curse.

"*Madre de Dios!* His blue eyes flashed fire but he was angry with himself. Another kiss and he would pull her down beside him on the ground despite all his honorable intentions. That was not what he wanted of her. For a moment he had lost his head but it would *not* happen again. "I am sorry. I apologize for what happened and for what I have done. My conduct was inexcusable." Every muscle in his body stiffened. "But rest assured that I will never show such weakness again."

"Rodrigo?" Angelica was devastated, humiliated as he moved away from her. She had despaired of his ever being drawn to her, had thought herself too plain to draw his eye, and yet he had kissed her. Why was he angry now? She stared after him in stunned dismay, poised to follow him but unsure of herself. "Rodrigo!"

He wanted to answer, wanted to renege on his decision to leave, but did not. For the first time in his life Rodrigo Delgado O'Hara knew fear, not for himself but for her. His was a violent kind of life that would destroy a woman as gentle as Angelica. Better to end this forever before it even began than to know that he had hurt her. The gringo, Jesse Harrison, was more her kind of man. One of her own. Never the devil. Never a wanted man, a bandit.

Moving towards the door he did not see the eyes watching them, or the silhouetted figure duck quickly into the shadowed darkness. He had turned around just once to look at Angelica again. There was no way he could have known the silent vow Bonita Mendoza had taken, to rid herself of the gringa once and for all.

Chapter Thirteen

The fiery morning sun blazed across the horizon like a torch, nearly blinding Rodrigo as he opened his eyes to the day. He had spent a sleepless night, uneasy about the situation with the woman hostage. Angelica. He pushed her name out of his mind, despaired of calling her that again even in his thoughts. It made her seem less desirable, less approachable to refer to her as "the hostage," yet after last night he wondered if he could ever look at her again without remembering that kiss. It had been potent enough to make him realize the potential danger of the situation. That was why he had left the hut and slept outside the door. It was where he was determined to sleep from now on. The farther away he kept from that woman the better!

Qué va!" he grumbled beneath his breath. He had kissed a hundred women, perhaps more. Why then did he yearn for *her* lips again? It was a question that bedeviled him. She was attractive, reasonably pretty, but she was not the most seductive woman he had ever seen. No, it had nothing to do with her looks. It was something more. It was as if her soul cried out to him, made him realize that there was another world outside the camp. A world of refinement and beauty without violence and hostility. "Angelica!" She brought the warmth of sunlight and the gentleness of a spring breeze to his tormented heart. If only . . .

There were too many *if onlys* in his life. He had learned to live without regrets, without a thought to the past. He was what he was *now*, a bandit. He and Luisa had to forget the way their lives had once been. Rodrigo knew he had a duty to perform for those in the camp, renegades like himself who had been unjustly accused of a crime. He was their leader. He wanted a better life for them. This and only this had been the motivating force in his life until *she* had been brought here and forced him to delve into the depths of his soul, to look at what he had become. Ruthless. A man with little conscience.

Rodrigo tried to put any guilt feelings far from his mind. He had been driven to become an outlaw by desperation and by lies. His mixed blood marked him. The gringos taunted him because of his Spanish blood, the Spanish *caballeros* didn't fully accept him because of his Irish father. Only in this camp had he found a sense of belonging, a secure feeling of being needed. He would do anything in the world for these people he had made his own, anything but kill innocent people because one pale-haired gringo did not keep his word.

How was he to know this would happen? It had all seemed so easy. Too easy. Just like all the other times when he had taken from someone rich to aid those who were poor. They needed the rifles. Needed the gold. He had thought at the time that what he was doing was right. He wanted to help the Californians push the gringos from the land, wanted to do what he could to end the injustice being done.

Angelica was always speaking about God, yet Rodrigo knew God could not have meant for there to be such suffering. How could He condone that while others starved there were those men who strutted and squawked about in their finery like bright peacocks? Just because he fought against the gringos, he had been branded with the devil's name. The men who followed him had been branded bandits and there had been a price placed upon their heads. That did not mean they were evil! Even an animal would fight to stay alive.

And yet he regretted what had happened every time Angelica looked his way. He could not blame her for the injustice done to him. It was no fault of hers. She had not stolen his lands. She had not scorned him despite all that he and the others had done. Even when he had bound her wrists she had not spoken hateful words or tried to harm him. Instead she had suffered her humiliation in quiet dignity. He had kidnapped her, held her captive, even tied her, but he would not take her virtue. That he would not do to her no matter how much he longed to hold her in his arms. He knew these gringa women and how highly they valued their honor. To make her his woman, even for a short while, would destroy her. She was a virtuous woman, of that he had no doubt. Virtuous and untouchable and she would remain that way.

Rising to his feet he was adamant in his resolve to push her out of his mind. There were more important matters to think about. Garcia, for one. The surly black-haired *bandido* seemed to enjoy making trouble, arguing with Rodrigo's decisions, constantly stirring up the fierce fires of discontent. He was goading the other bandits with his babbling tongue. Rodrigo worried about Margaro and the mission he had been sent on. Would he be successful? They had only a few hours left before he would know. When Margaro returned, the council would meet again and either the matter would be settled peacefully or Rodrigo would have a fight on his hands to keep the hostages alive.

Walking towards the communal fire, Rodrigo reached for the huge coffeepot that rested in the flames and poured himself a cup of the strong brew. It was just as he liked it, hot and strong, simmered with Najalayogua's spices. From his squatting position from across the fire he watched as the others in the camp rose from their evening's slumbering. One in particular seemed intent on watching him as well. Bonita Mendoza flashed him a forced smile as she hurried to join him.

"Rodrigo . . ." Her voice was low and husky, whispering like the wind. Rodrigo scowled in irritation. He had no wish to confront her now. There was nothing quite as bothersome as a former mistress.

"You have been neglecting me, *querido*. One would suppose that I had suddenly sprouted another head. Or is it that I am suddenly ugly, Rodrigo? I miss our love-making."

"You are far from ugly as you well know, but I have much on my mind, Bonita. And as I have told you, I believe it is time for things to cool between us."

"You do not mean that! You cannot."

"I do. I have no time for lovemaking. There are other matters that require my full attention. I am not some rich *caballero* with nothing to think about but moonlit nights . . ."

"Ha! You think me to be a fool?" As if trying to punish him for his lack of attention to her, she dug the tips of her fingernails into the flesh of his neck. "It is that *puta* of a gringa hostage that distracts you, the one who shares your bed!"

Rodrigo clenched his jaw as he met her eye to eye. "She is no *puta*. I will not have you talk in such a manner."

"You will not?" The reflection of the sunlight glittered in her eyes, making her look predatory, like a mountain lioness after her prey. He was suddenly reminded of how dangerous she could be when crossed.

"We will have no more talk about the matter." A sudden sense of protectiveness towards the gringa hostage flooded over him. She would be no match for Bonita's ire. "I have

102

told you once and I will *not* tell you again that I have much more important things to do than soothe a woman's vanity. I wait for Margaro, to find out the status of our request for ransom."

"I hope he comes back empty-handed. I would be interested in seeing what you would do then. How you would protect that pale little gringa." She spat the words, her eyes flashing fire. "Well, you will have your chance to talk with your lusty friend. Here comes Margaro now and he is not wearing a smile."

Rodrigo followed her line of vision and saw that she was telling the truth. As Margaro strode forward with his hands at his sides and a frown marring his face, Rodrigo felt a sense of unease take hold of him. The moment had come now that he had been fearing. His voice was harsh as he asked, "Well?"

"I made contact with the gringo. At first he laughed in my face. No guns, he told me. And most definitely no gold."

"No guns! No gold?" He stiffened as Bonita's high-pitched laughter filled the air. As if he were shooing away a stray chicken he waved his hands at her. "Go away! Shoo! Foolish woman, do not anger me." In a whirl of multicolored skirts she was gone. "Then your mission was unsuccessful?"

"Not entirely." Margaro hurried towards the coffee urn and poured himself a cup, relishing it with a smacking of his lips, then sat down to tell the story. He had ridden all night without stopping and had found his quarry in a *cantina* halfway between the camp and the abbey. Dressed like a Mexican woman complete with veil, Margaro had approached him and somehow managed to get Edward Howe outside. Behind the *cantina* he had pulled a gun on the gringo and growled his message. "I should have brought him back to camp. No doubt when he was in fear of his own scrawny neck he would have given us all that

103

we asked for. Instead I gave him a message his sister had written.''

"Angelica? I did not know that she wrote a message."

Margaro looked sheepish. "I did not tell you but you will be thankful that she did. You see, the gringo told me he was certain that she and the others had been killed. Because of this he had not gone for the rifles and the gold.''

"He thinks me to be a murderer? A man who would not keep his word?"

"You are a *bandido*. That is not surprising." Margaro pulled at his long, drooping mustache. "Anyway, we haggled, the gringo and I. He was most stubborn, but he does seem to have some affection for his sister. He told me to tell you that he will not give us any gold but he will give us *half* the number of rifles we demanded.''

"*Half* the rifles?" Rodrigo was incensed; still, it was better than coming away empty-handed.

"He says he does not care what happens to the other hostages. He said to tell you that half the rifles should be more than enough to ransom his sister from your hands."

Rodrigo's anger exploded. "He does not care about the others. He is less than a man! Does he not even care about the red-haired man who rode so bravely into our camp trying to rescue the señorita?"

"He cares only to get his sister released back into his care." Margaro shrugged his shoulders. "I am to meet him at the appointed place and give him your answer."

"Then tell him this. If we receive half the guns and no gold, that will buy him the life of two hostages. Let it not be said that Rodrigo Delgado O'Hara is not a fair man. Two hostages for half the rifles." His eyes narrowed to gleaming blue slits. "Tell him I will let the hostages themselves decide who is to go and who is to stay. Tell him that is all I promise. On his conscience will be the fate of the other three.''

Chapter Fourteen

Angelica took her place kneeling in front of the concave stone *metate*, taking the heavy stone roller into her hands to grind the corn for tortillas. Luisa knelt beside her, taking dough into her hands and patting it out flat, then placing it on the hot earthen griddle behind her. Supper was a community effort with all the women helping, a time when Angelica could put her fears and her anxieties far from her mind.

"We are having puchero and enchiladas tonight," Luisa said, cocking her head towards the fire where two of the other women were cutting up chili peppers. "Jesse is well enough to eat solid food and I have it in mind to spoil him."

"You think a great deal of him, don't you, Luisa?" The lovely young woman didn't need to answer. The truth of her feelings was clearly written in her eyes.

"He is kind and gentle. I have never before met a gringo quite like him. I hope that when it is decided who will go and who will stay that . . ." Luisa broke off suddenly, realizing she had said too much. From across the fire Najalayogua gave the younger woman a fierce scowl, warning her to keep silent.

The entire camp had twittered with some sort of news.

An atmosphere of tension had hung over the camp all day and Angelica had wondered what had transpired this morning to cause every eye to follow her as she moved about the camp. Why was Margaro avoiding her so fervently whenever she moved his way? What was he hiding? She wanted to question him about what transpired with her brother but he was as elusive as the sun on a cloudy day.

"Something has happened, Luisa. What?" Angelica dropped the stone roller with a thud, grabbing Luisa's shoulders and forcing her to look at her. "Tell me! I have to know. Is my brother sending the rifles and the gold?"

"Sí. He is sending the rifles but . . ."

"He is?" Angelica interrupted her, relief flowing over her like a warm tide. Her plea to her brother had been successful. Rodrigo would not have to face the gruesome task of ordering their deaths after all. Slowly she raised her eyes upward, mouthing a silent prayer. Their ordeal would soon be at an end. "I have been so worried. I feared . . . but now I can relax." Picking up the roller again she busied herself with the task of grinding the corn. She felt content and confident that all would be well, at least until she noticed that Juan Garcia was staring at her. It was such a malevolent glare that she nearly burned her hand on the grill as she met his gaze.

"Tell me, señorita, how it feels to have an axe hanging over your head. Tell me how well you like your amigos, when it is either your life or theirs."

"What do you mean?" she withered under the look he gave her. Those eyes, those hard cruel eyes which seemed to undress her with their stare.

He ignored her, turning to Najalayogua. "Ah, puchero. Such a feast we will have tonight. Onions. Potatoes. Veal. Tomatoes. Take care we do not use up all our supplies, eh? But soon we will have less mouths to feed, is that not so?"

His laughter was shrill and penetrating, destroying Angelica's new-found calm.

"What do you mean, it is either my life or theirs. What are you saying?" Rising from her knees, Angelica approached him. "Tell me! Tell me! My brother is going to bring the rifles and the gold. Luisa told me so."

"No gold but half the rifles, *sí.*" He spat in the dust at her feet. "Enough to ransom you and perhaps one more, but not the others." Again he laughed. "It is for you to decide who will live and who will die, señorita. It will be for me to decide the losers' fate." Reaching in his belt he brought forth a knife, toying with it in menacing fashion, watching the glare of light on the blade from the sun's radiation.

"There must be some mistake." Angelica could not believe that her brother could be so heartless. Didn't he understand that he was possibly condemning three other people to death? How could he put earthly gain above the safety of their lives? "You are wrong."

"*Vamos,* Juan Garcia. Go away. You have done enough ill with your rattling tongue." Wielding her spoon like a deadly weapon, Najalayogua chased him away but the harm had been done. Turning to Angelica, the old woman sought to soothe her. "I do not believe that Rodrigo will take the lives of the others. He is not that kind of man. I believe that he will keep them prisoner for a while longer, until the gringos relent. Do not worry, child."

"Then it is true."

"Your brother is sending half the guns and no gold," Luisa said gently. "But that does not mean that Rodrigo will not change his mind. I am hoping that I can persuade him to set all of you free. There will be nothing gained in seeking reprisal for your brother's betrayal. Surely . . ."

Angelica searched for Rodrigo across the camp. No one could answer for him. Not Najalayogua, not Luisa, not

107

Juan Garcia. Only he could tell her what she needed to know. Bracing herself for the confrontation, Angelica fought to retain her courage as she walked slowly and surely across the camp. At the sight of his gunbelt she cringed. It was an all too potent reminder of the power he held over all of them. God give her the strength to say what must be said, she prayed.

"I must talk with you." She could barely get the words out. Her voice sounded like a strangled whisper.

"Talk with me? Yes, there is much that must be said, though I had hoped to wait until after our evening meal." Taking her arm in a gesture that made her tingle, despite the circumstances, he led her away from the fire and the prying ears of the others.

Angelica came right to the point. "Juan Garcia told me that my brother is sending only half the ransom and that it is to be used for me and one other hostage. And that . . . that you will kill the others. Is that true?"

His jaw tightened perceptively. "Half is true. I will release two hostages and two hostages only. Your brother will get only what he paid for. As to what I have decided about the other hostages, that depends upon what the others say."

"The council?"

"The council." The harsh glare in his eyes softened. "I will do my best to temper their decision. My men are not cold-blooded killers. Perhaps I can convince them to keep the others here among us. Your brother has paid for your freedom, señorita, but the others will be . . ."

"Let one of the other hostages take my place." It was the only way, the only hope. Edward had paid once to set her free, she was gambling on the fact that he would pay the other half of the ransom when she was not among the two hostages being released.

"Let . . . ?" He looked at her as if she had suddenly

108

lost her mind. "Señorita, you do not know what you are saying. Your brother has secured your freedom. I was going to let you and the others decide who the second released prisoner was to be."

"There is no question but that Tom Cowdrey should be set free. He is only a boy. So many years of his life are still to come. And . . . and Jesse needs a doctor. Jesse and Tom." It was the logical decision.

"I will release the boy." Rodrigo was touched by Angelica's tender bravery, her concern for the others when she could have only been concerned about herself, but he would not let her put herself at risk. "But you must go as well. It is only honorable. The child and the woman. The three men will stay!"

"But . . ." Angelica thought to change his mind but he covered her lips with his fingers in a gentle touch.

"I will speak no more about it. When the rifles are received you and the boy will be escorted out of my camp. It is what I have decided." And I will watch the sun fade from my life, he thought sadly. He should have been glad that she was going, felt a sense of relief that the temptation he had felt to claim her would finally be sent away. Why then did he have this empty feeling when he looked into her eyes? Why did he wish that they had met before he had become a bandit?

She was prim, proper, and prudish, not at all the kind of woman who should attract him, yet she intruded into his sleep night after night. Was that because he glimpsed what their being together could be like? When he looked into her seldomly smiling face did he glimpse what he could be with her gentleness guiding him? Did he catch a peek of what *she* could be? She was cold, like the mountain in the high country far to the north. Or was she? Did he not sense a blazing fire beneath all that frost? Yes. A spark waiting to be ignited into a flame by the love he could give her.

109

Selfishly Rodrigo wanted her to stay but he fought against such thoughts. He could keep her here, ah, yes. He could protect her from the others so that she would not be harmed and yet it was a far more noble thing to set her free. It was what he had promised himself he would do. Rodrigo Delgado O'Hara would make his truce with God by releasing one of his angels.

Chapter Fifteen

The sky was dark, the full moon covered by a shroud of clouds. Only the faint glow of the fire's embers illuminated the faces of the men who sat side by side. Fifteen men in all formed a tight circle around Rodrigo as they cast their votes.

"I say we kill all the hostages, despite the rifles. Bah, the gringo mocks us by what he does." Juan Garcia's eyes glittered evilly like a ferocious wolf.

"And I say we release *all* the hostages!" Margaro's voice was louder than it needed to be as he sought to draw attention from the other man. "We will get no reward by killing them." He kicked a rock into the fire sending the flames into a bright dance.

"Kill them all!" Again Garcia shouted.

"Set them free!" Margaro insisted and Garcia argued back. Only Rodrigo's strong grasp separated the two adversaries as the other bandits entered into the discussion. It was, Rodrigo reflected, much like a tug of war, with two distinctive views on the matter.

"I say we compromise!" With the grace of a nobleman he walked around the campfire, pausing before each man. Now he was glad that he had listened to Margaro's suggestion that he, Margaro, suggest the freeing of all the hostages. It gave Rodrigo the air of a mediator, gave him some bargaining power just as they had foreseen. "The gringo paid for half the hostages and that is exactly what he will get. The woman and the boy. The other three men we will keep here in the camp to do our heavy labor. Perhaps the gringo will have a change of heart, no? Perhaps his sister can convince him to give us all that we have asked."

"Keep the gringos alive? No!" It was an answer that was echoed by the other men's grumbling.

"No!"

"Kill them. They would have killed our Luisa."

"Show the pale-haired gringo that we will carry out our threat, that we are not as foolish, cowardly women."

"I say we spare them. The woman and the boy shall be released, the others held here as hostages." Rodrigo was taller by three inches than the other men and used his added height to his full advantage. Coolly staring down at first one man and than another he quickly asserted his authority.

"Rodrigo is right." Always steadfast in his loyalty, Margaro turned an angry glare in Garcia's direction as if to tell the other bandit to hold his tongue. "If we kill them we invite vengeful gringos into our territory. If we spare them we prove ourselves to be merciful."

"We prove ourselves to be weak!" Garcia was not to be silenced. His eyes darted sparks of fire in Margaro's direction. "We must kill them."

"And be called murderers and butchers. That is not our way. I have said that once before, Garcia. We are not barbarians. I only seek retribution from those who have given me harm. To those who will offer us a small measure of peace I offer my hand."

"And you will have it cut off. Struck from your body by those who wish to dance upon your grave. Gringos. *Americanos*. They hate Mexicans. They wish us dead so

112

that they might steal our land. Are we then to show them how 'merciful' we are so that they will seek to destroy us, or prove to them that we will reward treachery with death!" Garcia challenged.

"We must prove to them that we are men, not animals. But I will leave the matter up to you." He gestured with his hand, sweeping from one to another of the bandits. "All of you. We will do this the right way. Each of you will have a say." Gathering a handful of small rocks Rodrigo gave one to each bandit, then drew a square in the dirt. Down the center of that square he drew a line. One side for yes, the other for no. "If you cast your stone to the left, that means you wish to see the hostages killed, to the right means you offer clemency."

One by one each *bandido* stepped forward to cast his vote while Garcia looked on with glaring eyes. Ramon, for keeping the hostages alive, Diego for killing them. Julio for the hostages, Margaro for the hostages, Pedro against them. On and on until each stone had been cast, ending with Garcia's vote.

"Four against the hostages and eleven in favor of keeping them alive. You lose, Garcia. We will release the boy and the woman, just as I have said," Rodrigo announced.

Gritting his teeth, his eyes blazing with pure venom, Garcia turned on his heel and stalked off, and though Rodrigo knew he had won a small victory tonight he could not help but wonder at what price. Still, just to keep Angelica safe he would have faced Satan himself.

Rodrigo was not to know of the danger that awaited Angelica at that very moment as a darkly clad woman stumbled about in the night, holding a covered basket at her side. Bonita Mendoza stumbled once or twice, uttering a husky oath of anger as she carefully readjusted the lid. Slowly she made her way across the hard earth, feeling the bristle of dry grass, the round hardness of pebbles beneath

113

her bare feet.

"Just one bite," she whispered, "the woman will not even know what struck her." It was a valuable treasure she carried inside the basket, one that would ensure her she need have no further worry concerning the gringa.

Hearing the chatter of several men, she ducked back into the shadows, her heart lurching in her breast. She thought of what she would say if she were caught walking about and decided she would tell them the basket contained food. No one need know of the snake inside, the venomous viper who would remove her rival once and for all. Thinking about the reptile made her shudder and she carefully adjusted the lid of the basket. She did not want to be the rattler's victim. Instead she had saved that fate for another.

Bonita waited until the coast was clear, then headed towards Rodrigo's hut, where the pale-haired *puta* slept in false security. Soon she would sleep the deepest of all slumbers. One from which she would never return.

Moving slowly towards the hut, keeping to the shadows, Bonita pushed the covering aside, relishing the soft sounds of Angelica's slumber. She had feared she might be awake but everything was going exactly as planned. Rodrigo and his foolish meeting had kept him away from his usual post of guard at the door. She had to act now.

Pushing the covering of the hut aside, she adjusted her eyes to the room, taking careful note of where Angelica lay. "Go, do your work, my precious one," she breathed, setting the basket down by Angelica's leg. She could hear the soft slither of the reptile as it burrowed into the woman's garments. Only the tip of the snake's tail remained as evidence that Angelica had a visitor.

I must make him angry so that he will strike, Bonita thought, searching about for something to touch the snake with. She found the perfect instrument in a decorative sword Rodrigo had mounted on the adobe wall. A memento of his life as a *caballero*, she mused, letting a

114

smile tug at her lips. It would be used for a far different purpose now.

Clutching the sword, Bonita fought against the trembling in her hands. Now was no time to be squeamish, to have second thoughts. What was to be done must be accomplished quickly before Rodrigo returned and she was caught in the act of vengeance. She raised the weapon high and brought it down on the serpent, hitting it enough to anger it. Again and again she used the same ploy until she heard the sound she wanted to hear—a loud rattling, a warning of danger. Only then did Bonita pick up the basket and flee into the safety of the night.

Chapter Sixteen

Angelica opened her eyes in the darkness. Something was wrong. Very, very wrong. First she had felt the sharp prick to her leg and now she felt violently ill.

Rising from her pallet she walked on trembling legs to light a candle near her bed. There was something about being in darkness that added to her anxiety. Perhaps the candle would make her feel more at ease until she managed to calm the strange shaking that had taken hold of her.

"Oh . . ." She was startled by the dizziness that swept over her, by the nausea churning in her stomach. Was it something she had eaten? The puchero perhaps? Or her nerves? The strain of the whole situation of her brother's reluctance in paying all of the ransom had eaten at her. "I must take hold of myself. I must," she muttered.

It was much easier said than done, for even as she tried such a simple task as lighting the candle her fingers trembled so violently that she had to make the attempt again and again. Pain pounded in her head, streaking down her back, but she did feel much better as the soft candleglow lit the room. Shivering convulsively Angelica sought the warmth of the candle. It was so cold in the hut and she scanned the area in hope of finding a serape. Then she saw the loathsome reptile, curled at the back of the hut.

A snake! Oh my God! It was the one thing that could completely make her lose her sanity. Surely they were Satan's creatures!

Angelica tried to move backward but it was as if her muscles had suddenly grown weak, as if she could not even think. As the reptile lifted its flat, ugly head and stared at her with its slanted, beady eyes she screamed, long and loud. Suddenly she knew what the sharp pain in her ankle had been.

"No! No!" She flailed about helplessly, certain that she felt the poison coursing through her blood. She would die! Most precious Jesus, she would die a most agonizing death.

"What is wrong? Why did you scream?" Like a hovering angel Rodrigo appeared in the doorway, anxious as always to help her. This time, however, she knew he had come too late.

"A . . . a snake . . . bit me!" she somehow managed to say. Her terror-filled eyes seemed riveted to the reptile. Putting her arms about her body she shivered again.

"A snake?" Rodrigo followed the line of her vision and saw the rattler. *"Dios!"* Quickly he found a rock and beat the unwelcome visitor to death, then just as quickly turned his attention to Angelica. Holding the blade of his knife in the candle flame for just a moment he asked quickly, "Where did it bite you?"

"My left ankle." Strange how his being near somehow calmed her, until she saw his expression.

"I am sorry, but I am going to have to hurt you." He cut an "X" on the spot where the rattlesnake's fangs had made a mark. Putting his mouth to the wound he tried to suck out the poison, hoping he was not too late. He'd been in the wilderness long enough to know that the lovely golden-haired woman was in terrible peril.

"I felt something sting my leg while I slept but I didn't

know . . . I didn't know."

"When did it bite you? How long ago?" His voice was sharp, not because of anger at her but out of fear.

"I . . . I don't know exactly. A . . . a short while ago, I believe. It woke me but I tried to go back to sleep. And then I felt ill and I got up to light the candle. That's when I . . . I saw *it!*"

A sense of awesome guilt swept over him. *He* had brought her here. On his head rested the blame. She was too gentle a creature for the harsh dangers of the camp. Now the possibility of her death tormented him. Let me not have been too late, he pleaded silently.

"Keep quiet. Do *not* move about needlessly. Try to remain calm so that your blood will flow more slowly." His hands were gentle as he laid her back on the pallet. Calm, he thought. How could anyone maintain tranquilty under the circumstances? Surely *he* felt the tension. He wanted to scream, he wanted to shout, he wanted to curse and lament that this had happened, but he had to keep a level head. "I will get Najalayogua. She will help you. For the moment, Señorita Angelica, just lie still."

"All right . . . I . . . I will, Rodrigo." Her face was pale, her skin felt cold and clammy. She fought against her fear as she obeyed him. He was right. She must somehow find the courage to do as he said. Moving about would only add to the danger of the poison spreading.

Rodrigo tore through the camp like a madman, locating the healing woman and dragging her unceremoniously from her hut. "Come! Come, old woman. The American woman has been bitten by a rattlesnake. You must help her!"

"Aheeee! To take a woman from her bed." Her eyes were still half closed from sleep.

"It cannot be helped. You must hurry." When they reached the hut he pushed her inside. "You must see what you can do." Pacing back and forth over the dirt floor, he

119

watched in helpless anxiety as he saw the play of expressions move over the old woman's face.

"It is not good," she said at last. "I do not believe there is much that can be done. If we had tended her sooner perhaps. But the poison will have seeped all through her. Look at her, Rodrigo. Already she has the pallor of the dead." She shrugged her shoulders sadly. "I cannot work miracles, Rodrigo."

"There must be something you can do! There must be!" He knew if Najalayogua was right, if Angelica died, he would never be able to be truly happy again. Her death would be on his conscience for the rest of his days. There was something he realized at that moment—how very deep his feelings ran for the pale-haired beauty. No matter what bargain he needed to make, be it with God or even the devil himself, he would make it. Somehow he must do everything in his power so that Angelica Howe lived.

Rodrigo stared at the face of the lovely woman lying so near death. She was in a state of shock—her pulse rapid, her breathing shallow. Still, she was alive and as long as she was there was hope.

Najalayogua had tended her with care, coaxing a potion of herbs down Angelica's throat. The old woman had applied a clay, moss, and herb poultice to the red, swollen wound, designed to draw out any poison that might have remained. Rodrigo had watched her collect her herbs together, her mortar and pestle, and mix them in a brew that warmed over the fire. A miracle, that was what he was hoping for, and though the strange-looking mixture did not look imposing he hoped it would save the American woman's life.

"She must drink this potion. It will flush out the poison. Force it down her throat if you must, but see that she drinks it," the old woman had said. Thus, Rodrigo had kept his vigil. All they could do now was to hope.

"So lovely, *pequeña. Querida.*" And she was, even in

her deep sleep. Her pale hair was spread across the pillows like threads of silk, framing the ashen face that had grown so very dear to him. *"Querida!"* Smoothing the hair from her feverish brow he watched as her eyelids fluttered open, then she fell back into unconsciousness. If only he had let her go, and yet had not his stubbornness been in part the fact that he secretly wanted her near him? Yes. He could have so easily let her escape with the others and yet he had been incensed when he had found her with them. Why? Because he had wanted her to stay, despite the insanity of such reasoning. He had wanted her to want him, even though all his instincts had cried out against such foolish thinking. The devil and the angel.

Slamming his fist into his palm, Rodrigo gave vent to his anger. He would not give up! Hour by hour he watched her, caring for her as gently as any mother does her child. Taking her hand in his he promised not to leave her side. It was a promise he kept.

Watching the motion of her gently rounded breasts rising and falling beneath the covers as she struggled for breath, he felt a wave of stark fear sweep over him. "Don't die, *querida.* Please! Please." As if hearing his voice, her breathing relaxed and Rodrigo felt such a tenderness and love for her that his eyes were wet. Never a devoutly religious man in the last few years, he nonetheless bent his head and knees to pray.

At last midday came, bringing with it bouts of delirium. Her garments were so wet that they clung to her and he quickly had Najalayogua strip them off one by one and towel her dry. As soon as she was finished Rodrigo wrung out a cloth in cool water and laid it across her forehead, soothing her with his words, telling her that she must get well.

The day was hot, humid, and muggy, yet he watched as she shuddered violently with chills. No matter how many blankets he piled on her she still trembled. Even so she complained of being too hot.

"Please! Please! I am burning up." Angelica fought raggedly for air, felt as if her throat would close and suffocate her. And all the while, the pain in her head, the weakness in her limbs, made her certain that she was dying. "Dear God, please give me strength," she whispered. "A priest! I must have a priest! Don't let me die without . . ."

"You are not going to die!" A low, husky, voice answered her. Her brother? Was there a priest by her bedside after all? She tried to focus her eyes, feeling so confused.

"Oh, Mother Bernadette, I will make a terrible nun. I must take my vows. Edward wants me to . . ." She started babbling, talking about the abbey and the contentment she had felt inside its walls. "Sister Theresa, Sister Mary . . ."

Rodrigo pricked up his ears to what she was saying and stared in disbelief. *Madre de Dios,* his sin was more grievous than he had supposed. Angelica, his lovely *querida,* talked of becoming a nun. What did she mean? His angel, a woman of the cloth? Angelica Howe? The thought deeply troubled him as he remembered all the passionate thoughts he had had. He had thought once before that they were a mismatched pair, now he knew for certain that they were. A nun! *Dios!* To think what he nearly had done.

"Mother Bernadette! Mother Bernadette!" It was a name she kept mumbling over and over. "Please guide me in making the right decision. I was doing as you bid me and giving all my thoughts to looking within my heart . . . I want to serve God. Please help me."

Rodrigo remembered what a pious little creature he had thought she was when he had first taken her to the camp. How he had seen her so frequently down on her knees. Now he knew why, and the potency of the revelation stunned him. Perhaps in his way God was mocking him. Taking away the only woman Rodrigo had ever loved and putting her on such a pedestal that Rodrigo could never hope to obtain her. Even were he the *caballero* he used to be he would not have been able to claim Angelica Howe. *Sister Angelica!"*

Despite his disappointment, however, Rodrigo could not deny his love. The very sight of her brought a quickening to his heart, a longing he knew would remain forever unfulfilled. He held vigil by her bedside, hoping beyond hope that he would see her open her eyes. When she did he would leave, but only then.

She must never know how much I love her, he thought. He made a bargain with God. If God granted her life, he would fight against the love in his heart with every breath. He had managed to put on a hard shell to hide his vulnerability several times before. He was a master at it. Now he would do so once again, hiding from Angelica what was truly in his heart. He would be distant, he would be cold, until that moment when she left the camp to return to her Mother Bernadette.

You must forget the kiss you shared, the soft words of love you whispered in your thoughts, he told himself. Running his fingers through his hair he gazed in anguish on her face. She was so small, so innocent in her tortured slumber, yet she had a strength that far surpassed any of the other gringos he had ever seen. Perhaps she even exceeded Rodrigo himself in courage.

Straightening her blankets each time she kicked them away, wiping the perspiration from her body with a soft cloth, he let his fingers linger in a farewell caress. They would never know her love and yet he would carry the image of her forever branded in his heart.

Daylight flickered and died, turning into night. Rodrigo lighted a candle in the hut and started a small fire. He had done everything Najalayogua had told him to do.

123

Making Angelica drink the potions, keeping her warm, bathing her forehead with cool water. He had watched, waited and hoped and now as night passed into day again he was nearly drunk with fatigue. Yet he feared to close his eyes even for a moment, fearful something might happen to take Angelica away. Permanently away where even her Mother Bernadette could not come to her.

"*Querida*. My lovely angel," he said again. Unable to resist temptation, he reached out to touch her again, feeling the silky softness of her skin. His gaze wandered over her in a lingering caress. She would never know how very much he loved her. She must never know. "And she never will!" he whispered.

Chapter Seventeen

Warmth and light. Far away in the darkness of her mind she imagined she heard someone calling her name. Angelica, a husky voice called. Live. Please live. Someone was with her. Rodrigo? She wanted to know but did not have the strength to open her eyes. "Please . . . help me . . ." she breathed.

Dreams haunted her. Strange dreams. She seemed to be walking down a long, dark tunnel, groping about, struggling to come back into the light. Someone waited at the tunnel's end and she reached out to him? "Edward?" No, it was not him. Instead another darker form awaited her, holding ropes that would bind her. Prisoner. The word echoed over and over again, yet as the man walked forward she suddenly had no fear. "Rodrigo . . ."

There had been such magic when he had touched her. She wanted to stay, wanted him to love her. "No . . ." He was the devil. The others. "Tom . . . Jesse . . . Will . . . Please do not harm them. Oh, Mother Bernadette, what should I do?" Thoughts swirled inside her head, thoughts she tried to push away. He was a bandit, a violent man. How then could being near him make her feel so content?

A chill swept over her and she shivered, only to be enveloped by the soft warmth again. She felt the touch of a hand at her temple, brushing the hair from her face. Unconsciously she reached out, touching warm flesh, grasping tightly. "Don't leave me." She tried to sit up but a gentle pressure held her back.

"Sleep, little one. Sleep," a voice seemed to say. Was it real or was she only imagining it?

"Sleep . . ." she mumbled. Somehow she felt secure and let herself drift off into the darkness that consumed her. The sensations of the ministering hands were glorious, relaxing. "Don't stop!" Every part of her body absorbed the tantalizing stroking, bringing peace and contentment to her once tormented body. No longer did she feel that she was burning up, no more did the chills wrack her body with shivering. The pain was gone and she was at peace.

"Is she going to be all right? Najalayogua, *por Dios*, tell me!" Looking down at the small huddled figure Rodrigo felt a profound tenderness for Angelica. For three days and nights he had hovered by her side. Sleepless nights and restless days.

"She is out of danger, Rodrigo. Aheee, it is a miracle. The likes of which I have never seen."

"Your herbs and potions."

She shook her head. "No, your love and care. It is you who brought her through this. She will be very, very grateful."

"She must not know. You must not tell her it was I who sat by her bedside. I do not want her to know."

"You do not . . .?" Lifting her eyes she studied him, knowing instinctively of the depth of his feelings for the woman with the pale-yellow hair. He was taken with this woman. Much more than that. The thought made Najalayogua smile. She liked the gringa, this *americana*. There was courage deep within her heart and a kindness that could soothe Rodrigo's troubled soul. A woman like this was a treasure. "You should tell her, Rodrigo."

"No! I have my reasons." He was determined to keep his

distance, to maintain a cool manner with the *americana* woman when she awoke. Until the day she left he would be polite but he would stay as far from her as he could. "She must not know that it was I who stayed by her side. What I do, I do for her."

Najalayogua did not question him nor did she argue. She knew Rodrigo well enough to know it would do no good. He could be a stubborn man. She watched in silence, therefore, as he reached for the dampened cloth Najalayogua held in her hand and gently brushed Angelica's face, then handed the cloth back to the healing woman.

"Remember what I have told you," he said, forcing himself to be stern. "If the woman asks, tell her it was you who nursed her back to health." With a jangle of spurs he was gone, leaving the old woman to watch over Angelica in silence, to hold vigil waiting for the gringa to open her eyes. After another hour of waiting a fluttering of eyelids told her the young woman was awakening.

Light flickered before Angelica's eyelids as she struggled to open her eyes. She imagined she would find Rodrigo towering over her, remembered it to have been his voice she heard and was therefore surprised to see the old woman's face hovering just inches from her own. In confusion her eyes swept over the contours of the room, searching for someone else. "Rodrigo . . . where . . . where is he? I thought that he was here."

The old woman hated to lie but knew that she must. "Rodrigo was not here."

"But I heard his voice, heard him talking to me through the mists of sleep." She tried to rise from the pallet but she was as weak as a newly born kitten. The room seemed to whirl about her head, and so in resignation she lay back down, burrowing her head in the crook of her arm. How long had she been here? And why? She suddenly remembered and cringed. The snake. It had bitten her, made her deathly ill, but someone had brought her back from the brink of death. She had thought it was Rodrigo. She put her confusion into words only to be met with the same answer.

"Rodrigo was not here. It was your imagination, nothing more, *pequeña*." Reaching out, Najalayogua took Angelica's hand in her own gnarled fingers.

"Then it was you who watched over me?" Angelica could not hide her disappointment. She had thought . . .

"*Sí*, it was me. I gave you potions and put a poultice on your leg to draw out the poison."

"Then I thank you."

Najalayogua shook her head. "It is God who must be thanked and not I."

Angelica felt a flash of guilt. She had been so disappointed in hearing that Rodrigo had not been by her bedside that she had forgotten to give her thanks to *Him*. Closing her eyes she whispered a prayer. She was alive! Miraculously alive. Oh, how precious was life! The most priceless of gifts. She had been bitten by the serpent who had intruded into God's Eden and still survived thanks to His mercy.

"You fought to remain in this world, *pequeña*," Najalayogua said at last. "You did not want to leave us. I think I know one of the reasons. The look in your eyes tells me that there is someone you hold in your heart. Rodrigo."

Angelica's eyes widened in surprise. "What do you mean?"

"I have seen the way you have looked at Rodrigo ever since you arrived here. I heard the wistful tone in your voice when I told you he had not been in this room with you. I have potions that will melt a man's heart. Shall I give you one for Rodrigo?" She smiled a gap-toothed smile that held a hint of kindness, yet amusement too. These two young ones were drawn to each other but were fighting so foolishly against their feelings. Did they not know the awesome power of fate? Taking Angelica's chin in her palm she turned her face up to meet her eyes. "Can you look me in the eye and tell me you have no feelings for him?"

"I . . . I . . . what do you mean?" The piercing eyes made it too difficult to lie. "All right, I am drawn to him. He fascinates me and I sense a certain sadness in him, but I am not the kind of woman who would ever attract him. He is so handsome and I . . . I am much too plain." She really believed that. Edward's insistence that she was not pretty had been whispered once too often for her not to think he told the truth. "And besides, as soon as my brother brings the rifles I will . . . I will be gone from here." A sudden thought alarmed her. "Has Edward brought the rifles yet?"

"Sí, Margaro went to retrieve them yesterday. He should be back any day."

"Good. Good." She cast her eyes from the old woman's face so that her expression would not reveal the conflict of emotions she felt in leaving. "Poor Tom, he will be so glad to be back with his parents again. And I . . . I will hurry back to the abbey. Perhaps in some way I can manage to find a way to free the others."

If Rodrigo really does let you go, Najalayogua thought. Somehow she wondered if the *bandido* leader would really part with his rare treasure. She hoped he would come to his senses before he made a foolish mistake. Perhaps in her way she might help. A thought crossed her mind, and hugging her knees to her chest she cackled in amused merriment. "Aheeee, we will see!"

Chapter Eighteen

"The guns are here! Margaro has returned." A tumult of voices outside the window told Angelica the news without her even having to move from her chair. The matter of the ransom had been paid and soon she would be leaving this hideaway. Instead of feeling elated, relieved to finally be free, she felt sad. The last few days had shown her that many of the women really cared about her. Maria, Elena, Najalayogua, and several of the other women had shown her a great kindness and she hated to leave them. She'd had very few friends in her life, even the other young women at the abbey had teased her. Somehow she felt that she could make a home for herself here. And Rodrigo . . .

Foolish dreamer, she thought. Always she seemed to have her head in the clouds, imagining how it might be if the bandit leader cared for her just a little. If she were honest with herself it was *he* she hated to leave. She'd grown used to his tall, manly physique hovering around her, his smile, even his scowl. The thought of never seeing him again pained her. And yet that was the way it would be. She would go on to Santa Barbara, would finish her assignment and then sequester herself in a room and think about the direction her life would take from now on.

Would she take her vows? A voice in the corner of her

mind told her *no*. Since meeting Rodrigo she had realized what it meant to love. It had not worked out between her and the bandit leader but nerverthless she had glimpsed a passionate side to her nature. For the first time she truly realized that she had never been meant to be a holy sister. God had other plans for her. Her life was to take a different path.

The sounds of the men's voices intruded on her musing.

"Guns. I have need of a new rifle."

"Are there also bullets, Margaro? Was ammunition part of the booty, eh?"

"Bullets and guns."

The voices of the bandit men had grown louder. Laughing and revelry. Angelica rose shakily to her feet and walked to the door. Even after two days she was still weak from her ordeal. Her head whirled dizzily and she felt nausea churn her stomach. She knew she must be pale and wondered if her appearance would alarm her brother when they were united. If so, she must assure him that what happened was in no way the *bandidos'* fault. Edward was quick to anger and she feared he would retaliate, blaming her ill health on her captivity.

Hanging on to the wooden pole beside the door, Angelica maintained her balance, watching as the children mimicked their elders, running around with sticks and pretending that they had new guns. How sad that the little ones were so quickly learning the ways of the world. They should have been playing other games instead of thinking of violence.

"Will you now be going?" A wide-eyed little girl who had followed Angelica's every move with her eyes asked the question. At Angelica's nod she said, "I wish that you could stay. You are so pretty with your sunshine hair, and I liked your story. You could be Rodrigo's señora, he needs someone to care for him. He does not have a wife like the others."

132

Angelica blushed to the roots of her hair. Making a pretense of cleaning her spectacles, she hastily looked away. The child had innocently spoken her own desires, to belong to Rodrigo. Such a foolish wish. He had hardly even spoken to her these past days, had in fact carefully avoided her. No doubt he was anxious for her to leave. His very aloofness seemed to tell her as much, that he wanted her returned to her brother as soon as possible. From the safety of the doorway she watched him now, coming up to greet Margaro, examining and counting the rifles. As he looked towards Angelica she quickly averted her eyes, fearful lest he be able to read the adoration she felt for him. Dear God, give her the strength not to give her feelings away, not to make a fool of herself with her tears.

"Bring me the boy. Tom Cowdrey," she heard him say. "The gringo has upheld his part of the bargain and now I will uphold mine."

And soon he will be coming for me, Angelica thought. It would be a long and harrowing ride across the rough terrain, a journey that would be doubly difficult because of her dizziness and lack of strength, but somehow she would make it. Would she ever be able to forget the days and weeks she had spent here? She sincerely doubted it. Rodrigo Delgado O'Hara would be embedded in her heart, her soul.

"Bring me the woman as well!" This time Angelica met the bandit leader's eyes and she was astonished by his expression. He did not look triumphant as she had imagined, but regretful, almost sad. "The gringo will be anxious to have his sister back within the safety of his arms."

"No. Rodrigo, no!" The croaking voice of Najalayogua startled the onlookers and the bandit leader as well. "You cannot let her leave. Not yet. She is not strong enough. The poison is not entirely gone."

"What are you saying, old woman?"

133

"It is my potions that saved her life. I did all that I could. Some of the venom is still within her and only by the potions that I give her each day is she able to fight against the spirit of the snake. If she goes away her spirit will be conquered and she will die. She cannot go. Not yet. Not yet." The old woman looked in Angelica's direction and she could have sworn she saw her smile. "Let her stay until she is fully recovered, until the snake spirit hangs his head and slithers away."

"I made a promise to her brother. I gave my word." Rodrigo's emotions were torn. On the one hand he wanted the lovely blond woman to remain in the camp, on the other he wanted the temptation she presented over. Still, he could not take a chance that the old woman was right. Spirits, he did not believe in such foolishness and ancient prattlings, but he did realize that Angelica was weak, that she needed to recover her strength. He thought for a long moment before he made his decision. "The woman will stay. I will send a message from her own hand to her brother explaining the matter. She will stay. For one more week she will remain among us. That is my decision."

Chapter Nineteen

It was hot. The merciless sun beat down on the roof of the hut, making it uncomfortable inside, stealing Angelica's strength. Rising from her perch beside the pallet she walked to the bucket of water Najalayogua had brought for her and washed her face and hands. The cool moisture refreshed her and lifted her spirits.

Two days had come and gone since the arrival of the rifles. Two days but it seemed like forever, the hours stretching endlessly as Angelica recuperated from her brush with death. Boring days of little or nothing to do. The women insisted she must not lift a finger and so she had only her thoughts to occupy her time. Thoughts that were always of Rodrigo, wondering where he was, what he was doing, why he still had not come within speaking distance of her. It wounded Angelica that he avoided her so diligently. What had she done to merit his cold, unsmiling disregard? Was it because he considered her a burden, wished he could be rid of her? The thought pained her.

Sighing, she crossed the dirt floor to stare out the doorway again. She saw him, standing by one of his men and couldn't take her eyes from his strong, well-muscled body. Dressed in tight leather breeches, his broad, powerful chest and shoulders stripped bare of his shirt, he was a stirring sight. Angelica thought how she could have stood for hours just watching him. His voice could be heard clearly as he gave orders to reinforce the wall around the compound. Angelica felt a small twinge of fear, wondering if Rodrigo thought that the camp was in danger of attack.

"Miguel, it must be taller, the wooden slats closer together. We will make it strong enough, just in case we find ourselves visited by guests." His voice belied a confidence that soothed her fears.

Angelica was transfixed as she gazed at him. His dark hair had grown much longer since her first incarceration in the camp. He kept pushing it back as it fell into his eyes. As he moved, the sun glinted red in that hair and reflected on the sun-bronzed flesh of his chest and arms. He moved with a sinewy grace, his muscles rippling with his every movement. Angelica was a bit shocked at the sudden longing she felt, hardly appropriate for a young woman who had once considered taking holy vows. Shaking her head she sought to clear her head of those thoughts, yet they came back again. It was alarming, yet exhilarating at the same time. Oh, to be held in those arms again. For just a moment she allowed herself to dream, at least until Rodrigo sensed her staring eyes and turned her way. She raised her hand to wave but he quickly turned his head, carefully avoiding eye contact with her.

"What have I done?" she whispered. Her lips trembled as she remembered again the coldness he had displayed, or perhaps it was more of an indifference. It was as if he had suddenly become a stranger to her, as if he wanted to keep a careful distance between them. Angelica wondered if it had all been just a dream, his kissing her that night, being held in his arms. His dispassionate scorn tore at her heart and she felt the urge to get away, anywhere, as long as she could escape this sadness that welled within her.

Hoping to take her mind off the bandit leader's rebuff,

she walked the short distance to the hut where Jesse Harrison was ensconced and opened the door. She thought she could sense Rodrigo's eyes on her but when she whirled around to look he was once more embroiled in his work. Perhaps it was just as well. Now her leaving would not be quite as heartbreaking. Knowing there was no chance at all in winning Rodrigo's affection it was possible that she could leave here without regrets. Or could she?

Stepping inside the small hut Angelica found Jesse and Luisa laughing, her hand held in Jesse's with a familiarity which clearly showed it was not the first time. Seeing her, they broke away quickly, as if a shot had been fired, then Luisa audibly breathed a sigh of relief.

"I thought . . . I . . . I feared you were my brother." She looked down at the hand that the red-haired American had touched and shook her head. "Rodrigo would not understand . . ."

"He wants to protect you, Luisa. There are times my own brother is much like that." Angelica felt uneasy, as if she were intruding, yet she did not want to leave and be subject to Rodrigo's snub once again. Walking over to where Jesse Harrison lay propped up on two pillows, she feigned a smile. "How are you feeling, Jesse? I would have visited you sooner but . . . but I was not . . ."

"I heard you were bitten by a snake, Miss Angelica. Rattler, or so I heard tell. You were mighty lucky. I've known a few men who are playing their harps in heaven after suffering a like fate."

"Najalayogua hovered over me like one of God's angels. It is to her that I owe my life." She stepped closer, her eyes scanning Jesse. He looked much better than he had the last time Angelica had seen him. There was a stubble of beard on his face, which was a bit gaunt and pale, but considering the way he had appeared when they had brought him into camp there was a marked improvement.

137

Luisa had given him excellent care. "You look much improved."

"And you do not at all resemble a woman who was so near death. You are a sight for sore eyes, Miss Angelica. Perhaps that bandit isn't as bad a sort as I first supposed." His eyes turned in Luisa's direction, despite the fact that he was talking to Angelica. Luisa looked up and smiled. Their eyes met and held, speaking for them. "He sure has a wonderful sister . . ."

They're in love, Angelica thought. Oh, Dear God, don't let there be repercussions from this attraction. Her heart went out to the two young people, but at the same time she was frightened too. Tom Cowdrey was safe, but the bandits still held Will and Jeremiah, as well as Jesse. One incident of hatred could lead to all their deaths.

"Yes, Luisa is very special. Right from the first she befriended me." What would Rodrigo think if he knew, she wondered?

"And me as well." A smile crinkled the corners of the red-haired man's eyes and softened the face that badly needed a shave. For just a moment, as Jesse and Luisa looked at each other again, it was as if they were in their own private world.

"You needed me. I knew it. How could I turn away?" Luisa blushed shyly as he captured her hand again. "I tended you most carefully, used the healing Najalayogua showed me. She too could have . . ."

"No. The sight of your pretty face is what brought me back from the dead. I couldn't die, wouldn't let myself leave this world and you." His arm crept up around her neck, his hand cupping Luisa's chin as he forced her to look at him. "You're very special to me, Luisa."

Angelica slowly moved to the door, intent on leaving the two young lovers alone, but her movement seemed to bring them back to reality. "Don't go, Miss Angelica." He laughed. "Perhaps it would be better if we had

138

a chaperone.''

Once again Luisa blushed. With mock severity she pushed him back upon the pillows and carefully saw to his wounds. Soon he was shirtless, uncovered by the blanket, his pale torso reflected in the dim sunlight. Not nearly as splendidly strong as Rodrigo but an attractive man all the same, Angelica thought.

At first Luisa had been so shy with Jesse that she could hardly look at him, much less talk to him. Now, after having spent many long hours alone together, the shyness had left her and she was able to carry on a lively conversation as she prodded Jesse's wounds. There was a lighthearted banter between them that seemed to hide thoughts of a more heated nature.

Once again Angelica felt uneasy about the situation. Maybe it would be better if Angelica insisted Jesse accompany her when she left. She had heard about the creed of the Spanish men. It had been bantered about the camp in undertones after Jeremiah had attempted to abduct Luisa to facilitate his escape. Death before dishonor, it had been whispered. The men protected the chastity of their women, whether it was wives or mothers, sisters or nieces. Even unto death. A man who disobeyed that unspoken law or brought shame was subject to death.

"There is still a little swelling, a remaining scab. Let me examine your shoulder more carefully.'' Luisa poured warm water on the bandage, gently tugging at it to pull it free. She repeated the process until the linen was loose. Angelica looked at the wound. It was healing well, was scabbed and red, but no longer was oozing blood. "It is much better, Señor Jesse.''

Luisa rubbed salve onto the wound with a flowing, caressing movement that couldn't help but stir Jesse's emotions, Angelica thought. Then, once again, Luisa replaced the bandage with a thin strip of clean linen. Wrapped in his own special enchantment, Jesse was

139

hardly aware of anything but Luisa's administering hands. He closed his eyes, and before long had drifted off into a peaceful slumber. Only when she was certain that he was asleep did Angelica break the silence.

"Luisa, I do not mean to pry, nor to interfere, but I could not help noticing the feelings you and Jesse share. It is dangerous. Your brother . . ." Her voice was a whisper.

"My brother? *Sí*, he will be angry at first, until he realizes how very strong my feelings are. Nearly as strong as his own emotions. He too is in love."

So that's what it is, Angelica thought. A painful shiver of jealousy shot through her. Rodrigo was in love. Was it any wonder he looked at her so scathingly? No doubt he could tell her feelings, knew she cared for him. Her weakness must have made him determined to show her exactly how little he thought of her.

"I hope he is happy. I would wish him happiness." The words came out in a croak of regret and she was ashamed of her selfishness. She had no claim on him, no right to feel betrayed. He had never shown her in any way that her attraction towards him was returned in any way.

"He will not have it! He is a foolish man to throw his happiness away. Well, I will not!" Luisa's angry voice nearly wakened Jesse, for he stirred in his sleep. "He is blind and does not see that hatred is an evil thing. And yet if you had seen the way he sat by your bedside you would realize what I know."

"Sat by my bedside?" Angelica's eyes opened wide in disbelief. "Oh, no. I asked Najalayogua and she told me . . ."

"That's what he made her promise to say, but I saw him and I know. He was beside himself while you were lying on that pallet. He crooned to you, guarded you as carefully as a shepherd does a precious lamb. He didn't eat, he didn't sleep. He kept whispering your name again and again."

"But why did he keep it from me? He has been acting so

140

distant, as if I were invisible. Why?" Was that her heart thumping so loudly? It sounded like a drum.

"Because he is afraid of what he feels. That can be the only answer. My brother is drawn to you, perhaps more than he even knows. That feeling awakens fear within him. He is afraid of you, señorita. Afraid of his feelings and fighting against them. But I am not like him. I love Señor Jesse with all my heart and with all my soul and I will not let my brother's prejudice and fear ruin my own life. If he will not reach out to love, then I will. And if you are wise you will do the same." With a rustle of her skirts, Luisa walked from the hut, leaving Angelica behind.

Chapter Twenty

The sunlight glared as Rodrigo squinted his eyes against its rays to watch Angelica moving gracefully about the camp. She would pause from time to time to rest, which told him that her strength had not fully returned. Najalayogua was right then in her determination to keep the gringa a few more days, and yet the way the old woman had smiled, the way she kept looking at him with such a knowing look in her eye, he suspected there was much more than Angelica's health on her mind.

She knows, he thought. Somehow that old woman can see clearly within my heart and this is her way of trying to make a match between us. The thought irritated him and yet remembering the old healing woman hovering over Angelica when she was ill caused the corners of his mouth to tremble in a smile. Najalayogua was a strange-looking cupid, that gringo symbol of love. He had not expected the bow-carrying imp to be an old gray-haired woman. But even Najalayogua could not work magic this time.

Rolling a cigarillo and sticking it in his mouth, Rodrigo could not help looking at Angelica. At least he could do that much, he thought sadly. He could feast his eyes on her until she went away. He studied her intently. He liked the pale-gold color of her hair, like rays of sunlight. If only she would let it just hang free. How he wanted to see it blowing about her shoulders . . . Quickly he pushed *that* thought from his mind. He must not allow himself to think of her as a woman. She had thoughts of taking the veil, of being a Holy Sister, therefore he must nullify in his heart the desire he felt for her. She was untouchable! Totally and irrevocably so. There were women a man made love to, women like Bonita, and there were women a man must honor. Mothers, sisters, and nuns. To think of her otherwise would bring calamity and trouble. So thinking he lit a match and puffed at his cigarillo.

Even if it were otherwise, if she had not chosen the path towards God, he would have been a fool to follow his heart. He was a man of Mexican blood and she an American, an Anglo. His mother had loved his father with a deep and burning adoration and yet there had been problems from a mixed marriage. His mother's people had never fully accepted his father, had always thought of him as "that gringo" despite all his efforts to earn their respect. His mother, on the other hand, had never known anything but scorn from her husband's relatives. Like must stay with like. He would meet and marry a woman like himself, someone who was at least half Spanish like Bonita. Luisa too would make an appropriate match. Like with like.

Slowly he rolled the cigarillo between his lips, savoring the taste of the tobacco, trying to take his mind away from his thoughts, but it did no good. His eyes continued to seek out the yellow-haired American. At last, in a flurry of anger, he threw the cigarillo down and extinguished its fire with the toe of his boot. His temper, that was yet another reason to keep them parted. Like a match to kindling, Rodrigo's temper had always been volatile while Angelica was soft and gentle. Even in their temperaments they were at odds. He knew that in his

144

mind. Why then did she intrude into his sleep, into his dreams? Why was he so haunted by her? Did he see another woman entirely looking back at him through those foolish windows she wore at her eyes? Yes he did. Though he knew all the reasons why he was wrong to feel so, he knew he wanted to be the spark to ignite the fire of her passion. He wanted her to be his woman.

"Bah! Rodrigo Delgado O'Hara, you are a fool." This time when he looked up at Angelica she boldly smiled. Scowling, he turned his head away. He did not want to talk with her, get anywhere near her for fear he might give into his selfish temptations. He would hide in his contempt for all gringos, his anger at what had been done to him.

"What is wrong with you, Rodrigo?" Margaro's knowing smile only irritated Rodrigo further.

"Foolish amigos who ask too many questions!" he blurted, then amended, "The situation. And Garcia. I do not trust him. I feel as if he is waiting to strike."

"He has been mumbling about the hostages again. The same old song. He is trying to stir up discontent by making it appear that you are a coward, afraid to be strong. He said that were it up to him he would retaliate against the gringos for cheating us out of the promised booty. He posed a question which I myself am wondering about. What are we going to do with the three gringos who are left in our care? Are you going to release them?"

"I don't know! I don't care at the moment!" Rodrigo put his hands to his temples, massaging at the pain that stabbed in his head. "For just one moment in my life I would like a little peace, is that too much to ask?"

Margaro reached out and touched the other bandit's shoulder. "I'm sorry, Rodrigo. We will talk no more about it." He motioned with his head. "Come, let me show you the new stallion I got on last night's raid. If you like him I just might be persuaded to make of him a present. No? He is a wild one. Perhaps too spirited a one for me to handle. We will see, eh?"

Rodrigo met his friend's eye, knowing full well that this was Margaro's way of helping him forget his troubles. "You want me to help you break him, isn't that so? I will do all the work and you will find some way to win him back again. I understand you better than you think, amigo."

"No, no, no. If you like him I *will* give him to you, Rodrigo." Margaro pretended to have hurt feelings. "You wound me with your ill-founded suspicions. I am a man of honor, not some dishonest gringo!" Margaro laughed as he led the way to the corral, but his mind was just as troubled as Rodrigo's. He sensed Garcia was more of a danger than Rodrigo even realized and knew instinctively that soon, perhaps very soon, there would be trouble between the two volatile bandits.

Chapter Twenty-One

Angelica looked upon the sunrise with sadness. Three more days before her brother would come for her. Her time in the camp was nearly over. She would go back to her world, leaving Rodrigo's. Walking to where a throng of women stood she decided to make the very most of the time left to her.

"I do not want to go. I always do it!"

"I went yesterday, I will not go again."

"Everyone must take her turn."

The women were arguing, and in an effort to soothe their ill humor, Angelica held up her hand. "Ladies. Ladies, what seems to be the problem." She remembered a similar argument at the abbey.

"It is a morning ritual to walk the distance from camp to the stream to fill the earthenware pots with water. I went just the day before but now no one else wants to take their turn." Juana put her hands on her hips in indignant anger.

"That's what I thought this was all about." Even the postulants and sisters at the abbey didn't always get along. Women were women, people were people no matter what language they spoke or the color of their skin. She remembered how angry Mother Bernadette had been at the postulants' sputtering. She had made them do penance for a week. "I will go. Since I have come to the camp I have never taken my turn. I will do so now."

"You are too weak!" Juana looked as though she felt thoroughly ashamed of herself.

"Najalayogua would never allow it."

"I am stronger now. Each day I have regained some strength. Please! I don't mind. The walk would do me good."

"I do not know . . .?"

"I have a long journey ahead of me when my brother comes. If I am treated like an invalid, if I am weak when I go with him, it will mean that I am a burden. And I would like to enjoy the scenery."

The women reluctantly agreed, nevertheless looking warily about for any sign of Najalayogua lest she scold them. Seeing that she was nowhere around they helped Angelica tie the earthenware pots on the small burro that would carry the burden of the heavy load. That being done, she went on her way leading the burro past the adobe huts, past the storehouse and corral.

"Rodrigo." His name sounded well on her lips so she said it again. "Rodrigo." Since Luisa's startling declaration of Rodrigo's vigil by her bedside while she was in danger, Angelica felt light of heart. He did care. He was trying to hide it, from himself, from her but she did at least mean *something* to him.

We come from two different worlds, she thought sadly, and yet she held a hope that love could conquer anything. Dreamer that she was she was certain that if Rodrigo loved her even a tenth as much as she did him they would find happiness. Children, they would have such beautiful children. Angelica longed for a child, it was yet another reason why she had been tortured by doubts of taking her vows. She let her mind conjure up the vision of Rodrigo sitting around the fireplace of their home reading to the

148

little ones. They would have three sons for him and two daughters for her. A man always wanted a son and she would give him several, though if the truth were told it was often the daughters who held a father's heart. Hadn't she been her father's favorite? She remembered how she had always followed after him, hoping that he would take her on his knee. He had called her his "princess," enfolding her in his arms which had been the cause of her brother's jealousy more often than not. She, however, would make certain that she gave an equal share of love to all her children and would caution Rodrigo to do the same.

Following the small path which twisted downward, Angelica at last found her way to where the water gushed over the pebbles and small rocks and paused. It was so beautiful here, an oasis of golds, reds, and greens. A grove of trees lifted their branches to the sky, shading the earth below and she remembered that Rodrigo had told her about how the Mexicans held the earth in reverence. "The earth is like our mother," he had said. "She nourishes us and gives us life. Our first memories are of the earth. By running dry soil through his fingers a man can tell much about the weather." Bending down, Angelica let a handful of dirt sift through her hand. "The bond with the soil is strong. It is a thing we will give our lives to secure, protect, and to keep. No one will take it away."

At that moment Angelica understood the love he had for this land. She felt it too at this moment. Suddenly she knew how very much she wanted to stay. She didn't want to go with Edward when he came for her. Somehow she felt that it was *here* that she belonged. Perhaps she had more of an affinity with Rodrigo's people than even she realized. She wanted to help them, and there was so much that she could do. She knew how to read and write and could teach the children, and she was good with her hands. Little by little she had been drawn into Rodrigo's realm, his emotions, his longings for peace and prosperity for his people and she had begun to understand just what he was fighting for.

So many thoughts ran through her head as she filled the pots with water, a myriad of reflections and contemplations. It was such a beautiful world that God had created. Why couldn't his children learn to share with each other? Why did there have to be such an evil thing as greed, rearing its ugly head, keeping people from living in peace with each other?

She heard the song of a bird and raised her head to listen, then watched as a ground squirrel scurried back and forth in search of its breakfast. A crackle in the brush behind her startled her but she thought it was one more of God's creatures. Turning around she found herself instead face to face with the one man in camp who posed a severe threat to her—Juan Garcia.

"Buenos días." He stared at Angelica with eyes gleaming in contempt. His voice was sharp, belying his courteous greeting.

"Buenos días, señor."

"So Rodrigo has at last let you out of his sight. That is very interesting." He twirled the ends of his mustache as he eyed her up and down, giving Angelica an eerie feeling of apprehension.

"You . . . you gave me quite a . . . a fright, coming up behind me as you did. But now that you are here you can help me fill the water jugs." Nervously Angelica held forth one of the clay pots but Garcia thrust it aside with such a vengeance that it fell to the earth and shattered.

"Getting water! Bah, it is woman's work. That is not what I came here for. I followed you, señorita."

"Followed me?" Anxiously Angelica looked about her. She had been foolish to come to fill the pots alone. There was no one to help her and at this moment she indeed needed help.

150

"I don't understand," she said in an attempt to stall him, while her eyes scanned the foliage for means of an escape. Could she outrun him? She doubted it. She had still not gained back all of her strength. Would her scream be heard?

"I think you do." His smile was evil, menacing. He and not Rodrigo should be called El Diablo, she thought. "I think you know exactly what it is I want."

"No, I don't." She forced herself to remain calm, to fight against the overwhelming terror this man inspired in her. Dear God, help me, she thought.

"Ah, señorita, I have waited for so long to have you all alone." The gleam in his eyes clearly communicated his hatred.

She sensed that to portray fear would only endanger her more, for a man like Garcia thrived on fear. Boldly she looked him in the eye. "If you touch me you will have to answer to Rodrigo. He promised my brother that I would be safe here, that I would be returned to him in exchange for the guns. Have you no honor?"

For just a moment Garcia's frown vanished and he threw back his head and howled. "Rodrigo! Do you think I am afraid of him? He is but one more little ant that I will stomp on. He is half Anglo and for that I spit on him." The scowl returned. "I hate anyone with such tainted blood, more anyone who is full-blooded Anglo. They steal our land, look upon us as if we were crawling insects and not men. I will murder every gringo who crosses my path. They are all my enemies." He took a step towards her. "You too are my enemy, but I have a far different way of revenging myself on you." He grabbed her arm. "I watched the way Rodrigo looks at you. He wants you but is too much the fool to take what he wants. I will enjoy thrusting myself into your body, knowing of his hunger for you."

"If you touch me in that way, I will kill myself! I will.

151

I will never suffer the humiliation of such a thing." Angelica's voice shook with a mixture of fear and revulsion. This man was an animal.

"Kill yourself? You know it is not permitted. God will expect you to bear your fate, however . . ." Slowly he reached for the knife in his belt, a smile curling his lips. Holding the knife up before his eyes he toyed with it, caressing the blade, tracing its sharpness with loving fingers. "A fine weapon, is it not?"

"What are you going to do?" Was he going to kill her? Perhaps it would be better than suffering that *other* fate. She watched in fascinated horror as he kept the knife only inches from her breast, twisting it in a hypnotizing motion. Then suddenly he threw it at her feet. With a soft whir it stuck in a piece of wood on the ground.

"Go ahead and kill yourself if that is what you wish to do. Your life means nothing to me. *Nada!* Kill yourself this very moment, for I assure you that the time has come when I will taste of your skinny white body."

Angelica looked at the knife. A weapon. She would not use it on herself but on this . . . No, she could not take a life. Not even to save herself. Killing was the greatest evil. In horror she drew away, watching as Garcia bent down for it.

"Just as I thought. Gringo women are cowards, no?" Garcia was scornful. His arms were steel bands as he grabbed her, tearing at her clothing with brutal hands. Angelica's spectacles fell to the ground and she made an effort to grab for them only to hear Garcia's laugh as he ground them beneath his foot. "You have no need to see, only to feel."

Angelica struggled with all her might against the arms that held her. His breath was foul and sickened her, his fingers were tearing at her flesh, bruising her, tormenting her. She felt the hot touch of the sun as her bodice was wrenched away. The Mexican bandit pinched the crests of her breasts causing her to scream.

"Shut up, gringa bitch!" A stinging blow sent whirls of black before her eyes and as he pushed her to the ground Angelica fought against the darkness that threatened to overwhelm her.

Rage exploded before Rodrigo's eyes as he witnessed the scene before him. He had scolded Rosa when she told him she had allowed Angelica to go off alone. He had feared she might have a dizzy spell, might be too weak yet to accomplish her tasks all alone, but he had never envisioned he would find her half naked in Garcia's arms.

"You *bastard!* I told you no one was to touch her. You vile, filthy . . ."

He lunged at Garcia, but he, the smaller and thinner of the two, danced out of the way, laughing uproariously as if it were all just a joke. His eyes flickered dangerously, goading Rodrigo.

"Half gringo coward!" He brandished his knife.

Rodrigo's temper was inflamed beyond caution. Striking out with his fist he caught Garcia on the chin, just missing the lash of Garcia's knife. Garcia staggered back but did not fall. He maintained his balance, holding his knife out threateningly.

"For that, O'Hara, you will pay."

With the reflex of a man who is used to courting danger, Rodrigo clenched his own knife, frozen in a crouching position, waiting to spring.

"Are you just going to stand there, half-gringo scum?"

Garcia obviously wanted Rodrigo to strike out in blind anger but Rodrigo refused to let his emotions goad him into foolishness, despite the thoughts racing through his mind. Instead it was Garcia who lashed out, narrowly missing Rodrigo, who kicked out savagely, striking Garcia in the leg. In answer, Garcia struck with his knife again.

Rodrigo side-stepped him again, remaining alert as he

153

circled his enemy. "If you had touched her I would have killed you," he said, looking at Angelica out of the corner of his eye. She was staring back at them and that was the only thing that tempered his anger. He would not kill a man before her eyes.

"I will finish with you and get back to your gringo *puta!*"

With a low growl Garcia launched himself at Rodrigo, slashing out wildly. Rodrigo ducked away but the tip of the knife slashed his shirt and brought a small trickle of blood. Thankfully it was just a scratch. Even so, he knew he was in mortal danger. Garcia was deadly with a knife.

Controlling his breathing, ignoring the pounding of his heart, Rodrigo somehow managed to escape any serious wounds, though he did receive several bruises from Garcia's deadly aimed kicks. Garcia, on the other hand, was not quick enough to miss Rodrigo's blade. Blood poured down his arm. Still, he fought on, lunging again and again, surprised that Rodrigo was putting up such a good fight against him. Perhaps any man would fight for his woman, Garcia thought. But he could only stand between him and the woman for so long. Garcia would be the winner and take the gringa woman.

Watching from where she had fallen, Angelica's blood froze in her veins. She was chilled with fear. Please God, do not let him kill Rodrigo, she prayed. Please. She looked around for a log, any weapon she could use, but in the end thought it best not to intercede. If she distracted him even for a minute he might fall victim to this evil man's blade.

"First you and then the gringa bitch!"

Garcia was overconfident, and that made him careless. Like a cornered and enraged bull Rodrigo struck, this time knocking the knife to the ground. Garcia fell, holding his arm. He was weaponless and yet he eyed Rodrigo with defiance. "Kill me. For if you do not I will one day kill you. There is no room for both of us here."

154

"You aren't worth killing. I will not stain my soul with your blood." Rodrigo clenched his teeth saying, "I should but I will not. Unlike you, I am not a murderer."

"Murderer? Bah. I only kill gringos. That is not murder. It is much the same as swatting at mosquitoes."

"You have been one of my men and so I will let you leave without giving you the thrashing you deserve, but do not let me lay eyes on you again. Never!" Rodrigo gestured impatiently. "Go! Get out of here." He knew Garcia would not have done the same had he been victor. Garcia would have killed him without hesitation. Would he regret his gesture of mercy? Looking towards Angelica he knew he could never have killed the bandit in cold blood. He watched as Garcia picked himself off the ground and sauntered up the winding trail. Then he was bending over Angelica, holding her to his chest.

"Querida! Chica! Are you all right?"

His fingers were strokes of velvet as he caressed her. The hand that gripped her shoulder made her feel warm and tingly inside. She wanted to cry yet she maintained her calm, staring into his eyes as she tried to pull the shorn remnants of her bodice together.

"My angel, my love," he whispered.

Rodrigo tried to avert his eyes from the soft mounds exposed to his eyes. He had suspected that beneath all that cloth she would be lovely, but he had never dreamed that she would be as beautiful as she was. Full breasts with rosy crests that he longed to reach out and fondle, skin smooth and unblemished like a summer rose, a waist tiny with no foolish contraptions to hold her skin so tightly that she could not breathe. He'd seen glimpses of Angelica while she was lying in her unconscious state, but now the full splendor of her breasts and stomach was presented to his eyes.

"Rodrigo?"

"You are *bella. Bella, querida.*" Feverishly his hands

155

caressed her body, seeking out the soft peaks of her breasts, stroking and searching. A woman this lovely was meant for loving not to be cloistered away, he told himself.

Angelica was transfixed by his words and his gentle caresses. She was aware of her body as she had never been before, experiencing a maelstrom of intoxicating, fevered, bewildering sensations. All she could think was that there was nothing shameful in these feelings. It was beautiful, stirring, and seemed at this moment to be as natural as breathing. Mesmerized by the look she saw in his eyes she lifted her face towards his as he caressed her lips with his own. His kiss spoke of hunger and of love and she clung to him for what seemed like an eternity of time, a blessed eternity.

"Angelica. Lovely angel." He spoke her name in a breathless whisper as he drew his mouth away. He had tried to stay away from her. *Dios,* he had *tried.* But he was only flesh and blood, not a saint. Nor at this moment did he want to act like one. He wanted her with a fever that stirred his blood beyond all reason. Yet that fire was tempered with a gentleness. Never before had anyone but his mother and Luisa brought forth such tender feelings. He felt a warmth in his heart as well as his loins. He would never hurt her. He might damn himself for a fool later but for right now he would let the intensity of his yearning guide him.

Hungrily his lips closed over hers again as he very gently drew her down to lie beside him on the hard, earthen floor. He wanted to fit her soft curves against the tightness growing in his loins. His body was betraying his reason but for the moment he did not care. Angelica's hair had come unbound from its chignon and he felt its silken softness brush his cheek like a lover's caress, stirring the fire inside him to a blaze.

"Do you want me, *querida?*" Angelica heard his voice through a misty haze but somehow couldn't answer. All she could do to show him that she did was to hold him close. She wanted his protection, his nearness. After what had nearly happened she needed an affirmation of love and warmth. What Garcia had intended to do had frightened her. Rodrigo's caress, his kiss, unburdened her heart and sent it on a wondrous flight. It was almost as if she were dreaming, but she knew that the man beside her was very real. She could feel the heat of his body like a fire where their bodies touched. And his hands . . .

"Rodrigo, I love you. You know that, don't you?"

"Shhhhh." He silenced her with his mouth, afraid that if they talked it might break the enticing spell woven around them. If he thought about what he was doing for even an instant he would be lost.

He held her chin in his hand, kissing her eyelids, the curve of her cheek, her mouth. His tongue gently traced the outline of her lips and slipped in between to stroke the edge of her teeth. She tasted sweet. He felt her tremble beneath him and opened his eyes, mesmerized by the potency of her gaze. The thought that this achingly innocent woman had never had another man filled him with a wrenching tenderness. He would make it beautiful for her, this much he vowed.

"You are trembling. Are you cold?"

She shook her head as she eased his shirt from his shoulder. She let her hands roam over the hard muscles of his flesh. He was beautiful, far more so than she, and yet he had said such wondrous things to her. Her palms slid over his flesh as if to know every inch of him. His masculine scent filled her nostrils as she put her lips to his hair.

"*Querida!* I should let you go. I have no right to . . ."

"I want you, Rodrigo. Please don't back away."

"But you were to be a Holy Sister. I will shame you . . ."

"The first time that you kissed me I knew I would never take my vows, and even before that I had my doubts. I want to be a woman. Your woman."

157

His hand moved down her stomach into the soft hair between her thighs and Angelica gave a strangled cry. Tremors shot through her in tumultuous waves as she pushed closer to him. She had lamented of ever having him make love to her but now he was going to consummate the yearning they both shared.

"Rodrigo? Rodrigo?" A voice not more than six feet away called to him. "Did you find Angelica?" It was Juana's voice.

"Madre de Dios!" The sound of the woman's voice brought Rodrigo crashing back to reality. He had saved Angelica from one lusting man only to make her suffer his own advances. He felt ashamed of himself as he stood up, yet he was gentle as he helped her to her feet. Standing in front of her he shielded her from Juana's eyes as she came upon them. "I have found Angelica, Juana. She . . . she stumbled and fell and tore her clothing but she is all right now. I will take her back to camp." Without another word, he put his shirt over her and led Angelica back up the hill.

Chapter Twenty-Two

The sky was a dark-blue velvet filled with thousands of stars that looked like diamonds as they flickered brightly. The air was warm with just a hint of a breeze. A perfect night for love, Angelica thought. The strum of guitars added to the magical allure of the night, soothing and haunting. There always seemed to be guitar music in the camp which had often lulled Angelica to sleep. Tonight, however, the music had a far different effect on her, a feeling of anticipation. After what had happened at the clearing today she sensed it was only a matter of time until her yearning for Rodrigo would be fulfilled. Had it not been for Juana he would have made love to her. Oh how she longed for him to do so.

Angelica had looked into his blue eyes and been awakened to a glorious sensation of what love could be like. She knew she would never be able to forget the taste of his kiss, the way her skin had tingled when he touched her naked flesh. Rodrigo had made her feel beautiful. Strange, but she had always thought of herself as plain, but loving him had changed her. She was nearly pretty without her spectacles.

Angelica was wearing a blouse she had borrowed from Juana, a low-cut garment which did little to hide the soft swell of her breasts. Once she would have been too embarrassed to wear such a thing but not now. She wanted to look different, seductive, daring. A full scarlet skirt fell in soft folds to the middle of her leg, her pale hair hung loose in waves down her back. A piece of mirror that Maria had in her hut had revealed Angelica's loveliness to her eyes. She wanted to attract Rodrigo tonight, wanted him to carry her off to the hut and bring to her again the wonder of this morning. Rodrigo was meant for her. She felt it deep within her heart. How then could what passed between them be anything but right?

She had thought once that she did not belong here among Rodrigo's people, that she was not one of them but now she knew the error of her words. She *did* belong. Loving him made her belong, had brought her into his world. Without him she could never be truly happy.

"Luisa, where is Rodrigo?" Looking over the heads of the others her eyes searched for him. At last, seeing him by the fire, she flashed him a smile. Even without her spectacles on she would have recognized him just by the proud way he held his head, the grace of his stride. Moving past Rodrigo's sister, then past the others, she came to his side.

Music floated delightedly to the ears, accompanying the soft refrain of one of the women's singing. It enfolded Angelica like the folds of a magical cloak. "Catalina sings like an angel."

"And you . . . you look like one, *querida*. You do not know how long I have waited to see your hair hanging free as it is now." He looked down at his hands, embarrassed. "About what happened . . . I . . . I am sorry. I should not have let myself get carried away. I was wrong . . ."

"No, what happened between us was right. You felt it and so did I. I'm not sorry for anything, Rodrigo, except that Juana came upon us. Had she not . . ."

"*Querida!*"

160

"I'm not afraid to let you love me. I know what I want. I want you. Maybe I am shameless for saying it, but it is the truth." She had made her decision and knew beyond a doubt that before the night was over she would taste his kisses once again. If she had to be the first one to make the move, then so be it. Love only came once in a person's life and she would not throw this precious moment away. For the first time in her life Angelica felt truly alive and at peace with herself. She had made the right decision.

"We must talk about this." His voice was stern, yet his eyes held a soft glow of love. "Come with me. We must be alone." He led her away from the others to a small shed that was used to store the grain. Gesturing towards one of the barrels he said, "Sit down." As he spoke he reached for a lamp, then lighting it and setting it on the floor, he took a seat beside her.

Angelica was potently aware of his nearness. It was a hot night and his open shirt gave her a glimpse of his powerful neck and his chest with its thick tuft of dark hair. She remembered the feel of that hair, of his flesh.

"There are a hundred reasons why we must not . . ." he whispered. "Somehow I must make you understand."

"And one reason that overrides all the others. I love you, Rodrigo, and I feel deep in my heart that you love me." The lamp light cast long shadows on his cheeks outlining the sculptured planes of his face and she gave in to the urge to touch his face.

"*Caramba!* You do not make this any easier." He reached up to pull the offending fingers away but ended in taking her hand. His eyes held hers as he moved his head slowly towards her. He brushed her lips with his own, his mouth incredibly gentle at first then moving hungrily as he pulled her into his arms. A moan slid from his throat as she closed her hands around his neck and moved into his embrace. Their lips caught and clung as he whispered words of love.

161

"Te quiero mucho," he whispered, telling her that he loved her. For the first time in his life he knew he truly meant the words. *All other memories fled from his mind.* Hers were the only arms he wanted around him, hers the only mouth he wanted to kiss. Even so, his caution warred with his passion. "I don't want to hurt you," he mumbled against her hair.

"You will not hurt me." She held his face in her hands, looking deep into his eyes. "Only if you turn me away will you break my heart, Rodrigo. I could never be afraid of loving you." This time it was she who instigated their kiss. Her mouth opened to him, the moist flesh of her lips trembling as his mouth caressed hers. Shyly at first, then with increasing boldness, Angelica moved her tongue to meet his, initiating a discovery of her own. She curled her fingers in his thick dark hair as she clung to him.

Rodrigo's fingers slipped down the front of her blouse, cupping her full breast. Angelica felt a jolt from his touch and flushed as the peaks of her soft breasts hardened at his touch. She trembled in his arms and he, thinking that she had changed her mind, pulled back. He moved away from her, expecting to put an end to this sweet torture, but Angelica sensed his thoughts and brazenly tugged at the shoulders of her blouse until her breasts were bare. Taking his hands she drew each one to the pliant flesh. This was what she wanted, to be touched by him.

"Querida!" Rodrigo's breath caught in his throat as he caressed her. Slowly bending down, he worshiped her breasts with his mouth, traveling from one to the other in tender fascination. He buried his head between the mounds knowing he could never move away from her now. And yet the pleasure had only begun.

Angelica's body was reflected in the light as he undressed her, slipping the skirt, blouse, and her cotton chemise down over the swell of her hips and legs. He paused only long enough to feast his eyes on the soft contours of her nakedness. Her waist was narrow, her hips gently flared, her legs long and gently curved. His hands followed his eyes, igniting Angelica's passion as he stroked her. Then he stripped away his own garments, throwing them on the ground to cushion their bodies. Lifting her up in his arms, he carried her gently to the roughly fashioned bed and knelt beside her.

Rodrigo's skin glowed golden in the lamplight and Angelica took her turn to appraise him with her eyes. She had never seen a naked man before, and he was more magnificent than she had imagined any man could be. His shoulders were wide, his rib cage lean, his buttocks taut and slim, his belly flat. Her eyes moved down to the dark hair from which sprang his manhood, and her gaze lingered there in fascination before it traveled again to his face.

"You are beautiful, Rodrigo. I had no idea a man could be so beautiful." Her hands reached out to touch him, as if to know every inch of him, caressing him as he had gently explored her. Winding her arms around his neck she drew him down to lay beside her, nearly shattered by the pleasure of lying naked beneath him. Angelica felt the rasp of his chest hair against her breasts and gloried in the sensations which swept over her.

They kissed again and again, smiling against each other's lips. Rodrigo moved his pelvis against her leg, allowing her to become used to the feel of his maleness so that she would not be afraid. "It will hurt at first," he warned her, "but then there will only be pleasure. His hands caressed her, warming her with their heat, then his hand was between their bodies, sliding down the velvety flesh of her belly, moving to the place between her thighs. Angelica gave a small gasping cry as his gentle probing created a sweet fire. Spirals of pulsating sensations curled deep inside her.

"You were made to be loved, my sweet Angel." His voice

163

was husky with passion as he moved against her. Then his hands left her to enter her. "I feel your heart pounding against my own. *Te quiero mucho*, Angelica." He supported himself on his forearms as he pushed a bit deeper within her softness. Taking her mouth in a hard, deep kiss he joined her in that most intimate of embraces as she arched against him. There was a brief moment of pain and Angelica stiffened, but the other sensations pushed it away. Pleasure and pain, yet the pleasure of being filled by him was far more potent.

"Rodrigo . . ."

"I don't want to hurt you." He paused as he felt the proof of her virginity but Angelica urged him on. Only by blending together with him could she appease the fire burning within her. She moved her hips upward, sheathing him fully within her, enjoying the sensation that danced through her. Lovemaking was like nothing she had ever imagined, beyond her wildest dreams. It was like a wave crashing over her, taking her under then hurtling her up again, like falling over the edge of a waterfall. Her arms locked around Rodrigo as she arched her hips hungrily to meet him, expressing her love.

It was a passionate mating and Rodrigo was amazed to discover that beneath the gentle, angelic-looking woman was a sensual woman who was his equal in passion. He had never dreamed that love could be so powerful yet such a tender emotion all at the same time. He sighed as he penetrated to his full length and moved within her. He held back his own pleasure, moving in her body in a way that held back his own release until he'd made certain that she had experienced the supreme joy of their union. When he could bear the tension no longer he carried her with him to a blaze of fulfillment, raining kisses on her cheeks, her eyes, her lips. She was his woman. She was all that he could have asked for, all he wanted. As a sweet shaft of ecstasy shot through him he closed his eyes and whispered her name. The devil's angel, that was what she was. She had tamed El Diablo as no one else dared and had claimed his heart, his soul.

Rodrigo and Angelica lay side by side for a long time in the aftermath of their lovemaking, each one hating to break the spell that had been woven. At last Rodrigo broke the silence. "We should get dressed," he said. His fingers touched her arm gently, moving down to entwine his hand in hers.

"Not yet." Relishing the warmth of his body, she leaned against his strength and turned her face so that he could kiss her, a gentle brush of lips against lips.

Rodrigo looked at her face, his expression one of great tenderness as he studied her intently. "You're not sorry?"

"How could I be? Why would I regret the most wonderful night of my life?"

"Your brother—"

"Will just have to face the fact that I do not want to return. I won't go back, Rodrigo. I have made up my mind. What happened between us changed many things." She had found happiness in his arms and she would not give him up.

"He will be angry. There will be repercussions. I doubt that he will be pleased to have his sister married to a wanted man, a bandit. But I do intend to *marry* you, just as soon as we can safely send for a priest." Reaching up he brushed a wisp of hair out of her eyes. "It will be a hard life being married to such a man as me."

Married. The word had a magical ring. To belong to Rodrigo forever. "I am much stronger than you think."

Raising himself on one elbow he smiled, his eyes fever bright as he caressed her breast. "I know you are, *querida*. Right from the first you intrigued me with your courage. Insisting that you take the place of your brother and the frightened nun as a hostage. Perhaps even then I sensed that you would be very special to me."

165

"I was frightened but I had to do what I thought was right. And then when I looked into your eyes I was lost. You were so handsome, so arrogant."

"I wanted to take off those windows that you wore at your eyes and see you as you are now. Such lovely eyes. Like an unclouded sky. I wanted you but I was afraid of losing my heart. And so I hid behind my anger." Bending his head down, he kissed the valley between her breasts, then found his way to her mouth again, trailing kisses from her chin to the soft flesh of her ear. His voice tickled, sending shivers through her as he whispered, "I love you, Angelica, though I have only my heart to give. I am a bandit, *querida*. Do you understand what you are giving up for me? It won't be easy. Mine is not a simple life. There are those who hate me, who would shoot me down without a second thought. Loving me will put you in danger."

"I will face it bravely if you are at my side. The only thing I could not stand is losing you." Her arms clung to him, afraid that something might happen to shatter this dream.

They lay quietly, kissing for a long time. The warmth in his eyes made her feel beautiful as they caressed her, then his fingers replaced his eyes as he explored her gently. He rose over her, his manhood seeking the blessed softness of her. For one blinding moment Angelica was aware of every inch of his body as they embraced.

"Love me again . . ." she whispered, parting her thighs so that he could glide into her. She sighed as he penetrated her again, arching and surging in a sensuous dance. Her long legs wrapped about his hips as he possessed her, her hands locked around his neck. This time their joining was like a storm, a delicious, arousing descent into passion. This time Angelica knew what to expect but nevertheless his lovemaking left her breathless. It seemed an eternity later when he spoke her name, cradling her in his arms.

166

They talked about many things, seeking to learn about each other. Rodrigo told Angelica about his early childhood, the happy memories he held as well as those that were not so happy. She in turn told him about the death of her parents and how it had shattered her young life. How she was still frightened by the sight of Indians and the thought of witnessing such brutalities again. She told him of Edward and how he had been forced to take on the responsibility for her welfare at an early age.

"Your brother is much like me. Perhaps I have misunderstood him. We will talk, he and I, and I will make him realize that I love you, that I will care for you. He and I should not be enemies."

Angelica averted her eyes, knowing it would not be as easy as that. Edward could be very stubborn and she knew he would not be easily reconciled to what she had decided. It was not going to be a simple matter and she could only hope that her brother would not stir up trouble on her behalf.

Sensing her pensive mood, Rodrigo touched her face. "Do not worry. It will be all right. I cannot believe that God would send you to me and then take you away. Somehow I feel that this was meant to be, Angelica."

With their bodies entwined, they were unwilling to bring reality crashing around them but at the faint stir outside the door Rodrigo pushed away. "There are only a few more hours left before sunrise. Someone might come." He helped her to her feet. "Get dressed and I will take you back to the hut."

Angelica relit the lamp, watching as Rodrigo picked up his discarded garments. Once again she relished the sight of his handsomeness, his magnificent body which had given her the ultimate joy. This man was going to be her husband! Her husband! Who would have ever thought that a bespectacled, plain young woman would ever meet a man like this one. A man who looked upon her as beautiful. Slipping on her own clothes she sighed as she thought of the wonder of it all. God moved in mysterious ways, but he answered her prayers. She was not lonely anymore. She had found a purpose in life and a man to share it with.

Rodrigo walked her back to the hut, reluctantly taking his leave of her. "Tomorrow I will move into this hut with you. Never more will we have to say good night."

"But the others?" In spite of herself she blushed.

"They will know that you are mine. My woman, my wife. You belong to me. Think on that, *querida*, and hold me in your dreams." With a kiss, he left her, striding back into the dark of the night, taking her heart with him.

Rodrigo did indeed move into the hut with Angelica, establishing beyond a doubt that she was his woman. It was the happiest she had ever been, a time that she cherished, a world spent laughing, talking, and making love. Rodrigo told her amusing stories of his escapades with Margaro who used his many disguises, of the way they had made fools of both wealthy gringos and rich Spaniards. She laughed with delighted abandon, yet there was an underlying sadness at times, as if both of them feared this moment of contentment was somehow more fragile than they realized.

Angelica was all too aware of the enemies she and Rodrigo had made. Bonita's eyes followed her wherever she went with a cold, haughty disdain that was unnerving. Jeremiah Adams too showed contempt, calling her a "whore" beneath his breath whenever she passed. Will Cooper avoided her eyes. The men of the camp were stiff and eyed her with suspicion. Only the women gave her their camaraderie. Luisa especially seemed to have taken an interest in her brother's affirmation of love for the American woman in their midst. Angelica could sense that

168

there was a ripple of unrest in the camp because of her decision to stay. Even so she would not have been able to do anything else. Rodrigo was her life and her place was here with him.

Angelica blossomed slowly, knowing deep within her heart that Rodrigo was her sun, her warmth. Their lovemaking was many faceted. Slow and gentle. Wild and wanton. Always passionate. Angelica never tired of feeling Rodrigo's hands on her skin, tasting his kisses. He taught her the ways to arouse him and she gloried in this new-found, sensuous skill. She was happy, and yet each time Rodrigo and the others left the camp she was engulfed by the fear that he might not come back. Each heartbeat of time that he was away seemed an eternity. Upon his return she would cling to him, pushing such fears away. She would lie cradled in his arms, giving herself up to the sweet sensations that shivered through the center of her being as they joined their bodies in love.

"Are you happy?" he asked one night.

"Very happy, Rodrigo. So much so that I am nearly afraid to open my eyes and find it is all a dream. I never want to go back. I want to stay with you forever." Reaching out, she traced the outline of his mouth with her finger, watching as his smile turned to a frown. "You haven't grown tired of me already, have you?"

"No!" He caught her hand, pressing kisses to her palm. "It is just that the note that you sent to your brother has been answered. He says that he will drag you out of this camp by the hair of your head if need be." He shook his head. "If it were my sister I would do the same thing. How can I be angry with him? He wants you back, safe within his sight. I hate to come between you and your brother, *querida.*"

"It is my choice to make. Edward will just have to understand. He can take Jeremiah or Will in my place."

"He has said he will accept no other but you, so I am

169

taking him at his word. Until the ill feeling cools I will keep the two gringo men here. Perhaps your brother will forgive my having taken that which is so precious to him."

Angelica bit at her lip, expressing the truth that she had kept hidden even from herself as she said, "Edward does not think me precious. I think he has always seen me as a bother. If I were honest with myself I would have to admit that is the reason why he was so fierce in his determination that I take my vows. To free him from worry about my welfare. He will soon forget all about me. You will see. He's angry now because of the rifles and not for worry about my honor. He gave you the rifles and in turn feels he got cheated. If he is honest with himself he will see that he was the one who did not fulfill the agreement and not you."

"At times I feel that I am selfish. I wonder if perhaps what I am doing is a terrible wrong. I have nothing to offer you. *Nada.*" Rodrigo wanted to give her the world, to spend the rest of his life with her. He wanted a home and respectability instead of an outlaw's life.

"Nothing to offer me?" Her arms wound around his neck and she buried her face in the warmth of his chest. "You have given me your love and made me a woman. And someday I will give you children . . ."

"Are you . . .?" His hands gripped her shoulders. "I will send Margaro for a priest."

"Not yet, but I want to be . . ." Rodrigo gave her no time to finish her sentence. Lowering his head, he captured her mouth with his, kissing her with a furious gentleness that engulfed them both in a maelstrom of arousing desire. Crying out his name, she gave herself up to the tempestuous floodtide of his love.

From the shadows Bonita looked towards the hut with anger, knowing very well what was going on inside. Rodrigo could hardly wait for the night to come so that he could return to the hut and his pale-faced *puta*. A savage flood of jealousy flooded over her like a tide. She had thought the snake would kill the gringa but that foolish old hag of a healing woman had saved her life. And now Bonita had learned that the woman had no intentions of returning to the gringo world. She thought to permanently entrench herself in the camp and share her life with Rodrigo's. It was even rumored that he would make her his wife.

No! She would not take Bonita's man from her. She would not be replaced in his bed. Bonita ignored the voice inside her head that said she had already lost him. She would win him back. She would not let Rodrigo cast her aside like an old sombrero. Was she supposed to stand docilely aside while he shamed her before the entire camp? Was she supposed to smile as he took the *americana* into his bed each and every night? No. There was only one way to rid herself of her rival. A snake was not the only creature who could use poison. Smiling grimly she turned away, knowing exactly what to do. There were herbs and roots that could work wonders if one only knew how to use them.

Chapter Twenty-Three

Luisa held the candle aloft as she pushed through the opening of the hut. She treasured these moments alone with Jesse. Even if he was asleep she felt content just watching over him. He'd called her his guardian angel and perhaps that's just what she wanted to be. To be close to him. To care for him.

Coming closer she looked down at the features of his sleeping face. His full mouth, the tilt to his nose, the cleft in his chin were all wonderfully familiar to her, as much so as her own features. The soft glow of the candle cast a reflection as his jaw tightened and relaxed, knotted and loosened again as he breathed deeply in his sleep. Though his strength had nearly returned to normal she kept that fact hidden from Rodrigo, making up one excuse or another, fearing what might happen to the American when he had recovered. That she would be forbidden to see him any longer she knew only too well. Already Rodrigo was grumbling.

He loves Angelica, has made no secret of his relationship with her, she thought angrily. How then was her feeling for Jesse any different? She was nineteen, hardly a child, and yet he treated her like one! When she told him she was old enough to marry he immediately mentioned

Miguel, Chuey, or Pedro. She had no feelings except friendship for them. Why couldn't her brother understand? He'd been free to let his heart go where it wanted. All she wanted was the same choice. To love the man she wanted to love. Jesse. Kind, gentle Jesse.

Hovering over the American man she reached down and touched his cheek. His eyes opened and locked on hers as his hand shot from under the covers and caught her wrist. "I was dreaming of you, Luisa. And here you are."

"I . . . I like to watch you while you sleep." She'd had dreams too, always of him.

"Luisa. . . ." He let her hand go and looked away. She'd been gently reared, despite the fact that her brother was a bandit. He had known that from the very first moment she'd blushed so becomingly when she'd stripped away his garments to tend to his wounds. She was a lady, naive about the ways of men despite the bandits surrounding her. To them she was Rodrigo O'Hara's sister, to him she was as alluring as a summer rose and just as lovely. But she was forbidden fruit. Loving her was madness and would ensure a bullet in his head, he thought.

"Are you hungry? You didn't eat much supper." She sensed the tension in the room. He had such a sad look in his eyes that she could not help but feel sympathy. It must be very difficult for a man to be a prisoner, she thought. And yet were her brother to set him free she would never see him again. It was such a selfish wish to keep him here and yet she couldn't drive the thought from her brain. He'd brought sunshine to her sheltered world, the warmth that only filled her heart when he was near.

"Am I hungry? No." He *was* hungry, but for her. He wanted her. God help him but it was becoming more difficult each day to remember all the reasons he must keep away from her. Oh, he could talk with her, laugh with her, even hold her hand, but beyond that he could not go. And yet this gut-wrenching need for her tortured him.

174

"I can read to you if you like. My brother has several books. Some of them in English." She moved closer to him just as he sat up and their bodies touched. Luisa was aware of a pleasurable tingle in the pit of her stomach, of the tightening of her nipples where her breasts touched his chest. She had the overpowering urge to press herself closer, to cling unashamedly to him but instead she moved away with a murmured whisper.

"Luisa . . . ?" His hands reached out to touch her hair. Take her, a voice whispered. Make love to her. You are alone. She wants you as much as you do her, you sense it. Her brother need never know.

She glanced at him questioningly, her heart hammering painfully in her breast. She knew instinctively that he would have kissed her if she had not moved away and scolded herself for her shyness. She wanted him to kiss her. Taking a deep breath, she moved forward again, on the pretense of checking his wound, offering him another chance. "It is nearly healed. Soon they will take you away from me. They will make you . . ."

"I don't want to think about that time, Luisa. You're all that keeps me goin'. I know I shouldn't be so bold but you've become very special to me. Your brother thinks of me as . . . But I don't want to be *your* enemy." Their lips were only inches apart, too much of a temptation to be ignored. Jesse gazed at her wordlessly, then with a mumbled imprecation, bent his head and claimed her lips with his mouth.

Luisa had never been kissed before. Nothing in all her life could have prepared her for the searing fire that swept through her as his lips caressed her.

"Señor Jesse!" Her hand rested shyly against his chest, a brand against his heart. He almost lost himself in the taste of her, the sweetness of her kiss.

"You're beautiful. So damned beautiful. I want you so . . ." His hands played along her back, he caught hold

175

of her shoulders and pulled her to him for another kiss. Somehow her soft, yielding mouth was far more powerful than any aphrodisiac might have been. His body exploded with a fierce surge of uncontrollable desire that made him heedless of anything but wanting her. He ached for her, she was lovely, and they were alone. Only their garments stood in the way of what they both wanted.

He pulled the blouse from her shoulders and Luisa didn't stop him. She opened her mouth to speak but no words came out, instead she leaned into their embrace. It might be the only chance she would ever have to taste of his love.

"I need you. Oh, Luisa . . ." He loved the smell of her hair, the warmth and softness of her breasts against his hands. His passion was like a dam bursting, yet even so he drew away from her. She was innocent of a man's physical desire. Taking her now would be like plucking the wings from a bird, crushing a rose, harming a butterfly. She had never known a man's body. The experience could devastate her. He knew the strict Spanish way. Their women were sheltered, guarded. Luisa was a virgin, of that he had no doubt, and he knew instinctively that she was capable of passion. He'd had proof of that tonight, but taking her virtue would shame her.

Her gasping breath mingled with his own as she wound her arms around his neck. She wasn't afraid. Lovemaking must be a wondrous thing, she thought. Wasn't Angelica always smiling now? "I need you too, Jesse. I want you . . ."

A noise outside broke the spell. With a start Jesse pushed her away. It was one of the bandits making his rounds. "You must go, Luisa. Go!" Pulling up the shoulders of her blouse, Jesse pushed her away. He'd very nearly made a tragic mistake, one that would have shamed this gentle Mexican girl and put him in grave danger. She was too much of a threat to him, no matter how fierce her

176

beauty. His features tensed in an unsmiling mask as he said, "Go, Luisa. And do not come back. This thing between us must end before it starts. For your good and for mine."

"No. I want you. I have from the very first moment I saw you. I am not afraid of my brother's wrath. Somehow I'll make him understand."

Poor, innocent, lovely girl, he thought. She just didn't realize. It was much more than kisses. The love they felt for each other could only cause complications. It would be much better to guard against such a thing now. "There will be nothing to say to him. I will not take your virtue, Luisa. You saved my life and now I give you something in return." Lying back down on the pallet he closed his eyes. "Now go. I am tired. We will speak no more about what happened." At her hesitation he repeated the word. "Go!"

Luisa fled the hut, blinded by her tears. If Señor Jesse Harrison had been one of her own kind she would have chosen him to be her husband. She sensed that he cared for her, knew instinctively that his dismissal of her did not mean he did not. He was thinking of honor, noble man that he was. But somehow, someway she would make him realize that the way they felt about each other was all that was important. The next time they were together she would not let him send her away.

Chapter Twenty-Four

Firelight flickered, pulsating in rhythm with the soft strum of the guitars. The laughter of the children and chatter of the women was a welcome melody as Angelica sat by Rodrigo's side by the fire. She was happy, totally content. It was a beautiful world made even *moreso* because she was in love. This was her home, she knew it now and so did the others. The smiles across the fire showed that they approved.

Angelica felt a great affection for the people in the camp. Najalayogua and Luisa were her greatest friends but little by little she was making strong friendships with the others as well. Even Bonita seemed to have put aside her resentment and was now showing overtures of friendship to Angelica, often sitting beside her as she ate, getting Angelica's food for her whenever she scooped up her own. With Juan Garcia exiled from the camp there was no one now who did not fully accept Angelica. Life was perfect, or nearly so. Only one thing marred her happiness—frequent bouts of nausea which had come upon her within the last week and Angelica assumed that she was with child.

"We will have the grandest wedding, querida," Rodrigo was saying. "A fiesta. Already Luisa and the others are putting the finishing touches on your wedding gown. Margaro will be back any day now with the priest and then you really will belong to me." He grinned at her, showing her the exuberance of a small boy. "I will have the loveliest bride in all of California."

"And I the most handsome husband." She felt ill again. Closing her eyes for just a moment she fought against the waves of nausea churning in her stomach. She didn't want to worry Rodrigo. It was nothing. Every woman experienced the same thing. She thought hopefully that after she ate she would feel better. A little food would soothe her.

"*Querida*, what is wrong? You look so pale." Angelica opened her eyes to see Rodrigo staring at her with worried concern.

"Nothing. Don't worry. I just feel a little sick to my stomach is all." She refused to think any more about the matter. If she was going to be a bandit's wife she would have to be strong.

"Perhaps there is going to be a little one." Rodrigo kissed her forehead. "It seems the priest is coming just in time."

"Just in time." She forced a smile, concentrating on the soothing music which swirled through the air. The Mexicans were a musical people, always singing. Their music could be wild, accompanied by dancing, or melancholic, as it was tonight.

Angelica sat very still, taking deep breaths, fighting the churning in her stomach. There was also an annoying pain that seemed to turn her stomach inside out. At last, fearing she might succumb to the queasiness, she rose from her place by the fire to get something to eat. Rodrigo sensed her intent and pushed her down very gently.

"I'll get it, *quierda*."

Large, blackened pots hung suspended over the fire, bubbling and spewing. A tantalizing aroma filled the air and Rodrigo's nose quivered at the spicy scent. Picking up

180

a clay bowl and a wooden spoon, he scooped some of the food from the pot.

"I'll get it for you, Rodrigo." Bonita was quick to pull the bowl away. "Food is woman's work."

"It's for Angelica. She's not feeling very well. I thought something in her stomach might help."

"Not feeling well?" Bonita's lips trembled as she hid her smile. "What a pity." Reaching into a pouch hidden in the folds of her skirt she brought forth a pinch of dried leaves and very carefuly sprinkled it on the contents of the bowl in such a manner that Rodrigo did not see. She was growing skilled in such maneuvering, she thought. A little of the poison at a time. Not enough to kill the gringa woman quickly, but enough to accumulate in her body slowly. Her death would not be sudden but would come after a lingering illness. Who then would ever suspect?

"*Gracias*, Bonita." Rodrigo touched her arm. "I have noticed your change of attitude towards Angelica. It is appreciated. I want her to feel at home here. It is important to me. What happened between you and me is over but we can still have respect and affection for each other."

"Of course, Rodrigo." Bonita averted her eyes, fearful lest he read her thoughts. She wanted him. She would never stop wanting him. When the woman was dead and he grieved, she would be there to comfort him and to love him. At last, allowing her lips to form a smile, she watched as he took his seat beside the pale-haired gringa by the fire.

Rodrigo held the bowl in his hands as he lifted a spoon to Angelica's lips. "Our spicy food is hard to get used to, but this is from the less spicy pot. Vegetables and beef."

Angelica relished the food, all the more so because Rodrigo was taking such tender care of her. She wanted to please him and so ate every bite, warmed by the stew. Who ever would have thought that first day she'd been taken hostage by Rodrigo that he had such a gentle side? He had seemed so fiercesome, so strong that she had been afraid of him. Never in her wildest dreams had she envisioned at that moment that she would marry him. God moved in mysterious ways, she thought. Who would ever have imagined.

"Do you feel better?"

"Much better." She did for awhile, until the terrible churning started again. Eating seemed to have made it worse, not better. Her stomach convulsed again and again, and she groaned. Saliva filled her mouth, sweat beaded her brow as she fought to keep down the food. She would not embarrass Rodrigo or herself by a show of weakness. If she kept her mind preoccupied it would pass.

She thought about her dress and how beautiful it was. Luisa had showed it to her only this morning. It was a white cotton dress with embroidered flowers and leaves, full-skirted and delicately done. She'd wear flowers in her hair, she thought, and carry a bouquet of the wildflowers that grew near the creek. She'd write a note to Mother Bernadette and . . .

"Ahhhhhhhh." A jolting pain seized her and she doubled up, falling to her knees.

"Angelica!" Rodrigo cradled her in his arms, motioning to Luisa frantically. "Bring her some water. Pronto!" Brushing her hair back from her face he crooned to her in gentle concern. "I think perhaps it is the baby that makes you ill. A boy, no, to give you such trouble?" His hand caressed her stomach reverently. "A son."

Angelica reached out to him, closing her eyes against the pain. Though it was warm she shivered, leaning against him. "I'll be all right." She was mortified to show such weakness in front of the others. She, who had never suffered illnesses before. She drank eagerly of the cool water Luisa gave her. It helped a little. Closing her eyes she sighed deeply as Rodrigo lifted her in his arms and carried her to the hut. Watching over her, he stroked her back and shoulders as she drifted off into a torturous sleep.

182

Rodrigo watched as she slept, his brow furled with concern. He had to believe it was a coming child that tormented her so. Bearing children could often take a toll on a woman, he thought. He'd never wanted to cause her any pain, would have suffered himself if he could, were it to lessen her grief. It had to be the child, for he knew he could never bear losing her. This pale-haired, lovely woman had become his life.

Chapter Twenty-Five

An atmosphere of gaiety hung over the camp. It was Rodrigo and Angelica's wedding day and everyone was anxious to do their part. The sound of laughter filled the air, and people were bustling about. The camp was strung with lanterns for the evening celebration. Today it did not look in the least like a hideaway for bandits but much like any other peaceful village.

Looking over the heads of the throng, Angelica's eyes searched for and found Rodrigo. Dressed in *calzoneras*, tight-fitting pants flared at the hem, trimmed with buttons down the side and a braided jacket, he looked more *caballero* than bandit, resplendently handsome.

"*Querida*, you look bella. Bella!" Rodrigo's voice was husky as he greeted her. "And not nearly as pale as you did two nights ago."

"Najalayogua has been taking good care of me." She did feel better. The healing woman's potions had calmed her stomach. It was either that or the fact that she had eaten little food today, only a little broth that Najalayogua had given her.

"You feel strong enough for the ceremony?" he asked showing her tender concern.

"Yes. But if I had to crawl on my hands and knees I

would do so, just to become your wife." Nervously she tugged at the bodice of the dress she was wearing, wondering if he approved. Looking up into his eyes the appreciative sparkle said that he did. Slowly she pirouetted for him, showing off Luisa's handiwork. The dress was a beautiful creation, hand-embroidered at the bodice with pink-and-red flowers and green leaves. The full skirt fell in soft folds to her ankle. Of oyster-white cotton it made a perfect wedding dress.

"You do look like an angel." His eyes touched on the soft swell of her breasts, the pale golden hair hanging in loose waves down her back. She was a most striking sight as the approving gazes of those who walked by attested to. The devil's angel, he thought with a grim smile. Dear God that she should ever regret this marriage. "Come, I will take you to the priest. It is time."

Taking her hand he led her through the crowd. The light from the lanterns reflected the brightly colored skirts, rebozas, sombreros, and sashes scattered about the brightly hued crowd. Everyone had put on their finest garments to celebrate and the guitars, handmade drums, marimbas, and maracas blended their sounds.

"They will spoil us, *querida*. We will expect such treatment every day." Pausing before the cooking area he breathed in the aroma of food, watching her warily to see if she had any sign of queasiness. When she did not he was comforted.

Indeed there was a mountain of food, Angelica thought. The women had outdone themselves, heaping pots, bowls, and plates on the roughly fashioned tables. Cauldrons of beans and rice, stacks of tortillas, roast pork crackling, chicken wrapped in corn husks, basted with a thick red sauce, awaited the hungry palate. There were vegetables—peppers, corn, and tomatoes, enough to give the impression the storehouse had been raided for the occasion. They would not want for variety tonight.

"They make a handsome couple, do they not, Pedro?" she heard one young woman say. "Nearly as fine a couple and you and me. So when are you going to marry me?"

Everywhere people were talking and laughing, some singing. The night, in fact, seemed to be filled with song. All the voices quieted, however, as Margaro held up his hand. Hiding behind him in the shadows was a portly man with gray hair and small dark downcast eyes. Angelica had no doubt that he was sorely afraid, and her heart went out to him as she remembered how she had felt coming to this camp. Her nod assured him he would not be harmed and she was the recipient of a trembling smile.

"The priest will waive the posting of the banns," Rodrigo whispered. "Margaro was most persuasive on the matter."

"Rodrigo . . ." Angelica's look was one of gentle reproach.

"He will not be harmed, of that you have my promise. In all my days as a bandit I have never seriously harmed anyone of the church. On that you have my word. A little teasing perhaps just to keep them in line, but no bodily injury." He knew she was remembering the raid on her brother's caravan. "The men who traveled with your brother were not really priests."

"But the two women *were* nuns. You nearly frightened poor Sister Theresa to death." She couldn't help but wonder what that gentle woman would think of Angelica marrying that very same bandit. Life had its surprises after all.

"For that I am deeply sorry. Perhaps someday I will make it up to her, eh?"

Margaro pressed forward, a grin splitting his face from ear to ear. "I told you that one would claim your heart, amigo. But I am glad that she has. Would that I could find such a woman we would make of this a double wedding, no?" He nodded towards the brown clad priest. "I hope he

187

is not too nervous to proceed with the ceremony. On the way here we were nearly intercepted by Indians. It scared the poor Father all the way down to his toes. Then when I insisted he be blindfolded before we entered the last mile to the camp it was the final straw." His voice lowered to a whisper. "I think he feared we were going to eat him. Perhaps the Señorita should tell him that we are *not*." He looked at Angelica. "His name is Father Sebastino."

"Father Sebastino, welcome to our camp." Angelica pushed her way to the nervous priest, bestowing on him a smile that came from her heart.

"You are to be the bride?" He looked from Angelica to Rodrigo and back to Angelica again. "My child, my child, are you certain that you know what you are doing?"

"I am certain." The very air crackled with tension and Angelica thought he might refuse to officiate at the ceremony. Instead he took her hand.

"Come. Let us proceed if that is your wish. I want to get out of this troublesome camp." He shook his head impatiently. "I have another wedding and a funeral mass to officiate at tomorrow morning. I must finish with this and be on my way." His eyes touched warily on Margaro. "*He* was dressed like a fisherman. Told me I was needed to give the last rites. He *tricked* me. I would not like to be in his shoes when he stands before the Almighty. Indeed I would not."

"I cannot help but think that God understands," Margaro answered back. "But you have my apologies for any discomfort I may have made you suffer. Pray for me, Father. A bandit always has need of prayers."

Rodrigo led Angelica, Father Sebastino, Margaro, and the others to the middle of the camp where an improvised canopy had been erected. "No church, no stained-glass windows, no chapel, *querida*. Just the stars overhead to be our candles. I wish I could offer you more." His hand, in the middle of her back, caressed her.

188

"An outdoor wedding beneath God's heaven. I don't think any surroundings could be more beautiful than this." Indeed it was very romantic, she thought.

He moved nearer, drawn by the happiness in her voice, his eyes appraising her with sincere appreciation. "I am glad that you are my woman, *querida,* for I would want no other." Reaching out, he brushed the hair back from her forehead.

Holding a bouquet of wildflowers in one hand and a prayer book in the other, Angelica took her place at Rodrigo's side before the priest. From out of the crowd two hands reached up to place a lace mantilla on her head, a beautiful white lace veil that Juana had once worn at her own wedding. Clutching her rosary, Angelice listened to the deep voice of the priest as he droned the sacred words in Latin. She repeated the words in an awed whisper, her hands cold and trembling, and Rodrigo turned towards her with a smile.

Suddenly the night was shattered by a loud explosion. *"Madre de Dios,* what was that?" Rodrigo's head snapped around as Margaro's voice boomed the question. The sharp crackle of gunfire gave proof that the sound they had heard was no accident. From out of the crowd a bloodied figure emerged, staggering as he made his way to Rodrigo.

"What has happened?"

"The . . . the gringo has escaped." Manuel was frantic, shaking his head from side to side. "He somehow . . . the gunpowder . . . set it off while we . . . were distracted."

"The gringo? Which gringo? Rodrigo had a gut feeling that he know which one.

"The one with no hair. He killed Chuey, stole your horse, and escaped . . ."

"Merciful God!" Angelica gasped. "Jeremiah Adams." She had feared for a long time that he might make such an impulsive move. Her hands trembled as she saw the fury in Rodrigo's eyes. Jeremiah Adams had sealed his fate.

"Rodrigo. No! Don't stain our love with blood."

"He has taken a life and for that he must pay the price." Strapping on his holster he pushed her aside. "Wait here for me, *querida*. When this matter is finished we will continue our ceremony."

"No!" Furiously she shook her head. She could understand his anger but she could not condone the spilling of blood. With an agonized sob she watched as he strode away.

Like a shimmering ribbon of light, the moon guided Rodrigo, Margaro, and the others as they rode in pursuit of the escaped American gunman. Anger goaded Rodrigo on, anger as much at himself as for the man with no hair. It was his indecision that was to blame, his stubborn pride in the matter of the prisoners. Yes, it was true that Edward Howe had insisted that he would take no other hostages in his sister's place, but Rodrigo should have decided what plan to adopt nevertheless. Instead, he had been in limbo, not wanting his pride to be stung by letting all the hostages go free but not wanting to harm them either. Thus he had kept them in the camp, a potential danger to the others. Jeremiah Adams was a dangerous man who could do a great deal of harm. Rodrigo had realized that and yet had been so wrapped up in his happiness that he had not viewed the situation and taken action. Now Chuey was dead, a boy of little more than eighteen. Chuey, who he had taken into his camp as a boy of thirteen. A young, orphaned Mexican boy who had idolized him, who had obeyed his every word. He had made him promise that he would not let the American escape, that he would guard him with his life. And he had.

"We will never find him. You know that, don't you?" Margaro grumbled.

"We will find him" Rodrigo insisted.

"There are hundreds of rocks, thousands of bushes. He might have gone north or south, or even east. We have no knowledge of which way, amigo. It is dark. A clever man, especially one in peril of his life, will blend with the darkness and use his wits to great advantage."

"If you want to go back you may, Margaro." Rodrigo's voice was sharper than he intended. At the back of his mind was the fear that Jeremiah Adams was a far more dangerous adversary than he had realized. What would be the reprecussions of his escape?

"Go back?" Margaro was indignant. "No. I ride with you, by your side. That is the way it has always been and most likely always will be."

Silently they rode through the dust, the only sound the soft rhythm of their horses' hooves striking the earth. More than the desire for vengance motivated Rodrigo. Until now his hideaway had been a secret, known only to a few. It unnerved him to have the American wandering about freely, marking a trail that might enable him to lead other gringos to the camp. He had to find him before danger came to the encampment. He and his people had always been wanderers before they had found this haven which Rodrigo hated to leave.

"The gringo must be found." Rodrigo eased his weight in the saddle, pausing as he reined in his horse to appraise the terrain. The moon passed behind a cloud, shrouding the earth below in eerie darkness. There was no sound, except for the howl of a lonely coyote, the hoot of an owl. Though he hated to admit it, he knew that Margaro was right. Finding the gringo would be as difficult as finding a dried bean in a haystack. They were just wasting their time. Just like a speck of dust in the wind, the gringo was gone.

Swearing beneath his breath, Rodrigo waited as Margaro caught up with him. A sudden gnawing fear took hold of him. "We have left the camp poorly guarded. What if the gringo was not alone in this deed?"

Margaro preened himself like a proud rooster. "I already thought of that, amigo. I left Rafael with the old gringo and Pedro with the red-haired, wounded man. If it was indeed a plot, they won't get very far. Besides, I would venture a guess that the red-haired gringo is not very anxious to leave. I have not missed the looks he gives our Luisa. Enough to set her on fire." He laughed gently. "He may become a permanent part of our camp if he has his way."

"Never! I will have no gringo gunman for a brother. Luisa is a gentle girl. I have in mind a rich *caballero* for her. I want the world for her. *Dios!* She has had nothing but sorrow these past few years."

"Mmm. We shall see. I think, however, that you have a surprise in store. Luisa is very protective of that one. She hovers over him like a mother hen with her *chico*, spending more and more time with him."

"Too much time." Rodrigo decided that when he returned to the camp he would put an end to the matter. The gringo was strong enough to do a day's work. He could not hide behind a woman's skirt forever. "Bah!" he swore. Luisa had outfoxed him and now he understood her motives. It was just as he had feared. But no gringo would touch his sister. At the thought his mouth narrowed into a grim line. "Come, let us go back. We have wasted enough time. Leave it to fate to punish the gringo who killed Chuey, for it is apparent that we will not."

They had traveled quite a distance, galloping across a wide expanse of barren shrub and sand. It was a long and uncomfortable ride back to camp, made even more grueling because they had not been successful in their quest. The gringo had been using the cover of darkness and the distraction of Rodrigo's wedding to break free.

My wedding, Rodrigo thought. He had been ready to say the final words that would have bound him forever to

Angelica, had been ready to slip the ring on her finger but his insistence that they take up the chase had put a halt to his dreams. He remembered the look of reproach on her face when he had pushed past her, the fear that if he killed her countryman it would put a permanent wedge between them that even love could not breach. She at least would be relieved that the gringo had not been found.

The air was warm, the moon had at last come from behind its shroud as the riders arrived back at camp. Bone-weary, aching from head to toe, dusty, they were met by curious eyes and whispers.

"No, we did not find them."

"Yes, he escaped."

"We will have the priest say a mass for Chuey."

One by one, Rodrigo answered the questions. The exuberance of the camp was shattered, a sadness hung over the throng as each said a prayer for their dead comrade. Rodrigo searched for Angelica, finding her at last by the priest, deep in conversation. Looking at him, her eyes questioned him.

"I did not find him."

She looked relieved but kept her silence. Taking his hand she drew him to sit beside her on the ground. The night was filled with song, but they were mournful now as the singers recalled the life of the young man who had lived and died among them. Slim bottles of tequila and mezcal were passed from hand to hand as some of the bandits preferred to dispel their sorrow in a far different way. Father Sebastino looked on in frowning disapproval, reminding Rodrigo that the night was slowly dwindling. Taking Angelica by the hand, Rodrigo motioned for the priest to follow him.

"Our ceremony was interrupted but we will begin where we left off. Are you ready, Father?" Rodrigo's eyes scanned the camp for Luisa. "My sister, where is she? I would not have her miss this for the world."

"I don't know, Rodrigo. She cannot be far. Perhaps down at the spring or in the storehouse. If you wish I will go find her."

Angelica's offer was met with refusal. 'No, I will seek her out. There is something I wish to speak with her about." Kissing her lightly on the cheek, Rodrigo went in search of Luisa.

Chapter Twenty-Six

Luisa's only thought was of Jesse as the camp sprang to action. What if he had been hurt by the explosion? What if the others in their anger took out their frustrations on him? Moving through the crowd, she pushed and shoved her way to the hut where the American was confined. There she found Pedro standing in the door, pointing his rifle at the prisoner.

"What are you doing?" she snapped indignantly. "Pedro, put down that gun."

He gripped the weapon tightly. "Oh, no! The gringos think they are very smart, but I will not let this one escape. Margaro gave me strict orders to keep my rifle aimed at him lest the escape by the one gringo is a plot. I will not suffer Chuey's fate."

"A plot? A plot?" Luisa pushed her way into the room. "Look at him. It is only by a miracle that he is alive. Your bullets nearly killed him that day he was brought here. Only now have his wounds fully healed. He is hardly strong enough to be involved in a *plot!*"

"He could be playing possum."

"Think, Pedro, think. He has not even had the chance to speak with the other men. You are a fool if you really think Señor Jesse plans to escape." Picking up a pile of bandages and ointments from the floor she looked scathingly at him. "It is Rodrigo who needs you not this poor gringo."

"I don't know . . ." His face was marked with confusion.

"I would suppose that you at least trust *me?* I will watch him. I promise you he will not escape." She flapped her hands as if shooing away chickens. "Go! Go! Leave me, Pedro, so that I may tend his wounds. With the entire bandit camp searching the area I doubt that this man could get very far." She sighed. "Please go."

"Well . . ." He scowled, tugging at his bottom lip as he made his decision. He obviously hated to have Luisa angry with him but neither did he want to incur Margaro's wrath. "If you give me your word that you will watch him. That you will yell to me if he even looks as if he wants to step out that door . . ."

"I will not even let him move one muscle." Luisa tapped her foot impatiently, watching as Pedro at last turned and pushed his way through the torn curtain.

"Thank you, Luisa. I was sure my goose was cooked." The smile that Jesse gave her was filled with gratitude. "I've had enough bullets pumped into my ornery hide, I don't need any more." His expression sobered. "What's happened? I heard the explosion, the shouting. What on earth riled that fella enough to point a gun at me?"

"One of your amigos has escaped. He somehow managed to get a gun. He killed one of us. Chuey, a young man. A very young man." She wrung her hands nervously. "Now there will be trouble, a great deal of trouble. My brother has gone after the man."

"The poor bastard, the man who escaped, I mean. Was it Will?"

"The man with no hair."

"Jeremiah Adams. Well, he's mean enough and tough enough that he just might make it. I hope to God that he does, for his sake." He sat up from his pallet and looked about him, his face illuminated by the lamp at his side. "I can understand his need to get away. Being caged is not agreeable to a man."

His soulful voice tore at her heart. "That is how you feel, caged?" Of course he would. He had been confined to the hut since his arrival in the camp. Luisa's own fears for him had been partly responsible. She had insisted that he was much too weak to do any work. She had made an invalid of him because of her selfish desire to have him close to her.

"I'm not the kind of man who can stay a prisoner for long, Luisa. Sooner or later I will flee. Somehow I'll manage a way out of here."

"I suppose you must." Her eyes were misted with tears as she looked at him. "Be careful. I could not ... I I would ... if ... if anything were to happen to you."

"Would you miss me, Luisa?"

"You know that I would."

He thought a long time and then he said gently, "Come with me. Livin' amongst bandits is not the kind of life for a gentle young woman like you." As he spoke he reached for the lamp, holding it out before him as he stood up. The light played across his features, accenting the strong planes of his face. It was a hot night and the front of his shirt was open, giving her a glimpse of the powerful neck and his chest with its thick hair. "Come with me."

"I can't!" Her voice was a wail. She couldn't leave her brother. If anything happened to him and she wasn't there to guard him, she would never forgive herself, and yet ...

He moved nearer, drawn by the sadness in her voice. He wanted to hold her in his arms. to comfort her and never let her go. "Luisa ... I wish so many things. If we were not on opposite sides of this silly ... perhaps ..."

"But we are ..." There was a crazy leap in her pulse as he touched her arm. Her heart contracted painfully in her chest with a feeling she had never felt before. She wanted to

197

be held in his arms. That was the only thing she could think of at the moment. To feel safe and protected and loved, even if it were just for a short while. "I wish . . ."

"So do I. Oh, God, so do I . . ." He took a step forward, his pulse fluttering wildly as he took her in his arms. For a long moment he stood embracing her, relishing her warmth, the scent of her hair. He had seen her every morning with the other women, washing it with the soft-milled soap her brother had brought back with him from one of the raids. It reminded him of roses, a garden in flower.

Drawing strength from the warmth of her body, Jesse could feel the steady beat of her heart against his own. He had tried to tell himself why he could not care for this woman, but day by day the barriers he had built had crumbled. If only for this one night he could admit to himself that no one had touched his heart before like this woman, this lovely, gentle woman who was so very different from the others he had known.

Luisa felt secure in the circle of Jesse's arms. From beneath her lashes she studied him, so intent and unsmiling. She missed his smile.

He held her in his arms like the precious being she was. He found himself telling her things he'd never revealed to anyone else. About his father's death at the hands of Indians, his mother's grief, and the way she had slowly faded away until the loneliness and hardships of her life had taken her from him. Jesse had been on his own from an early age, living on the streets of Texas by his wits. There were the years of wandering the streets, homeless and hungry until Edward Howe had taken pity on him and given him a job. He hated to call it a "hired gun" but that was what he had been.

"But I have this dream of having my own land, Luisa. Now that I've met you that dream somehow seems even more important to me. To have a good woman who loves me, who will share my life." Slowly his head bent down to hers in a kiss that told of his longing.

The moment his lips touched hers, Luisa felt a surge of desire, a longing that touched her soul. It seemed that for just an instant the earth fell away, leaving her suspended in midair, clinging to him, loving him. There was nothing in the world except the two of them as she clung to his strength. No hatred, no sorrow. There was no room for such things in the world where they lived.

Dios, if that were only so, she thought. For a moment she *was* able to believe such a fantasy as she trembled under the warmth of his mouth. She responded to Jesse with a passion she hadn't even known she possessed. Nothing had prepared her for this wonder, this chaos of the senses that left her head spinning.

"I want to make love to you," Jesse said at last. A coil of her dark-brown hair had come free and he felt its silken softness brush his cheek like a lover's caress. He fought an inner battle, but something much stronger than reason tugged at his senses. Hungrily his lips closed on hers as very gently he drew her to lie beside him on the hard earthen floor. He wanted to fit her soft curves against the tightness growing in his loins.

Slowly, gently, he tugged at her blouse, exposing her breasts. Feverishly his hands caressed her, seeking out the soft peaks, stroking and searching, inflaming them both to an even fiercer desire with every caress.

Luisa could not even think clearly. It all had come so quickly, these new sensations, Jesse's sweet assault, her own reactions to his nearness. It was as if she were dreaming, but she knew that the man beside her was very real. She also knew that she loved him with all her heart.

"Do you want me, Luisa?" She heard his voice through a misty haze but could not answer. All she could do was hold him close so that he could not move away. Not now, not ever.

Blowing out the light, Jesse held Luisa, stripping off her garments like the petals of a flower. When she was naked he explored her with the reverence of a man for a cherished treasure. "Do you ache for me, Luisa? I do for you." Taking her hand he laid it flat against his hard chest, letting her fingers tangle in the prickly hair. "My heart is yours, feel it beating?" It beat in triple time as her small hand moved over his chest, then glided down to his stomach. Groaning, he took her mouth hungrily. He had gone beyond the point of turning back. Stripping away his own clothes he rolled onto his back, taking her with him.

"I don't want to hurt you."

"I'm not afraid." Her whisper tickled his ear.

Reaching up he spread her legs and lowered her as their bodies embraced. He would go slow with her, initiate her into lovemaking very gently. The first time was painful, he thought, but he would make it beautiful for her nonetheless. He would take it slowly. Giving her pleasure was all that he could think of. With his mouth and hands he aroused her with that thought in mind.

Luisa opened like a flower to Jesse's love, not even crying out when he touched her in the place covered by her maidenhead. She followed his whispered words and lowered herself on the hard flesh of his manhood until he was pressed into her. He gave her a moment to adjust to his invasion, then raised his pelvis. Her body was stretched taut, ready for him, welcoming him with murmurings of love, giving him her most precious gift. They entered a spiraling world together, of blinding light and quickening hearts. His arms clamped her to him, his mouth covered hers in a kiss that muffled her cry.

"*Madre de Dios!* What is this?" The shout of outrage shattered the darkness as a raised lantern flooded the hut with light. Luisa and Jesse lay on their sides clinging to each other, embracing hungrily as Rodrigo walked in the

200

door. *"Bastardo!* I will see you hung for this." Jesse was lifted by brutal hands and hurled across the room. "I will give you only enough time to get dressed and then I will hang you myself!"

An atmosphere of tension and unease hung over the area as Rodrigo paraded a half-dressed Jesse Harrison to the middle of the camp. Dogs barked, children whimpered, the men stared in anger, the women chattered in nervous surprise. What was happening, they all seemed to be asking as they stared at the two men.

Angelica gave a horrified gasp as she saw Jesse slump to the ground. "Rodrigo, what is this? Why . . . ?" She pushed frantically past the staring crowd to come to Jesse's side.

"This gringo scum has taken my sister's virtue!" Rodrigo's eyes focused on Jesse's face, his jaw ticked in fury. Nudging the red-haired man with his foot he snarled, "Get up. Get up and face your punishment like a man."

"What are you going to do? Answer me, Rodrigo!" The unwavering look of anger on his face frightened Angelica. This was not the Rodrigo she had come to know these past few days but a stranger capable of violence.

"I am going to hang him! Like the dog that he is! I will string him from the nearest tree and watch him dangle in the air. Gringo! Pig! *Bastardo!* You shame Luisa and you shame me." His fingers bit into Jesse's arms as he lifted him up. "Walk, gringo. Walk."

"You cannot hang him!" Angelica grabbed Rodrigo's arm. "You cannot kill him. Luisa loves him, Rodrigo. She . . ." He ignored her pleading, giving Jesse a brutal shove.

"No! Rodrigo . . . !" Luisa's shriek shattered the air as she flung herself forward. "If you do this I will never forgive you, never. I love him. He did not take what I did not freely give. I am not a child, I knew what I was doing."

"Bah! You know nothing. You are innocent of men's

deceitful ways. This man used you to soothe his lust. Stinking pig that he is . . ."

"He loves me and I love him. He wanted to take me away with him . . ."

"He wanted to use you to help him escape. Gringo dog is what he is!" Rodrigo gave his captive another fierce shove. "We will see how he likes hanging from a tree. Eh, gringo."

"I . . . I love your sister. I was not using her as you say. Do what you will to me but spare her your anger. You are right, I should not have touched her, it's just that . . ."

"Love." Rodrigo's voice was full of scorn. "I doubt you know what the word means. I know what you gringos think of Mexican girls. You will lie with them but you will not marry them."

"I would marry Luisa!"

"You will not have the chance. A marriage between a gringo and a woman who is half Mexican will never work out. It has no chance. Luisa will marry one of her own. If I can find a man not shamed by her lack of virtue." His angry gaze fell on his sister, who met him eye to eye defiantly. "Now you will have to choose."

"I will never marry. I love Señor Jesse."

Angelica felt her heart turn cold, as if an icy hand had gripped it. She was a *gringo*. Did Rodrigo hold the same scorn for her that he did for Jesse? He had taken her virtue. She, like Luisa, had given it freely. How then was the situation any different? In a whispered voice she put her thoughts into question.

"It is different between us, *querida*. You are choosing to live in *my* world. Here you will be welcomed. It is the gringos who would not accept Luisa into *their* world. I know. My mother was scorned until the day she died."

"And so was our father, if you recall," Luisa cried out. "But their love was strong enough to conquer the insults of others. I love Señor Jesse the same way. You have no

202

right to live my life for me, to make my decisions. Of all the women in the world, you wanted Angelica. You chose her as your mate. I choose Señor Jesse. The only difference is that I am not pigheaded. I let you love where you please without trying to run your life!" Tears flooded her eyes and she angrily dashed them away. "Little Luisa! Little Luisa! You have always treated me like a child. But in this *I* will do the choosing." Encircling her arms around Jesse she glared at her brother.

"Rodrigo . . ." Angelica knew she had to be the mediator, had to do something to help the young lovers. "Let them marry. We will make it a double wedding." She offered a gentle reminder. "If . . . If Luisa and Jesse . . . made love there could be the fruit of their joining already planted in Luisa. You could not think to hang your nephew's father . . ."

Her words stunned Rodrigo into a stony silence. If his sister became pregnant with the gringo's child who then would want to marry her? Her life would be ruined. "I will wait a month and if her monthly courses flow then I will hang him!"

"A wonderful solution!" Now it was Angelica's voice that was tinged with scorn. "Hang him and break your sister's heart? How can you be so stubborn? So cruel? Luisa deserves the same chance at happiness that we've been given. If you cannot understand that then you are as pigheaded as Luisa proclaims!"

"Pigheaded?" He raised a brow in frustration. He could handle one or the other of the two women but what was he to do when they joined forces against him. "And would I be understanding if I let my sister throw away her life on a useless gringo. He would soon break her heart. Am I then to gather the pieces and try to soothe her grief?"

"You are so sure that he will break my heart? Have you no faith in me as a woman?" Luisa's voice was low, just a whisper. "Do you think I am unworthy of his

203

love, Rodrigo?"

He threw up his hands in exasperation. "You just will not allow yourself to understand. It is not how I see you but how *he* sees you that is important."

"I see her as a very beautiful woman. A woman I love very much and wish to share my life with. Here in this camp or outside its walls, it makes no difference to me." Jesse's plea was impassioned as he met Rodrigo eye to eye. "Give me the chance to make your sister happy before you judge me so harshly."

"Agh . . ." Rodrigo grumbled. He didn't like the situation one bit but it was beginning to look as if he had lost the argument. If he hung this man, which he realized he really did not want to do as his anger cooled, then he would have earned both Angelica's and Luisa's ill will, possibly her hatred. As he saw the protective way Jesse clung to his sister his doubts began to flounder. He loved Angelica and she loved him. Should he give the gringo a chance?

"We have a priest . . ." Luisa said quietly.

"*Caramba!* Women, they drive a very hard bargain. I will be damned for eternity if I do not give in to you on this." He tapped his foot impatiently. "All right! All right! A wedding there will be." He clutched the lapel of Jesse's shirt. "But if you do one thing to make my sister unhappy I will carry out my warning and hang you. Do you undertand?"

"I understand." Jesse's mouth trembled as he eyed Luisa. "But I do not plan to bring her anything but happiness."

"Bring forth the priest." Rodrigo clapped his hands in impatience.

A huge bonfire licked its bright tongues of flame towards the black velvet sky as Rodrigo and Angelica said the final words that made them husband and wife. Angelica looked in awe at the large topaz that had been his

204

mother's as he slipped on her finger. From this moment on until the day she died she would belong to the man at her side. Until death parted them she would be Rodrigo's wife. Such a heady thought. Such a wonderful, spiraling ecstatic realization. She watched as Luisa and Jesse Harrison whispered the same words she and Rodrigo had spoken only moments before. Two pairs of lovers joined in happiness. God grant that they would all be content, that peace would reign in this encampment and within their hearts.

"Here. Drink. Celebrate. Tonight we show joy for the living. Tomorrow we will mourn the dead." Margaro winked as he handed Angelica a gourd filled with bright liquid. She started to take a sip but Rodrigo brushed it away as she raised it to her lips.

"Careful. Even one gourdful can make you drunk, *querida*. You stomach has not been well. I would not advise partaking of the 'Pulque'."

She deferred to his advice, and instead reached for a plate. The tortillas—pork crackling, chicken and vegetables—made her mouth water. Now that the excitement of the evening was over she felt the need to fill her stomach.

"So, the blushing bride?" With a forced smile Bonita held out her hand. "I hope you will be happy with Rodrigo for the *rest* of your life." Hopefully that would be very short, she thought.

"*Gracias*, Bonita." Angelica welcomed the gesture of friendship. Now that she was going to be living in the camp as Rodrigo's wife she wanted all the women to accept her.

"We will drink together you and I. No?"

"I . . . I don't think I should, Bonita. I haven't . . ."

"Just a few sips."

Fearful of causing insult Angelica took the proffered cup and held it aloft, then drank it down. It was bitter and she nearly choked as she swallowed it. Tequila, Bonita called it. From now on she would only drink wine. Angelica wiped her mouth and quickly sought a drink of water from the water bucket.

"You do not like our tequila, *querida?*" Rodrigo was amused.

"It tastes terrible." Angelica made a face and he laughed. Taking his arm, she led him to the planked table, feeding him out of her plate as he fed her out of his. The food was delicious, the music soothing. Except for what had happened to poor Chuey it seemed to be a perfect night. Rodrigo and Angelica could not take their eyes from each other. It was as if they hadn't already spent several nights of love together in the hut. All they both knew was that they wanted to be alone.

"Do as your heart asks," they heard a voice say. It was Margaro. "Take her to the hut and make love to her now. The others will understand."

"We will wait a little longer. I do not want it said that Rodrigo Delgado O'Hara is rude to his guests." Rodrigo answered his friend with a smile that soon melted to a frown as he looked at Angelica's pale face. She was clutching at her stomach, writhing in pain. *"Querida,* what is wrong? What is it?" Picking her up in his arms he carried her to the hut but not for a night of passionate love. Instead he hovered by Angelica's side as she spent the night in misery, holding his hand as she groaned. The terrible haunting fear that something was very wrong nagged at him. Perhaps it was not because Angelica was with child that she suffered these pains, this torment. He knew the agony of not being able to help her, to soothe her. Knew the all-encompassing fear that he might be losing the only woman he would ever love.

Chapter Twenty-Seven

"Najalayogua. *Por Dios*, you must help me. You saved Angelica's life once before with your potions. You must do so again." Rodrigo was beside himself with worry. Three days and nights had come and gone and still there was no sign that Angelica was getting any better.

"She still has the sickness of the stomach?" The old woman raised one gray eyebrow in question.

"And pain."

"When she eats or when she does not eat?"

"That is what is so puzzling. I thought perhaps it could be the food, that her stomach was in a delicate condition, but her symptoms have no pattern. There are times when she gives in to her hunger and feels the better for it and at other times her eating causes the symptoms again. I have monitored what she eats, thinking perhaps it is one of our hot, spicy dishes that makes her suffer so, but again there is no pattern."

"You said before you thought she is going to have a little one. Have you changed your mind?"

"The monthly course came upon her yesterday. There is to be no child." Rodrigo's expression, the tinge of sadness in his voice were proof of his disappointment. "Had it been so, I would have been the happiest of men."

"Hmm." Najalayogua crinkled up her eyes and pursed her lips as she thought about the matter. "No baby. I was so sure . . . But of course there are other reasons. A sickness of the body. In my village once there was a man who wasted away despite all my healing herbs." Rodrigo's face turned a deathly pale. "Then there was a woman who lost the contents of her stomach every time she ate corn. It did not agree with her. No corn, no sickness. And there was the man who suffered much because of his wife. She was trying to kill him, you see. By using *poison*. A very little at a time so that no one would suspect, eh? There are many innocent looking plants that are deadly. The egg-shaped fruit of the jimson weed for one. The leaves of the tomato plant. Some wild mushrooms. Berries. The bright red berries of the nightshade plant . . ."

"Angelica is loved by everyone. No one would try to harm her." Rodrigo refused to believe that poison could be the cause, nevertheless he questioned several members of the encampment. Was it possible that one of the children might have picked some poison mushrooms by mistake, or seasonings that had been used in the food?

Rodrigo watched carefully as the food was prepared that night, tasting all the ingredients used in the food. He watched as Luisa and Juana ground the corn dough for tortillas, supervised Elisia as she chopped the chili peppers for the puchero. But everything was as it should be.

"I have been cooking for fifty-five years," one old woman snorted defensively as she noticed Rodrigo's intent stare. Her voice trembled with annoyance. "I do not need you to tell me which way it should be done." Wielding her spoon, the old woman tried to chase Rodrigo away but he stood his ground, placating her with a smile and a kiss on the hand. At last, when he had satisfied himself that nothing was amiss, he retreated to the corral.

Swirls of pink and lavender touched the sky. The day

was waning as Rodrigo leaned against the bars of the corral appraising the horses. He smiled at the boy who had followed him and gave him a wave as he took his favorite perch on the wooden bars. Avidly the child watched him as he saddled a sorrel stallion, a spirited animal that no one else could tame.

"Do you think that someday I could learn to break a horse, Rodrigo. Do you?" Ricardo was a shy boy whose parents had been killed in a fire a few years ago. Spending his days and nights in a self-imposed seclusion he was more like a shadow than a being of flesh and blood. He moved quietly, said little, and usually went unnoticed.

"I will show you how. Would you like that, Ricardo?" His bright smile showed that he would. Finding a gentler horse for the boy, Rodrigo helped him onto its back. The boy seemed to take to riding with a natural grace that made Rodrigo very proud. "You do very well, niño. Someday I will show you how to rope as well as ride, eh? On the next raid I will see if I cannot find a horse that is just your size."

"Would you, Rodrigo? Would you?" The boy's eyes opened as wide as coins.

"And I will have my Angelica sew for you a jacket like mine, the one with the silver buttons and the braid trim." Rodrigo's mouth tugged in a grim frown. "That is, if she is not ill. Poor Angelica. It worries me, Ricardo. Were I to lose her . . ."

"She will get well, Rodrigo. I know that she will. Najalayogua will help her and Bonita as well."

"Bonita?" Rodrigo wondered what the buxom woman had to do with the matter. Bonita was hardly the kind of woman to act as a nurse. "I doubt that Bonita would be of any help."

"She is trying. Just like Najalayogua, she has her special potions. I have seen them in her hut, hidden in a pouch under her pallet. She uses them when she thinks that no one is looking. I have seen her take just a pinch of them to put in your señora's food.''

"To do what?'' Rodrigo's blood ran cold as he considered what the child's revelation might mean.

"Perhaps it is a special seasoning or spice for the food. I do not know. All I do know is that it is only the señora's food that she . . .''

"*Sangre de Christo!*'' So that was it. Anger bubbled fiercely in Rodrigo's blood. In a thunderous rage he ran back to the living quarters. Pushing his way into Bonita's hut he fumbled under her straw bed for the pouch and came up empty-handed. Was the boy imagining things? No, he didn't think so. He had never known Ricardo to tell a falsehood.

But of course, he thought. It was the hour for cooking. The time Bonita worked her evil. Leaving the hut, he found Bonita standing over the largest pot, her hair in a tangled mass around her eyes. Sweat beaded her forehead as she stirred an iron cauldron of beans.

"Rodrigo . . . ?'' Her voice was a purr as she saw him appraising her. "Have you tired so soon of your new wife?'' A seductive smile played on her lips.

"And if I had?''

She made no attempt to embrace him but moved to within an inch of where he stood. "I could stir a fire in your loins. We could meet in our secret place, you and me. Away from the eyes of the others. There was fire between us, Rodrigo. I am more of a woman than the pale-faced gringa could ever be.'' She thrust her large breasts out temptingly. "She is not one of us. She cannot eat our food. You were a fool to marry her.''

"I am not a fool. It is you.''

"What?'' The harshness of his tone took her by surprise. Searchingly she looked into his face. What she read there made her heart grow cold.

"You are a fool if you think I do not know what you are up to.'' Before she could react he grabbed her wrist,

210

twisting her arm behind her.

"What are you doing? Let me go!" She gasped, but not with desire, as he let his hands roam over her roughly. He searched the waistband of her skirt, her bodice, and found what he was looking for in the stiff folds of her gown. A small leather pouch, tied around her hips with long leather ties. "Give that back to me." Bonita cried her outrage as he yanked the pouch free.

"And what have we here?" Rodrigo's eyes narrowed suspiciously.

"Herbs and spices, nothing more. Give it back. Give it back to me, Rodrigo." She fought him to get the leather pouch back in her possession, biting and scratching. Rodrigo skillfully dodged out of her way.

"Herbs? Spices. Let us see what Najalayogua says. What will she say, Bonita? Eh? Do you want to tell me or shall I embarrass you before the whole camp."

"Najalayogua is an old fool. She knows nothing. Nothing." She shook her head wildly. "Rodrigo . . . !" Her last plea went unheard as he gave her a brutal shove and walked in the direction of the old healing woman.

"I found this pouch in Bonita's possession, Najala-yogua. She insists it is only spices and herbs." He thrust it into the old woman's hands. "Ricardo says he has seen her putting this in Angelica's food." Was he being unreasonable in his accusation? Now that his anger had cooled a bit he wondered. Perhaps it was nothing but dried roots and leaves after all.

"Ehhhhh?" Sifting through the brown leather bag she took a handful and held it to her nose, sniffing it carefully, examining each and every particle, took just a pinch and cautiously tasted it. With a loud exclamation she spit it out. "Devil's root, jimson weed, and I think a bit of poison mushroom." Her eyes focused on Rodrigo's face. "Not for flavoring our chili. If, as you say, she has been putting this in your woman's food, then it is with evil intent."

211

"Just as I suspected." So there was nothing so vile that Bonita would not attempt to get what she wanted. Even murder. When he thought of the agony she had put Angelica through, what might have happened if he had not found out in time, his blood boiled with fury. "Margaro! Bernardo! Felipe! Bring Bonita to me!"

That was a command not easily carried out. Knowing all too well the punishment that awaited her, Bonita was a yelling, spitting, scratching cat, trying her best to escape the hands that held her. Even as she was dragged along she hurled epithets at the men who imprisoned her with their hands.

"*Bastardos!* Let me go! I am not some filthy peasant to be so treated. I will cut out your livers. I will scratch out your eyes. Leave me be. Let me go! I am one of *you,* not some gringo dog." Her attitude changed the minute she was face to face with Rodrigo. "I have done no wrong, *querido.* The old woman is addled in her wits if she says otherwise."

She reminded him of a snake, hissing and spitting one moment, capable of poisoning her victim, then turning to a lamb, all innocent baaing in the attempt to save her skin. He might have been fooled by her once but not now. Najalayogua would not lie. Nor was she "addled", as Bonita claimed. No one was more skilled in the knowledge of plants and their uses than the old healing woman. If she said the concoction found on Bonita was poison then he had no reason to doubt that she spoke truth. Even so, he gave Bonita one last chance.

"You say the contents of this pouch are harmless?" Rodrigo's eyes squinted, his jaw clenched as he suppressed his anger. He even managed a smile.

"*Sí! Sí!* It is a misunderstanding, nothing more. I know that the gringa woman is not always fond of our food, and so I was merely adding spices to her portion to make it more palatable. If that makes you angry then I will do it no more." Thinking that she had won, she flashed the old healing woman a triumphant grin.

"Then you would not be afraid to taste of these 'harmless herbs and spices' yourself?" He cocked his head in the direction of the cooking pots. "Felipe, bring me a bowl of the stew."

"Of course I would not be afraid . . ." Bonita watched warily, knowing what Rodrigo intended to do. She was trapped. If she did not eat the poisoned stew she would confirm her guilt, if she did she would condemn herself to agony. Either way, she could not win.

Rodrigo took the clay bowl from the young Mexican bandit's hands. The stew was piping hot, sending forth tantalizing smells from its steam. Taking the pouch, he measured out a handful of the dried leaves, stems, and berries and stirred it in the stew with a churning motion. With an ominous smile he held it out to Bonita. "The herbs and spices should make this suitable to your taste. I put in an extra portion just for you." His words left no doubt as to their meaning. If it truly was poison he had put in enough to kill a horse, much less a human. Bonita had only put in a pinch each time and that had been enough to sicken the American woman.

"It is too hot. You would not have me burn my delicate mouth?" Taking the bowl she looked nervously from left to right, hoping for a chance to flee. She was not fool enough to poison herself just to prove her innocence to these gawking fools. To the devil with them!

"Too hot? Then we will wait for it to cool. All of us *together*, Bonita." All was quiet as the minutes passed.

"Rodrigo, you can't insist that she . . ." Bernardo, who had always been attracted to the buxom woman, shook his head. 'No."

"Stay out of this, Sanchez. It is none of your concern." Angrily Rodrigo shoved him aside. "Bonita has a chance to prove her innocence. In this I have been fair. It is more

213

of a chance than she gave my wife." He turned his cold eyes on the object of his scorn. "Eat, Bonita. *Eat!* Or be condemned in front of all."

Picking up the spoon Bonita lifted it slowly to her mouth, her breathing loud and raspy. Perhaps one spoonful would satisfy him. It would not be enough to kill her. Putting it in her mouth, she chewed slowly and said a silent prayer as she swallowed.

"Eat it all, Bonita. The whole bowl." Rodrigo was ruthless in his anger.

"I . . . I am not hungry." Bonita trembled, imagining that a fire was coursing from her throat to her stomach. She would die! And all because of her desire for this man. No, she would not! The devil take him before she would sacrifice herself. Picking up the spoon again, she dipped it into the stew, looking down with an air of resignation. "All right. If you insist."

Suddenly she threw the contents of the bowl in Rodrigo's face, taking to her heels with a violence that stunned the four men surrounding her. With the swiftness of a gazelle she pushed her way past the women, beyond the storage huts to the corral. Rodrigo wiped the sticky mess from his face and eyes and followed, catching up with her just as she pulled herself onto his favorite horse. Tumbling over and over on the ground with her, he fought to subdue her. Her fingernails tore at his flesh, her feet kicked out ruthlessly, but at last he held her down.

"You have proved your own guilt beyond a shadow of a doubt, *puta!*" he raged at her. "You thought to kill my wife. That I would console myself in *your* bed. Ha! I would never have a woman such as you. You could never have taken my Angelica's place. You are as poisonous as the roots and herbs you used to get your way. You are evil. And you will pay for what you have done. By my oath, you will!"

At last Margaro and Felipe caught up with the

struggling pair. As they reached down to pull Bonita to her feet she spit at them.

"Take her to the area where we have the gringo prisoner. The old man. Take her there and by the devil's breath, do not let her get away. First thing when the sun sets tomorrow we will decide her fate."

It took a long while before the camp settled down. The whisperings of Bonita's doings were the talk of the camp, spoken so loudly that even she could hear from her perch beside the locked door of the storehouse. Not one of the bandits condoned what she had done so there was no one to take her side.

"A gringa woman has turned them against me," she mumbled to herself, casting an angry glare towards the old man incarcerated with her. His snores were unnerving, keeping her from the sleep she so badly needed. Gringos, she hated them all. Now because of a gringa she was the object of ridicule and scorn.

What would the verdict be? Bonita sincerely doubted that it would be death, for the woman had not died. If she had and Bonita's guilt had been revealed, then because she was Rodrigo's wife and thereby considered one of the members of the encampment, Bonita would have faced the severest punishment. It was the law of the encampment that anyone who caused the death of another of the bandit camp would, in turn, forfeit their own life. A harsh law, a brutal rule, and one she dreaded now. The other possibility was being branded so that anywhere she went it would be marked upon her what she had done. Running her hands over her smooth skin she shuddered as she thought of that possibility. Then again she could be sent out into the rugged wilderness with no food and little water, to find her way on foot to another camp. Humiliated. Openly scorned. It was better to take her chances on her own, to escape on horseback.

Over and over again in her mind, Bonita toyed with a

plan. Perhaps fate had been kind after all. The gringo man. Perhaps he could be used to help her accomplish her purpose. If she was crafty she could create a diversion so that her own escape would not be detected. It would be no easy task to break free. Since she was awaiting sentencing she would be heavily guarded, and she had heard Rodrigo threaten anyone who was responsible for her getting away.

How was she going to free the gringo? He seemed to be sleeping so peacefully she wondered if he even wanted to leave the camp. The old fool. Since he was beyond his youthful years he had been given the job of seeing to the horses during the day, under guard, of course. He was given plenty of food, always taking second helpings, then was given a soft pallet on which to sleep in this storehouse. Only the fact that the door was locked at night gave proof that he was still a captive. It would be just her luck if she did all she could to free him only to have him say he wanted to stay. Her own escape depended on his bungling attempt to flee.

Nudging him none too gently with her foot she awakened him. "Señor Cooper, I am going to help you escape. Would you like that?"

"Escape? I'd get my damned fool head shot off. Jeremiah was lucky that he left here in one piece, but I'm not as fleet of foot as he is." Stretching, he eyed her warily. "Why would you want to help me? How could you when you're as much a prisoner as me?"

"We will help each other, no?"

"Don't know if I trust you. Someone who would try to poison a young, beautiful, innocent girl like Angelica . . ."

"It was a misunderstanding, señor. Surely you would not condemn me without knowing the truth." Bonita feigned one of her most innocent smiles. "I admire the señorita. I would never have tried to harm her."

216

"Well . . ."

Before he could object too strongly, she outlined her plan. In the morning when the young guard Felipe came to bring them their breakfast and take Will Cooper to the corral to do his work, she would distract him. It would not be hard to do. There was not a man in camp who did not desire Bonita. With the exception of Rodrigo, she thought with a snarl. She would make a show of seducing the young bandit, then, while he was contemplating her charms, Will Cooper would come up behind him and hit him over the head.

"You will go to the corral. No one will think it strange, señor, to see you there. You will turn all the horses loose. All except one for you and one for me. While the others are trying to catch their fine stallions we will ride away."

"And you do not think they will shoot me?" Will Cooper was nervous about the matter. It was one thing to attempt an escape with Jeremiah Adams giving him aid, quite another to trust a woman who was the consort of bandits.

"They will not shoot. They will be much too busy gathering up their precious horses to care about one lone gringo." If they did shoot him, what did it matter, she thought. She did not care about one gringo's life. All she cared about was her own.

Bonita did not sleep one wink that night. Instead she forced herself to think out every detail of the plan. The only flaw in her scene was that it was Margaro and not Felipe who took the early-morning turn at guard and Margaro was not so easily fooled. Instead of meeting her amorous advances with youthful ardor he merely laughed.

"We have been in this camp together for two years, Bonita. Not once have you ever cast me a second glance. Now you try to make me think that you are wild for me? Could it be the key I carry that you are wild for?" He

217

clenched it securely in his hand as he set down the tray of food. Nevertheless, he seemed to take pity on her. "If it makes you feel any better, I will plead leniency for you today. Your penalty will not be as frightening as it might have been." He laughed. "Perhaps your only punishment will be to be stuck with me as your lover, eh?"

"That would be no punishment, Margaro. In your way you are nearly as handsome a man as Rodrigo." She did think him handsome in a peasant kind of way. Not like Rodrigo. She and Rodrigo both had white Anglo blood, were descended from old aristocratic lines. "You are very much a man, Margaro."

"And you hope a big enough fool to succumb to your charms. No, Bonita. No."

"Margaro . . ." She purred his name, brushing against him sensuously like a cat. "Would you deny the pleasure I can give you?" Wrapping her arms about him, she sought his mouth but Margaro pushed her away. *"Vaya Ud a pasear!"* In anger she told him to go to hell.

"I may, *chico*. I very well may. But at least I will have Rodrigo's good will. You may pout all you like but I will not set you free, if that is what you are thinking . . ." His eyes looked stunned for just a moment as he was hit from behind, then, with a loud thud, Margaro slid to the floor. Will Cooper's well-aimed blow had hit its mark.

"I thought you would never silence him," she chided peevishly. "But no matter." Impatiently she shoved the old man out the door. "Now, remember all that I have told you."

It was more easily accomplished than she might have ever dreamed. She watched as Will Cooper opened the gates of the corral and set the horses galloping. Like ants in a disturbed anthill the bandits gave chase, and in that moment Bonita made good her escape, Will Cooper following close behind.

All along the way Bonita thought of her revenge.

Bastardo, she thought. Rodrigo would pay for his treatment of her. How she would make him pay. She would bring down the gringo's wrath on the camp if need be. Ah yes, she thought, the yellow-haired woman's brother would be very anxious to exact vengence on the bandit who had taken his sister's virtue. She would lead him to the camp and watch what happened.

Chapter Twenty-Eight

Bonita was gone! The news buzzed about the camp. Bonita had escaped and taken the old gringo man with her. Rodrigo was outraged, doubly more so at Margaro because he had warned him to beware of her.

"She charmed you. Seduced you into letting down your guard. *Idiota!* I should have your head."

"She did not! We were talking, and I was watching her every move. How was I to know she had included the old man in her plan. It was he who hit me from behind. Bonita. Bah! I would never look twice at one such as her. You do me a great wrong, my friend, if you think otherwise." Squaring his shoulders, Margaro looked every inch the offended party.

"Then I will forgive you, amigo. The large lump on your head is enough punishment for being caught off guard."

Margaro rubbed his sore head. "But perhaps I can amend my stupidity. I will find her for you. A woman will not go far, I think. She will stop to rest."

With a swagger Margaro called the men together, forming a search party to scour every inch of the surrounding area for the woman and the old man, only to return several hours later in embarrassed disappointment.

There was no sign of them. The fiery, tempestuous woman and the gray-haired man had seemingly vanished. Rodrigo shouted; he raged. It took several hours for his anger to cool but at last he succumbed to Angelica's pleading.

"Perhaps it is better that she did go, Rodrigo." She trembled at the thought that anyone could hate her enough to want to kill her. Even so, Angelica would have loathed to have anyone punished because of her. In her mind she thought that Bonita must have loved Rodrigo very much to hold such resentment. It made her feel a twinge of guilt for having caused the other woman's unhappiness by taking him from her. She would remember in her prayers and hope that someday Bonita would be as happy as she was now with Rodrigo. Taking him by the arm she led him to the hut, hoping to find a way to calm him.

"My gentle angel," he whispered, taking her in his arms. "You would forgive Satan himself." He looked deep into her eyes. "Anyone else would be crying out for Bonita's blood for making them suffer as she did you these last few weeks. Instead I can read forgiveness in your eyes."

"Punishing her would not undo what happened, but only make her hate me all the more. She will find another place to live, among people who will give her a fresh start. And . . . and perhaps another man. Though I cannot imagine her finding another man like you, Rodrigo. I stole you from her. For that she would always have resented me. Away from here she will get over her hatred." Reaching up, she curled her fingers into his thick, dark hair and brought his head closer so that she could kiss him. "But for the moment I feel strong, in love and very, very happy, my dearest husband." Her kiss held all the longing of her soul. There had been so much precious time wasted, but now they had the rest of their lives to make up for it.

222

Gently Rodrigo lay her down on the soft pallet, kissing the soft hollow at her throat as he pulled the blouse from her shoulders. "You are mine, *querida*. I will never let anyone hurt you again. You are the only beauty in my life, the only woman I have ever loved." He sighed. "Sometimes I wonder why God rewarded me with such a precious treasure when I have not always obeyed his laws, and I think at these times that I must be dreaming. If I am, then I never want to wake up." Lying down beside her he stretched his long length out beside her, just contenting himself with caressing her as he watched the rise and fall of her breasts. His lips followed the path of his fingers, kissing the soft warmth of her breasts, which had slowly come free of the restraint of her garments. With a deep sigh of pleasure he kissed each taut peak, then without another word rose and took off his shirt, pulled off his boots, and discarded his trousers. Angelica's clothing followed, joining his in a heap on the hard, earthen floor.

They lay quietly kissing for a long while, gazing silently at each other each time their mouths parted. Love. Such a potent emotion. It transcended boundaries, thoughts, cultures, society's restraints, and sometimes even reason, she mused. She loved this man with all her heart, could never imagine a time when she would not give him that love. Her husband. What a wonderful thought that was, to belong to him.

"I love you, Rodrigo." Her whisper sent shivers up his spine as their bodies caressed.

"And I adore and love you with all my heart." He laughed gently. "There are some who might say that I do not have a heart, and yet in this I prove them wrong. You have captured it and hold it right this moment in your hand."

She smiled, laying her hand on his firmly muscled chest. The pounding of his heart was strong, nearly as fierce as her own. Feeling emboldened in her touch, she explored

223

the magnificent expanse of his chest and his hard, muscled shoulders. Her eyes moved down to the dark hair from which his manhood sprung, showing proof of his desire for her, and she marveled at the wonder of it all. How could anyone have ever made her think that what went on between a man and woman could be embarrassing? It was beautiful. Loving him made it so. Reaching out, she touched him.

"Angelica . . ." They were both aroused, wanting to consummate the lovemaking that had been denied to them because of Bonita's foul plotting. It was the first time in a long while that Angelica was not consumed by her illness; thus it was nearly like the first time they had made love. With all the anticipation and all the passion.

Rodrigo rose over her, then slid into her warmth, her softness. She moaned as he penetrated her to his full length, locking her hands around his neck, opening her legs, arching against him. Tenderly he brought her to the peak of fulfillment yet there was a certain frenzy in the lovemaking as well. Having come so close to losing her she was all the more precious to him.

With Angelica their lovemaking was always a sharing, not a giving or a taking, Rodrigo thought. Gentle as well as passionate. Wild and wanton. Always a matter of the heart.

Angelica never tired of feeling Rodrigo's hands on her body, of tasting his kisses. He had taught her the secrets of her body as well as his own. Now exploring every curve, every secret of her with his hands and mouth, he taught her to be bold in her appraisal of him as well. They were in a world of their own. No matter what happened outside they could for a time forget. Even so, a slight frown flickered over Rodrigo's brow. He was a bandit. The life he asked her to share was one of danger and he found himself regretting his way of life. He wanted so much for this woman at his side. He wanted to give her the world, to spend the rest of his life just making her happy. He wanted a home, a rancho and respectability. Perhaps he would never be able to give her the life she truly deserved. Perhaps there would never be peace and contentment. Loving her had changed his view of things and yet he was trapped by the past. What if someday this happiness was taken from him? How could he live now without Angelica by his side? Beyond the walls of this hut was reality. He could not hide from it forever. Reality. Brutality. Pain.

Trying to forget, he buried his face in the warmth of her breasts, whispering her name. Kissing her with a gentle fervor, he sought to push his fears from his mind. She was here. They were together. It was all that they had for now. For the moment it had to be enough.

Chapter Twenty-Nine

The fiery rim of the sun crept above the dark line of the horizon as Bonita at last located the gringo trader's camp. The foolish old man riding beside her had at last remembered where it was. Had he not she would have ridden off and left him to find his own way. He had been her guide, nothing more, and more of a hindrance than blessing as they traveled the hilly and very rocky roadway.

Sweat trickled down her forehead and into her eyes. Reaching up, she wiped the perspiration away, swearing beneath her breath. The gringos had better make it worth her while. Without her to lead them they would never find Rodrigo Delgado O'Hara. Never. Certainly the old man could not lead them. He could barely find his nose, she thought angrily. Stupid gringo! Foolish old man. Men. When their manhood had withered they were of little use to a woman.

"Straight ahead," she heard the old fool say now as if she had not eyes to see. With a muffled oath she followed him, riding at a quickened gallop despite her aching bottom. Revenge drove her on, the need to see Rodrigo lose what he valued the most. She would laugh when they hung him. Laugh until the very sky rumbled. Then see what his precious Angelica could do for him. Or what her God could do for him for that matter.

The landscape was splashed with hues of green, mingling with the barren soil. Bushes, wild grass, and an occasional tree stretched in a never-ending rolling plain, rising and falling until it met the sea. A breathtaking sight if one had time for such nonsense, she reflected. She took no time to relish the scenery. Her mind was on only one thing. Finding this Edward Howe and making certain her betrayal was profitable. She wanted money for something she would have done anyway.

She found him sitting like a king on a throne in the large tent of the gringo encampment. Bonita had never envisoned that he would be so handsome. Hair as light as his sisters, eyes just as blue. A handsomeness marred only by his once broken nose. Licking her lips, hastily straightening her hair, she moved towards him.

"Who are you, and what the hell are you doing here? Sam! Sam! Who let this woman in?" The greeting was not what she had anticipated.

"Señor Cooper brought me here. I have brought him back to you."

"Will?" Taking a thin cigar from a gold case he lit it by striking a match with his thumbnail, then he tilted his head and looked up at her. "You brought him here? Why?"

"I wanted to talk with you and he knew the way. Or at least he told me he did. If the truth be known, señor, I more or less found it myself. You friend is a bit senile it seems."

He threw back his head and laughed. "Senile? Will Cooper? Why he's the wiliest old fox I know." Hearing his name Will Cooper stuck his head through the tent flap. "Is she telling me the truth? Did she bring you here?"

"Sure as shootin'. Them bandits were riled at her. Put her in the storehouse with me." He shook his head. "Few years ago I would have done something far more than snore in her ear but . . ." He sighed regretfully.

"So you incurred the bandits' wrath and had to escape. Did you think I would welcome you?" His eyes were bold in their appraisal and she could tell he liked what he saw.

"I thought that a man as rich as you would pay very well to have the head of the man who raped his sister."

"Raped? Angelica wrote to me . . ."

"Of course." She smiled sweetly. "What was she supposed to say? Rodrigo can be very menacing at times. I should know. I was once his mistress. Like your sister I too was once innocent and untouched by a man. Now, I am a match for any woman."

"I would not doubt it. And what of Jeremiah Adams? Do you know what happened to him?" Edward cocked his brow.

"He escaped but I do not know where he is," Bonita answered.

"So what do you want from me?"

"I am a woman in need of a protector. Now that I have met you I think I have found the perfect man. I will help you and in return . . ."

"I understand." He gestured to a wooden crate and bid her sit beside him. "You intrugue me . . ."

"Bonita. Bonita O'Riley Mendoza. My mother was Irish, my father a *caballero*. My ancestors were here long before yours ever had their feet touch the shore. I had a great-great-grandfather who was a Spanish missionary. But unlike your sister, I never had thoughts of taking the veil. Poor Angelica. Rodrigo's lechery put an end to all her dreams. How sweet then will be your vengeance." And my own, she thought angrily. "I will give you that chance for a very small price."

"Me?" he asked, half jokingly, half in earnest.

"If that is what you offer." She ran her tongue over her

229

lips, bending down to give him an ample view of her large, full breasts. "I think we will deal well together." Meeting his eye she boldly smiled. Leaning closer she whispered a plan.

They would attack when it was dark, that time when the camp was in repose and unwary. It would be like shooting at sitting ducks, Edward Howe reasoned. He would ride in and rescue his sister. Take her from the hands of that thieving bandit who had the gall to double-cross him. And when all was said and done he'd have the bandit's head. He'd hang him or shoot him, whichever happened to suit his mood at the moment. Rodrigo Delgado O'Hara was as good as dead.

"We'll leave first thing tomorrow morning." He smiled as he thought of how happy his sister would be when he took her from the hands of the man who had so vilely defiled her. Yes, sir, happy indeed.

Chapter Thirty

The moon hung like a large golden coin, and flickering stars pulsated against the black velvet of the sky. It was a warm night, a lover's night. Leaning into Rodrigo's embrace, Angelica traced the strong lines of his face, which had become as familiar as her own. He had brought her so much happiness the last few weeks that somehow it seemed they'd always been together. She loved him. There could never be any doubt, and he showed her in a hundred small ways how much she held his heart.

"We should go back to the camp, *querida.*" He pressed a kiss to her neck regretfully, as if he would like to stay much longer in the secluded clearing where they had just made love. It had become their lovenest, the only place where they could be totally alone, without prying eyes.

"Mmm, just a while longer." It was like a paradise here, she thought. Just like the garden of Eden must have been. The air was fragrant with blossoming flowers, the nightbirds had begun their serenade. Lying on a thick blanket of leaves, she sighed in contentment. If only it could always be this way. She here with Rodrigo while the world around them was at peace.

It had been peaceful. In an effort to please her, Rodrigo had instigated less raids on the rich *rancheros* and wealthy

American settlements. He had told her quite earnestly that he wished to forge a new kind of life for his people, had played with the idea of going farther south and settling there.

"How would you like to be married to a farmer?" he had joked, half seriously, "or a fisherman?"

"I would love it. Just as I love you," she had answered. "Wherever you go, whatever you choose to do with your life, I will be beside you."

Perhaps God had sent her to these people to work a miracle in His own way. Angelica knew in the last few weeks and months she had been a positive influence in their lives. The last few days she had even been instrumental in having the men of the camp erect a small dwelling which they could use as a chapel. One of the newer members of the encampment had once had thoughts of being a priest, had been trained as one, and so gave to the tiny community a tentative link with God. It was a beginning.

"*Te quiero mucho*," Rodrigo whispered now, nibbling on her ear in the way he knew always stirred her. "We will stay here much longer, eh. Long enough to make love again."

Opening her eyes, she found his face only inches from her own as his mouth met her lips in a light, caressing kiss. Strange, but even after all this time his kiss still made her tremble. A mesmerizing languor always swept over her whenever he was near.

A sharp staccato pop interrupted her reverie, and Angelica sat up with a start. "What was that?" It sounded again. Gunfire.

"I hope it is not a quarrel. Playing with guns can lead to tragedy." Hurrying to don his calzones and shirt, Rodrigo was visibly agitated. "I was a fool perhaps to think the quiet could last for long. My men are violent men. Used to fighting."

232

While Angelica dressed he lit a cigarillo and stared into the darkness, as if trying to see the camp. "I cannot leave them alone for even one hour." Puffing on the cigarette in frustration he paced up and down.

More gunshots shattered the silence, and smoke billowed upward, hanging over the area like a cloud.

Throwing the cigarillo to the ground and grinding it beneath his foot he swore. *"Madre de Dios!* Something has happened." He ran from the clearing, ordering over his shoulder, "Stay here!"

Stay? Angelica could not do that when he so obviously needed her. Her place was by Rodrigo's side, not clinging to safety in some sheltered grove. Stumbling blindly along in the dark she followed him. She was cautious, very careful as she moved from tree to tree. Still, she managed somehow to keep him within her sight, his white shirt her only aid as she pushed through the undergrowth.

The closer they came to camp, the worse the smell. Smoke. Gunpowder. Angelica had a frightening premonition of what was happening but she forced it from her mind. Dear God, please. Please do not let what was happening be in any way because of her.

The night exploded around her. Horses' hooves pounded and the crack of rifle fire echoed in the stillness, and for just a moment Angelica felt her heart stop. Reflected in the light of the fires was the enfolding tragedy. She looked on in horrified silence at the sprawl of bodies.

Rodrigo was barking out orders. "Margaro, Felipe, Bernardo, take your places on the wall. José, see to the women and children. Pepe and Ramón, come with me. Esteban, keep us covered!"

Bullets struck the ground all around Rodrigo as he moved forward, but he barely seemed to notice. His thoughts were on one thing and one thing alone, saving the people who trusted him.

233

"O'Hara!" A voice cried out Rodrigo's name, a familiar voice. "I want the woman you so brutally kidnapped and ravaged. My *sister!*"

Dear God, Angelica thought. It was her brother who had wreaked this carnage. Frantically she ran forward. "Edward! Edward, no! I'm here of my own free will. I'm not a prisoner. Not now. I wrote you . . ." She screamed as a volly of fire struck the ground around her. "Dear God, stop this shooting. Please! Please!" She fell to the ground but picked herself up again. Tears blinded her but she somehow managed to get to her brother's side. Throwing herself at his feet she pleaded with him. "You can't let them die. You can't do this. Rodrigo . . . Rodrigo is my husband."

Taking her hand, Edward lifted her to her feet. Instead of understanding there was only anger in his eyes. "Your husband? Then we will soon make you a widow!"

Surrounding Rodrigo, Edward Howe grinned evilly as he prepared to capture his prize. Angelica realized at that moment that it was not just to free her that they had come. At that moment the love she held for her brother died, to be replaced by another emotion. In anger, Edward gave her a shove.

"Leave her alone, gringo! Do not touch my wife. Brother or not, I will not let you treat her such . . ." As Rodrigo ran forward seeking Angelica, Edward pointed the pistol and fired.

"Aghhh . . ." Rodrigo cried out as the bullet struck him in the leg. The force of the impact sent him tumbling to the ground, yet he struggled to rise. Another gun fired, this time hitting him in the shoulder, setting his flesh on fire. Gasping for breath, he reached up to close his fingers over the wound. Blood poured over his hand, and through the darkness that threatened to engulf him he could hear Angelica cry out his name. Fighting the fog that clouded

234

his vision he tried to drag himself to where she was.

All around him he could hear the hoarse curses of his men, the sobs of the women, the groans of the dying, accompanied by the staccato fury of gunfire. *"Bastardos!"* he cried. "Women and children." It was one thing to fight man to man but in all his days as a bandit he had never injured or killed children. This man in his quest for vengeance had done just that. The whimpering sound was agonizing. The fact that he was helpless was like a knife at his heart, as devastating as any bullet wound. All around him his people were dying and he could do nothing to offer help. He had been caught unaware and for that he could never forgive himself.

"Rodrigo!" Angelica struggled in her brother's hold. "Rodrigo!" Reaching out, she heard his frantic cry. Anguish rose in her throat. Once again she begged her brother, but her cries fell on ears that did not want to hear her pleas. "You killed him! You killed him!" she screamed.

"A bullet or a hangman's noose makes little difference to me." He pushed her along with him to where a horse was tethered. "You have been through quite a trying time, a shock, but I will see that you are taken safely back to the abbey."

"The abbey? No! I will not leave Rodrigo." Her place was here with Rodrigo, not with the nuns. Not now. Not after all that had happened. Rodrigo was wounded. He needed her. Without her he might die. She wouldn't leave him. He had been by her bedside when she needed him, had tended her so lovingly, carefully.

"Sam, Reedy, take her with you. I don't care if you have to tie her, make certain she doesn't cause any trouble. I've got my hands full as it is." Edward turned his sister over to two burly men who pushed and shoved Angelica towards the horse.

Like a cornered animal she fought them as she watched them set the camp on fire. "You are worse than animals. You are butchers. Vultures." Opening her mouth, she screamed, venting her horror, her grief. She felt something strike her head and fought the haze that swirled before her eyes. "Rodrigo . . ." Her last thought was for the man she loved.

Chapter Thirty-One

It was like a nightmare. Wounded and wimpering people lay on the ground. Long, shuddering groans, never-ending prayers for the dead, agonizing cries wailed through the night. Men, women, and children had been killed, the encampment destroyed, its crude huts put to the torch. It was like some macabre painting, Margaro thought as he crawled on his hands and knees to where Rodrigo lay. A terrible dream.

The stench of smoke was like a smothering blanket, choking him, yet he fought against the urge to cough as he moved like a snake on his belly. He had to reach Rodrigo before they killed him. This was Margaro's only thought. Rodrigo had saved his life countless times and now he would return the favor. He would die himself before he would let the gringo bastard finish him off.

Voices laughed, arguing and planning their next move while all around them lay the wounded and dying. Margaro watched as Edward Howe searched through the ruins for anything of value. Like a vulture he picks our bones, Margaro thought angrily. Even so, he used the man's greed for his own advantage. While the gringos fought over the spoils he inched closer to Rodrigo, at last grasping him by the leg.

"Easy. Easy." If any of the Anglos realized what he was doing he would be shot, and Rodrigo as well. Though he felt a frantic urge to pick Rodrigo up in his arms and flee, he knew to do so would be stupid. Thus, Margaro was conscious of every breath, every minute as he moved along the ground, tugging the wounded Rodrigo behind him.

Laughter rang out and Margaro stiffened in wary alarm. All he could do was lie there near a pile of bodies until he was certain no eyes were turned his way.

"Look at these books and painting, Sam. Our bandit must have thought himself a gentleman." Again the laughter.

Margaro raised his head to look in the gringo's direction, knowing instinctively they were huddled together in Rodrigo's hut, the only one that had not been set afire. In their desire to load their wagons with spoils they had forgotten Rodrigo, at least for the moment, no doubt thinking him already dead or most certainly dying. It was just the chance Margaro was waiting for. Taking advantage of the distraction, he sprang to his knees. Grasping Rodrigo around the waist he moved in the direction of the clearing. There was a small cave there where he and Rodrigo could hide out until the danger was gone. Let the gringos have Rodrigo's treasure, one day they would suffer for it, he vowed. There would be other bandits who would follow them, other days. Edward Howe would pay for what he had done, Margaro Bautista Renaldo swore on his mother's grave. Gringos were poison. Every one of them would be driven from the land. It was a promise that drove him on as he slipped through the trees leaving the smoldering ruins behind him.

Part Two:

A Storm in the Heavens

California Territory—1846

"To take arms against a sea of troubles."

—William Shakespeare,
Hamlet, act 3, scene 1

Chapter Thirty-Two

As Angelica looked out the tiny window of her room at the Mission of Santa Barbara she thought how the day matched her mood. Dark and dreary. A never-ending ocean of tears had fallen from her eyes just as the rain fell from the heavens. Rodrigo was dead.

Angelica had spent the last few months in a haze of grief with little awareness of the time or of those about her. With little concern for her emotions, her brother had callously made good on his promise, taking her not back to the abbey, however, but on to the Mission. To rid himself of her, Angelica thought as the bitter reality hit her anew. Edward had never cared for her, never loved her. To him she had always been a burden. His insistence that she take the veil had been nothing but a way to put the responsibility for her welfare in other hands. She knew this now. Not that it mattered. Edward had destroyed her happiness, had proven himself a heartless murderer. She had no love for her brother. On her arrival she had viewed the Mission's adobe walls and courtyard with relief. Maybe she would find peace there if not happiness.

Nevertheless it had been weeks before she could go through the day without crying, months before she slept through the night without tortured visions of that fateful day, that tragic moment when her happiness had been destroyed with Rodrigo's callous murder and the attack on the bandit camp. When sleep did claim her, Angelica woke up screaming from her nightmares only to find Sister Maria's comforting arms wrapped around her, her soothing voice telling her that everything would be all right. That she was safe. Someday she would find happiness again, she would tell her, but Angelica knew that she was wrong. How could she ever smile, ever laugh when Rodrigo had been taken from her?

Cloistering herself away like a nun during those times when she was not teaching the Mission's children, Angelica had been nearly oblivious to anything but her memories. Wearing her widow's black she had mourned her husband, had tried to come to terms with her unrighteous anger with the God she felt had forsaken her. Questions were raised in her mind that had never been there before. Why had God allowed Rodrigo to be killed when she had begged so fervently? How was she going to find it within her heart to forgive her brother and the men who had unthinkingly and unemotionally carried out his orders? What was to be her purpose in life now? Just what did she believe about God and his mercy? Was her faith diminishing little by little? Was what had happened to Rodrigo in any way her fault? Was what had happened punishment for her giving her heart and soul to a bandit, a man who boasted of being called the Devil?

Forgiveness. That was a word which had been whispered to her over and over again by the priests, nuns, and friars the last few weeks and Angelica was grim each time the word was spoken. She would never be able to forgive her brother. Never. She remembered how all along the road to Santa Barbara Edward had crowed and gloated about his triumph over "El Diablo." He had boasted of shooting the infamous bandit to all who would listen. He never seemed to tire of telling the story, even to those who lived inside the Mission, making himself out to be a hero. A hero? Angelica thought. A man who had swept down upon a peaceful village of women and children and fired his guns before the men of the camp had even had time to arm themselves. There was another name she would have called him. Killer. Murderer. That he had profited by his raid on the camp was all too apparent. Edward had taken rifles, horses, cattle, and any gold and coins that he had been able to find. Included in his booty had been Rodrigo's books and paintings. The sight of those objects had torn at her heart.

"Why didn't you shoot me too, Edward?" she had cried, wondering at the strange expression that had glinted in his eyes. For just a moment she had held a hope that he was lying. That somehow, miraculously Rodrigo had escaped. His chilling laughter had put an end to such dreaming. Rodrigo *was* dead. She had to face that fact and carry on with her life. Mourn him, love him, but do what she could to right the tragedy her brother had instigated. Perhaps teaching the Mission children would be a start. So she had thrown herself into a relentless routine. Up before the crack of drawn to help in the cooking and cleaning of the Mission. Prayers. Breakfast, after which work was apportioned to the friars and the Indians who lived within the cloister of the walls. Then that time of day, the only time Angelica could even hope to keep her mind from her own unhappiness, when she taught the children how to read and write. Illiteracy was rare in California as most people knew the wonder of the printed language. It was Angelica's determination to make a better life for these little ones so they could blend in.

One boy in particular reminded her of Rodrigo, a boy of mixed heritage as he had been. Paulo was an apt pupil, the joy of her heart. It was much like seeing Rodrigo as a boy. What might he have become if circumstances had not led him to become a bandit? That question gnawed at her over

243

and over again. If only she had met Rodrigo sooner, before his world had come crashing down. Would there have been a chance for them then?

The light shower of rain ended, the sun peeked through the clouds as Angelica left the *monjerío*, the sleeping quarters of unmarried women and girls. She passed in front of the main building that was designed in a quadrangle. It contained a kitchen, grainary, servants' rooms, the chapel, missionaries' residence, and a magnificent library. It was here she spent a great deal of time, among the leather-bound books, reading the treasures. For just a short span of time she could escape from the tragedy of what had happened and immerse herself in learning. One of the friars, skilled in making lenses for the magnifying glasses needed for the mission's scriptorium, had fashioned her a new pair of spectacles. The frames were made of gold, prettier by far than her old ones. In fact, everyone at the mission had shown her a great deal of kindness.

Angelica remembered her first sight of the Mission, wishing she had the spectacles then. Nevertheless she had enjoyed its beauty. Though she had viewed magnificent scenery since coming to California the beauty and majesty of this Santa Barbara Mission always took her breath away. The long sandstone structure stood on top of a rising slope overlooking the valley and Santa Barbara Channel below. Placed against the background of the towering Santa Ynez Mountains, the Mission's two bell towers also seemed to reach the sky. All around were flowers, palm trees, and various shrubs that reminded her of the Garden of Eden. If only she were not Eve without her Adam, she thought.

Appraisingly Angelica's eyes took in the splayed Moorish windows. They seemed indented into the very walls with a front arcade of Roman arches completely enclosing the entire quadrangle. She counted sixteen arches in all. A peaceful, beautiful place to spend her exile.

The friars and bishop understood her anguish, had tried to heal her soul as best they could. The friars belonged to the Order of Our Holy Father, Saint Francis of the Observance. Truly they did practice the example of poverty, chastity, and obedience and took full pride in exerting Christian influence as did the few nuns in residence. They had been very kind to her, had given her the assignment to teach those children who were unschooled how to read, write, and do their sums.

Angelica spied some of the children now gathered at the Moorish fountain in front of the Mission. Beside them were several of the Indian women. The fountain's huge basin was used as a *lavandería* to wash clothing. Water was abundant here in the Mission. The Río Pedregoso, which flowed through Rattlesnake Canyon, carried water to the Mission through stone aqueducts to a storage reservoir. Walking towards the fountain Angelica was reminded of the bandit camp and the camaraderie among the women. She wanted to put her unhappy memories from her mind but she doubted that she ever would. It seemed there was always something to remind her of Rodrigo and the short period of happiness they had shared.

"Oh, Rodrigo . . ." She closed her eyes to a fresh wave of pain that clutched at her heart. She heard the clang of the bell from the tower announcing the hour of siesta. A time she dreaded. As long as she was busy, preoccupied with other thoughts, she could push away her heartache. Now, as everyone scurried to find a soft, quiet resting place she was left all alone. As usual, she found she was not in the least tired, knew she could not sleep. Instead she busied herself with doing some of the washing that had been left behind.

Such turbulent times. Rumors of what was happening farther east disturbed her. News had been leaked into the Mission by way of the grapevine. The murmurings had come slowly at first. There was talk that President James Knox Polk of the United States thought war with Mexico was a possibility. Certainly a man named John Frémont was creating quite a stir in Monterey. Supposedly his intention was to incite revolt. The friars and nuns had increased their prayers, asking for God's help in avoiding such a calamity, but for the most part little thought was given to a problem so far away. The people of the village said that it didn't concern the Santa Barbara Mission. Angelica sensed they were wrong. The United States was eager to get its hands on California Territory, had been bargaining to buy it, or so her brother had said. How terrible it would be if war ensued and lives were lost because of a desire for this lush, green land. War was a terrible word. She'd seen enough death and destruction to last her lifetime.

It was inconceivable that the mission system would continue if California came into *americano* hands. The two Franciscan padres worried that the new governor, José Figueroa, favored gradual secularization and the lay inspectors of missions seemed greedy and incompetent to Angelica. Even they seemed to look at church lands as future sites for *ranchos* and *haciendas*. If that happened what would be the fate of the Indians who had been embraced by the padres? Surely Rodrigo would be against it. Why, he would . . .

Rodrigo was dead! Silently her lips formed his name. He had been aware of the tensions mounting in this country, had espoused his opinion to Angelica. Even so the camp had been an oasis where they had pushed away their apprehension. News of the outside world had seemed to evaporate like the early-morning fog during those last few weeks they had enjoyed together. Now suddenly Angelica had come face to face with the actions of her countrymen. Men who, like her brother, were greedy and ambitious.

246

The relations between Texas and Mexico had been tumultuous for nearly two decades, yet now it appeared that they were on the brink of war. If war erupted, how could California not be involved? Guns. Cannons. Destruction. The tranquility of the Mission destroyed. She wondered if Brother Antonio was right in what he envisioned. "California will be the prize, but it will not be the cause of war," he had said. "Texas will be where war will begin."

And what would happen then to Jesse? Bernardo? Margaro? Or any of the others of the bandit camp who might have escaped. Would they be drawn into the conflict? Questions troubled her. Since she had not seen any of the bandits or their women after that day the camp had been destroyed, she could only wonder at their fate. Maria. Rosa. Luisa. Her friend, the old healing woman. Where were they now? Oh dear God, that she might be assured that they had not been harmed.

Filling a large water bucket, Angelica was immersed in her thoughts, and was hardly aware that Paul watched her, or that he was by her side until he tugged at her arm. "Señora O'Hara. Please. You have a visitor. One who says for you to come pronto."

"A visitor?" The fear that Edward had come for her quickened her pulse. He had mentioned taking her with him when he went into Mexico on business but Angelica had hotly argued against going with him. Being with Bonita, her brother's lover, and Edward was just too painful a reminder of Rodrigo and all that had happened. Still, Edward was her guardian, upon the death of her husband. It was his right to take her with him if he so determined. He was her only living relative. She might argue but he would get his way if that was what he wished. Not even Brother Antonio would be able to protect her.

Edward, she thought, of course it would be him. No doubt he felt she would be useful to him in some way. It

247

was most certainly not because of any love for her or a wish to be in her company that had made him write to her just last week. Oh no. Something sinister was afoot, ever fiber of her being told her. Why oh why couldn't he leave her alone?

"Please, Señora. Come with me . . ."

"If it is my brother, tell him . . . tell him I will not see him. Tell him to go away. I am content here. Let me have at least a little peace for the love of God." Angelica closed her eyes as a wave of fresh grief washed over her. As long as Edward badgered her she would never find tranquility.

"It is not your brother. It is a visiting nun. One who is very, very tall . . ." The child gestured with his arms.

Mother Bernadette! It had to be that most compassionate of sisters. She had heard the story of what had happened to Angelica, the incarceration in the bandit camp, her marriage, her widowhood, and had come to comfort her. Setting down the bucket, Angelica hurried to the courtyard, anxious for a reunion with the one woman who would understand her feelings. She found her standing in the Cloister Garden, her back turned as she gazed in to the depths of the fountain. "Mother Bernadette! Thank God you have come."

Running towards her with the intent of finding security in the kindly nun's embrace, Angelica gasped as the figure in the black-and-white nun's robes turned around. It was not Mother Bernadette but a man, one whose face was very familiar despite the missing mustache. "Margaro!"

Angelica blinked, certain the figure standing in the garden was an apparition. Or were her spectacles causing her eyes to play tricks on her? "Margaro?" She moved uncertainly towards him. Why was he here?

"We have little time, Señora. I must be quick about what I came to tell you and then be gone." He drew her with him into the shadows. "Rodrigo is alive!"

"Alive? He is alive?" Her heart rose in her throat to

248

choke her. "Where is he? Take me to him. I must be with my husband." Anxiously her eyes scanned the slumbering figures huddled in the corners of the courtyard, fully expecting him to materialize as magically as Margaro had done. Her heart was beating rapidly, her breath coming in short gasps of excitement. Rodrigo had not been killed. Her brother's cruel boasting had been a lie. She took several steps forward only to find Margaro blocking her way.

"He is not here."

"Where . . . where is he?" A chill of apprehension swept over her. Something was wrong. Why else had Margaro come alone? Dear merciful God, what was going on? Though the sun had come from behind a cloud she found herself shivering. Reaching out, she clutched Margaro's arm, studying him intently. "Tell me . . ."

"He was badly wounded. Near death. So full of wounds that he had very little blood left. I watched the gringos until I saw a chance to save him. They were distracted by dividing the spoils, certain that he was dead." Margaro clenched and unclenched his hands, reliving the moment. "While their backs were turned I took Rodrigo to safety. Dead or alive, I would not let the gringos have him. It was, Señora, a matter of honor."

A tremor passed through Angelica's body as he unfolded the tale. The words seemed to echo hollowly in the chambers of her brain. A fearsome story of survival. Margaro had pushed and pulled Rodrigo to the shelter of a small cavern in the rocks and had removed the bullets and tended his wounds. Using the ocean's water to cleanse the torn and bloodied flesh, he had stayed right by his side.

"I was fearful that I was watching him die, attuned my ears to hear the death rattle. Instead Rodrigo clung to life." Margaro's lips curled up in a half-smile. "He thought, Señora, that I was you. Called me *querida*. Held my hand. I did not mind as long as his determination to survive

249

made him able to withstand death's angel."

"No man could have a better friend. Rodrigo owes you his life. And I . . . I owe you my gratitude. You have given me back my heart." In a gesture of thankfulness Angelica grasped Margaro's hand, giving it a fierce squeeze. "And now you will take me to him."

"No." Margaro shook his head. "It is too dangerous. Your brother has men watching. I have Rodrigo hidden away. He is weak, unable to protect himself from his enemies. You must wait, and when he has regained his strength he will come for you."

"Wait? How can I wait when my soul cries out to him. I must be with him, Margaro. He needs me and . . ."

"To go to him might very well mean his death. We cannot take the chance. The only reason I came to you was at his prodding. He couldn't stand the thought of your pain, your anguish. He wanted me to come to tell you that he is alive. That he will come for you. You must be patient."

"Patient . . . !" The word was a wail, yet in the end she conceded to Margaro's wisdom. By the grace of God Rodrigo had escaped death. She must not endanger him because of her selfish longing to be with him. Edward knew several people in the surrounding area, Spanish, Indian, and American. If even one of them became suspicious it could lead to tragedy.

"I found Najalayogua. Together she and I have been taking care of Rodrigo, moving about, staying only a short time in one place." Margaro squarred his shoulders cockily. "I have made use of my talent for disguise to find out information and to procure money and food. A beggar, a farmer, a gringo. And of course this most Holy Sister who came to you today." He bowed graciously.

"Do you need money? For food?" Though he denied that he did, she sensed that it was pride answering for him. "I will give you what I have. The Indians here have been

250

taught to farm, oversee the livestock, and tend the fruit trees. Surely God cannot be angered if you take what is necessary." Gently she pushed him in the direction of the storerooms, hoping kindly Padre Duran would forgive her. Hadn't he always espoused the necessity of sharing with the poor? Most definitely the displaced bandits belonged in that category.

"I will take only what I can carry on my back. Though I am tempted to load up my horse, I cannot risk attracting attention." His lips twitched in another smile. "Nor would I want it whispered that I was a greedy sister." Nevertheless he worked side by side with Angelica, filling two sacks with corn, rice, dried beef, and peppers. Tying the sacks with a rope so that they clung to his body, the once slim nun emerged from the storeroom looking very, very fat. The provisions, Margaro assured her, would last at least a week or more. Looking carefully over his shoulder, he wound his way through the courtyard. "I thank you. Najalayogua thanks you, and Rodrigo . . ."

"He will get well, won't he? The image of Rodrigo lying wounded wrenched her heart. He was such a proud, strong man. "I don't think that I could bear it if after knowing he was alive he was suddenly taken from me again." Her hands clutched at her heart. "Oh, Margaro, I love him so."

"I know that you do, Señora. Had I not known that I never would have come. Since that day at the camp all gringos are my deadly enemies. But not you. Never you!" He seized her hand between his large calloused palms, tightening his fingers in a gesture of affection.

"Tell him of my love . . ." Padre Duran had given Angelica a small, delicately shaped cross, a gift to soothe her tortured soul. Unclasping the chain she put it into Margaro's hand. "Give him this. Tell him . . . tell him that I wait anxiously for him to put it around my neck again. That until we can be together, this will be a token of God's mercy and my love . . ."

251

A bell tolled, signaling a call from siesta to prayer. Slowly the sleeping figures of the courtyard stirred. Following Angelica's lead, Margaro ducked through a narrow passageway, passing from the large quadrangle of the Mission's walls. "I will send you a message. Until then, dream of Rodrigo. Soon you will be together. I will see to it." Margaro's heavy black brows arched upward. "On that you have my word." Passing through the bushes he found his horse peacefully grazing the wild grass that grew in abundance. Angelica gave him help in managing his newly acquired girth to mount into the saddle.

"Luisa, was she . . . was she killed?" All these weeks she had held on to the hope that she had survived.

"I don't know. After the carnage she disappeared."

"Jesse?"

"He too vanished. I like to think that he took her far, far away to safety. It is what Rodrigo chooses to believe." He grabbed the reins, complaining beneath his breath at his need to ride side-saddle. "Perhaps one day soon we can all be reunited. Like old times, no?"

"Miracles do happen, Margaro. One happened today." Rodrigo's name reverberated over and over again, sending her heart on a wondrous flight. He was alive. As she watched Margaro ride away she smiled for the first time in a long, long while.

Angelica returned to the fountain, dipping her hands in the cool water, splashing it on her face. She tried to maintain some semblance of calm but the knowledge that Rodrigo was alive, that she would be reunited with him again, kept echoing over and over again in her head. She could have sworn that even the animals carved in the fountain's stone smiled with her.

"So . . . Señora, you had a visitor."

Angelica whirled around, her reverie gone as she came

face-to-face with Father Narcisco Duran. His eyes sparkled with amusement as he regarded her, and she was instantly filled with guilt. Giving Margaro supplies from the Mission's storehouse had been perilously close to stealing. She hung her head, afraid to meet his stare.

"You should have introduced me to the sister. I have been around for many years, know all of those of her order, and yet she did not look familiar."

"She . . . she is from a northern abbey. She . . . she brought me news from Mother Bernadette but could not stay with us for longer than a moment because . . ."

The father's gray eyebrows shot up in surprise. "A northern abbey? Well then, of course it is good that she went on her way." Putting his hand under Angelica's chin he forced her to look at him. "It must be a very poor abbey indeed if she came all this way for food. I must scold Mother Bernadette when next I see her. She should have told me what dire poverty has afflicted them."

He knew. There was no use in carrying on with her charade. Bowing her head she made her confession. "It was one of the men from my husband's camp." She knew she could trust Father Duran with the truth. "He came to tell me that although my husband was gravely wounded; he is alive. Alive, Father Duran."

"And in hiding . . . ?" His brows furrowed.

"There are men searching everywhere for him. Margaro would not let his pride admit it but I could tell by the weight he has lost that food is scarce. I . . . I had to help him and Rodrigo. Forgive me."

"There is nothing to forgive. It is God who gives us our bounty and he who declares that we must likewise share it." His thin lips drew up at the corners. "We will speak no more about it. We were blessed with a plentiful spring. The sacks that your compadre took will not be missed."

"Nevertheless I will work very hard to make restitution for what was . . . was loaned." Angelica thought that it

253

was no wonder she had come to love Father Duran so quickly. His wisdom and genuine love of his fellow man showed in everything he did. Certainly the Indians all loved him. He had seen to it that they were taught trades such as shoemaking, saddle-making, carpentry, black-smithing. He instructed them in how to make adobe, stone cutting, spinning, weaving, making soap and candles as well as agricultural skills. He wanted them to become self-sustaining. Under his supervision they had planted the surrounding fields with maize, wheat, beans, barley, and chick peas.

Father Duran had been president of the missions for thirteen years. He was a man who always sung, and was gifted in music. It had been his idea to form the band of Indian musicians who contributed so greatly to church services and celebrations. Also in residence was Frey Francisco Garcia Diego, the first Bishop of California, though Angelica had remained aloof from him. He was as strict as Father Duran was loving. Together they were in charge of the Mission. They had to manage farms, oversee the raising of livestock, keep accurate accounts, give religious instruction, administer sacraments. Time at the Mission was divided between work and prayer; study, service, and recreation.

It was the time for prayer now. As Father Duran led her towards the Mission church, asking all about her husband and this mysterious friend of his, she whispered a silent prayer. God had not forsaken her.

Angelica took her place near the main altar, listening to the Latin being sung by the Indian choir. It was a song she had helped Father Duran teach them. Once the canticle had sounded mournful to her but now it made her feel peaceful and calm. She found herself humming softly, looking at the beauty of the church interior with a different perspective.

Before, she had been so immersed in her sorrow that she

254

had been immune to its beauty but now she gave her eyes full rein. On the flat, plastered ceiling were carved and painted wooden designs, flowing scrollwork. Imitation marble was painted on the pilasters, the wainscoting, and the door frames. Much like a Greek temple, she thought. The six columns and statues near the entrance of the church had been carved by the Indians out of local stone. Under the friars' tutelage they had displayed their talent.

The painted wooden statues of Saint Barbara, Saint Joseph, the Immaculate Conception, Saint Francis, and Saint Dominic found on the reredos, and the figures of the Holy Archangels had come from Mexico and looked alarmingly real. The statue of Saint Barbara seemed to be scolding her for not paying careful attention to Father Duran's words as he began his droning Latin. Kneeling, Angelica forced herself to listen, but once or twice her mind wandered to thoughts of the future. How long would it be before Rodrigo came for her? Where would they go? Father Duran would unquestionably give them shelter and sanctuary if she asked for it.

Could Rodrigo be convinced to give up his nomadic style of life? For just a moment she had fantasies of a vine-covered cottage or a large sprawling rancho. They would have five children, all of them tugging at her skirts as she went about her daily chores. Angelica sighed audibly. There was a price on Rodrigo's head. Unless he was vindicated he would always be in danger. Without the security of the bandit camp he would always be on the run, and yet as long as they were together she knew they would find contentment.

Angelica felt a moment of embarrassment as she realized that she was the only one who had remained kneeling. Rising to her feet she touched her rosary mumbling her prayers. She would have made a terrible nun, she realized. She could not keep her mind on the sacraments even for a moment, but so much had happened.

Expecting Father Duran's chastisement when the mass was over she nevertheless pushed through the throng of Indians to come to his side. "I am gratified that you are so pious, Angelica." Father Duran brushed at the robe of his vestment. "You will set a good example for the others, being constantly on your knees." He led her into the chapel room, motioning to an ornately carved bench. "I will miss you, Angelica, when you leave. It is unfortunate that you have not been happy here."

"Oh, but I have. You have been very kind to me. Without your teasing, your smiles, I don't think I could have survived." Angelica found herself opening up to the priest. Telling him about her first meeting with Rodrigo, her attraction, her fear. "I think I fell in love with him then but I wouldn't admit it to myself. He was so proud, so fiercesome and yet I sensed the gentleness beneath his harsh demeanor." She revealed the vigil the supposedly brutal bandit had kept by her bedside when she was near death, the joy of their marriage, the devastation she had felt when her brother had descended on the camp.

"And now you know he is alive. Is it any wonder, my child, that you were distracted just now? I understand and I want you to know that if you have need of me I will do what I can . . ." They were interrupted by a loud slam as Paulo pushed through the door. He was too excited to remember to knock. Father Duran shook his head, intending to give the boy a severe reprimand but the expression on the child's face silenced him. "What is it, Paulo?"

"A messenger from Mexico. The American President has declared war. No one is allowed to leave the Mission grounds, by order of General José Joaquín de Herrera."

Part Three:

On Wings of Love

Mexico—1847-1848

"Love is a smoke raised with the fume of sighs;
 Being purged, a fire sparkling in lovers' eyes;
 Being vex'd a sea nourish'd with lovers' tears:
 What is it else? a madness most discreet,
 A choking gall and persevering sweet."

—William Shakespeare,
Romeo and Juliet, Act 2, Scene 1

Chapter Thirty-Three

It was the kind of day that withered a man's strength. A hot, humid, sweltering summer day. Sitting in the corner of the small hut Rodrigo tried to garner as much of the fresh air as was available from the doorway. The mud and straw hut belonged to a relative of Najalayogua's who had endangered himself to hide Rodrigo and Margaro. The old Indian man had proclaimed it his "Christian" duty to do so. Most of the Indians living in the small village were Christians and were by nature lively and industrious.

At least they are useful, Rodrigo thought. His convalescence severely frustrated him, made him feel helpless and unproductive. He was used to doing, not sitting or lying around being waited on. Though he was appreciative of Margaro and Najalayogua's loyalty, his temper was short more often than not lately. It was just that he was not used to being housed within walls like a captive canary!

Rodrigo counted the notches he had carved in a wooden post that supported the wall, each one marking the days since the attack on his camp. Twenty-five days and still he was as weak as a newly-born kitten. It was discouraging, irritating. Worst of all was being without Angelica. If she had been with him, even the incarceration would have been bearable.

"Angelica!" He whispered her name like a benediction. Loving her had given him the will to survive even when Margaro had given him up for dead. Najalayogua had been certain that he would die. He had heard her mumbling to Margaro that they should be prepared. Rodrigo had tried to speak, tell them that it was too soon to plan his funeral. Calling on some inner reserve of faith and strength he had fought against the dark fog that threatened to enfold him permanently. He would not leave Angelica. She needed his protection and his love.

Angelica. He wanted to see her so desperately. His insistence that he must go to her, tell her that he was alive, had prompted Margaro's stern refusal. They had argued with Rodrigo, admitting he could barely walk across the hut much less travel. In compromise Margaro had made the short journey to the mission, having found out Angelica's whereabouts from a wandering friar. From what that holy man had said the O'Hara widow was taking her husband's death very hard, was shrouded in a cloud of grief. Rodrigo commiserated with her pain, insisting that Margaro go at once to give her the message that just as soon as he was able to travel he would come for her.

Rodrigo reflected on his narrow escape from death. It haunted him just as surely as Angelica haunted his dreams. He had come so perilously close to dying just at a time when he had everything to live for. So close that Angelica's brother had not even bothered to shoot him again. They had left him on the ground like a worthless piece of garbage, and had it not been for Margaro dragging him away he might have been buried in the mass grave that had entombed his people.

Margaro had taken Rodrigo to a small cave by the spring and tended him there. They had stayed hidden there for five days until Margaro had been able to find Najalayogua hiding in the shrubbery. She had heard the marauding gringos say that they would be back to search the area for the missing bandit leader, and thus in the cover of the darkness Margaro had procured a wagon that had been used to carry the corpses of their people to the grave. Harnessing his horse to the death cart he had taken Najalayogua and Rodrigo to a secluded village sympathetic to the bandits. There Najalayogua had tended him, watching him slip in and out of consciousness.

For the first time in his life Rodrigo had been totally helpless. All he could do was to lie still. To watch and to listen. Angelica's face had loomed before his eyes, beckoning him to stay among the living. Of all the reasons for dying, the thought of losing her had been the most potent source of pain. But he had not died. God had spared his life, given him another chance. Rodrigo vowed that from that moment on he would no longer allow himself to be called "El Diablo." The devil was gone and in his place was a man determined to do only good from now on.

Rodrigo had escaped his brush with death, yet there were new dangers on the horizon. Angelica's brother was intent on capturing him, had made it a vendetta. Margaro, Najalayogua, and Rodrigo had begun a hectic period of traveling around, never staying in one place for any length of time. Now at last it seemed they had found a permanent haven in the Indian village, at least he hoped so. That the village was only a few miles from the Santa Barbara Mission and Angelica lightened his heart. At least he was coming closer and closer to her. One day soon they would be together again to live as man and wife.

Rodrigo turned his gaze towards the doorway as he heard the squawk of chickens. Striding in, looking a bit comical in his attire as a nun, Margaro greeted him. "She is fine, she loves you, and she was made very, very happy by my news," he said before Rodrigo could ask the question. "She is a bit thinner but still as lovely a Señora as she ever was. Her new found smile made her even more so."

"You did tell her how very much I love her . . ."

"Sí! Sí! She already knows that." Margaro looked hesitantly over his shoulder. "But I have no more time to speak. I have a feeling I was followed, an eerie intuition. Perhaps I am not too convincing as a nun, eh?"

"You make a very *ugly* one! The sisters of the abbey will be very angry that you give them such a bad name." While they were traveling they had passed by a small abbey and Margaro had smuggled the nun's garb from the laundry in case he had need of it at some future time. It was the only disguise he could think of that would get him safely to the Mission, though he begged God's pardon for masquerading as one of the holy sisters.

"Ugly? Me? Hah! Surely your fair señora looked upon me as if I was the most beautiful thing she had ever seen, but we will talk about that later. Right now I have the feeling that we should hide." Helping Rodrigo to his feet he supported his weight as the two men hastened towards a small copse of trees. Hiding in the foliage, they waited a long while.

"You are getting paranoid, amigo," Rodrigo whispered, anxious to hear all about Margaro's journey and Angelica. He was just about to move from the shrubbery when a cloud of dust gave warning of a horseman. As the rider approached it became apparent that he was a soldier.

"So now they have the Mexican Army looking for us! This does not bode well, amigo."

Both men watched as the soldier dismounted and walked from one hut to the other, speaking to each villager in turn. Waving his arms about wildly he seemed to be frantic about some matter and Margaro and Rodrigo could only suppose that word of Margaro's visit to the Mission had been reported. A nun traveling such a distance on horseback would no doubt have been noticed.

"My fault, Margaro. I should not have tempted you to be so bold, but I had to know that Angelica was safe . . ."

"It is not important. Not your fault. I have been a bit too brave with my disguises lately . . ." He stiffened as he saw the soldier corner Najalayogua. Her description had been posted at every village, town, and soldier's camp throughout California, as well as Margaro's and Rodrigo's. Would the soldier recognize her? Perhaps he would see her as just one more old Indian woman. And then again, the large mole on her ear could give her away.

"If he realizes who she is we are as good as dead," Rodrigo expressed both their thoughts. "He will know that we are nearby. He will start up a search for us . . ."

He stopped speaking as the soldier's gaze turned towards the trees. Margaro and Rodrigo held their breath, fully expecting a calamity, but with a shrug of his shoulders the soldier left Najalayogua, and with a heated taunt over his shoulder moved back towards his horse. Pulling himself up in the saddle, he was gone as quickly as he had appeared. Even so, Rodrigo and Margaro stayed safely hidden for a long, long while, watching as the shadows of evening closed around the sun.

They cautiously returned to their hut after waiting more than two hours in the undergrowth. Gathering together their few possessions, Margaro was intent on leaving, certain the soldier meant danger to their security but Najalayogua detained him. "It was not bandits the soldier had been inquiring about but *americanos*. He said he had been told that a gringo had been seen in the area. At first he wouldn't believe me when I said there were no gringos here." Najalayogua drew herself up proudly. "But I argued with him and told him I would not lie, that I would as soon spit in a gringo's eye as to shield him."

"Gringo? The soldier was after a gringo? We were in hiding while . . ." Throwing back his head, Margaro gave in to a storm of laughter at such irony. "So the hunter has turned into the hunted," he proclaimed. "How I would like to see that pale-haired gringo hanging from

263

a tree."

"Why was the soldier after an *americano?*" Rodrigo was stoic on the matter. Any kind of turmoil endangered his freedom. He slumped to the ground in exhaustion, balancing on one elbow as he looked up at the old woman.

"Ahhhhhh, a great deal has been happening since we have been jumping around from place to place. The name Frémont is enough to startle the soldiers. That gringo has caused trouble even though he is so far away. The Mexican soldiers are afraid that the word of his doings will incite the *americanos* here to rebel. The gringo they are after was said to be heading far, far north to a place called Sacramento to join this Frémont, journeying by way of the coast."

Waving her arms about, Najalayogua told them all she had learned. Thirty-three Americans had attacked the northern outpost of Sonoma. Civilians had been arrested, their arms confiscated, and a makeshift flag of independence, a "bear," had replaced the Mexican flag. The soldiers were apprehensive that California would fall into American hands.

"They fear the Californians will welcome them."

"Welcome them? Bah! The *americanos* are far outnumbered here. Our people will fight to the death if need be to defend their land. Too many gringos already have pushed their way in here." Pulling at his chin, Margaro strode back and forth across the dirt floor.

"Perhaps not." Rodrigo was more realistic, knowing more about the matter than Margaro. There was little loyalty to Mexico in the Californians' hearts. Many of the citizens felt a sense of isolation from Mexico City and had enjoyed cordial relations with the Americans. Rodrigo remembered the days when he too had welcomed the gringos, only to be turned on viciously by a man he had befriended. His property had been stolen, his honor besmirched by lies the man had told. The man's deceit had made of Rodrigo a bandit. Others who had not suffered the same fate, however, would still be friendly to the interlopers in their midst.

"They will fight, I tell you. They *will* fight to drive the gringos from our land." Margaro's eyes blazed fire, remembering the cries of the dying members of his camp. He knew he would never be able to chase away his hatred. It was too deeply embedded in his soul. Men of Edward Howe's kind were like locusts on the land, destroying everything in their path as they moved. He'd seen their kind before.

"Only time will tell, Margaro." Rodrigo closed his eyes in weariness. He did not have the strength to argue, nor at the moment did he care what happened. Let the Mexican Army and this ragtag band of Americans fight like dogs over a bone. When both sides were bloodied from battle the Californians might very well be free of both foreign elements. If he was strong by then perhaps he would be able to aid his people. Perhaps there could be a new beginning for himself and for Angelica.

Chapter Thirty-Four

Rodrigo stood on the hill, staring in the direction of the craggy bluff where at high tide the sea went rushing over the rocks. There were ships on the horizon. American ships. Margaro had gathered what information he could in a village infested with Mexican soldiers. Ships had been sighted off the coasts of San Francisco, Monterey, Santa Barbara, and a few of the other coastal towns. It appeared an invasion was imminent.

"The villagers are troubled, but fools that they are, will not fight." Margaro spat at the ground in disgust as he came up beside Rodrigo, turning his gaze to follow his friend's. "The soldiers? Bah! They are too few. I was wrong in thinking there were men enough in California to push the gringos back. Soon they will be crawling all over our shores."

"Much too soon." The past few weeks had been enough time for Rodrigo to regain some of his strength, enough to walk and ride short distances, but not the stamina he needed. All he could think about these last few days was Angelica. If there was fighting he wanted to be certain she would not be in any danger. The mission would be safe as long as California was in Mexican hands. They would not dare go against the church officials, but what if the

Americans were victorious? Angelica was of American descent to be sure but a rampaging, violent group of men were often oblivious to decency. Men who were not Catholic themselves could show disrespect for people and officials not of their own belief. He had seen anti-Catholic lithographs alleging that Mexican clerics were corrupt and sinful. One had even said that Catholic priests openly enjoyed their wine and women, flaunting their behavior with tight-lipped smiles. Lies of course, and yet such malicious falsehoods could often stir up trouble.

"They think these *americanos* will be amiable and I say that they are wrong." Margaro casually toyed with his pistol. "This, this is all they understand!"

"Perhaps they will be peaceful. My father was." Rodrigo remembered his father with a feeling of warmth. He had stopped at the province to do business and had ended up falling in love and making California a permanent home. He had died and been buried here.

"Peaceful? Ha." Margaro gnashed his teeth. "I heard that this gringo named Fremont seized the village of Sonoma and San Francisco and in the doing proved himself bloodthirsty and utterly ruthless. An amigo of his, a . . . a Kit Carson shot an elderly Californian and his two nephews for no good reason. Only because he said he could not take any prisoners. That is not the act of a peaceful man." He laid his hand on Rodrigo's shoulder. "Come away from here. There is nothing that you can do, amigo. Nor I. We cannot fight the villagers' battle for them. Once we might have gathered our men together but those days are gone." He shrugged his shoulders. "Me, I talk foolishly. I would like to take my pistol and show the gringos, but to do so would be insanity. I am not *loco!*"

Rodrigo watched as the sea rushed noisily over the shore. The rocks were quickly disappearing under the incoming tide. It reminded him of what would happen to his people when the Americans came. "Get your belongings together. Tell Najalayogua to come quickly. We must go to the Mission. Angelica . . ."

"Will be safe with the padres. You are not yet strong enough to travel all that way." Margaro mumbled incoherently beneath his breath, swearing about "stubborn *hombres.*"

Rodrigo turned and his soul was in his eyes. "We must go. A great turbulence is coming. I must protect my wife!"

Putting his index finger to his head, Margaro rotated it in a circular motion. "It is not *me* who is *loco* but *you.*" He scuffed at the dirt with the toe of his boot, growling and grumbling, but in the end he said, *"Está bien, bueno."*

A mist hung over the ground as the rickety old wagon rumbled along the road. Najalayogua and Margaro had flung their meager possessions and the two sacks of food in the large cart, making a comfortable bed for Rodrigo. The old woman had thrust a tattered blanket into his hands with the instructions that he was to cover himself up if he felt chilled.

"If we see any soldiers along the way, you had best hide that all-too-recognizable face of yours, amigo," Margaro taunted, "lest we find ourselves decorating the gallows." With a slight show of nervousness, he tugged at the big sombrero, pulling it down to cover his own face. "Ha, they will think us to be only *peones.* At least that is what I hope."

For himself and Rodrigo, Margaro had procured the white pants and tunic worn by the poor peasants of the area, sandles, a multicolored serape, and two of the largest straw hats he could find. Najalayogua was dressed in a plain brown skirt, white blouse, and a long cloak wrapped about her head and shoulders to hide her graying hair. Just to add authenticity to their appearance Margaro had stolen a pig and three chickens, which he placed in the back of the wagon with Rodrigo.

"They will keep you company, amigo, until you are

with your Angelica again."

As the wagon proceeded over the bumpy pathway the pig grunted and the chickens cackled, causing an unnerving clamor. Rodrigo winced each time the wheels hit a hole or rock and jostled the wagon. His wounds still pained him but he wouldn't admit it to his companions. A miserable journey, yet one he did not regret if it would lead him to his wife. Determining to keep up his good humor he bandied jokes about with Margaro. They talked of old times, asked each other riddles, pushing from their minds the danger that lurked behind each bush.

Looking over his shoulder Margaro guffawed as he saw that the pig had burrowed its head beneath Rodrigo's knee. "I think that she likes you, amigo. But then, you always did have a way with the women, no?"

"That has changed. There is only one woman for me and that is my wife." As he flexed his knee he heard the pig squeal. "I apologize, señorita."

"You have hurt her feelings. She thinks you do not like her. I am told that these are very affectionate animals, Rodrigo. Very sensitive. You must not hurt her pride."

"Her pride be damned." As the pig nestled even closer, Rodrigo pushed it away. "I'm only concerned for my comfort at the moment. Go away *puerco!* Shoo!" His muttering only succeeded in frightening the animal. Burrowing beneath him, it hid its head. With a sigh of resignation Rodrigo leaned back against the wagon and closed his eyes. Somehow, despite the bumps, jolts, sqwaking chickens, he managed to rest.

At last they came to a small village, equidistant between the Mission and where they had been in hiding. Dogs, pigs, chickens, and children meandered in the street blocking the wagon's path. Impatiently Margaro alighted from the wagon and waved his hands. *"Vamos! Vamos!"* At last the pathway was cleared and the wagon proceeded, passing a ramshackle building that served as a combination bar, rooming house, and general store.

"Are you thirsty, Rodrigo?" Margaro licked at his lips as he spied two young men sharing a whiskey bottle in the doorway of the building.

"Not thirsty enough to take a chance. Ride on, Margaro. There could be danger here."

With a regretful look Margaro nodded. "As usual you are right, and yet oh what I would not give . . ."

They passed another Indian village. The adobe houses with tile roofs contrasted sharply with the grandeur of a nearby wealthy *hidalgo's* rancho. Rodrigo grimaced at the reminder of the injustice that abounded. Rich and poor. No in between. Surely the rich Mexicans were as great or perhaps an even greater enemy to the poor than the Americans. The wealthy kept down the poor with a hardness of heart that had seldom been equaled. While the Indians and poverty-stricken toiled, the rich *hidalgos* and *caballeros* played. He could see several horsemen cavorting now, each making a game of bending down low over their mounts, trying to pluck a buried chicken from the sand. All were dressed in colorfully embroidered boleros and silver-buttoned *calzoneras* unfastened over their boots to make room for their gleaming silver spurs. Rodrigo eyed them with scorn. Peacocks. Useless, vain, preening birds.

"You! *Pordioseros!* We need another chicken. This one has died of fright." Rodrigo had played the game before, he knew the rules. A live chicken was buried in the ground up to its neck so it was helpless. Each rider took his turn trying to grab the fowl by the neck and pull it up without falling from his horse. It was no wonder the chicken had died.

"Ride on, Margaro. Ignore them. Pretend you do not hear." Rodrigo lowered his head as if in submission as a rider came thundering up.

"*Bastardos,* did you not hear me?" One of the young

271

men was particularly arrogant. "I said I need one of your chickens to continue our game." His eyes regarded them coldly, his left eyebrow raised in question.

"Give him the chicken, *Chuey*." Margaro's fingers trembled on the reins, not from fear but from suppressed anger. Purposefully he addressed Rodrigo by another name. "Give it to him, *Chuey*."

Rodrigo grasped the floundering hen by the neck and held it out, keeping his head down for fear he might be recognized.

"Look at me, *campesino*. Show a little respect for your betters." There was no way Rodrigo could keep his face hidden. For a few moments they regarded each other before the man grabbed the chicken and moved away. "Arrogant. Do you see the way he's looking at me. He hates me."

"No, no, he likes you." Margaro's teeth flashed in a mocking smile. "I like you. Take another chicken if you wish. It will be our gift to you. Now, let us pass on." Instead the cocky young Spaniard summoned his companions forward.

"We need, I think, to teach these *campesinos* better manners. What do you say? We do not want to make a bad impression on Señor Adams."

Rodrigo and Margaro started at the same time, remembering the man by that name who had been their prisoner a long time back. A relative perhaps? They watched warily as a light-skinned, heavyset man dressed in a black suit trimmed with gold braid rode forward. Sweeping a flat, wide-brimmed hat trimmed with tassels from his head he exposed his bald pate. Jeremiah Adams! It *was* the American. He had escaped the wilderness and the danger of Indians to arrive safely here.

Of all the unholy coincidences, Rodrigo thought glumly. With all the hundreds of people inhabiting California they had the misfortune of meeting this man of all men on the road to Santa Barbara. Surely he would recognize them. Tugging at his sombrero Rodrigo sought to pull it down over his face.

"Pardon, señor . . ." His manner was the epitome of obsequiousness.

"You are too lenient with your peasants here, Joaquin. Why, in Texas insolence would earn a fella twenty lashes. Got to know to show respect for their betters. Why, just look at the way that old woman is staring. And those two should be standing up straight and looking you in the eye, not slumping like cornered hounds." Dismounting, he walked over to the wagon for a closer look, his gaze settling on Najalayogua. "Damned old hag looks familiar."

"All old women look alike, Señor Adams. When the blush is off the rose . . ."

"No, I mean it. I've seen her somewhere before." He gestured to Margaro and Rodrigo. "Take off your hats so that I can see your faces."

Margaro's arm snaked out in answer, catching the bald-headed man around the throat. Pushing him to the ground he gave the reins a vicious jerk, sending the wagon hurdling forward. "Hang on, Rodrigo, this is going to be a shattering ride." It was a daring cavort across the rolling hills with the horsemen in pursuit. "*Caramba*. I should have been more careful. But how was I to know there would be a watchdog on *this* road?" Margaro threw over his shoulder. "I wish now that I had killed him while I had the chance. He will be the death of us." Though Margaro led the horsemen on a merry chase a wagon was no competition for swift horses and skilled riders and it was soon overtaken. Though Margaro used his pistols, aiming a shot that send one hidalgo flying from his horse, they were outnumbered, surrounded by the ten horsemen. Even so, Margaro, Najalayogua, and even Rodrigo, as weak as he was, put up a fight.

The melee was soon over. Two other men had suc-

273

cumbed to Margaro's well-aimed gun and lay sprawled on the ground. Another had been felled by Rodrigo's knife. The sound of groans filled the air as the well-dressed Spaniards held their swords at Rodrigo and Najalayogua's throats.

"Run, Margaro. Save yourself." Rodrigo's croaked order was ignored.

"Leave you? Never." Such loyalty was rare and yet Margaro refused to desert his friend. "If nothing else, you will need a partner for chess, no?"

Jeremiah Adams rode up in a thunder of hooves, a malicious grin on his lips. "So Edward was not wrong. You were spared. How lucky for me to be at the right place at the right time. Now I can collect the reward."

"Reward?" One of the *hidalgo's* eyebrows shot up in surprise.

"Yes, a reward, gentlemen. You see before you two of the most notorious bandits in all of California." His eyes were slits of laughter. "I swore someday I'd get even. Yes siree! How I hate you, O'Hara. Nor have I any love for your friend. I'll pay you back for all those days of imprisonment by returning the favor." He motioned with his head towards the village from which Margaro, Rodrigo, and Najalayogua had just come. "Take them away!"

It was cramped in the cell and dirty. Rodrigo lay sprawled on the rancid straw, staring fixedly at the wall with frustration. What hour was it? Time moved so slowly that he couldn't be quite certain. There was little to do but think and reflect as one hour blended into the next.

"You were right. We should have stopped at the *cantina* in the village and had that drink," he muttered irritably to Margaro who was also lying on the straw. "Then we would be riding the road now instead of being companions for the rats." Seeing one scurry over his foot

274

he grimaced.

"We had no way of knowing." Margaro hit the adobe wall with his fist. *"Madre de Dios,* what bad luck! To think we have been moving about so stealthfully right beneath the gringos' noses and why do we get caught? Because some imbecil of a *hidalgo* wants a scrawny chicken!"

"Fate, I suppose. We'll find a way to escape."

"Do not be too certain, amigo." Margaro toyed with a piece of straw. "They guard us as diligently as if we were dangerous. Ha! Am I not always a gentleman?'

"Gentleman!" Rodrigo was in no mood for light banter. He was trapped and there was nothing he could do. Would they hang them, shoot them, or keep them in prison until they withered into very old men? None of the choices was appealing. Angelica would wait for him, wondering why he never came for her. *"Sangre de Christo!"*

They had spent the night under guard, listening to the tramp, tramp, tramp of boots beneath their lone window. Rodrigo had considered escape but had changed his mind. He had heard Jeremiah Adams give the strict instructions that if such an attempt was made they were to be shot. It was not his intention to make Angelica a widow. Perhaps if they waited there might come a more opportune time. Now they were being watched every moment.

"I wonder how Najalayogua is . . ." She had been jailed in an adjoining cell with only a thick stone wall between them. No windows, not even a crack in order to communicate. Jeremiah Adams had been certain the old woman had magic powers, had called her a witch, insisting she be kept apart from the two bandits.

"Ha! I wish she really was a witch. I would have her cast a spell turning that ugly, bald gringo into a toad." Rising to a sitting position Margaro relished the idea. "A toad or a chicken. We could give him to those *hidalgos* to use in

275

their game, no?"

"An amusing fantasy, Margaro." Rodrigo had dreams of his own that were of a more amorous nature. Turning over on his side he stretched, envisioning Angelica lying beside him. He wanted to touch her velvety skin inch by inch, explore her loveliness. Closing his eyes, he remembered what they had shared, each movement, each word, her response to his ardent lovemaking. She was the perfect woman.

"You will see her again, amigo." Margaro could read his expression.

"I have to believe that, Margaro. And what of Luisa? Somehow I must find her too. I had hoped that after we went to the Mission we could go in search of my little sister." He wondered how the conflict between the Americans and Mexicans would affect his sister's marriage. Would her Jesse be steadfast? Or would he leave her? If the red-haired gringo dared to break his sister's heart he vowed he would have his head.

His musing was interrupted by a grating sound. Standing by the rusty iron bars, Jeremiah Adams appraised the prisoners. "Thought you'd be interested in knowing that I made a mighty good profit out of bringing you in, O'Hara. Five hundred dollars."

"Go to the devil, señor."

"Oh no, I'm not going anywhere. You may very well be going to hell, however. Yes siree. Bang! Bang! Gonna put you up against a wall, blindfold you, and have a little target practice. Then I think I just might pay a little call on your poor, bereaved widow and see if I can give her a little comforting."

Rodrigo jumped to his feet, lunging at Jeremiah Adams before he could step back. Sticking his hands through the bars, he grabbed the grinning man by the front of his shirt. "Touch her and I'll . . . I'll . . ."

"Come back from the dead to haunt me? I don't think

so." Pulling away, Jeremiah Adams brushed off his shirt. "Keep your filthy hands off me, Mex, or I'll have you shot right now." Picking up a stick, he nudged Rodrigo roughly, reopening one of his wounds. Wincing against the pain, Rodrigo sank back down to the ground.

"Careful. Careful, amigo." Margaro uged caution.

"That's right, Mex. You're a hell of a lot smarter than your friend. He's gonna get himself killed quickly when I had plans of letting him stay alive, at least for a while . . ."

"How very gracious of you, señor."

"Gracious? Oh no. I want to see you so miserable that you'll get down on your knees and beg me to intercede for you with the *alcalde* of this village." He took out a roll of bills. "I could make things a hell of a lot more comfortable for you, Mex. Money talks here just as it does anywhere." He laughed.

"What do you want, gringo?" Rodrigo demanded.

"I want you to squirm. I want you to go to sleep at night wondering if tomorrow at dawn you will be shot. I want you to think about that pious, pale-haired wife of yours and know you'll never see her again. Maybe then you'll know how I felt." Turning his back he started to leave but paused in the doorway. "The Bible says an eye for an eye."

"If you ask me, there could be a lot of men running around blind." Rodrigo sat in the corner of the cell. The stale odor of the straw assailed his nostrils and he wrinkled his nose in disgust. He had to get out of here or lose his mind.

"Come, forget that *idiota*. We will while away the hours with a game of chess."

"Chess?" Rodrigo laughed. "You think they will be so generous as to give us a board and pieces?"

"No, but in such circumstances as this a man needs to use a little imagination." Picking up a stick Margaro drew a chess board in the hard dirt of the floor. "See, no man ever had one finer, amigo." He gathered a handful of stones and pebbles which had come loose from the wall. "The round pebbles are pawns. The jagged ones knights . . ."

Rodrigo got into the spirit of Margaro's inventive illusion. "We'll scratch a face on the two largest rocks and fashion a king and a queen."

"And a bishop . . ."

If there was no leaving this filthy, putrid place at least they could manage to amuse themselves, Rodrigo thought, and he still had Margaro with him. Tap. Tap tap. The sound came from the other side of the wall, reminding him of Najalayogua's presence.

"We will get out of here. Najalayogua is wiser and craftier than we know." Margaro clucked his tongue as he set up his makeshift chess pieces. "You wait. You'll see. You will see your Angelica again."

"I *will* see her again!" Rodrigo whispered it over and over. In saying it it seemed somehow possible. He had escaped death. Perhaps anything was conceivable. If he was patient and held rein on his temper perhaps his greatest wish would come true.

Chapter Thirty-Five

It was a brutally hot day, and Angelica paused from harvesting to wipe her sleeve across her forehead. She was exhausted. Thirsty. Even so, she refused to complain. It had been her intent to make good on her promise to Father Duran to work for the food Margaro had taken, and work she had. After her teaching duties were completed she worked in the fields beside the Indians. It had covered her hands with blisters, but at least it had given her back a measure of her pride. The debt had been paid ten times over.

But how long before Rodrigo would come for her? It had been a month and yet she had heard no word. She had watched and waited to no avail. Patience might well be a virtue, she reasoned, but at times it was so very hard to maintain. Surely her patience was waning but not her worry. Dear God, where was her husband? That Santa Barbara and other coastal towns had been occupied in quick succession by landing parties from United States naval vessels increased her concern. What if Rodrigo had fallen into danger? Surely southern California was becoming the main battleground for the insurrection of the Californians. They had won a series of encouraging triumphs but at what price? Her only consolation was that the Mission itself had not been touched.

Angelica had been kept abreast of what was happening by the messages sent to Father Duran. General Mariano Arista, commander-in-chief of Mexico's Army of the North had given the order that triggered the war with the United States, insisting provocation abounded. American soldiers from Texas had crossed the Nueces River invading the Mexican province of Tamaulipas. They had marched one hundred fifty miles south to the Rio Grande and had begun building a fort across the river from the Mexican garrison in Matamoros. Repeatedly the Americans had been warned to return home but had refused. Arista had thought it necessary to bring the trespassers to battle. Angelica's feelings were at odds. She was American and could not wish her people ill and yet her love was for Rodrigo and the people that had adopted her country. She had learned while living in the bandit camp just how fine and loving these people were. And what of this invasion? At times she was in a quandary as to what to think.

The United States naval blockade of Mexico's gulf and coastal ports was creating hardship for the Mission, making it impossible to get some of the necessary supplies that came from Mexico City. Father Duran had become inventive and the inhabitants of the Mission had to do without things once taken for granted. Tools. Clothing. What hurt Angelica the most was not being able to procure books.

"Contentment is a state of mind," Father Duran had told her more often than not of late. Nonetheless, she had noticed the worry lines creasing his face. He had been saddened by the death of Bishop Diego, his companion these past months and his friend. The bishop had died after an illness and been buried in the sanctuary of the Mission. Angelica was concerned about Father Duran. He too had been ill, though he would not admit it to her. He was pale, much thinner than before. The worry of what might happen to his Indians if the Americans took over California had begun to take a toll on his health. Angelica watched over him as best she could, but a premonition of his death could not be pushed away.

Father Duran's Indians, Angelica thought, glancing at the toiling men and women by her side. The padre was a fierce defender of his Indians. His love for them had been beneficial for Angelica's own peace of mind. Little by little she was overcoming her fear of all Indians which had haunted her since her parents' death. When first coming to the Mission she had been nervous whenever any of the Indians were around, had found it difficult to be at ease around them. Once she had nearly been frightened to death when she'd taken a basket of fruit to an ailing Indian woman of the village and had come upon a group of Indians wearing plumage and war paint. She had mistaken a celebration for an Indian raid and had gone fleeing back to the mission to inform the padre. Taking her by the hand he had led her back to the village and sat beside her as they watched the colorful dancing. Now Angelica was becoming as fond of these peaceful and friendly people as Father Duran. She had learned a little of their language, their customs, and their history.

She learned the Indians inhabiting the coast were nomadic in the early days of the Mission. They had, however, well-laid-out semispherically shaped villages, slept in beds, and were skilled at fishing and fashioning canoes. Father Duran insisted they were industrious and had directed their energy towards agriculture. Now the Mission grounds were thicklyt settled with these members of the Chumash tribe. Once they had embraced Christianity they were not allowed to leave Mission grounds.

Angelica returned to her work, picking up her basket and filling it with ears of freshly picked maize. She was anxious to hear the bell announcing the end of the day's labors. First thing she would do was quench her thirst, then she'd enjoy the luxury of a long, leisurely bath before she went to bed. At least in her dreams Rodrigo belonged to her again. It was then she would remember the glorious moments of her marriage to Rodrigo, his gentleness, the dizzying passion he awakened in her.

Oh, Rodrigo, when are you going to come for me? she cried silently. It was torture counting the days. Over and over again she chided herself for being so agreeable to staying at the Mission. She should have insisted on going back with Margaro. He had disguised himself, why couldn't she have done the same? Perhaps she could have guarded Rodrigo, made certain that he came to no harm. Looking out towards the rolling hills and green valleys of the Mission as if she might see him riding towards her, she sighed. Everything comes to those who can wait, she had read in a book, but God only knew how difficult it was.

The last hour before sunset moved slowly but at last the tolling bell drew Angelica towards the Mission. Washing her hands at the water pump in the kitchen she set about husking the ears of corn she'd picked. Father Duran's favorite was a dish she prepared with onions, peppers, kernels of corn cooked together. It was a concoction she'd learned from Luisa while staying in the camp. It was a nutritious food and she hoped it would put back some of the weight he had lost these past few weeks. As he entered the kitchen she smiled at him in greeting.

"Angelica . . ." Something in his tone of voice alarmed her. It was the way he spoke when he was going to gently scold or tell somebody something they would rather not hear.

"What is it?"

He came directly to the point. "Your brother is here. He has instructed me that you will be leaving with him the first thing tomorrow morning."

"No!" Once she might have been obligated to go but not

282

any longer. Rodrigo was alive and that changed everything.

"He is insistent. I think you might change your mind when you speak with him . . ."

"Send him away. I never want to see my brother again. God has granted me another chance at happiness and I will not let Edward interfere." She clutched so tightly at the ear of corn in her hand that she broke it in two. She had to get rid of her brother quickly. What if Rodrigo were to come tonight for her and meet her brother, his enemy, face-to-face? "We have nothing to say to each other. He has chosen his way of life and I have chosen mine."

"You must see him." He hated to be the one to tell her but perhaps it would be better this way. "Your Rodrigo was captured on the road to the Mission by a band of *caballeros*. He will not come for you, Angelica. He has been put in jail."

"What?" The shock and grief of his news hit her so hard she was winded. She couldn't breathe, couldn't think. "No!"

"It is true, my child. I sent one of the Indians into the village to verify your brother's words . . ."

At that moment Edward Howe pushed his way into the kitchen, a triumphant smirk on his face. "Jeremiah Adams caught him. Good old Jeremiah, I should have known I could count on him. Of course it's up to you what happens."

"Up to me?" Her voice was so choked she could hardly get the words out.

"If you promise to be a good girl and not put up a fuss, to be obedient and do exactly what I say, then no real harm will come to him. No firing squad, no hanging . . ."

Angelica clutched at the table for support, fearing her legs would give way. "Don't harm him. Please, Edward. I thought I lost him once, I could not live if I thought he had been taken from me a second time." She was a proud woman, yet she went down on her knees. "Spare his life. I beg you. I will do anything you say."

Putting his hands behind his back he strutted arrogantly before her. "Anything?" It seemed to give him pleasure to see her groveling.

"Anything."

He snapped his fingers. "Then hurry to your quarters and pack your things. Tomorrow at the first glow of sunrise we must be on our way." At her questioning expression he explained. "We, dear Sister, are going to Mexico."

"Mexico? You must be mad, there's a war going on."

"Precisely. One the Americans cannot possibly win. Why, the Mexican Army is awesome. There isn't a chance they can be beaten." He stroked at a scar on his chin. "I am not a fool. I intend to align myself with the winning side."

"By being a traitor to your own?" Though Angelica didn't support the American invasion she nonetheless loathed her brother's disloyalty. How could she ever have admired Edward? All he ever thought about was money. Even when her life was at stake he had been concerned with his finances and not her well-being.

"By being astute. The Mexicans are skilled disciplinarians when it comes to strategy but they lack the weapons. They are poor in comparision with the Americans. That's where *I* come in. My occupation is as a trader. I have the weapons they need. If I use my wiles I could become very, very rich . . ." He tapped his foot in impatience. "But I don't have time to stand here all night telling you my plans. You'll soon find out." His tone carried a threat. "Tomorrow at the first crack of dawn be packed and ready . . ."

Chapter Thirty-Six

The twin towers and walls of the Santa Barbara Mission were outlined against the bright pink of the sky. Angelica looked over her shoulder from time to time to catch glimpses of the Mission and a great sadness welled up within her. For a little while at least she had found peace, now all her happiness would be just in her memories. Not only was she leaving California but Rodrigo as well. To save his life she had no other choice but to go with her brother.

"Hurry up, Angelica. You are holding us back." Bonita's voice was peevish as she tossed her long, thick dark hair. "You act as if you think Rodrigo was going to come galloping over the rise to carry you off. Well, I assure you he will not."

"I'm coming . . ." Angelica took one last look at the Mission. Would Paulo continue his lessons? Would Father Duran remember to take his medicine? Would he eat a second helping at dinner as he had promised? Would he give Rodrigo the note she had written? "Please Rodrigo . . . take care of yourself, my love." Father Duran had promised to explain to Rodrigo what had happened. She knew that they would meet again as soon as he was safe, and then would have the rest of their lives to be together. Someday when this was all over they would sit side by side in their rocking chairs telling their many grandchildren this story. Someday . . .

It was a peaceful day, so deceptive in its quiet. The sky was blue, tinged with faint streaks of pink, and white-fluffy clouds moved across the sun. The smell of the ocean was in the air. Looking up, Angelica watched as a flock of seagulls winged homeward after catching their breakfast. She didn't want to leave! She wanted to guide her horse back, wanted to return to the Mission. What if she never saw Rodrigo again? What if . . . ?

"Angelica!" Edward's voice thundered her name. "If you do not stop gaping up at the sky and come along I'll send back a message instructing Jeremiah Adams to have your fine bandit husband whipped within an inch of his life. Believe me, I'll do it!" He brushed at the sleeve of his shirt in irritation.

"So, you will use my husband's welfare as an axe poised above my head. All right. So be it. Have it your way . . ." Angelica nudged her horse, sending it into such a rapid gallop that she was nearly unseated.

They rode in silence, following a rough coastal road that gave them a splendid view of the ocean. At least the scenery was pleasant, Angelica thought. She caught a glimpse from time to time of sandy beaches, hidden coves, and the endless blue span of water that seemed to go on forever. The sun was hot and sweat trickled down her forehead and into her eyes, blurring her vision. She reached up to wipe her eyes. Was it really so surprising that she was crying? Her tears mixed with the trickles of perspiration as she dabbed at her cheeks.

Her brother surprised her with his abrupt changes of mood. He was laughing one moment, sullen the next as he carefully scanned the terrain. There were moments when she believed he was deliberately trying to frighten her, that he was playing a game, maliciously toying with her.

Remembering the fears she'd had as a child concerning Indians he talked as if there was a painted brave behind every bush. Once she might have called it teasing but now . . . ?

"After living at the Mission, the Indians no longer frighten me, Edward," she said at last. "Indeed, I find them far more civilized than you. At least they have a sense of family honor." Her barb struck him as she had intended, for he scowled.

"And is your bandit husband so very honorable?"

"He was the kind of man you would never understand." Shaking her head, she left her brother in a cloud of dust, riding up ahead of him.

"Not so quickly, dear sister. You will take the wrong road." Edward indicated a fork in the road that led to the beach. "We are not traveling by land, Angelica, but by sea. A much more comfortable ride." He pointed out at the horizon where the outline of a ship was visible. "We will be carrying two flags, American and Mexican, just in case . . ."

The turbulence of the sea gave proof that it would not be the comfortable ride he proclaimed, yet Angelica thought it was calm compared to the tumult that was coming. Letting the breeze blowing her hair, she felt suddenly chilled. There was death on the wind . . .

Chapter Thirty-Seven

Rodrigo counted the notches scratched into the adobe of the prison wall, seven to a cluster, marking the weeks he and Margaro had languished there. Five weeks. At least Najalayogua had been spared. Since she was an old woman, the *alcade* had released her, an act of kindness that had been repaid when she had nursed his mortally ill daughter back to health.

"You know, I miss that old woman," Margaro was saying, as if somehow reading Rodrigo's mind. "I had even worked out a code so that I knew what her tapping meant. She promised to find a way to free us, you know."

"Free us?" Rodrigo flexed his arms, practicing the exercises he'd developed to hone his muscles. At least the weeks spent in the dank, dirty jail had given him time to regain his stamina. He was nearly up to full strength again. He had not spent the days brooding. When the chance for escape came he would be ready. "Why on earth would we want to leave, amigo?"

"You have been driven *loco*." Margaro slapped Rodrigo on the back. "Stop fooling . . ."

"All right. Even if we could open the door, just how are we going to get away?" Rodrigo had considered all the options and come to the unwelcome decision that escape was nearly impossible. They were too closely guarded, not by one or two prison guards but by four. The only unpatroled area was the ocean. "If we were fish we could swim, but since we are not . . ."

"A boat."

"Ah, now you are talking, amigo." For the first time in a long while Rodrigo's hope was renewed. "But just where are we going to get a boat? Eh?"

"Steal one."

"Ha!" He stamped his foot against the hard, earthen floor, startling a rat who scurried across his boot. Staring at him with beady eyes, the rodent chattered a rebuke, then sought a hiding place in the straw. "You see, even he knows the impossibility of leaving this place. A boat. How I wish it could be done."

Sitting down on a hard wooden bench, he assessed the cell. It was damp and cold but he had become used to that now. The moistness of the adobe might make it possible to dig their way out. Rodrigo had kept two metal spoons with that in mind when the jailer brought their food. Taking them from their hiding place, he handed one to Margaro. "First we get out, then we worry about a boat."

Both men spent the day chipping away at the soft mortar, taking turns watching for the guards, only to be thwarted by those oafish men when their chicanery was discovered. Men of little intellect, the jail guards unfortunately had lots of brawn, were veritable giants of muscular strength. Rodrigo received a blackened eye, Margaro a bloodied nose before the day was over.

"So much for escape, amigo." Margaro wiped his face.

"Those guards are just waiting to pounce on us again, grinning like cats with sparrows." Rodrigo ran his fingers through his hair. "We will waste away in this stinking place until we rot and become food for the flies." Walking to the bars, he looked out. "I have another idea. Distract the guard when he comes with the food. I will do the rest."

Rodrigo waited until he heard the familiar jingle of keys. Lying down, putting his knees up to his chest, he closed his eyes and pretended to be asleep. He knew the routine very well. The guard would open the cell, put the food on a small wooden stool by the door, then turning his back, would make a swift exit. Such a brief amount of time to strike yet not an impossible feat. Even so, that attempt at gaining freedom also failed. Unlike the other jailers, this one was no simpleton. He did not turn his back, or did he take his eyes off Rodrigo for even a moment.

"You are playing possum, señor. But I tell you there is no reason for such a trick."

Swearing beneath his breath, Rodrigo opened his eyes. "I beg your pardon?"

The man's voice lowered conspiratorially. "I bring you news. You have friends on the outside who have it in mind to set you free. Tonight when it is dark . . ." He disappeared quickly before either Margaro or Rodrigo could question him.

"It's a trap," Margaro insisted. "When we go out that door we will be shot. Perhaps they are tired of feeding us."

"And then again perhaps Najalayogua is more persuasive than we know." Rodrigo grinned. "Is it possible that some of the villagers remember our most generous aid?" There had been a time when their banditing had helped the peons in the surrounding area. Rodrigo interceded in the punishment of one young villager. He had taken him to his camp, thereby cheating the hangman.

"We are quite infamous! It is possible. I hope it is not that he is having his fun with us and that we have no friends at all." Margaro sat down on the ground, motioning for Rodrigo to sit across from him. "We will know soon enough. In the meantime I have it in mind to beat you at chess this time. Eh, amigo?"

It was six chess games later when they heard the grating

sound. The rusty hinges creaked as the door to the prison was opened. A tall, thin youth stepped inside, making his way slowly to the cell where Margaro and Rodrigo were incarcerated. His finger was held to his lips to gesture silence and it was only when he came into the lamplight that they recognized him.

"Bernardo!" Margaro and Rodrigo mouthed his name at the same time. It was too good to be believed. They watched as he took a ring of keys from his pocket and unlocked their cell. He led them through the shadows to the alleyway, stepping over the prone bodies of the guards as he came to them.

"Najalayogua found me and told me you had been captured. One of your guards is a cousin of mine. He bribed two of the guards. The others, as you can see, were . . . uh . . . disposed of. Najalayogua knows the right ingredient to be added to a bottle of wine. They will have very bad headaches in the morning, however."

As they weaved their way in and out between the small adobe buildings Bernardo told them of how he had been saved by Luisa the day of the raid on the bandit camp. "She and the red-haired gringo rode out in a wagon beneath the other gringos' noses. I was hidden under a blanket and brought here."

"Then my sister is safe?"

"*Sí.* The last I heard, she and her *esposo* were headed for Los Angeles. She thought you were dead. We all did. When Najalayogua found me and told me I . . ." He seemed inclined to enfold Rodrigo in a bear hug but changed his mind, turning away in embarrassment. "But come, we can't take time for chatter. All too quickly there will be other guards to take these *hombres'* places. No gold was ever kept under such a watchful eye. I had feared we would not be able to help you. As it was, it took a very long time."

"But at least we're free. Thank you, Bernardo. Will you

come with us?" Rodrigo felt a moment of nostalgia for the past.

"No." Bernardo's blush was revealed by the moonlight. "I have taken a wife and she is expecting our first child. I lead the dull life of a farmer but I am content." He paused to listen. Voices. Shouting. The sound of running feet. "They've discovered your absence much too soon. Come! They will be expecting you to go by land." He led them towards the beach where a small rowboat was tied.

"The boat you wished for, Margaro, though not as large as we had intended." Rodrigo eyed the tiny vessel with apprehension. Hang or drown, which was it to be?

"It was all we could procure for you . . ."

"It will do. *Gracias, amigo.*"

"Go with God, Rodrigo." This time Bernardo gave in to his urge to hug the man he had long respected.

"Take care, Bernardo. May you have many fine children."

"I will name them all after you . . ." Bernardo held the boat steady as Margaro and Rodrigo climbed aboard. A mist hung over the shore, hiding the three silhouettes from view of any unfriendly eyes; but it also posed a danger to navigating.

"I do not like this, Rodrigo. I do not like this at all. I have changed my mind about a boat. Let us take our chances walking, crawling, but at least staying on land. We will be killed, washed overboard." The boat rocked precariously as the waves battered it. "It is much too dangerous!"

From the top of the ridge came the unmistakable sound of voices. The pursuers were coming closer. "It is the only choice we have." Crossing himself, taking a deep breath to quiet the pounding of his heart, Rodrigo took up the oars and began to row.

The ocean was tumultuous, pummeling the boat unmercifully. Margaro clung to Rodrigo's legs, bracing

293

him as he pushed and pulled the oars. A wave crashed over them, nearly sending them over the side and only by sheer strength of will did they manage to fight against the watery fist.

"*Madre de Dios*, we *will* be killed!" Margaro prided himself on his bravery, yet in this battle with the sea he was afraid. As the rowboat bobbed threateningly he was certain that they would be swallowed up by the water.

"We will *not* be killed. I have beaten death once and I will do so again!" Rodrigo was stubborn in his determination, struggling against the waves in an attempt to guide the rowboat closer to the shore. If they were swept out to sea they would be lost. With no compass, no drinking water, their chances of survival would be slim.

Bright splashes of foam curled around the oars, pounded at the boat's side, sending a spray of water into Rodrigo's eyes and mouth. Coughing, he fought against the sting of the salt to open his eyes. The wailing wind sounded like a mournful cry and shivers crept up his spine. He had been bluffing Margaro, pretending to be brazenly brave in an attempt to ease his friend's fear. In reality, Rodrigo had his own doubts about their survival.

Eastward as far as the eye could see was a shimmering, rolling, frothing, spuming endless body of water. Awesome. Frightening. Intimidating.

"What possessed me to get in this boat? At least if I had been hung I would have had a decent burial." Margaro grabbed at the boat's side as another wave assaulted them. "And . . . and Rodrigo, there is something I did not tell you. I . . . I cannot swim."

"What!" Rodrigo stared at his companion in angry disbelief. "I hope that you are playing with me. If so, this is no time for joking, Margaro. Any moment we might find ourselves paddling in the water."

"I tell you truthfully. I have never been in the water before. Had I been, I would have realized and not said such

294

a foolish thing. Go up the coast by boat. Ha! If I had it to do all over again I would have faced our enemies on that shore." He groaned. "Suddenly that jail cell seems very dear to me. I wish we were there again, I wish . . ."

"*Silencio!*" Rodrigo sat upright, motionless as he listened intently. "A ship's whistle." The loud toot pierced the enshrouded quiet. "There is a ship nearby."

"A ship?" Margaro attuned his ears to the sound. "They are looking for us. What are we going to do now?"

Rodrigo ran his hands over the bottom of the boat beneath his bench, pushing another set of oars forward. "We row! Take these, Margaro."

They labored for nearly an hour, struggling against the waves, seemingly gaining nothing. The small boat rocked from side to side moving forward, but each crashing wave of water sent them hurtling back, countering their force with its own current. Still, they pushed on until they were exhausted, looking behind them, trying to see through the fog. Was the ship still there? Had they been seen? Margaro was smugly sure that they had bested their enemies. His fear had evaporated for the moment and he had returned to his jovial bantering.

"I knew that if I helped you we would . . ." A loud splintering crash, a jolt interrupted him. "*Dios!* What was that?"

The bow dipped, the stern lifted from the water, throwing them forward roughly. The small boat shuddered and for a moment both men were certain it would fall apart, yet in the end it stayed together, though it had sprung a leak.

"Bail! Bail, Margaro." There was no bucket in the boat so both men frantically scooped at the steadily seeping water with their hands. "We have to reach the shore before this old barrel sinks." Taking up the oars again Rodrigo worked them as best he could, trying desperately to maneuver the tiny vessel through the violently churning waters. Wind chilled him to the bone and whipped at his face as he pulled and pushed with all his strength. Margaro, meanwhile, had taken off his boot and was filling it with water.

Mumbling curses beneath his breath Margaro was distracted for a moment as he looked over his shoulder. "The ship. It's coming this way. I think they've seen us. Perhaps we should wave them down, eh, Rodrigo. We . . ." A large wave buffeted the boat and Margaro cried out as he was thrown into the icy blackness.

"Margaro! Margaro!"

Rodrigo hurriedly scanned the dark waters. Seeing his companion's head bobbing up and down he peeled off his shirt, stripped off his boots, and without a second thought, dove into the ocean. The swirling water was freezing, debilitating. Ignoring his discomfort, he strained again and again against the waves as he searched for Margaro but he was gone. "No!" he shouted into the wind, then whispered a prayer. As if his words were answered he saw the dark-haired head bob up again. With surprisingly strong strokes he approached the sinking form. Grabbing Margaro's waist, pulling him towards him, he fastened his arms around him.

"Hang on to me, Margaro and don't let go no matter what happens!" he ordered between gasps.

Rodrigo thought surely his strength would give out. The watery prison appeared almost endless as he put one arm before the other. He was winded yet somehow he found the courage, and at last the flow of the tide rose to aid him in his combat with the elements. They were drifting towards the shore. "Just a little farther. Easy. Easy. Don't fight me, Margaro."

Stumbling on to the shore, crawling across the slippery rocks, Rodrigo at last dragged his friend to safety. Setting Margaro down, he pushed at his back, pounded him on the chest trying to help him dispel the water that had filled his lungs. Mumbling incoherently, Margaro seemed to be scolding him.

"Don't . . . don't beat me to death!" he said at last.

"I should, Margaro. Your stupidity nearly cost us both our lives." He wanted to be angry but the reminder that Margaro had saved his life when he had been near death silenced him. They were safe, at least for the moment. Stretching out his arms, Rodrigo sank down on the rocks, breathing hard, gathering his strength.

The two men rested for a long time, then glancing in the direction of the ocean, Rodrigo stood up. The tide was coming in and if they weren't careful they would be swept back out into the sea again.

"Come. We must hurry." They scrambled over the slimy seaweed and jagged rocks. At last they came to a leveled-off area covered with sand. It seemed they walked endlessly, until their legs ached and their feet were blistered and bleeding.

"Where are we?"

Rodrigo didn't know exactly. Looking up at the sky he tried to calculate by the stars where they were. They had been headed south towards the Mission, yet he didn't know where the ocean's waves had deposited them. "We'll keep going south."

Dark, ominous clouds ringed the moon and rain fell in heavy sheets. The wind shrieked and groaned, and the two men were chilled to the bone, with no hope of finding shelter. There was no shrubbery, no caves, no rocks. It was a never-ending acreage of nothingness so they pushed on until they nearly dropped from fatigue. They traveled all night, pausing to rest only a few times along the way. At last the sky grew clear again, and the sunrise lightened the sky.

"Rodrigo, I think I know where we are. I've been here before. Over that hill. The Mission . . ."

Inspired by Margaro's words, Rodrigo started to run.

The Mission and Angelica. Despite all the dangers, all the odds that he would never see her again he had made it here. Love was a potent force, he thought.

Laughing, his eyes misting with unshed tears, Rodrigo crested the hill and gazed at the horizon. Against the backdrop of the sunrise rose the twin towers of the Mission Church. He had never seen a more beautiful sight. Despite his exhaustion he ran, yet nearing the quadrangle of the Mission he became more cautious. Surely someone would have guessed that he would come here. He looked around for any signs of soldiers and was relieved to see that the Mission was quiet.

"I know the way. I will take you to the priest's quarters." Margaro pushed ahead, entering by a side door.

He motioned with his head for Rodrigo to follow. They found the inhabitants of the Mission in a state of melancholy, because Father Duran had taken to his bed; he was dying. Brown-robed friars were on their knees in prayer.

"Señora O'Hara, where is she?" Margaro hated to intrude upon their mourning but he had to know.

"Not here," a tall thin friar said.

"In her quarters?"

Again the man shook his head.

"Where?"

"Gone . . ."

"Gone?" Rodrigo stepped forward. "She can't have gone! She is waiting for me here."

Panic seized him. Running up and down the corridors, he searched each room, apologizing to their occupants when he saw she was not inside. "Where is she? *Where* is she?"

Timidly a dark-haired, brown-eyed boy tugged at his sleeve. "My name is Paulo," he said. "I know where she is. Her brother came and took her away. Father Duran knows where." He led Rodrigo through the maze of rooms,

298

entering a small, dimly lit chamber where a pathetically thin man lay in a narrow bed. "Father Duran, you said if the señora's husband came I was to bring him to you . . ."

"Yes . . . yes, Paulo." The voice was a breathy whisper. Raising his head, Father Duran looked searchingly at the wet and tattered man who stood in the doorway. "Come . . . come in."

"I do not wish to disturb you . . ." Rodrigo was unnerved by the frail figure, felt ill at ease. "My wife was to meet me here. I have been told that she has gone. The child says that her brother took her away, but to where?"

Father Duran licked his parched lips, trying to sit up. In resignation he lay back down. "Paulo . . . in my . . . my desk. A letter. Get it for me." The child did as he was instructed to do, placing the letter in the old priest's hand. Father Duran in turn gave it to Rodrigo. "For you, my son." He struggled to sit up.

Rodrigo read the missive silently, cursing beneath his breath. Angelica spoke of her love for him, expressed the hope that they would be together after the tumult of the war had ended. What she was doing had to be done, she wrote, to ensure their happiness. "She leaves with her brother and thinks to make me happy?" Rodrigo crumpled the note in anger. "I told her to wait. Why didn't she?"

"Because . . . because her . . . her brother was threatening your life. She did it to save you, my son." He collapsed in a fit of coughing, lying back down. "Her brother said he would have you shot if she did not comply with what he wished of her."

Grinding his teeth, Rodrigo swore again. "But where has he taken her? I will go and bring her back."

"Mexico. They were going to Mexico, though I do not know the exact destination."

"Mexico City." Paul exclaimed loudly. "Her brother spoke of selling guns. I heard him talking. He goes to meet with El General."

"Mexico!" At the moment it seemed an impossible journey, yet Rodrigo knew that had Edward Howe taken his sister to hell Rodrigo would have followed. "Margaro, we have a journey to undertake, you and I." Clenching and unclenching his fists, Rodrigo thought to himself that with the war heating up the border he might very well be going into Satan's lower kingdom after all.

Chapter Thirty-Eight

From the deck of the *Scorpion* Angelica watched the ocean. It was so peaceful now, but as she knew it could be violent. Last night there had been such a storm that she had feared the ship would topple over and throw them all into its mighty depths. She remembered seeing a small rowboat being tossed about by the ocean's waves last night and wondered at the fate of its occupants. She had pleaded with Edward to help the two men she had glimpsed from afar but he had, as usual, been stubborn, thinking first and foremost about himself.

"If we go too close to shore we might run aground on the rocks," he'd told her. "If you ask me, anyone who would go out in such a boat on a night like this deserves to be drowned." He had, however, blown the ship's whistle thinking to alert the two men to the ship's whereabouts so that they could try to reach it. Instead, the boat had gone in the opposite direction, disappearing in a mist of fog. "Stupid Mexican fishermen! Well, let the sea have them."

"At least they won't have to suffer your company," Angelica had responded angrily. "Oh that I did not."

It had already become a stressful journey. Being forced to travel with a man she found to be loathsome, brother or not, had taken a toll on her nerves. She was in her way just as much a prisoner as Rodrigo except that, unlike him, she had no bars to hold her in. And Bonita's presence made the atmosphere even more strained. The woman had tried to kill her twice, once with poison. Was it any wonder she was careful in what she ate or drank? When she expressed her alarm to her brother, he merely laughed.

"Bonita is spirited, yes, but she is not a murderer. She is an exciting, sensual woman, Angelica, and you could do well to learn from her."

"Learn what? How to lie? How to lead a man you supposedly love into danger." She could never forget or forgive what the woman had done to Rodrigo. Only by a miracle had he survived. "How to enslave a man with the use of my body? She has you wound around her little finger, Edward. Someday she will betray you just as she did my husband. Wait and see."

The breeze tore at Angelica's hair, whipping it around her face and into her eyes. The salt spray splashed her face as she gazed out at the ocean. Mexico. It was so far away. Even if Rodrigo did manage to break free it would take him nearly an eternity to reach her. So much precious time wasted. Time they could have been together. Still, each day of pain, each moment of sadness and disappointment would be worth enduring if they could see each other again. Love each other. What she wouldn't have given for a moment with him. Just to touch him, tell him she loved him, look into his eyes.

The sudden cry, "All hands to quarters" startled her. She watched as her brother strode across the deck, his blond hair whipping about his face as he shouted out his orders.

"Edward? What is it?" She tried to control her fear.

"None of your concern. Go below."

Angelica looked in the direction of his gaze. White sails and the round shape of cannons declared the ship following them as a warship.

302

"Reedy, come here!" Edward's shout reverberated in the air. The short, fat little man came running. "Is it a Spanish ship or American?" With impatience he grabbed the spyglass out of the pudgy hands that held it and looked himself. "They're flying the Stars and Stripes. Hoist up the American flag, you fools. Quickly!"

All hell broke loose at his order. Men swarmed across the deck and into the rigging. Two men vied with each other to put up the flag. They were not quick enough. Before Edward could issue another order, several puffs of smoke billowed from the warship as she fired a volley of cannon fire. The deck shuddered as wood splintered from the railing.

"Angelica, watch out!" At least Edward held some affection for her after all. As another thunder of cannon fire rained down on the quarterdeck, he pushed her out of the way. "Jesus Christ, we've been hit. The flag! The flag, you idiots. And while you're at it, throw up a white flag of truce too. We can't outrun that vessel and we sure as hell can't fight." The *Scorpion* was ill equipped to make a stand. Unlike its name, it had no stinger.

The acrid smoke and stench of burnt wood permeated the ship, and several of the crew members were wounded. Angelica acted as a nurse, carefully tending the men. Though her brother shouted at her to go below, she held her ground. She was needed above deck.

While Angelica stared at her brother, a long, jagged gash cut across his forehead. He had been hit by the flying debris and putting her emnity aside, Angelica bandaged him. He had done things that had hardened her heart against him but they did share the same blood. He was her brother.

"They're going to board us. I'll be Gawd damned." Reedy, one of the shipmates, leaned so far over the railing that he nearly toppled overboard. "What shall we do, Boss?"

303

"Let them come aboard, but I warn you. If anyone even hints at what we are about or where we are headed, I'll have their head. That includes *you!*" He looked at Angelica meaningfully.

"I know when to keep my silence, though I cannot help but think that some time your perfidy will get you hung." She grew silent as the American ship ranged alongside the *Scorpion.* Four men armed with swords and muskets, came aboard.

Rising to his feet, adopting his most sophisticated demeanor, Edward was eloquent in his greeting. Before ten minutes had passed he had the four men apologizing ardently for their attack on an unarmed merchant ship headed for Los Angeles. Angelica could not help thinking that her brother's blond hair aided him. No one would even conceive of the fact that her brother had sided with the Californians.

"You have our sincere regrets, ma'am." A handsome man of medium height, a dark beard covering his face, stepped forward. "John Charles Frémont at your service." Taking her hand, he kissed it in gentlemanly fashion. "Major Frémont."

So this is John Frémont, Angelica thought. He didn't have the appearance of a man who could stir up such trouble. His buckskin-garbed companion was an altogether different thing, however. His swagger and swearing and lack of concern for the carnage that had been dealt the ship put her on guard, as did his leering appraisal of her.

"I deem you, please be our guests, at least until your own ship has been repaired. We're stopping briefly at a port near Los Angeles, then will be pointed in the direction of San Diego."

"Make it a heap more interestin', havin' a woman aboard." Once again the frontiersman appraised her. "Carson's the name. Kit Carson."

John Frémont was contrite. "Our lookout swore you

304

were flying a Mexican flag, and, as you know, our two countries are at war. We fired. It was an unfortunate incident but one which can be corrected. Please allow us to do just that."

Angelica expected her brother to say no, therefore she was astounded when he accepted the invitation for them to stay on Frémonts ship while the *Scorpion* was disabled. When she pulled him off alone he told her the reason.

"If I can find out just what they're planning the information could bring a high price. A very high price. Besides, we can't sail until our ship is repaired." He eyed his sister distastefully. "For God's sake take off those stupid spectacles, and find yourself something more frivolous to wear. That pale green poplin hardly becomes you."

"You've never worried about what I wore before now." If her assortment of dresses was meager, if they were plain, it was because he had always been so stingy.

"I've never had to count on your charms before now." He gave her a shove in the direction of the cargo hold. "If you can't find something among the dry goods I've brought along, then perhaps Bonita could help you."

"I do believe I'd go naked before I'd wear anything that belonged to her."

"Don't tempt me. I'm certain I could get the information I needed then . . ."

"I won't spy for you, Edward . . . !"

He curled up his lip. "What was the name of that Mexican you seemed so fond of? Ah yes. Margaro. I forgot to tell you that he was also captured." He reached up to touch his head wound, wincing as his fingers made contact. "He is nothing to me. I would as soon see him dead. But perhaps if you are a very, very good girl I might decide to spare him too . . ."

It was blackmail. Edward would use Rodrigo and Margaro to manipulate her into doing anything he wanted. But she would not have it. Somehow she would think of a way to thwart him.

Angelica found in the following days that she had no need to spy. Edward was so successful in his ploy as an American patriot that John Frémont talked freely in his presence. The *Californiano* general, Castro, was said to be in Los Angeles, the province's capital and its most populous area. Together with Governor Pico they had raised a force of five hundred. Frémont was traveling to join Commodore Robert Stockton in taking Los Angeles for the Americans. From his conversation Angelica supposed that Frémont's motivation was a grudge against Castro, the Californian military commander who had accused him of agitating a revolt, and ordered him to leave San José.

"I have heard it rumored that the Californians are pitifully short of gunpowder and lead." Sitting at dinner, John Frémont dabbed at his mouth with the edge of his napkin. "And their weapons. Antique." Noticing that Angelica had hardly touched her food, he was concerned. "You do not like the sauce? I had the cook prepare something I thought you would like."

The talk of weaponry had unnerved her. As Angelica's eyes met her brother's gaze she read his mind. He intended to make use of the Californians' lack of guns for his own profit before moving on to Mexico. If Frémont was not cautious he'd find he had on his hands a more furious battle than he supposed.

"I . . . I'm just not very hungry. A bit of seasickness perhaps. The rise and fall of the deck . . ." She didn't want to offend the American. He had most graciously invited her brother and herself to dine in his cabin. Despite all that she had heard, she liked Frémont. He seemed genuinely convinced that what he was doing was right. Unlike her brother his motivation was not money.

"Seasick? I'm sorry." The lips above the beard curled in a half-smile. "But don't feel too bad. I've seen Kit weather storms, fight Indians, face a grisly bear, and yet right now he's puking his guts out over the rail. Looks a bit green, as a matter of fact."

"I'm sorry. Would a cup of tea help him? It's helped me."

Frémont shook his head. "No. If he knew you realized his malady it would embarrass him. Just leave him alone. He's conquered just about everything else. I guess he can conquer this."

Though Kit Carson had been bold on their first meeting, Angelica hardly saw him at all as they continued on their journey. She did, however, see a great deal of John Frémont, who enjoyed himself in her company. He was an educated man who had a world of stories to tell her of his exploration. He was intent on mapping the lands west of the Rockies, had endured danger to do so. He was an intriguing man, if a more than slightly ambitious one. It seemed, however, that he was marked by an almost too-powerful urge to prove his worth and a quickness to perceive slights where none were intended and to take offense. Once or twice Edward had agitated the major and only Angelica's quick thinking had avoided a scene. Frémont had a personal bodyguard of Delaware Indians who looked as though they would use violence to protect him if a quarrel broke out.

"I tell you, Angie, this Frémont has high aspirations but he'll never subdue California. He is a balloon full of hot air. And that Commodore Stockton he talks about must be the same. There are eight thousand Californians to seven hundred American settlers. Their small invading force cannot think to win. I tell you it is just a matter of time." In an attempt to make certain of that, Edward smuggled a small load of guns and bullets to the coast aboard a small rowboat, sending Reedy to deliver the booty. Nonetheless, his effort was wasted. Instead of become rich and making himself a hero who would be rewarded with rich grants of land, Edward found out much to his dismay that he had been tricked. Frémont had suspected him all along. Instead of going to Los Angeles, he sailed directly to San Diego.

"I regret that I must put such a lovely woman under surveillance but I have no choice," John Frémont said sternly. Thus ensued Angelica's second captivity. Looking out the porthole of their quarters she couldn't help but chide her brother.

"How does it feel to be a prisoner, Edward? To wonder at your fate? Now you know how Rodrigo feels."

"We will be released soon. When Reedy realizes what has happened he will come to our aid. The streets of San Diego will run with blood when that bearded buffoon marches in." He watched sullenly as the *Scorpion*, which was being towed behind the *USS Cyane*, pulled into the quay. "The residents of San Diego will fight to the last man."

He was wrong. Taking San Diego was easy for Frémont. Indeed, it required little more than putting his men ashore. There was scarcely a shot fired. The same was true when they pulled into the port a few miles west of Los Angeles. It too fell without much opposition. The people were not cordial in meeting the Americans but they did not put up much of a fight either. The Californians had abandoned their arms and gone home. From the talk she heard bandied about, both Castro and Pico were on their way to Mexico. By nightfall the American flag flew over all of California.

"What is going to become of us now, Edward?" Bonita walked back and forth angrily across the deck of their prison quarters.

"Wait . . . Someone will come to help us." For once he was right. Reedy came back, and he brought a small armed band with him, enough men to take over the ship while Frémont and his men were ashore celebrating. One familiar face made Angelica cry out in joy. Jesse was with the men.

"Jesse! Where is Luisa?"

"She's on board the *Scorpion*. We're going with you to Mexico. There is nothing for us here. Besides, I owe your brother a debt."

"You don't owe Edward anything. He would have let you stay in the bandit camp until you grew to be an old man. And what of Luisa? Surely she is not agreeable to this . . ." Angelica supposed that Luisa thought her brother to be dead, just as she had before Margaro's visit to the Mission.

Jesse turned his head away from her searching gaze. "It was a matter of contention between us on our way here, but when I heard your brother was in trouble I decided to accompany him. Luisa and I can begin a new life away from all the turmoil that has taken California by storm."

"But you don't know anything about Mexico."

"I know that after today we have no future in California. Your brother and I are marked men as long as the United States holds control here. Being American and having fought on the Californians' side makes the threat of punishment even more certain. So we gotta flee, Miss Angelica." Seeing her distressed expression, he touched her hand. "But I would think you'd move heaven and earth to reach Mexico City. Rodrigo . . ."

"Is in jail in a small village outside Santa Barbara. That's why I'm going with Edward. The only reason." She bit her lip to keep from crying.

"Rodrigo broke free! He sent a message to Luisa. He went to the Mission at Santa Barbara and was told you were on your way to Mexico City with your brother. He's on his way there to meet you when you arrive and . . ."

"Rodrigo going to Mexico City?" Suddenly that city

seemed to be the most important place in the world. Angelica broke into a run, longing to hasten their departure for that destination.

"Miss Angelica . . . ?" Jesse ran to catch her, bounding up the ladder to the upper deck right behind her.

"We've no time for talk, Jesse. We must hurry before Frémont and the others come back. I think I relish this ocean voyage." She winked at him, feeling carefree despite the danger they were still in. Suddenly she felt confident. Being with Rodrigo again was meant to be. "Hurry, Jesse," she said again. Mexico City. Mexico City. It was there that Rodrigo was headed. She wanted to laugh, to cry, to shout out loud. Her arms had been empty too long. She was on her way to be with her husband.

Chapter Thirty-Nine

The flickering pink glow of sunset reflected on the turrets, domes, and spires of Mexico City welcoming Angelica with the brightness of a shimmering star. The magnificent city was breathtaking, so much so that Angelica forgot her exhaustion as she stared at its beauty. She had never seen anything that could compare to the tall, opalescent buildings that towered high in the air, the long, spacious streets, the iron grills that covered the windows and balconies of red lava brick and gray, volcanic rock-constructed haciendas. Some of them rose four or five stories high, touching the sky. The city showed the influence of the Spanish architectural genius that had belonged to those living here centuries before the Anglos had come to the New World. It was here that the *hacendados* and silver mining grandees had built their noble palaces. Foundations of carved stone, artistically carved stone doorways, and abundant arches gave the city an artistic touch.

"You thought we would never make it but we did." Edward smiled smugly. "I said I would get us all safely here and I *did!*" He guided his horse into a strut beside the wagon.

"Yes, you did." It had, however, been a grueling

journey. First there had been the frantic escape over the sea, down the coast and around the tip of California to the gulf. That the *Scorpion* was a crippled ship with damage done to its stern and hull made the traveling all the more difficult. They had been in fear of being captured by Frémont, always looking on the horizon to ascertain that there were no ships following them. Then the hot, dusty trek on land through an area that was little better than desert. Crossing a mile-high plateau, working their way through sleepy Mexican villages, they had been wary of marauding bandits or rampaging Indians. Angelica and Luisa had been so exhausted they could hardly sit atop the wagon seat without slumping. Bone-weary, thirsty, miserable, they had somehow endured. Over rough roads, through canyons and over the mountain passes of the Sierra Madres they had arrived in the heart of Mexico.

"We'll have the kind of life-style we deserve here. The Californians were barbarians compared to this!" Edward's eyes were as large as silver dollars as he appraised their new surroundings. Though it was late the cobbled streets were filled with people—soldiers in gold-braided uniforms, women in rebozos and colorful skirts, priests and friars in their browns and blacks.

The horses trotted along the street and Angelica leaned over the side of the wagon, taking in the sights and sounds. While Edward was in awe of the ladies covered with jewels and the men smoking long black cigars, Angelica stared at the half-naked *mendigos,* the beggars plying their trade or begging in the streets. Her heart went out to the boys and girls in ragged dress, performing acrobatics for a few coins. Wealth and poverty seemed to walk hand in hand.

From churches, convents, and monasteries the city bells rang out, reminding Angelica of her stay at the Mission in Santa Barbara. Father Duran had once mentioned his journey to this Mexican city and the wonder of the constant bell-ringing. Angelica had heard it said that while the bells pealed, souls in purgatory were in peace from their torment. Crossing herself, she whispered a prayer for those souls and for the ragged poor.

"And if I may be so selfish, please send Rodrigo to me," she breathed. Her heart skipped a beat as she thought that perhaps he was already here. Oh, when would she see him?

"You seem overly pious today, Angie." Edward bent low from his horse, meeting her face to face. "Have you in mind to become a nun, dear sister? If so, there are many abbeys and convents about, I would wager."

"I'm thankful we've made it safely, that's all."

Taunting her, always taunting her. Edward had been loathsome company all the way across the desert. Angelica had begun to think that Bonita was perfect for him. A scorpion and a tarantula. Bonita had not chosen to ride in the wagon with Luisa and Angelica but had traveled the roads on horseback dressed in tight leather breeches, a silk shirt, and a large-brimmed hat. Though she had kept distance between them, Bonita seemed to be watching Angelica as if trying to read her mind. Angelica feared that somehow, someway the buxom woman sensed the change in her mood, knew it was because of Rodrigo. She would have to be very, very careful that Bonita was not given a chance to vent her jealousy and anger on Rodrigo again.

"If you ask me, we have a lot to be grateful for. Seems it was a boon to have someone along who is in God's favor." Following Edward on horseback, Jesse swept off his hat. "Think we all ought to do a heap of prayin'." He looked Luisa's way, hoping for a smile, but just as she had done all along the journey, Luisa avoided his eyes. She was still angry with him for his insistence that they join the caravan of the very man who had meted out such destruction. She hardly spoke to him, slept apart from him, and showed him her displeasure by her icy aloofness.

The wagons, ten in all in the caravan, passed on through the city, by fountains and trees, past a towering cathedral to the open stalls of the market. The air rang with the cries of craftsmen and artisans hawking their wares. Edward halted the wagons so that they could look and listen. There were stalls hung with strings of dried peppers, onions, and dried corn, others with flowers. The scent of blossoms and savory smelling herbs permeated the air. There were baskets filled with fresh fruit and vegetables that reminded Angelica and Luisa how very hungry they were. There were delicacies to eat as well—tortillas, sweet breads, and nuts.

Exhibiting his large appetite, Jesse sampled several culinary offerings, sharing his purchases with the ladies. As he reached across the wagon, his hand touched Luisa's just briefly but long enough to make her tremble. All coherent thought fled from her mind and she could only remember how it had been between them before they'd gone on board the American ship and rescued the man she so detested. If not for her love for Jesse she would have stayed in California, yet she had tagged along after him like an obedient, lovesick child. Infuriated more at herself and her emotions than at him, Luisa nonetheless turned her back.

"Luisa . . . don't be too hard on him. He's doing what he thinks is right." Angelica was determined that if it was the last thing she ever did she would bring these two together again. Moments of love were too precious to waste with dour looks and frowns.

Children abounded in Mexico City. Wide-eyed innocent children who were unaware of such things as hatred and war. The sight of a small baby cradled in its mother's arms made Angelica wish for a child of her own by Rodrigo. Her eyes met Luisa's and she read the same longing in the dark-haired young woman's. For just a moment Luisa let down her guard and smiled.

"Perhaps I am not really so angry at Jesse as I was before . . ." Luisa conceded. Her gaze shifted to her husband but when he glanced back she looked away. When Angelica slid down from the wagon seat to tour the marketplace, she followed.

Indian and mestizo vendors squatted along the streets nearby selling beads, handwoven baskets, and straw hats. A jeweler displayed bracelets, necklaces, and rings made of finely wrought silver. One old Indian woman held forth a basket of medicinal roots and Angelica listened to her drone. Luisa told Angelica that the Indians spoke several different dialects so she wasn't surprised when she couldn't understand one word of what the old woman was saying. Still, she took one of the roots from the old woman's hand, exchanging it for a coin.

"Why did you buy that?" Luisa giggled.

"Oh . . . because she reminded me so very much of Najalayogua." Angelica rolled the root around in the palm of her hands. "Why are you laughing? What is this for?"

"It is for treating warts!" This time when Luisa laughed, Angelica joined in.

"Well, I dare say I'll be prepared if I ever get some." While Bonita amused herself trying on the rings and bracelets, Luisa and Angelica busied themselves with more practical matters. Hats, sandals, and brightly painted pottery. With the little money Edward had given her, Angelica bought a white cotton dress, embroidered in threads of blue, red, and green, to wear when Rodrigo paid court. Holding it up she asked Luisa's opinion of the dress and was given an enthusiastic nod. Taking the purchases back to the wagon, she was puzzled to see Edward taking several bundles out of the head wagon. On closer inspection she was mortified to see what they were. Rodrigo's paintings and books. Her brother was selling them, bartering with an old toothless man.

"That's not high enough. I can sell them for twice as much elsewhere," he was saying. As Angelica tugged at his

315

sleeve, he pushed her away like a bothersome insect and continued his haggling.

"You can't sell those. You have no right! Those are Rodrigo's things." She was incensed that he could be so heartless. "You stole them from him. You are nothing but a thief!" She had envisioned returning them to Rodrigo but nothing she could say or do could sway her brother. They needed money, he said, and the paintings and leather-bound, gold-engraved books would bring a high price. Many foreigners—American and English—frequented markets such as the one they had stopped at, and such treasures were at a premium.

"I have no time for sentiment!" he said sharply. "Besides, you will never see that bandit again. He'll be shot by a firing squad if I have my way. Then there will be no need for an annulment to your ill-timed marriage."

"Shot? I think not. He's not in your power any longer. He'll come for me and he'll . . ." Angelica quickly covered her mouth with her hands, knowing she had already said too much.

"Come for you?" Edward threw back his head and gave vent to a wave of chilling laughter. "He'll be captured again before he gets halfway." Thrusting the books and paintings into the old vendor's hands he muttered beneath his breath about woman's foolishness, then busied himself in counting his ill-gotten money. "I'll give you a few of these coins back if you can direct me to the closest and most resplendent inn," he said, "for me and my party."

In rapid Spanish the man complied, pointing excitedly to a red lava brick building about a block away. Several carriages pulled up out in front, depositing richly dressed men and women. "Visiting Californians . . ." the old man exclaimed. "Fugitives."

"Mmmm, a Californian inn or at least one frequented by them," he said pensively as he mounted his horse and led the way to the well-kept stables.

Unhitching the horses from the wagons he gave instructions to his men to take care of them, then, taking Bonita by the hand, led the small party across the patio, up the stairs, and to the rooms he had arranged for. It was an awkward situation. Angelica felt uncomfortable when her brother said he would not let her stay alone. At last the matter was settled that Luisa would stay with her while Jesse took a room next door. Angelica whispered her apologies to Jesse with a knowing smile.

"I may not be as handsome a companion as Jesse," she confided to Luisa, "but at least I do not snore." Jesse did, as proven time and time again when he had been reposing in the adobe hut, recovering from his wound.

"Ah, but I do. . . ." Luisa said, laughing.

Their beds were comfortable, and as they settled down for the night they both were too exhausted to make any further jests about sleeping habits. How good it was to sleep on feathers instead of on the hard ground, to bathe in warm water, not cold, and most of all, to sleep as late in the morning as one desired. Sinking down into the feathers, both women closed their eyes and were instantly asleep. They were unaware of the man who was frantically searching for one of them at this moment.

"It's no use, Margaro. It's much like looking for a peso in a haystack. It's a huge city. How can I hope to find her?"

"You will! You will. All we can do is to wait. A woman so fair of hair will be noticed. Miracles happen when they are least expected. Angelica told me that." He led Rodrigo towards a *cantina*. "We will drink on it, eh? Tomorrow may be the day." His words soothed Rodrigo's pique. Tomorrow. It was both a hope and a promise.

317

Chapter Forty

The sun was unmercifully hot. Rodrigo and Margaro pulled their wide-brimmed hats down lower on their foreheads to shade their eyes as they sat astride their horses viewing the city from a hilltop. The last few days their routine had been the same, up at the crack of dawn, breakfast in the *cantina*, and then the unrelenting search for any sign of Angelica. Surely she would have arrived by now, Rodrigo insisted. She had left long before they had begun their journey.

"Ah yes, but they could not have traveled so fast, amigo. You practically set fire to your horse's hooves in your hurry." Margaro sought to reassure his friend. "Nothing has happened to her if that is what you are afraid of."

"There are bandits. Indians. That fool brother of hers is just the kind to incite danger. Just as he did before. I would never have captured her if not for his idiotic scheme. And what of Garcia? You know that he is preying on the area between California and Mexico."

They had learned that information on entering a small Mexican Village near San Diego. Seeing Margaro and Rodrigo ride in on their "borrowed" horses, the villagers scampered to their huts, hiding fearfully. It had taken Margaro nearly one hour to convince them that they would not be harmed. Slowly they had come out of their adobe dwellings to tell the story of Garcia's rampage and destruction. Rodrigo's jaw tensed as he remembered.

"No, I don't think your Angelica has fallen into Garcia's hands . . ." At least Margaro prayed that she had not. "She is possibly safe right now inside one of the missions." Though he did not believe that for a moment, he thought that it was the perfect thing to say to soothe Rodrigo's apprehension.

"I hope so. With all my heart I hope that she is safe." Rodrigo gazed out on the city, wondering if the woman he so loved was somewhere within its walls. He had to admit that it was a beautiful sight. To the southwest the stone walls of the Chapultapec Castle rested on its hilltop, and he remembered all that he had read about it in books. It had been the summer home of the Aztec leader Montezuma, later of the Spanish viceroys, and was now a military school. Even from this distance its cannons were visible, guarding the city from invasion. Mexico City was built on what was once the capital of the Aztec civilization; then it had been the main city of the Spaniards who had come from beyond the sea. He wondered if some conquistador had once looked out at the hills and mountains as he was doing now. Turning his mount around, he looked to the north of the city at the mountains. The snow-capped head of Popocatepetl soared high like some old Aztec god.

"Let us wander again through the *americano* section of the city, Rodrigo. Surely it is there that Angelica will stay."

Margaro led his horse down the hill and Rodrigo followed to the noisy, crowded streets. It was obvious that many foreigners inhabited the city. The distinct cut of their garments, their dialects, proclaimed them as such. Oblivious to the war raging to the north of them, many Americans loitered on the streets, enjoying the delights Mexico City had to offer. Rodrigo scrutinized each face but

Angelica's was not among them.

"Another lost day." Dismounting from his horse, Rodrigo wandered aimlessly in and out among the vendors' stalls.

"Buy, Señor Americano?" Mistaking him for an American because of his blue eyes and the glint of red to his hair, one old vendor approached him.

"I am not an *americano!*" Rodrigo gently pushed the man's clinging hands away.

"A *caballero* then? You have the look of one. I have just what you need to make your hacienda more beautiful. Paintings." He held one out for his inspection. "See . . ."

"I have no need for . . ." Rodrigo gasped, staring at the scene of his own hacienda. It had been painted by his mother. There could be no mistaking it. "Where did you get that?"

"You do not like this one? I have several more. And books. With leather covers. Books are very hard to come by these days, with the war going on up there." He bent down to pick up two, running his fingers over the smooth leather covers. "Very fine . . . and for you I will give a very good price."

"*Dios!*" Rodrigo's fingers trembled as he opened the cover of the largest one. There, scrawled in his own handwriting, was his name. There could be no question as to ownership or to the fact of who had sold them. "Tell me where the *hombre* is who gave you these." In his excitement he grabbed the man by the front of his shirt and held him, fearful lest he run away. "Tell me!"

"Please! Please, I have done no wrong. I bought these, señor. I paid many pesos." The dark brown eyes were round with fear, his voice was a hoarse croak. "Please. I have a wife and many, many children . . ."

"I will let you go if you tell me where the man is. The pale-haired gringo. Where is he?" His thunderous voice shattered the air. People turned to stare at the scene.

"Rodrigo! Amigo, take care. We do not want to incite attention." Margaro put a hand on the old man's shoulder as Rodrigo loosened his grip. "We are looking for the man. If you can help us find him, and the yellow-haired woman who was with him, we will be very grateful."

"I do not want to cause the man harm . . ." The old man looked as if he wanted to escape, but Margaro blocked his way. "At the inn. He is at the inn." His hand shook as he pointed the way. "The red lava building. There. He was with, as you say, a pale-haired woman, a man with fire-red hair and a dark-haired señorita. He had several men in wagons following him but they went in the opposite direction to an inn that was just adobe."

"Angelica, Jesse, and Luisa," he said to Margaro as Rodrigo started to walk towards the inn but the sight of a small group of parading lancers held him back. He eyed their gold-braided blue-and-red uniforms, their glittering scabbards, and their plumed hats with caution. He was a wanted man in California and he could not be sure that his posters had not been nailed to trees and doors in Mexico City as well. He would have to be careful. Meeting his eye, Margaro sent a silent message that he was thinking the very same thing. Both ducked back in the shadows until the horsemen had passed.

"You cannot go to see her. Not in the daylight!" Margaro's usually jovial-toned voice was stern.

"Sangre de Cristo, I must! All these weeks and months, Margaro . . ." His voice echoed his loneliness, his agony at having found her only to have to deny himself. "I must . . ."

"There is a way . . ." Dropping a peso into the old man's hand, Margaro led Rodrigo away from the market stalls. In the alleyway he paused. "I will go to see her and I will give her a message to meet you beyond the city's walls. There is a secluded spot there that I saw when we rode in. A place far from prying eyes or soldiers."

"Margaro . . . !"

"*Silencio.* It is the only way." Whispering his plan, Margaro related that he would dress like an old man, complete with graying whiskers, and would somehow get to Angelica's room.

"An old man?"

Seeing a wine merchant gave Margaro an idea. "I will dress like a servant and I will insist that the señoras have asked for some ice."

"Ice?" Rodrigo violently shook his head, dismissing Margaro's idea as foolish.

"I have heard that the *ricos* in the *americano* haciendas and inns desire it above all things. The ice comes from the snowy peaks of Popocatepetl and is brought here by Indians who sell it to those with money to pay . . ."

"But we are running short on pesos, Margaro." They had just enough for food and lodging.

Margaro's smile was wide. "I will take care of that too, amigo. There are so many rich in this city. It would not hurt them to share with those of us who are poor, eh?"

"Margaro . . ."

"I will be doubly careful. Leave everything up to me." He pushed Rodrigo playfully. "Now, go to that small clearing we passed on our way down the hill." He reached in the small leather pouch that hung at his waist, pulling forth a few pesos. "Here! A man awaiting his *novia* must have new clothes. Amuse yourself while I am on my errand." He winked. "And a shave, Rodrigo. that stubble of beard at your face is much like sandpaper, eh? I don't mind but perhaps Señora Angelica will." Again he smiled.

Margaro watched as Rodrigo sauntered off down the cobbled street, then set about obtaining his own purchases —a tattered hat, a small sack of flour to dust in his hair, a shirt similar to those he'd seen the servants at the American inn wear. Most important was the ice, though

323

much to his regret he had to steal it when he found he had not enough pesos to spare. Dressing himself, powdering the flour in his hair and on the month's growth of beard on his face, he set out. Ignoring the protestations of those at the inn who tried to detain him, he shrugged his shoulders and insisted in rapid Spanish that he was merely following someone else's orders.

"Hielo! Hielo!" he insisted, pointing towards the large basket he had hoisted on his shoulder. Slowly he inched his way towards the stair.

"Oh let him go, Gregory. He doesn't look like a thief to me. Only some silly old man. I have no doubt that he's on a feasible errand," one of the servants said. Turning their backs on him the two men busied themselves in the dice game they had been playing.

Margaro paused only a moment before he ran up the stairs, knocking at the thick wooden doors with impatience. He knocked at seven different doors before he came to the right one. Luisa opened it, shaking her head when she saw the servant.

"You have the wrong room!"

"No I do not, Luisa." Margaro pushed inside before she had time to say otherwise.

"Now see here . . ." Luisa frowned, pointing towards the door. "My husband will . . ." As he grinned at her, sweeping off his hat, she started to laugh. "Margaro! Margaro!" She hugged him. "How did you get here? Where is my brother? Why are you dressed like that? Oh, I'm so glad to see you. Angelica has been so worried, as have I." She pulled away. "but we must be careful. Señor Howe is most formidable. He is keeping Angelica a veritable prisoner. If he even suspected that Rodrigo was anywhere near, he might—Rodrigo is here, isn't he?"

Margaro threw back his head and laughed. "You have not given me time to tell you. He is here. And he wants Angelica to come to him at sunset." Margaro looked around the room. "Where is Señora Angelica?" He started towards an inner door but Luisa blocked his way.

"She is taking a bath . . ." She laughed delightedly at the blush that stained his usually swarthy face. "But sit down. Tell me all about your journey while you wait. I would not deny you the pleasure of delivering your message to her." Pouring him a glass of wine she found the most comfortable chair and settled down with him to listen and to tell her own tale of all that had happened.

Chapter Forty-One

Angelica found Rodrigo waiting for her near the west wall of the city, silhouetted before the stars. Tall and handsome, dressed in tight black pants with silver buttons down each side, that flared at the knee, and a white shirt embroidered with a rainbow of threads, he made her feel suddenly shy. They had been apart for so long that he seemed suddenly like a stranger. A virile, awe-inspiring stranger. She felt nervous and tongue-tied. All she could manage to say was "Rodrigo!" in a small, choked voice.

He whirled around, seemingly as bereft of words as she. All he could do was stare. His breath caught in his throat as he stared at her loveliness. Her hair was haloed in the moonlight and hung in soft waves down her back, the fine structure of her facial bones made her look fragile and very, very beautiful. She looked like the angel he remembered, though even more beautiful than the vision that had haunted his dreams. Reverently he worshiped her with his eyes, the long curve of her neck, the lips that were now curved in a smile, the large blue eyes which shone with love.

"Angelica!"

"I'm . . . I'm sorry that I am so late . . ." she managed to say. "Edward has been watching me like a hawk." She tugged at her skirt nervously. "Luisa exchanged clothes with me and gave me her mantilla to wear so that I could slip away." She laughed nervously. "At this moment she is pretending to be me, huddled under the bedcovers feigning a headache-induced sleep."

"You look beautiful in that pink dress. Soft and glowing, like a rose . . ." She was framed in the moonlight, the soft swell of her breasts as they strained against the bodice of the dress teasing his eyes. Desire choked him as he took a step forward.

Rodrigo's throat went dry as she returned his stare. She was mesmerized by the potency of his stare. In his face she read her own longing. She started to say something, to thank him for his compliment, but the words failed her. All she could do was run to his arms and seek the warmth and comfort of him as he cradled her tenderly.

"Por Dios, Angelica. *Querida."* He buried his face in her hair, content for just a moment to do nothing else but hold her. The night air was cool yet she trembled for a far different reason. "Cold?" He tightened their embrace. The stars were full and bright, the sky untouched by clouds. The trees swayed very gently in the night breeze.

"I'm not cold . . . Oh, Rodrigo, I thought you were dead! I thought my brother had killed you . . . and . . . and then when Margaro came to the Mission . . . but . . . but my brother . . . and I thought . . . I feared."

"Hush. Hush, *querida.* Everything is all right now. We are together." He looked down at her, touching her with his eyes before his lips met hers in a deep, probing kiss. His mouth was hungry as it claimed hers, his lips and tongue urgent.

Angelica returned his kisses, her lips parting as she welcomed the sweet bolt of fire that always jolted her whenever he made love to her. She was trembling in his arms, on fire for him, wanting to savor the raging desire that overflowed her as he ran his hands up and down the curves of her body. She was like the long-slumbering volcano, Popocatepetl but now, as she felt the heat and strength of his growing desire, she was awakening to her own long-suppressed passion.

Angelica surrendered to him totally, twining her hands around his neck, holding him tightly as if fearful that he would somehow slip away from her, elude her like her haunting dreams. She was afraid to close her eyes for fear he might vanish and she find out it was nothing but a dream. "Rodrigo . . ." His name was prayer on her lips. As her eyes met his gaze she saw the passion in the endless blue depths of his gaze.

Groaning, he pulled away from her. "If only we could be alone." His voice was husky, regretful. "But we cannot make love here without fear of being taken unawares. Our love is much too precious to share with any watching eyes."

"I'm willing to take the chance."

"But I am not. There are soldiers in the area who would be much too tempted by your beauty. I would not want to fight the entire Mexican Army for my own wife!" His smile was rueful.

"Have we no place to go?" She certainly could not take him back to the inn. It would be suicide. Her brother would take the greatest pleasure in stirring up trouble, not to mention what Bonita might do. "You could take me to your camp . . ."

"I have no camp. Only a pitiful, broken down hovel where Margaro and I sleep."

"Take me there."

"No! It is no place for you. It is totally unacceptable. I would be shamed." It was little more than a shack in the poorer section of the city. Margaro and Rodrigo had found it a haven of safety, for the *mendigos* had a code of honor that forbade betraying anyone considered a friend. "The bed is lumpy, the roof leaks. It is . . ."

329

"It will be a paradise if we are there together." She reached for his hand, squeezing it tightly. "Please . . ."

"Angelica . . . !" Her name was muffled as he spoke it against her mouth. His hand slid beneath the neckline of her dress to close over her firm, high breast. His calloused fingers teased her sensitive flesh, relishing the feel of her. "*Dios*, you would tempt a saint as I am tempted . . ."

"Take me there . . ." She wanted him with a fierce passion that was foreign to her usually docile nature. There was nothing in the world except his hands caressing her, his mouth doing wondrous things to her lips and tongue. At that moment she would have risked anything, braved rain, sleet, or the desert sun to have him make love to her. Palace or hovel, she didn't care.

"All right, but we must be careful not to be seen by your brother or any of his men."

He took the white lace mantilla from her shoulders and secured it around her pale-blond hair, then, reaching for her hand, led her from the clearing, past the city gate to the plaza. Moving quickly past an old *cantina*. It was a dangerous time to be walking, with the soldiers lurking about. Several times he pulled Angelica with him into the shadows as he spied the red, blue, and white uniform of a Mexican soldier or the stark white of the peon soldiers. Moving in a crouch, he led her past a clattering carriage.

At last they came to a tiny adobe building and Rodrigo pushed their way inside. The door squeaked from the rust on its hinges. Inside it was dark and dank yet with Rodrigo beside her Angelica failed to notice the hut's imperfections. As her eyes adjusted and she looked about the room, her eyes were drawn to the bed. The bed was old, made of leather straps tacked to a framework of two-by-fours and covered with a straw mattress. There was a tilting table, two wooden chairs, and a pottery washbasin. Also inside were the books and paintings that she recognized as belonging to Rodrigo.

"Rodrigo . . . you got them back!" Moonlight shone through the one lone window illuminating them.

"That was how I knew where you were. The old man told me. Once they were my most treasured possessions, now they are special because they led me to you." He closed the door, positioning a chair and table in front of it. "To insure against Margaro's intrusion. When he tries to open the door he will know . . ." He stepped to her, his hands encircling her waist, his fingers tracing a sensuous pattern across her neck and shoulder. "I could stand looking at you forever."

Her nearness was a healing thing, washing away all the pain and bitterness the last months had brought him. He gazed down at her face, tracing her features with the fingers of his left hand as if to memorize them. "Dreams of you are what kept me alive. Margaro dragged a half-dead man from the camp, had given me up for dead, but the hope of seeing you again gave me the fortitude to fight death. Even in the darkness of that jail I'd see your face and know that somehow I had to find the patience to keep my sanity." She started to speak but his fingers silenced her. "You are so precious to me, *querida!*"

Rodrigo's hands closed about her shoulders, pulling her down with him to sit on the bed. They talked for a while, reacquainting themselves with each other. They had been separated for a long time and in some ways being here together was like making love for the first time. Rodrigo felt the need to woo Angelica all over again and did with soft words and gentle caresses.

Angelica lay back on the bed and watched as Rodrigo pulled off his boots and removed his shirt. He was even more magnificent than she remembered. The bronze skin on his hard-muscled shoulders glowed in the moonlight, rippling as he moved. Only the faint reminder of his scars gave hint of all that he had gone through.

Angelica's hands fumbled at the buttons of her bodice,

freeing herself of the cumbersome material. Her face flushed at the all-consuming need she felt to be naked against him, to feel the strength and potency of his love. "I never dreamed love could be so . . . so . . ." In sudden shyness, she averted her eyes.

"So powerful? Stirring?" Bending down, he lent his fingers to aid her in slipping the skirt and bodice from her body. He knelt at her feet and removed her shoes and stockings, then tugged at the strap of her chemise. He let his eyes drop to her full breasts, then to her slender waist and flaring hips. "Oh, *querida*, I burn for you!"

He kissed her and drew her closer, feeling her shudder, then with a smile he stepped away to remove his trousers. Angelica caught her breath as her gaze traveled from his shoulders to his rib cage. His long, muscular legs gave proof of his strength as did his manhood, erect and proud. Angelica hurried to discard her chemise, pantalettes, and corsellete, then held out her arms to him. Rodrigo enveloped her, embracing her, caressing her, kissing her feverishly as their bodies embraced intimately. Her hair was soft and pleasant against his eager flesh and he buried his face in her hair, whispering her name over and over again.

His warmth and power, straining so hungrily against her, filled her with an aching pleasure, a sweet pain curling deep inside her belly. Her arms crept around his neck, her fingers tangling in his hair. She opened to him as he rose over her, his manhood seeking, then finding her softness. They moved with the grace of those entranced in a dance. It was as if at that moment their hearts rose up to embrace, touching as fervently as their bodies were entwined. Merging. Blending. Loving. He was strong and powerful, yet he was gentle. Ardent, yet tender as he guided her to the heights of passion. Together they made love as the night shattered into a hundred stars, experiencing the blaze of fulfillment. They were a man and a woman coming together with passion, desire, love, and ultimate joy. There were no more words needed for the rhythm of their passion, the meeting of their eyes said all that needed to be said. She loved him and he loved her and no one could ever part them again.

They lay quiet after their explosive lovemaking. Then Rodrigo propped himself on his elbow, lying on his side, looking down at Angelica almost reverently. He smoothed the tangled hair away from her face, trying to discern her fathomless expression. "What are you thinking, *querida?*"

Nestled in the strength of his arms, she tried to smile but the expression was more of a grimace. "I want to stay here with you, never to leave, but I know that if I did Edward would move heaven and earth to find me. He has a way of arousing people. He would go straight to the authorities and have them hunting you. As it is, he doesn't even know you are here." She sighed. "I was thinking how much I wish I could close my eyes for just a minute and open them to find ourselves back at the camp. We were so happy then, despite Bonita's tampering. If not for my brother I think we could have been content . . ."

"No! Not as long as I was a bandit. We would have been living with a gun to my head, knowing that at any moment I might be captured, that I would not come home from a raid." Taking her hand, he kissed her palm, then looked deep into her eyes. "I want something much better for you, Angelica. I want to make love, to plant my seed in your belly and know that I will be there to nurture it, to watch it grow." He groaned, burying his face in the warmth and softness of her breasts.

"I want that too. I want your child."

"If I could only be exonerated from my prior banditing! If only there was a way so I did not have to look behind me every time I walked down the street. Fear that someone would see my image on a poster and turn me in for the reward. I want to give you the world and watch you reach out for it. I want you to have a husband and not a fugitive lover who must part from you after our brief times together. I want to wake and find you beside me . . ."

"I love you just the way you are. Being with you for one night, one hour is enough. It has to be . . ." Putting her arms around him, she pulled herself up to his kiss, showing him with the caress of her lips how deeply she cared. Desire sweet and warm flowed through them, encompassing them once more, but Rodrigo pulled away.

"You must go. As you said, your brother . . ." Gathering his clothing together he dressed as quickly as he had shed his garments, then stood up. "I will take you back, though I wish in my heart that I could take you by the hand and flee this city."

"Why can't we? Why can't we take Margaro and run away? We could go back to California and . . ." Angelica's voice was a whisper.

"The California we knew is gone. It is in the undisputed military possession of the United States." He crossed his arms across his chest, scowling.

"But Edward said that the Californians had won it back." Angelica pulled her chemise over her head with an impatient tug, then looked up at him.

"Their show of courage was belated. They thought that being under *americano* rule would be preferable to Mexican domination but the men who took over the city openly showed their disdain for anyone not of pure Anglo blood." Rodrigo's tone of voice showed his anger.

Angelica remembered witnessing the instinctive feeling of superiority the people of her race displayed. A condescending, often contemptuous attitude. They forgot how long the Spanish culture had flourished or that the Spaniards and their missions had carved beauty into the wilderness.

"But they took up arms against the invaders. Southern California was the main battleground for the insurrection.

The Californians quickly won a series of triumphs, pushing a small American force from Los Angeles and winning a brief skirmish twenty-five miles to the east. I heard that one hundred Californians with one cannon repelled an attempt by four hundred Americans to recapture Los Angeles. It was all that Edward talked about a few months ago. He would have returned to California if not for the fact that he is a wanted man and feared he might be captured when he crossed the border." Her eyes were questioning. "How then . . . ?"

"A General Kearny arrived from New Mexico and in union with other American forces won a victory. Perhaps had General Pico acted quickly . . ." Rodrigo shook his head. "But it does no good to reflect. Besides, to the Californians and the Mexicans I am wanted. By this time the *americanos* too will have seen my wanted posters and will be on the lookout for me."

"Maybe not!" A glimmer of hope shone in her eyes. "Perhaps there is a chance . . ."

Rodrigo was afraid to hope. "More likely there is not."

"But we have to try." She laughed quietly. "I wonder what Edward will do when he finds out he was on the wrong side. He was so certain that Mexico would win this war that he's been selling guns and ammunition to General Paredes. He will probably change sides in the wink of an eye. Ah, such loyalty. Certainly it is touching."

"Most touching." Rodrigo tried to smile. He watched as she dressed. "And then he will take you away with him."

"I won't go! It's as simple as that. I could go to one of the missions. Then we could go to Monterrey or Buena Vista or perhaps Veracruz."

"No, it is much too dangerous. The Americans are swarming as thick as flies there. I will not put you in any danger."

"Then what are we going to do?" Running to him she threw her arms about his neck feeling a sense of desolation. They were trapped in this desperate, stupid war.

"I don't know. But I will think of something. Until that time I want you to be very careful. Your brother offers at least a measure of safety for you here in this tumultuous city at the moment, but if it appears that he is being foolish, or risks your safety in any way, I want you to leave him immediately. Pronto. And come here. When we go back to your inn I will show you the shortest, quickest way here." He cupped her chin in his hand. "Until I think of a plan, *chica*, we must be content with an occasional meeting. This poor excuse for a house will be our love nest, eh? I am little more than a peon but I am rich in love."

"And that is all that matters. I don't care about anything except our love, Rodrigo." She ran her hands over his chest, longing for him again. "Edward is a very sound sleeper. He never wakes before eight o'clock in the morning. By this time he thinks I am in bed. I could stay here for a little while longer. It's hard to say when we will be together again . . ."

"Mmm." He nuzzled her ear. "I have only one thing to say on that matter, wife."

"And just what is that?"

"That we dressed much too quickly. Tonight there is a lover's moon in the sky. This time I want to watch your face when we make love." He smiled as she blushed and drew her once again down on the bed.

Chapter Forty-Two

Luisa tugged at Angelica's hair, putting the final touch to her upswept hairdo. The long pale-blond waves were held in place by pins and an ornately Spanish comb set with clusters of pearls. Adjusting a black lace mantilla over Angelica's head, she stepped back to view her handiwork and clucked her tongue triumphantly.

"No señor or señorita ever looked more grand. Edward certainly didn't spare any money when he told you to buy yourself a new dress. You look like the wife of the finest grandee in all of Mexico."

"Rodrigo *is* the finest grandee!" Angelica adjusted the bodice of her dark-blue and black flower-patterned dress. It was all planned. Tonight she, Margaro and Rodrigo were leaving the city to go to Veracruz, far from the reaches of her brother. It had taken much persuasion on her part to convince Rodrigo, but at last she was to have her way.

They had met every night during the past week at his hut; enjoying delicious nights of love, forgetting for a time their peril. Rodrigo had been stubborn, as usual putting her safety above his own happiness, but little by little Angelica had made him see the feasibility of her idea, to disguise themselves as wealthy Spaniards, hire a carriage and travel the road to Veracruz in style. Who would ever

337

suspect that the carriage hid two wanted men? Rodrigo would be dressed like a grandee and Margaro like his servant. Perched atop the carriage as the driver, Margaro would keep his guns hidden in case there was any sign of trouble.

To allay her brother's suspicions, Angelica had been as docile as a lamb the past few days, obeying his every word. Edward had been so pleased that he had rewarded her with a new fan, one with inlaid mother of pearl. She thought with a slight smile that in his way he was aiding her escape, for she would use the fan to hide her face when she made her way through Mexico City's darkened streets to her appointed meeting place with Rodrigo.

"You be careful, Angelica . . ." Luisa adjusted the comb, then busied her fingers lacing up Angelica's bodice. "There are soldiers along the road and . . ."

"Rodrigo has given me the very same warning over and over again. I will be careful, I promise." She squeezed Rodrigo's sister's hand affectionately. "And . . . and thank you for being my friend. Without you pretending to be me these past several days Rodrigo and I would never have had the precious time we shared." Angelica met Luisa's eyes. "I wish . . . I wish that after I go, you and Jesse would make up. His being with my brother is out of his desire to help the Californians and not out of loyalty to Edward. Jesse did what he thought was best. Sometimes decisions are complicated and a person can't do exactly what they would . . ."

"We have made up!" A flush started at Luisa's cheeks and spread over her entire face as she confided, "I made use of those times when you were gone to spend time with him. We . . . well . . . well, his bed is so hard and this one so soft that . . ."

"I'm so glad!" The two young women stood for a long moment, then embraced each other. "Be happy, Luisa. Jesse is a good man. As fine a man as Rodrigo."

"I will be and you also. I know my brother can be as hard-headed as a mule at times but he loves you. Someday, when this war is all over, we will all meet again and you will have so many stories to tell me that . . ." Both were startled as the door was flung open. Edward Howe stood in the doorway.

"Well, Angie . . ." His eyes roamed over her questioningly and for a moment she feared all her carefully wrought plans were to be ruined. Blessed God, if he suspected what she was up to Rodrigo would be in terrible danger. Worse yet, she would be put under lock and key and never see Rodrigo again.

"I hope you are pleased with my new dress and mantilla, Edward." Taking a deep breath, Angelica stepped forward with a carefully etched smile. "You are always telling me the importance of being accepted by the people of respectability who can be of influence to you, and at last I have conceded." She twirled around, letting him inspect her dress. "Do you like it?"

"Of course I like it. You . . . you look lovely, Angie." He grinned. "I couldn't be more pleased. It's about time you stopped mooning over that damned bandit bastard and got some sense. Why, there are hundreds of men down here who would be aching to ask me for your hand." He whistled. "I told you to throw away those stupid spectacles and to dress in style. You are really something. And to think I wanted you to become a nun. That was foolish of me."

Yes, foolish, Angelica thought sourly, when you think you can use me to further your own ends. It was difficult to maintain her smile but somehow she did. "There are so many handsome men in the city, how could I not be tempted." She caught herself, adding, "Luisa and I watch them pass from our window. Once in a while we even wave at the most dapperly dressed *caballero*." She affected a giggle and Luisa mocked her with a mischievous glint in her eyes.

Edward grunted, "Yeah, well, I hope you can make use of your wiles tonight. We're having dinner with a very important man of the city, a cousin of Santa Anna himself."

"Santa Anna?" From all she had heard he was a scoundrel but then she supposed it wasn't surprising that her brother would align himself with such a man. Santa Anna had caused quite a stir in Mexico a decade ago, she remembered. His name had been mentioned over and over again when anyone spoke of the Alamo. He had been living in exile in Havana, devoting most of his attention to cockfights and his lovely seventeen-year-old bride, it was said when he had been approached by the United States to return to Mexico. They had paid him millions in hope that he would aid them in winning the war, and so like a bad penny he had landed at Veracruz then traveled on to Mexico City. He had been handed the government by the popular acclaim of the Mexican people who had forgiven his past blunders in hopes that he could help them beat the Americans. Hardly a man to revere.

"I'm hoping to arrange a meeting with him. He needs guns and I can get them for him." At Angelica's incredulous look he added, "I'm going to try my hand at blocade-running!"

"You'll get yourself killed and all for what. The Americans are going to win this war, Edward." He was her brother. She didn't want him to die.

"The Americans have had a few victories, I will admit, but they won't win the war. They are up against one of the greatest armies in the world. Besides, they have to win or you and I will be tilling the soil down here for the rest of our lives as peasants!" He gave her a push for the door. "I was going to tell you to get ready, but since you are we'll go right now to Señor Gutierrez's *casa*."

"But I'm not quite ready. I . . . I . . ." She didn't want to

340

go with him. Rodrigo was going to meet her in a half hour. Somehow she had to stall.

"You look fine. I won't let you primp and fuss for another hour like some damned women do." That he meant Bonita was obvious by his frown. She spent hours preening and had nearly driven Edward into poverty with her demands. Angelica suspected that Edward's fascination with the woman was waning but he wasn't certain how he could rid himself of her. Bonita knew too much for him to cast her off easily. For the moment her place as his mistress was undeniably secure.

"But, Edward . . ." The pressure on the small of her back told her he would brook no resistance. "All right. I suppose I will have to keep my hair just as it is . . ." Her eyes gave Luisa a silent message to find Rodrigo and tell him what had happened. Their departure from the city would have to be detained but not postponed. It was five o'clock now. She knew her brother would be in his cups by seven or eight and then she would be able to safely slip away. So thinking, she held up her fingers, declaring the appointed time.

Following her brother out the door and down the stairs, she once more feigned obedience. Once inside the carriage, she allowed herself the leisure of examining it in detail. There were barred doors of a porte-cochère and a grilled peephole that would allow Rodrigo and herself a great deal of privacy as they traveled. Yes, it would be perfect. Hopefully Margaro would be most persuasive in obtaining one like this.

The carriage rumbled to a stop before an imposing gray stone building with red Spanish tile roof. Surrounded by an adobe wall and a forest of nopal cactus, the lawn took up an acre or so. Tall trees huddled protectively around the house as did several uniformed guards. As the carriage door was opened one guard stepped away from the red iron gate, his rifle prepared should he find the occupants foe and not friend. A difficult place from which to slip away, Angelica thought in alarm, and yet she must somehow manage.

"Ah, Señor Howe. It is good to see an amigo." The man's gap-toothed grin spread over his face. "You are expected inside."

"Why such tight security? What has happened?" Edward was slow to descend from the carriage, moving cautiously.

"Ah, it is nothing. Nothing. Well . . . everyone here is on edge. Nervous, you understand. There are those who are worried and therefore overly cautious. Now I think it will only be a matter of time before we push them out but . . ."

"What are you talking about?"

"The *americanos*. A General Scott has captured the port of Veracruz. I am surprised you have not already heard. The city was verging on chaos a few hours ago when the news was reported. There was a five-day naval bombardment that left over half the city in blackened ruins." He detailed the story to an apprehensive and glowering Edward. Two weeks after a supposed victory at Buena Vista, in which Santa Anna had taken a few captured flags and called it a triumph, the citizens of Veracruz had seen the American general's men coming ashore in specially built surfboats. The city was a fortress and had stood up to more than two weeks of bombardment by field artillery and naval ships lying at anchor in the bay. "The people felt honored that the *americanos* would make war on civilians, and so they were inspired. Women made bandages out of bed sheets for the wounded. Every capable man enlisted in the National Guard, but . . ." The guard shrugged.

"And . . . ?" Edward was growing increasingly more irritated, Angelica more disappointed. What were the

342

chances of escaping with Rodrigo now? Surely security would be doubled on the roads that led to Veracruz.

"When it was over Veracruz belonged to the new invaders. I heard a cousin who was there told his sister, who whispered the news to a friend of mine, that the citizens watched in pain and foreboding."

"So Veracruz is in American hands."

"*Sí.* But that is not all. There are messages that say that the Americans have started marching up the steep, winding National Road which runs the many, many miles between Veracruz and Mexico City. Is it any wonder people are annoyed?" He managed a slight strut. "I do not believe they will do it. They would have to be *loco*, these *americanos*. But apparently Santa Anna is not so certain. He is on his way to Mexico City to calm the people."

"Santa Anna is on his way here?" Edward saw a chance to perhaps make a profit out of the city's distress after all. "When will he be here?"

"Any day."

Angelica could nearly see the wheels turning in her brother's head as he concentrated on furthering his own aims. She saw him fish about in his pockets, at last palming a twenty-dollar gold piece. Placing it in the surprised guard's hand, he said, "I will give you more if you advise me of the exact time he arrives."

"Ah . . ." The guard bit down on the large coin then grinned. "I will tell you the very *moment* he arrives." He led them up the cobbled walk to the door where a brightly dressed majordomo welcomed them with a stiff bow. He ushered them into a mammoth room with gilded ceilings and a marble floor. The velvet-covered settees and lavish decorations indicated the owner of the *casa's* wealth. "I will tell the señor that you are here."

As soon as he had turned his back, Edward faced her, his manner stern yet pleading. "You must help me tonight, Angie. I need Señor Gutierrez's good will. That's one

343

reason why I brought you with me and not Bonita. Bonita is beautiful but she is at heart a whore. You will dazzle him, charm him. He is said to have a penchant for beautiful women. If you aid me in this I will be grateful. More so than you will ever know. If I am successful, if he decides to become my patron I will see that you benefit."

"No more shackles?" She cocked a brow.

"I will allow you to come and go as you please. But if you anger me . . ." He clenched his jaw. "Somehow, someway I have to think of a way Santa Anna can whip the Americans. If I do and help him to attain more power than he ever dreamed possible, we will both be doubly rewarded."

To help you become an even worse traitor than you already are, she thought but only smiled. There was no more time to talk as a tall, cadaverously thin man in burnished splendor made his way down the red-carpeted stairway. His silver hair shone in the light of the chandeliers as he took her hand and kissed it.

"So this is your lovely sister of whom you have spoken?" Despite his polite manners, he openly leered, leaving no doubt about the conversation he had had with her brother. "You brighten my humble home with your luminescence." His fingers were cold and clammy as he placed her hand on his arm and led her to the dining room. All Angelica could think of was how quickly she wanted to get away from this house, her brother, and this man. She would have to be very careful but their host's intentions made her leaving quickly decidedly imperative.

Chapter Forty-Three

Five lamps, their wicks turned up to full blaze, illuminated the haughty, angry face of the woman staring in the mirror at her image. "Edward Howe is a pig. *El puerco!*" she spat in fury. Leaving her behind tonight as if she were no more than his *cantina* whore! Taking that pale-faced *gorrión* of a sister with him in *her* place. Ha! "As if he were shamed by me. As if he feared I would disgrace him before his important friends," she muttered.

Bonita was disappointed beyond tears. She had overheard Edward talking to the red-haired *americano* about his invitation to the *casa* of Santa Anna's cousin and she had been thrilled at the prospect of at last being treated in the manner she deserved. She had looked forward to tonight, had even bought a new dress—red with black lace that clung to her well-bosomed form. She had spent hours before this very mirror only to find that Edward had gone without her, taking the silly, dowdy Angelica instead.

"I should have poisoned her while I had the chance," she mumbled, drenching her hands with perfume and spreading it over her neck and the globes of her half-naked breasts. "Edward would not have minded. She is useless. A nuisance. We would all be well rid of her!" She regretted now that she had failed. Had she known that once more the sniveling, always praying gringo woman would stand in her way, she would have moved more quickly to remove her permanently from her path. Now she wished that she had.

Bonita touched a glittering earring. Edward had up to this time been very useful to her in giving her the things that she wanted. He was an ardent lover, though at times a bit too rough even for her. He was insatiable, bringing her to fulfillment time and time again. Handsome. At times generous. His ambition promised to make him a very successful man, even if he made a few mistakes in judgment. The dinner tonight at the Gutierrez *casa* was proof of that. Even so, there were times when her body craved another man's touch. Rodrigo! She had never really gotten over him. Though she had wanted him dead, had raged at him, had betrayed him, she couldn't get him out of her mind. There were times when she closed her eyes during Edward's lovemaking and imagined it to be Rodrigo, kissing her, stroking her, only to know the pang of disappointment. No man had ever made her fly to the stars as Rodrigo had. What she would not have given to have him back as her lover again.

But he was that yellow-haired gringa's husband, and that rankled her beyond bearing. At first, on the way back from the camp the night of Edward's raid, she had felt triumphant, then sad at the thought of Rodrigo's heart stilled forever. Vengeance was a two-edged swored and she had suffered its prick. Then she had overheard Edward's mumblings, his frenzied nightmares of facing the bandit leader again. It was the first time she had learned of the possibility that Rodrigo might be alive. Alive to return to his wife! That angry thought had plagued her and she had sent a few of Edward's men in search of him. They had not disappointed her. But then Rodrigo had escaped. The missive had annoyed her, for she had held the fantasy of becoming the grandest lady in Mexico City, a wealthy, splendorously dressed woman who would return for him and show him her mercy by having him released.

But he had seemingly vanished, though she often wondered if Edward's sister knew his whereabouts. It was a question which had pricked at her the last two days after seeing Angelica return mysteriously one afternoon. She had been tempted to tell Edward but had relented, thinking perhaps the information might be more useful to hold back. "Now I would not tell him anything. *Bastardo!*" she grumbled.

Picking up a hairbrush, she stroked the strands so violently that her head ached, then pulled her hair back in a bun. She would go to the *casa* tonight, invited or uninvited. Once she was there she would challenge Edward to have her thrown out. What could he do once she was there? The thought intrigued her. And perhaps she might even find another man more important than he to share her bed? Perhaps Señor Gutierrez himself. What potent revenge. She would be late, but what would it matter if her entrance dazzled everyone there?

Bonita laughed softly to herself as she put the finishing touches on her toilette, fastened her gown, and adjusted her lace mantilla. Around her neck she clasped a sparkling necklace which looked like rubies but were only paste. No one would know, and the red fire flashed against her golden skin, emphasizing the beauty of her neck.

"I will make Edward's sister look like a colorless moth!" she declared to her reflection in the mirror, licking her lips. She would have the very last laugh and see what the night brought. Flouncing from the room she ran down the stairs and hailed a carriage.

Chapter Forty-Four

Flames flickered in the wall sconces and chandeliers, illuminating the silver and gold dishes that were piled high with food. Sitting between an officer of the Mexican Army whose gilt epaulettes glittered in the light and Señor Gutierrez, Angelica was very uncomfortable. The hours were passing so slowly. She wanted to be far from this room, in Rodrigo's arms, but with every eye in the room watching her she had had no way of escaping. What made her even more frustrated were Señor Gutierrez's blatant advances. He rubbed his knee against her leg, pinched her beneath the table, made use of every excuse he could to touch her. Even so simple a thing as passing a glass platter piled with well-spiced beef was used to his advantage, his elbow rubbing against the tip of her breast. Another time she would have rebuked him, but fearing to cause a scene and therefore anger her brother, Angelica merely smiled. Let the old lecher fantasize. As soon as it was possible she would flee.

"I hear this General Zachary Taylor, this 'Rough and Ready' *americano* is an uncouth barbarian," the officer at her left was saying.

"Indeed. He and those 'Los Diablos Tejanos,' those devil Texans, are frightening the soul out of the poor peasants. Monterrey, Saltillo, Veracruz . . . where will it all end?" A sour-faced Spanish matron waved her fan frantically.

Gutierrez stopped his ogling at Angelica long enough to answer, "A few fortunate victories. Luck only. My cousin is en route to the city to raise an army that will squash the *americanos* like bugs. He has it in mind to meet them at Cerro Gordo. Such a narrow pass that not even a rabbit can get through." He laughed merrily, obviously certain that his cousin would win the battle.

Angelica was not so sure. She had heard that the frontiersmen and Texans fighting on the American side were fearsome, frightening when they hooted their rebel yell. She felt a faint prick of pride despite her self-declared neutrality on the matter. She hated to see the Mexicans run off land they had held for years yet she hoped that the invading Americans would be fair. When this fighting was over, the two peoples would have to learn to live together in peace and tranquility. If they could not then what hope was there for humanity? If on the other hand, the Californians won she could not help but think that the experience of what was happening would make them better able to govern themselves.

"What do you think, Señorita Howe? I understand you once lived in residence at the Santa Barbara Mission. Do you think the *americanos* will be just to the Indians? We have allowed them the security of the missions but if . . . if the worst happens and the *americanos* win, do you think they will do the same?"

"What . . . ?" Angelica was still surprised that he had addressed her by the title of an unmarried woman to hear the rest of what he had said. So Edward had been up to his little games. No doubt he had sold her to this old man for the assurance of patronage. How much had he found her to be worth? How many pesos?"

"What is your opinion of missions and Indians if the

350

americanos by some dastardly miracle win the war?" He patted her hand. "Ah, just like a woman to be more concerned with happy artless chatter than matters so serious. We will talk of other, more pleasant things." He reached for his tall-stemmed goblet, plucking it up for a toast. "To women," he said. "To beautiful women. *Dios,* how they make this world such a much better place to live."

Angelica saw her chance to get out of the room. As Gutierrez raised the glass to his lips, she bumped his arm, sending the contents of his goblet splashing all over the front of her dress. "Oh . . . !" Putting her hand to her mouth, she pretended distress. "My new dress . . . it . . . it will be ruined. I'm drenched!"

Gutierrez was embarrassedly horrified. Taking his napkin he dabbed at the wine stain. "I am sorry, señorita. I am clumsy. Stupid. Forgive me."

"The fabric will be ruined if I don't wash it out at once." Angelica rose to her feet, touching his arm caressingly. "And I wanted to look pretty for you." The words sounded ridiculously phony but he seemed pleased. As she worked her way around the seated figures of the guests, he boldly winked. Pausing in the doorway, fearful lest Edward follow her, she was relieved to see him immersed in concentrated discussion. Her ruse had been successful.

Walking quickly through the *sala,* nodding to the majordomo as she passed through the archway, she made her way to the front door. Pushing it open, she breathed in the fragrant night air. She boldly approached one of the guards and told him of the headache that made it necessary for her to return to her rooms at once.

"Of course, Señorita Howe." He was very obliging, even going so far as to signal for the carriage, take her by the arm, open the door, and help her into the vehicle. As he did so, another carriage pulled up alongside. It was Angelica's misfortune that Bonita was nestled inside, peering out the

351

window. Spying Edward's sister leaving without him piqued her curiosity. Suddenly, making her grand entrance at the *casa* was unimportant.

"You. Driver. Follow that carriage. Discreetly, *por favor*, so they do not know that we are behind them, eh?" She tapped her fan on the side of the carriage. *"Date prisa!"*

Unaware of the danger that lurked behind her, Angelica leaned out the window, staring ahead as the carriage left the Gutierrez estate, passing several other *casas* before coming to the area where the church domes and spires rose high in the air. It was seven o'clock. She knew that Rodrigo and Margaro would still be at the hut, and asking the driver to stop the carriage, she walked the four long blocks, past the market to the poor section of town. Seeing Rodrigo's hut from a distance, she gave a sigh of relief that there was a light in the room and ran the rest of the way.

Both he and Margaro were inside. If they had grown impatient with waiting they didn't show it. Rodrigo rose from the wooden bench by the door to enfold her in his embrace. "I was worried, *querida*. I thought perhaps you might be unable to get away." He ground out the cigarillo he had been smoking with the toe of his boot, then concentrated on her. Lifting her chin with his finger he kissed her gently. "You look *bella. Bella*, Angelica." His hands caressed her as Margaro coughed gently and turned his back. Rodrigo pulled back in surprise. "Your dress, it is wet."

"It's a long story. Let me just say that the cause of the accident allowed me to escape. Wine."

"Wine?"

"I initiated the spill so that I could leave the room and now I am here. I hope I have not come in vain, Rodrigo. Have you heard that the Americans have taken over Veracruz?"

"Yes. To my way of thinking it is going to be very

dangerous. Perhaps, however, the *americanos* will not be as relentless as their Mexican and California counterparts, eh? Though I hate to see the city of my grandmother's birth overrun, it is better for us."

"Then we are still going to go?" Angelica had been afraid that he was going to decide otherwise.

"I will leave it up to you. You are a woman of courage, but can you accept whatever happens? If the worst happens and I am captured and shot, can you . . ."

"Never! That will never happen. It must not." She was suddenly scared. "I couldn't live without you, Rodrigo. Not having known such happiness these last few days. I lost you once but never again!"

Throwing her arms around his neck, she clung to him and Margaro, peeking at the couple over his shoulder, smiled. He wanted happiness for these two. Most certainly they deserved it, he thought.

"I have bribed a carriage driver to meet us at seven-thirty at the fountain," he mumbled. "Several pesos. I told him that I wanted to impress a very wealthy señorita. He thinks I will just be borrowing it for a few hours. By the time he realizes, we will be far, far away." His tone was regretful. "I hope he does not face very much trouble. I would hate for him to be too severely punished."

"What time is it now?" The chiming, ringing bells answered. Seven o'clock. It was not as late as Angelica had first supposed. "We have twenty minutes to wait."

"What if Edward suspects?" It concerned Angelica that he might search the Gutierrez household, and not finding her might think to question the carriage driver. She fidgeted nervously.

"He would have to search the entire city. He would never find you here. Unless you were followed? You weren't, were you, *querida?*"

"No! I came by carriage and I instructed the drive to stop several blocks from here." He looked so handsome in the

353

lamplight that she could not help but stare. His trousers were cut in the Spanish style, nearly too tight over his muscular thighs, the white ruffled shirtfront contrasting with the dark golden skin of his face. The fine broadcloth of his black jacket fit smoothly over his shoulders. Who would ever suspect he had once been the most notorious bandit in the West? Even she found it hard to believe.

"You are certain no one followed you. Not the driver or any soldiers . . . ?" At her vehement assurance he smiled. "Then we are safe, for no one would ever guess that you were in such a humble *hacienda*." His breath tickled her ear as he whispered, "Someday I will give you much better than this. Someday."

Their silhouettes were etched against the light of the window as they shared a passionate kiss. From where she stood a short distance away, Bonita snarled in anger as she watched. Such hatred welled inside her that she was nearly poisoned by it. Rodrigo and his mate. Rodrigo and his wife. So, he had come to Mexico City to find his bride.

Well, we will see how content he is when he is put back inside a jail cell, she vowed. Oh, she would make a grand entrance at the *casa* tonight! She would have some very important news for this supposed cousin of Antonio Lopez de Santa Anna. Turning her back, she ran down the roadway, anxious to pull the snare on the two lovebirds who were cooing so contentedly inside their adobe nest.

354

Chapter Forty-Five

The guests at the Gutierrez *casa* were still at the table, partaking of chilled fruit and caramel pudding when Bonita swept through the door. Her gown drifted in deep flounces as she walked towards the table. The women stiffened at the sight of her décolletage and she smiled smugly. Cows! she thought. Every one of them. Cows whose silly, artless chatter reminded her of mooing. Well, she would soon show them.

"Bonita!" Edward's face was fused with anger at her intrusion. "What are you doing here? I told you . . ."

"Why, I came to take Angelica's place. It seems she has disappeared." Her eyes squinted her rage at him.

"She . . . she spilled some wine on her dress and went to wash it off." The way he kept looking at the door told of his anxiety at the length of time it was taking her to return. "As for you . . ."

"She is not washing off her dress. She is not even here! At this very moment she is making love to her husband in some dusty, broken-down adobe shack in the peons' part of town." She turned her attention to the man she immediately sensed was the host of the *casa*, offering him her most seductive smile. "Edward's sister is married to the bandit El Diablo!"

355

"No!" Miguel Gutierrez could not believe it. Such a soft, gentle, beautiful woman would never have married a bandit.

"It's true. But we have no time to stay here and argue the matter. If you hurry with your men you can capture him. I have no doubt but that there is a substantial reward in pesos being offered." Swaying her hips, she moved closer to her quarry. "Just think of the fame you will win then . . . but you must hurry!"

"A bandit!" Miguel Gutierrez looked daggers at Edward as he rose to his feet. "And to think I nearly soiled my reputation by taking up with the little *puta*." He motioned to several of the soldiers. "Come, and do as she bids you. Hurry! I am anxious to take a look at this infamous El Diablo!"

"I . . . I didn't know he was here, I swear it. My sister was foolishly naive. The marriage was all a mistake. I should have told you but it was such a trivial matter . . ." Edward glared at Bonita. She had ruined him, she and that hot blooded sister of his who stalked after that half-Mexican bastard like a bitch in heat. He snarled threateningly at her as he passed by but she returned his denunciations with a toss of her head. She was not afraid of him, nor was she sorry.

"I will lead the way," she exclaimed, passing in front of the men. She climbed inside a waiting carriage, pressing herself intimately close to Miguel Gutierrez. Let Edward go to the very devil, she had a far more influential lover in mind. "Gringos, bah!" she whispered.

It was a jolting ride over the cobblestones. At each lurch of the carriage Bonita skillfully threw herself in the arms of Gutierrez, brushing her breasts against his chest, looking coyly up at him. With a few smiles she ensnared him. Within the ten minutes it took to reach the marketplace she had him completely smitten with her. This time when the carriage bumped them together she didn't bother to pull away.

"The third hut to the right!" As the carriage pulled to a stop on the dusty, gravelly road Bonita watched from the safety of the window as her mischief was carried out.

Inside the hut Margaro saw the approaching soldiers and instinctively reached for his guns. Rodrigo, however, stilled his hand. "No! Don't shoot. Angelica might be harmed."

"Don't shoot? They are soldiers. I doubt most seriously that they are paying a social call, amigo. One. Four. Six. Ten of them. Must they bring an army to capture us, eh?"

Angelica clutched at his hand. "Oh, Rodrigo, why? Why now?" It was her fault. Somehow Edward had found her and now he was going to punish her by striking out at Rodrigo. Hopefully she ran toward the door, peering out. "Maybe they are looking for someplace for their soldiers to quarter. If we are cautious and don't do anything to alarm them, perhaps the only thing we will suffer is their company."

The sight of the gold-braided soldier who had sat beside her at dinner dashed her hopes. She knew full well what his presence meant and yet she would not accept the reality of it.

"No! No! Not when we have at last found peace, when we were so close to happiness . . ." Closing her eyes she whispered a prayer, then quickly opened them. She could not really expect God to interfere in this. He wouldn't. He hadn't before. When all was said and done He gave men courage and wisdom but seemingly left such matters into mortal hands.

Rodrigo watched as the soldiers swarmed through the door. Ensuring Angelica's safety, he held forth his guns and ammunition belt and barked out an order for Margaro to do the same.

"Which of you is El Diablo?" Pushing past the others, Gutierrez made his way inside, hissing the word "whore" at Angelica as he passed her. He was irritated at the situation, never a good loser in matters of the bedroom.

"I am El Diablo!" Seeking to protect his friend, hoping that were he to convince them that he was the wanted bandit Rodrigo might yet enjoy some happiness, Margaro stepped forward. "I am the one you are looking for."

"No!" Rodrigo could not let Margaro take his punishment. "I am El Diablo. This man is merely my servant."

"I *am* El Diablo!" Margaro jabbed Rodrigo in the ribs. "This man is but a young *caballero* having a bit of fun, thinking to make the acquaintance of a skilled bandit so that he can tell many a story around his banquet table."

Gutierrez was not amused. "Arrest them both in the name of General Antonio de Lopez Santa Anna, soon to be Presidente."

Angelica watched in horror as Rodrigo was poked and prodded with guns, then securely bound. It was as if her worst nightmares had suddenly materialized.

As they pushed Margaro and Rodrigo out the door, holding a torch to light the way, she ran after the soldiers. "Keep away!" one of them ordered.

"I won't! He is my husband and I intend to stay by his side. If that means sharing a jail cell with him, then that is exactly what I will do." Elbowing her way to Rodrigo, she rested her hand on his arm. "If he is guilty then so am I."

"Angelica, go back. I won't see you enmeshed in this. Whatever happens, remember that I love you now, have always loved you. *Por favor, querida.* Think of yourself . . ."

She ignored his pleas, walking beside him with her shoulders back, her chin held high, reminding Rodrigo of a carved figurehead. She was fearless in her love. Stubborn but so very appealing. He had never loved her more, yet even so he scolded, pleaded, begged her to change her mind. Angelica refused. The priest had bid her to obey her husband when he had spoken the wedding vows, yet there were other words spoken as well. To love, cherish, and be with him until death parted them. Angelica had made up her mind that only death could part them.

"Angelica . . ." Rodrigo's voice was a wail. His sweet, beautiful, brave angel was making a terrible sacrifice. All along the road he argued with her but to no avail. They were thrown into a small cell together, Margaro incarcerated in a similar cell adjoining theirs, all to await their fate.

It was stark black in the cell, with no windows to let in even a beam of moonlight and not even one candle lit. Rodrigo and Angelica lay side by side, cradled in each other's arms, listening to Margaro's snoring through the thin walls. Unlike them he slept soundly even at such a harrowing time as this.

"I wanted so much for you, Angelica, and what have I brought you to but this sorry plight. Caramba! What am I to do?" He had wracked his brain trying to think of a way to save them, at last admitting there was none. Bernardo or Najalayogua could not help him here.

"We'll see this through together, Rodrigo. I have to believe that things are not as dismal as they seem." She was determined to keep up his spirits, to be brave, but the truth was she was frightened. The sound of rifle fire coming from the courtyard outside made her remember stories about prisoners being shot before firing squads.

The walls were cold and damp, the stale odor of rotting straw assailed her nostrils. Clutching tightly to Rodrigo to share his warmth, she fought against her tears, tears not for herself but for him. He was at heart a good man, despite what he had done in the past. She had seen that for herself. He had been forced into the life of a bandit by one man's treacherous lies. They had talked over and over again of beginning a new life. Now he might never have the chance.

How had Rodrigo's hut been found tonight? She

pondered the question, blaming herself, but did it matter? What was important was doing everything possible to set him free. Edward she knew would not help, his resentment of Rodrigo ran too deep. Gutierrez? Not unless she was willing to barter her body for his favor. The Church? Therein lay a possibility. Perhaps Father Duran might help her if she could get a message to him. There were dozens of churches in the city to which she might turn for comfort and aid.

"You are quiet, so quiet. What are you thinking, *querida?* Are you sorry you came with me?"

"Never! I love you. Our love will free you somehow and . . ."

His kisses drowned out her words. Tomorrow was an uncertainty, but they had tonight to be together. Angelica's heart hammered so loudly that she feared it would awaken Margaro in the next cell, yet she needed his reassuring love, needed to feel his hard warmth against her, reassuring and strong. She moved against him in a manner that wrenched a groan from his throat. They couldn't waste any of the precious time they had together.

Reaching down without any trace of modesty, she pushed the bodice from her shoulders, baring her breasts to his touch. "So soft," he breathed, cupping her full breast in his hand. With hands and mouth he explored her body, searching out her most sensitive places as she writhed under his touch. Like a flame, his lips burned over the soft peaks of her breasts. He pulled away only long enough to strip off his shirt and other garments and when he came to her again he was naked power and throbbing strength.

Rodrigo worked a powerful magic and Angelica felt as if she were floating. Let the sunrise come, she thought with a smile, they had the nighttime, and for now that was enough. Pulling the remnants of her dress from her slim body, spreading it down on the straw for their bed, she reached up to bring him to her. He kissed her again, slowly with a fierce yet tender demand. She was enflamed with his kiss, her desire raging like an inferno. Naked and burning with passion, she flung her arms around him, holding him close as her mouth returned his kisses with a frantic urgency. All the days of anguish, of searching, of wanting, all the questions in her mind drifted into oblivion as he stroked her. He was maddeningly gentle, bringing her to a fever pitch before he covered her body with his own. Entwined, she slid her fingers across the broad, hard-muscled shoulders, thrilling at the ripples of strength which emanated from him. She never got tired of touching him. Her hand explored, stroked, and enclosed the shaft of his manhood, arching to him, opening to him.

He took her with a powerful surge as she drew him to her, needing her as he had never needed anyone or anything before, sheathing himself in her satiny flesh.

Angelica's cry was smothered by his mouth as they plunged together over the abyss and into the flames of desire. Over and over she whispered his name as he took her with a tender urgency. Clinging to him, her arms about his neck, she answered his movements with her own, like a wild thing, her shyness and reserve shattered by their passion. Only the magic of the moment was real. The darkness of the outside world was forgotten with the beauty of their joining. Lying naked, their limbs tangled, they sealed their vows of love and knew at that moment that the love they felt at this moment could never be destroyed.

In the aftermath of their love, Rodrigo's hands were gentle as they caressed her. "No matter what happens to me, Angelica, I have this to remember. If I die, I will die a happy man, knowing that we have loved, you and I."

They slowly dressed and then settled once again in each other's arms. Rodrigo continued to hold her until at last she fell into a restless sleep. He stared into the darkness, lightly resting his chin on the top of her head, his arms holding her close against his heart. She had loved him enough to follow him to jail to be with him. His heart ached with love. She had sacrificed her own freedom for him. Was there any greater proof of love than this? If he lived, he would never forget that fact. Never.

"Angelica . . ." He whispered her name caressingly, then settled himself more comfortably against the cell wall. Closing his eyes he murmured her name again before he slipped away into sleep.

Angelica awoke, the rattle of keys jarring her from sleep. The sound reminded her all too brutally of where she was and what had happened. Shivering, she moved closer to Rodrigo, the heat of his body warming hers. His arm was heavy across her hips, his legs, slightly bent, resting intimately between hers, a reminder of the soul-stirring passion they had shared last night. Easing herself up she stared into his face, memorizing it just in case . . . No, I don't even want to think about it, she thought. The idea of being without him was much too painful. A dark wave of hair had fallen across his brow and she brushed it out of his eyes. Again she heard the jingling noise and this time when she looked up saw the face of a long-nosed guard peering at her through the grille of the wooden door. Rodrigo heard the sound too, for he bolted up and reached towards his belt. Realizing he was without weapons, he swore.

"What do you want?" Rodrigo snapped out at the overly curious soldier. He didn't like being gawked at.

"I have never seen a *bandido* before. I have lived all my life in the city where they dare not come." He snorted disdainfully. "You do not look so dangerous to me."

"And you do not look like much of a soldier," Margaro

grumbled through the bars of his cell. "You are much too young. Bah, you are a boy who should be home with his mother."

"I'm twenty." Another guard joined him at the grille, one who looked far more menacing. "My companion has just given me an order that you are to come with us."

"Are you taking us to breakfast?" Margaro's voice was mocking.

"No. No breakfast." The heavyset, scowling guard opened the door with a grunt. "Santa Anna himself wants to see you."

"Santa Anna?" Rodrigo looked at Angelica as they both wondered the same thing. Why would a man as important as the newly declared president of Mexico want to see them?

"Sí, Santa Anna." The youngest guard flung the doors open wide, holding a lighted torch and then unlocked Margaro's cell. Angelica could see the guard's shadow as he came towards her. "Come with me. Quickly now. All of you."

With rifles pointed at their backs, they were hurried along a dark corridor and Angelica glanced over her shoulder from time to time to familiarize herself with her surroundings, in case an opportunity presented itself for escape. There was none. More guards joined the others until it was a veritable procession. They were ushered into the Mexican president's presence with as much ceremony as if they were about to come face-to-face with a king.

As Rodrigo approached him, he appraised the man who held all Mexico in the palm of his hand and who, the people seemed to think, was the only man who could save Mexico from the Americans. By all accounts he was a courageous man, but Rodrigo wondered if, like his uniforms, this Santa Anna was more show than substance. Certainly for all his love of challenge and discipline he had been unable to keep the Americans away

363

from Mexico's shores. Santa Anna was a failure in war. His own ineptness? Or was he plagued by slow-witted soldiers? Rodrigo had heard the matter argued even among the beggars on the street corners.

"El Presidente!" The soldiers at Rodrigo's side snapped to full attention. Angelica bowed her head, Margaro and Rodrigo stood tall and proud. Rodrigo would not bend his knee to any man.

"So you are this El Diablo my cousin was so upset about." Santa Anna took a step forward, then circled the three prisoners with an uneven gait. Rodrigo suddenly remembered that this dark-haired, graying ruler had lost one of his legs fighting the French nearly nine years ago. He wore a wooden leg which Rodrigo supposed was the reason that the left leg of the dun-colored trousers Santa Anna wore were unfashionably baggy. They were cut wide to slip more easily over his inflexible, false foot. He felt a twinge of pity for the man.

"I am El Diablo!"

The piercing black eyes measured Rodrigo man to man. "Huh!" He ran a hand through his dark hair as he paced back and forth. "And this is your . . ."

"My wife!"

"Ah . . . I see." The thin lips curved up in a smile that was far from reassuring. He was a stocky man, paunchy in physique from indulgence in the delicacies of life. Wings of gray in his hair declared his age, yet he was still formidable. More so since he held Rodrigo's and Margaro's lives in his hands, and possibly Angelica's as well. "I welcome you to my most humble quarters, Señora El Diablo." Like a preening rooster he moved his shoulders, affecting a bit of a strut despite his wooden leg as he walked towards her. The decorative scabbard at his side clunked against his wooden leg as he walked, but he failed to notice. Taking her hand, he kissed it in the manner of a gentleman. "I heard from one of the soldiers that it was at your insistence that you are here. I am flattered that you were so anxious to make my acquaintance."

Angelica curtsied. "I have heard what a just and fair man you are. I thought for a certainty that you would listen to my plea concerning my husband. He is a brave man . . ."

"Who led both the Mexicans and Californians on a wild chase." He cocked a thick black brow. "I myself lost a shipment of gold at his hands." He tugged in irritation at the elegant royal-blue cape he wore over his shoulders. He looked much like the eagle embroidered in gold along the edges of the velvet cape.

"If I could, I would give it back to you at this moment." Rodrigo moved closer to where Angelica stood as if to protect her.

"Bah! Gold, gold, gold. I have more than I need of that." Santa Anna grunted in pain. "If you could give me back my leg then I would be tempted to show you gratitude. Cumbersome thing, this wooden one I wear." At Rodrigo's shrug he added, "Ah, I knew you noticed because of the direction of your eyes." He waved the soldiers away impatiently. "Go, you fools, I wish a private conversation." Only two men remained, their rifles cocked and aimed at Rodrigo just in case he had bold ideas.

"You can put down the guns. I can't go far."

Santa Anna's gaze rested on Angelica. "No, I don't imagine that you can. I have seen the looks you give your señora. What is more, I think I like you. I have need of men with your courage and stamina. Instead, I am surrounded by fools." He plucked at the gold buttons on his dark-blue jacket. "I am sure that you have heard that the *americanos* have taken Veracruz. It calls for vengeance. Follow me and I will make it worth your while. I will not rest until the *americanos* are bloodied and beaten, crawling with their tails between their legs all the way back to their own land." A manaical gleam came into his eyes. "I want to kill

365

them all!"

Rodrigo was wary. He didn't want to become involved in this war. He was a bandit who swore no allegiance to either side. It was a Californian who swore false witness against him, a man of American heritage who had led the attack on his camp, the Mexican government who had hounded him unmercifully. He viewed the war much like a dogfight, both canines squabbling over a bone. His only loyalty was to his people and they would be victims no matter which side won. The Americans looked down their noses at them, the wealthy Mexicans kept them in dire poverty. Santa Anna had no concern for his people, merely his pride and own well-being.

"Did you hear what I said, *bandido?*" Rodrigo's silence angered El Presidente.

"I am not a soldier. I lack the discipline you need . . . and. . . "

"Silence! I do not think to make you a soldier, fool! I intend for you to do what you do best. You are a bandit with knowledge of fighting in the hostile back country. You understand ambush. My soldiers do not. They are not inventive or savage." He snorted in frustration. "I want you to act as a guerrilla fighter." He forced his lips into a wide smile. "I have freed many prisoners, granted many pardons to make use of the right men. Men like you, El Diablo. In return for their loyalty to me. Their fighting."

"No, please." Angelica was fearful that Rodrigo would be killed. It had been whispered that United States troops had been sent to hunt the guerrillas, meting out ruthless punishments. Far more brutal a way to die than Santa Anna implied.

"Does your señora speak for you, señor Bandido?" He laughed mockingly. "If so, then I will put this to you another way. You *will* fight for me, you and your tall, mustached friend." His dark eyes narrowed to slits. "For if you do not, she will be the worse for it."

366

"What do you mean?"

"That she will be my *guest.*"

Rodrigo shook his head, understanding too well what Santa Anna was saying. Angelica would be kept as a hostage to ensure his pliability in the matter of this war. He and Margaro must join the fighting on the Mexican side or see Angelica come to harm.

Chapter Forty-Six

Chaos reigned in Mexico City. Despair had been sweeping through the capital since the occupation of Veracruz. No wonder Santa Anna was so insistent on his aiding him, Rodrigo thought. He viewed the coming campaign and his part in it with frustration. Even so he had to grant the president of Mexico grudging admiration. Santa Anna's commanding presence revived the hopes of his citizens. In an amazingly short time he was able to restore order to the government, raise money, and start to build a new army that eventually reached thirty thousand men.

"The nation has not yet lost its vitality," he proclaimed before roaring crowds. "I swear to you I will bring triumph to Mexico. Veracruz calls for vengeance. Follow me and I will wash out the stain of her dishonor."

No sooner had the speech been delivered than Santa Anna set out at the head of a sixteen thousand man group of soldiers to stop the Americans from marching up the National Road. Rodrigo's and Margaro's assignment was to sabotage the American lines and to act as intelligence scouts, keeping the general informed of American whereabouts at all times.

Rodrigo observed the Americans astutely, seeing enough

about their manner of fighting to know the deadly peril the Mexican Army faced. The American fighting men were expert with the rifle, even though many had not been trained as soldiers. Many were frontiersmen who fought Indians and were crack shots. They fought bravely as individuals, not in unison, and placed their musket fire with deadly effect. After watching them for several days, Rodrigo told Margaro that he was not at all surprised that the Americans were winning. They were fiercesome and courageous.

Among the Mexican soldiers, on the other hand, morale, as could be expected, was devastatingly low. It was a class army in which gentlemen officers from highborn families looked down on the soldiers, considering them to be little more than peons. Even in their efforts at war there was no sense of camaraderie, only mutual scorn. The soldiers hardly knew their officers and understandably resented them. Rodrigo could read the hatred and bitterness in the soldiers' eyes, and at times felt the same way himself. If the officers treated the soldiers like peons, he was treated like a *mendigo*, the lowest of the low— dirt beneath their feet. A bandit. An outlaw. They openly scorned both him and Margaro.

"If Santa Anna did not hold Angelica captive, I tell you, Margaro, I would be gone. I have no liking for this."

"Nor have I, amigo. But we are much like two roosters tied by the leg to a stake awaiting a cockfight, no?"

Urging their horses forward on their surveillance mission, they cautiously scanned the countryside of the mountain passes separating Santa Anna's troops from the American General Scott's soldiers. Cerro Gordo, a sleepy little mountain village between Mexico City and Veracruz had been chosen for the confrontation because of its vantage point. It offered the Mexican commander a broad choice of easily defended terrain where he might block the American advance.

370

Dismounting from their horses and leading them for the remaining distance, Rodrigo and Margaro moved with the stealth of panthers as they approached an area near the American camp. What he saw alarmed him. The Americans were hauling cannons over the crude path and up the sides of the ravines, letting the artillery down each steep slope on ropes and pulling up the opposite sides.

They were going to outflank the two hills and strike Santa Anna from the rear, and Rodrigo and Margaro duly reported their findings only to be met with scorn. Rodrigo reiterated his opinion that not even a rabbit could get through.

"Are you a fighting man or a coward?" Santa Anna asked of Margaro, threatening him with disciplinary action if he spread such subversive rumors. The Americans would have to be crazy. "If you are trying to trick me, just remember your señora," he said to Rodrigo with a chilling smile. "You are trying to tell me this General Scott is a rabbit? Ha!"

Not a rabbit but a mountain of a man, nearly six and a half feet tall. Somehow he had found a way to squeeze himself and eight thousand five hundred troops through the woods and ravines behind the lofty Mexican defenses. Rodrigo marveled that the Americans had cut a road through the woods down the full length of the Mexican line. Frantically the Mexican gun crews swung their cannons around and began firing. The Mexican guns, loaded now with the American style of ammunition, did terrible damage but it was too late to save the mountain. The Mexicans fought desperately between and among the two American assault forces, not even being able to tell who was friend and who was foe. The Mexican officers hastily ordered a bayonet charge but the surviving troops were falling back. And all the while Santa Anna viewed the carnage from the safety of his carriage.

"He spoke of cowards?" Margaro said scornfully, doing

his best to man one of the cannons.

It was a fiercely waged battle, but after a few hours the first hill was at last taken by the Americans. The Mexicans retreated. Tomorrow would be a better day, Santa Anna promised. At first it appeared that he was right, but after an initial attack up the steep slope of the second hill the next day, the Mexicans were again put to flight. The Americans drove Santa Anna's army off in a furious assault of rifles, pistols, and clubbed muskets, all the while giving their blood-chilling rebel yell. The once proud Mexican Army had been brought down to a pathetically disoriented gathering, totally shattered. The Mexicans broke in confusion when a force of Americans suddenly appeared at their rear, having made a long march completely around the enemy position. The entire Mexican Army broke and ran.

"So, he is going to have the Americans run like dogs with their tails between their legs, eh?" Rodrigo said to Margaro as they held their ground until the last, fighting furiously.

Using the manner of fighting of their bandit days, they managed to hold several of the American soldiers at bay. At last, however, they were pushed back. Seeking out Santa Anna they found that he had fled, making good his escape by leaving behind the carriage and all his personal baggage, including a chest containing twenty thousand dollars in coin and his wooden leg.

"*Dios!* What are we going to do now?" Rodrigo knew a fear that somehow Angelica would be the brunt of the general's disappointment and anger.

"Try to reach Mexico City before he does, amigo. He will want to find a scapegoat for this. It is his way. What better victim than two bandits, eh?"

Thoughtfully Rodrigo looked toward the battlefield where hundreds lay dead. It was a grisly suggestion, yet with Angelica's life at stake he proposed it. "Were we to confiscate two officers' uniforms, I wonder . . ."

"Quickly. We must do it before the Americans find us and take us prisoner with the others."

The matter was accomplished with surprising ease. Rodrigo and Margaro were used to such dangerous missions. Crawling around on their hands and knees, remaining perfectly still whenever a sound reached their ears, they moved stealthily. It reminded Margaro of that horrible day when he had crept among the bodies of his slain comrades to save Rodrigo. That the American soldiers were pursuing the shattered division of Mexicans for a distance of ten miles to keep them from regrouping made the matter all the easier. When night fell, Rodrigo and Margaro eased their way on horseback among the bushes and trees of the terrain. They had come to Cerro Gordo clothed in linen and leather. They were leaving dressed in the gold, red, and blue of a captain and a lieutenant.

Chapter Forty-Seven

Waiting, not knowing if Rodrigo was alive or dead, was torture for Angelica. Standing at the window of the large room she had been unceremoniously pushed into and locked within, she watched as the dark shadows of dusk shrouded the sun. Church bells tolled crazily, ringing out their message and she shivered as a sense of foreboding crept up her spine. The bells seemed to be chiming a woeful song.

Running to the door, she tried for the hundredth time to force it open, incurring bruises for her efforts but little else. She had thought herself so very brave in coming with Rodrigo. Instead, she had given Santa Anna a weapon to hold over his head. Rodrigo would never have gone to Cerro Gordo if not for her. It was a thought that brought the bitter taste of bile to her throat.

In desperation, she walked the length of the room and back again. At least in the prison he had chosen for her, Santa Anna had been generous. It was not a cell with a hard stone floor but a spacious boudoir with decorative wooden furniture and a large, canopied bed. A gilded cage, she thought with a sigh. She would have preferred a pallet in a dungeon if Rodrigo were safe. Putting her face in her hands, she sat down in one of the plushest chairs to wait for any news.

The scraping of the door against the floor as it opened and a mumbled oath startled her. A thin woman with a sallow complexion and a long nose entered the room, accompanied by a scowling soldier. "Some food."

"I'm not hungry. I couldn't eat a bite, but thank you." Angelica's eyes moved to the open door wondering if there was any chance at all that she could get away.

"I would not try it, señorita. Besides, with your pale hair you would be marked for trouble the moment you stepped outside. The citizens are angered by what the *americanos* did to our soldiers and might make of you an example, eh?" The soldier closed the door with his foot, standing directly in front of it in case she failed to listen to his advice. He was unarmed, but his girth and strength made him formidable.

"What did the Americans do?"

"Mauled our army without mercy. A messenger arrived only a few hours ago with the news. General Santa Anna was defeated most soundly at Cerro Gordo. Three thousand captured and several thousand more killed or wounded." He grunted scornfully. "For the second time within two months Santa Anna has presided over the liquidation of an army. Savior of Mexico indeed. We will soon have the *americanos* marching through our gates. There is a clear route and . . ."

"Thousands wounded or dead?" Putting her hand to her throat, Angelica felt as if she might faint. Dear God, don't let Rodrigo or Margaro be among them. Please, she prayed silently.

"Señora, perhaps a drink of cool water will soothe you." Pouring a cupful from a large pottery pitcher, the woman held it forth. "Here, drink." Angelica gulped the cool liquid down, choking in her haste. "Careful. Not too much. Not too much. Men! Have you no feelings at all? Must you always talk of war? It is your fault that we may

376

soon be an invaded city.''

"War? It was a rout. As complete as it was shameful.''
Seeing that Angelica was not going to touch the food on
her tray, he moved forward and snatched up an apple.
With his mouth full he related all he had heard about the
battle. "The soldiers surrendered their arms almost
without a fight.''

"Surrendered? Then there were several prisoners taken?
What about the two bandits who were traveling with
Santa Anna?''

"Bandits?'' He belched. "I have not heard anything
about any bandits.'' Finishing the apple, he threw the core
on the marble floor and reached for a large leg of chicken.
"May I, señora?'' As she did not protest he took a bite,
smacking his lips. "My brother tells me that our cousin
declares the *americanos* are invincible. The soldiers are
telling terrible tales. Some say that the enemy soldiers are
such huge, strong men that they can cut an opponent in
two with a single sweep of their swords but I do not believe
it. It is also said that the Americans discharge shots which,
once they leave the gun, divide into *fifty* pieces, each one
fatal and well aimed.'' He laughed. "The next thing you
know they will be saying that the *americanos* can walk on
water, no?''

"Perhaps they can, or maybe it is that El Presidente is a
fool!''

"Hush, old woman! Keep your thoughts to yourself.
You will bring down a thunder of trouble upon yourself
with such words.'' He scowled at Angelica as if warning
her to hold her tongue. "Whatever has happened, Santa
Anna is our leader. He can be easily angered and . . .''

"Leader? Bah. He always makes such grand promises to
us and always he is the one to run away from the
battlefield. In the streets they are denouncing him as a
coward and a traitor. There is talk that he has sold out to
the Americans, that it was planned that he hand Mexico

377

into the hands of the enemy. He fills his pockets with gold. He is as bad, maybe worse than the *bandidos* he sets loose upon the Americans to blow up their supply trains and cannons," the old woman said with disgust.

Again Angelica paled. "Where is Santa Anna and his army now?"

The old woman shrugged her shoulders. "Who knows?"

"I heard he is riding through the city of Puebla. In hopes of rounding up the survivors. It will be a long time before he comes back to the city."

"If he even comes at all. I would not were I him." Hearing a noice outside the door, the woman quieted, clutching the tray against her chest. "Who is there?" she asked, fear in her voice. Again she called out, "Who is there?"

"Open up. We have been sent by El Presidente to bring the woman prisoner to him." A loud knocking accompanied the order.

"El Presidente's guard. If they heard your foolish words, old woman, you will get us both a hard lashing." The paunchy soldier hurried to the door and flung it open. "Ah, El Capitán. *Teniente*. El General was not expected . . . I heard he was at Puebla, but I was wrong . . ."

"We rode all day and night. El Presidente is a few miles behind. He will be here shortly and wants the woman awaiting him in his quarters. We are to take her there." The captain boldly strode through the open doorway, and in that moment Angelica caught a glimpse of his face. She gasped. It was Rodrigo. His eyes warned her not to show even an upraised brow that she knew him. "Which one is the señora?" Rodrigo asked, moving towards the skinny woman who held the tray. "Is *this* the bandit's wife?"

"If she was, I fear this El Diablo will never return." Slapping his thigh, the heavyset soldier gave in to a belly laugh. "No. No. It is the other one. The gringa with the pale-yellow hair."

Rodrigo affected a bow. "Ah . . . ! This bandit *hombre* has very good taste. It will be most pleasurable to escort her to El Presidente. Shall we go, señora?" In a gallant gesture he offered his arm. It had been so easy, Rodrigo thought. With the exception of a minor skirmish with a small band of buckskin-clothed Americans, he and Margaro had ridden through the countryside and over the roads unmolested. The uniforms they had absconded had gotten them without question through the gates of the presidential palace and up the stairs to the area where Santa Anna's political "guests" were kept. Perhaps the blood and torn cloth of their uniforms lent them even more credence. "Come, señora."

"Un momento." Like a puffed-up toad, the rotund soldier stepped in front of Angelica. "I must see your orders. This woman is a political prisoner. How can I be sure that you are taking her to Santa Anna?" He held out his hand, his stubby fingers clicking together in a snap. "Your orders, El Capitán."

Rodrigo eyed his adversary. It would take both Margaro and himself to beat him. Better to use persuasion. "Orders? You dare speak to me of orders, you . . . you . . . you *peon!*" He affected the manner he'd seen the officers use with those of lower rank. "I will have you hung up by your toes as an example. I will have you put in a tiny cell for so long that your fat belly will wane from lack of nourishment."

"And if he does not, I will." Margaro put his hands behind him, walking round and round the soldier. "It looks to me as if you could live a very, very long time without food." He bent down to pick up the apple core. "Who threw this on the ground? You? You know how El Presidente loathes men who act like *pigs.*"

"No, not I. The . . . the woman."

Margaro threw the apple core on the floor again. "Pick it up. Pick it up, you groveling, idiotic . .

Used to following orders, the soldier did as he was told. When he stood back up, he clicked his heels together and saluted. "As you ordered, *Teniente. Capitán.*"

"Stay as you are. Discipline, *soldado*. Discipline." Rodrigo gestured for Angelica to inch her way towards the door. "Had the soldiers shown discipline at Cerro Gordo, we and not the *americanos* would now hold that small village. Do you understand, *soldado?*"

"*Sí, El Capitán.*"

"Good."

"But I still must see your orders."

Rodrigo felt frustration well up inside him. At any moment a real officer who would recognize him for the fraud he was might come through the door. Fumbling around in his pockets, he felt for and found a folded-up piece of paper. Quickly he scanned it. It was a missive to lure American deserters to Santa Anna's army. Rodrigo had heard that there were several Americans who had deserted because of harsh treatment. Santa Anna no doubt thought to take advantage of the situation by offering cash and land to deserters. That Santa Anna's name was scrawled at the bottom offered Rodrigo a chance.

"If you must be stubborn, then here!" He thrust the paper in front of the soldier's nose, gambling that the man could not read. "Are you satisfied? Bah, you cost us valuable time. El Presidente will hear of this."

Seeing the scrawled signature the soldier cowered. "I am only doing my job. I was told not to let the gringa woman leave unless I saw a signed order." His eyes were pleading. "Please . . . tell El Presidente that I did my job . . . that I am a good soldier. He will be in a foul mood and you know how he is when in that frame of mind."

"*Sí*, I know all too well. And he will have my head if I do not hurry." Rodrigo grabbed the missive out of the soldier's hand, then pushed Angelica forward. "Hurry, señora."

Angelica, Margaro, and Rodrigo slipped out the door and ran down a flight of stone stairs. It was easier getting in than out of the palace, however. In just the time it had taken Rodrigo to convince the soldier to let them go, the bleeding and limping army slowly appeared at the palace. Angelica's long hair would instantly give her away. There had been a lot of talk about Santa Anna's beautiful prisoner. One soldier had fallen for his story, but an army?

"Rodrigo, watch out." Margaro recognized one of the officers who had been so openly scornful of the president's "bandits." He pushed Angelica and Rodrigo behind a pillar as the officer walked by, fearing they might be recognized. "We will never get away from here," he bemoaned as the moments dragged on. At last the officer walked away and the threesome stepped out of the shadows. More soldiers sent them scurrying back. This time the soldiers were carrying a wounded companion on a stretcher. The blanket pulled over the body and face indicated that the soldier had not survived.

"Margaro, are you thinking what I'm thinking?" Rodrigo quirked a brow.

"I think so, amigo." Margaro slipped away for just a moment and when he returned he was lugging a stretcher behind him and carrying a blanket under his arm.

"Lie, down, Angelica."

She knew immediately what he had planned, though having a blanket over her face was severely unnerving. She could hardly breathe. The dust nearly made her sneeze. The pitch and sway of the litter made her feel as if she were going to be catapulted to the ground at any moment. She feared what would happen to them all if this subterfuge was discovered. Closing her eyes tightly she pushed the thought far from her mind. Margaro was a master at fooling his pursuers. Somehow she sensed he would get them out of this danger. "This one to the morgue," she heard him say.

"That wagon. Put her in the wagon," she heard Rodrigo say, then she was plopped into a pile of hay as a horse nickered nervously. The bump of the wagon wheels against the rutted ground jostled her bones but she was free, Rodrigo was with her, and she couldn't ask for much more than that. But where would they go? The whole city would be looking for them. Her brother, Gutierrez. Santa Anna. The Mexican Army.

"The church. We must go to the mission church. It is our only hope." Peeking out from under the blanket, she made the suggestion. "I saw an old church on the outskirts of the city." They just had to make it, she thought in alarm.

The whitewashed adobe walls were a welcoming sight as the wagon crested a hill. It was a small, humble church presided over by Father Juan Diego, a rotund, jovial priest with a cherubic smile. Without their even saying a word he knew they were on the run and offered them sanctuary. "You will be safe here. As you can see, there is a wall surrounding us with a gate that is always guarded. There is a narrow parapet from which you can see for miles and I have an Indian bell ringer who watches from the tower. At any sign of trouble he rings the bell . . . and rings and rings . . ." With a nod of his head he beckoned them inside. "There is a tunnel, leading from beneath the altar to a spot behind the wall just in case . . ." He led them up the stairs to the church proper.

Angelica tried not to show her dismay as she looked about her. It was such a contrast to the churches she had been in before. The altar cloths were in tatters, a great wooden cross was warped and cracked from rain leaking through a hole in the roof, pews had been tipped over, the wooden floor was caked with dirt. It was a church for the rag-clad *mendigos.* Until this minute she had not realized the gulf that lay between the rich and the poor. This was a far cry from the cathedral she had glimpsed from the

382

wagon on her journey into this city. Even so, she could tell that Father Diego was contented here. He showed them about as if the altar and shrines were decorated with gold and silver and the pews upholtered in velvet. He spoke of his "people" as if he were a proud father talking about his children.

"Are you hungry?" Sensing that they were, he led them to a small, rectangular room. "You can eat in the rectory, with me. It will be good to have your company. And you can tell me all about who and what you are running from, my children."

The table was set with simple food, and as they sat and bowed their heads he whispered a brief grace, then looked up. "You are an American?" he asked Angelica.

"I'm from California. I came here with my brother. He . . . he is selling weapons to Santa Anna."

"He is a Mexican patriot?" He eyed her quizzically.

"He is doing it for land and for gold. It's a long story. He brought me here against my will, making threats against my husband if I did not come. My . . . my husband is . . ."

"He has the look of a wanted man. A furtive manner with his eyes. Always looking behind him. I might even think he was a bandit . . ." Picking up his fork, he attacked a slice of beef while holding his gaze steady on Angelica's face. "Is he?"

"Please . . . don't turn him in. Rodrigo is . . ."

"No better or worse than any of us. Bandits, ha! There are many bandits here, only they mask their stealing with respectability. Kindness and pity are too neglected here." He took a bite of meat, chewing as he talked. "I will not judge you. I will, in fact, help you if I can. Something drew you here tonight, I think perhaps it was God."

"We need to find a way out of the city, but I'm afraid they will be looking for us." Rodrigo eyed the priest warily. Could he be trusted? "We will need two horses. One came with the wagon. In return I will pay you."

Reaching inside his money pouch, he pulled several coins from within and laid them on the table. "Enough perhaps to replace the horses and buy a new altar cloth as well."

"Gold coins?" The priest scowled. "Stolen?"

"It is money that Santa Anna left behind when he fled Cerro Gordo. Margaro and I did not want to see it go to waste."

"No, of course not. Santa Anna's gold. That makes it all right. He is one of those respectable bandits I spoke about. He cares nothing for his people, except to bleed them dry for his own pleasures." There was an emotion in his voice that bordered on anger. "If you are a foe of Santa Anna's, then you are twice a friend of mine. I will do all that I can to help you. In the meantime I will find you somewhere to sleep." His eyes were mischievous as he said, "I suspect you will be needing *two* rooms."

"Just for tonight, while the dogs are hot on our trail. First thing at dawn tomorrow we will leave Mexico City far behind. Unless . . ." Rodrigo left his fear unspoken.

Chapter Forty-Eight

All the roads leading to and from Mexico City were blocked. Rodrigo, Angelica, and Margaro were effectively locked within the walls of Mexico City as thoroughly as the Americans were seemingly blocked out. At least, however, they were safe for the moment within the church's walls. Father Diego had taken them under his wing, giving them sanctuary, feeding and clothing them and keeping them informed about what was happening. Mexico City had been given a reprieve, at least for a while. Scott's army had made a detour of the capital to capture Santa Anna's home town of Jalapa. From there they had moved on to Puebla, regrouping and bringing in reinforcements from Veracruz. Father Diego was certain that they would march to the capital very soon.

There were moments when Rodrigo and Angelica could shut out the world, when the only thing that mattered was their love, but always in the backs of their minds was the danger. They couldn't step outside for a breath of fresh air without fearing they might be seen, thus they kept to their rooms in the old church tower or watched the glowing embers of distant campfires from the parapet knowing the Americans were moving closer and closer. If Mexico City was captured, how would it affect their lives? It was a question they pondered over and over.

"Selfishly it would be better for us if Santa Anna was defeated," she whispered to Rodrigo one night as they stared eastward towards the rosy dawn rising and coloring the skies with a brilliant hue. "Santa Anna has proven himself to be our enemy. Yet knowing what might happen to the people here makes me feel ashamed of such thoughts and I try to push them from my mind."

"It is such a beautiful city. I would hate to see it lie in ruins. I have found great happiness here with you . . ." Indeed, they had found moments of contentment just being together. It was the first time since their wedding that they had been able to spend any amount of time in each other's company. Before, there had always been one thing or another that had separated them. "Are *you* happy, *querida?*"

"Mmm, very happy." The familiar warmth she always felt at his nearness raced through her like a fire. An aching in her breasts gave promise of the delightful sensations that were to come when they were once more in their bed. Father Diego had been a hospitable host in granting them the room he had been using as a study. He had moved in a large bed and decorated the room with flowers just to please her. He was a very considerate man who in some ways reminded her of Father Duran. Poor Father Duran, she thought, surely the stress of this war had killed him.

"It is like a honeymoon. A time when I have you all to myself." Rodrigo laughed gently. "Except for the times when Margaro is hovering near. He can be a devil of a nuisance sometimes when I want to be with you."

"But I like him." She settled herself in his embrace, resting her head on his chest as he brushed the light strands of hair from her forehead. "How long have we been here, Rodrigo? I have lost track. How long has Father Diego shielded us?"

"Weeks and weeks . . ."

"So long?" She raised up on tiptoe to kiss his lips. "You will soon be growing tired of me."

"Tired of you? Never, *querida*. Never. I love you. Never doubt it." Rodrigo nibbled at her ear, causing sparks of flame to to flicker up her spine. "Shall we go back to our room, eh?"

"In a moment." She was suddenly pensive as worry over the future intruded. "Rodrigo, what is going to become of . . ."

He silenced her with a kiss, setting them both aflame. He didn't want to think of all that now, wanted to forget. Thinking about the war and their isolation in the church threatened to sometimes drive him crazy. If not for her . . . "We will think of that later, right now all I want to do is make love to you."

"And I to you."

He carried her back to their room and stripped away her garments. Once more the world was held at bay. There was no time for talking, only for making love. Sweet, hot desire fused their bodies together as Rodrigo made love to her with a fierce possessiveness. His lips burned over the soft peaks of her breasts, stirring desire in her loins. Her whole body quivered in answer to the intoxicating sensations he always aroused in her. Desire raged like an inferno, pounding in her veins. Then she was parting her thighs, guiding him to her with an ardor she had never shown before, rising and falling with him as he moved with the relentless rhythm of their love.

It was a wondrous night. Rodrigo worshipped her with each caress, each kiss, as if it might be the last. In the aftermath of their lovemaking, when all their passion had ebbed, they lay entwined, contenting themselves with each other. Rodrigo was stretched out beside her, his eyes closed, but every one of his senses was aware of her. He could hear her heart beating in a syncopated rhythm with his, could smell the fragrance of the roses she wore in her hair. His hands stroked her body, relishing the softness of her skin.

"I would be content to stay here like this forever," he breathed.

"Maybe if we try hard enough, we can chase away tomorrow. Do you think we can, Rodrigo?" Settling into the circle of his arms, she sighed.

"We can try, *querida*. We can try."

"Rodrigo . . ." His name was a prayer on her lips.

"It will be all right, Angelica. Somehow we will get through this together." The hoarse words were a promise. No matter what happened he would make certain that Angelica would be safe. Even if that meant sacrificing himself. Bending his head to kiss her once again, he sealed that vow.

Over the next few days and weeks, they tried to forget about the war but were unsuccessful. Soon the world came crashing in on them as the war raged fiercely all around. Soldiers died, both Mexican and American. The Mexicans lost the battles at Puebla and Contreras, the Americans endured heavy casualties at Churubusco. All the while, the American Army moved closer, determined in their drive to enter the city. That the battle at Churubusco had involved a convent in the carnage made both Rodrigo and Angelica uneasy. A man like Santa Anna seemed not to recognize the right of sanctuary. Were he even to guess that they were being sheltered in a church would he seek them out or was he too preoccupied with other matters? That he was cannily bargaining for peace did not soothe Rodrigo's apprehension, it only increased his fears. Santa Anna was a very devious man. Worst of all was the news Father Diego gave them one night at dinner.

"You asked me to find out news of Rodrigo's sister Luisa. She and her husband are happy, still living in the inn." His brow furled. "As for your brother, Angelica, the news is not so good." Father Diego had learned that a woman who had once been Angelica's brother's mistress had seemingly denounced him to Santa Anna as conspiring with the Americans. Realizing that he had chosen the wrong side in the warfare, Edward had sought to endear himself with the conquering American general only to be discovered in his plotting.

"Bonita! I warned him," Angelica said, her face red with anger.

"He has been threatened with the firing squad. His execution has been set for eight days from now," Father Diego added sadly.

"Eight days!" Though Edward had done a great deal to instigate Angelica's unhappiness, he was still her brother. The thought of him being shot was painful.

"I know it hurts, Angelica, but for me I can feel no pity. He had no qualms in shooting my people down like dogs." It was the next day, the rainy weather adding to a sense of gloom as Rodrigo and Angelica stood side by side looking out the tiny kitchen window.

"He is my brother."

"Angelica, there is nothing you can do. Were you to try and save him, you would only bring danger to yourself . . . to me." It was a bitter truth. "He made his choices and now he must live by them."

"Or die because of them." Angelica felt grief squeeze her heart. At a moment like this she remembered the fair-haired boy who had led her by the hand to hide among the bushes as a rampaging tribe of Indians had attacked their mother and father's caravan.

"Don't worry, Angie, I'll take care of you," he had said. Though he might have made more than a few mistakes, he had kept that promise. She had had clothes to wear, a roof over her head, had never gone to bed hungry. Perhaps if their parents had survived, Edward would never have become so ambitious and grasping. What if . . . ? She shook her head. A person could go out of his mind asking that question. All she could do was to pray for him, to hope for a chance of his escape.

Even so, the agony and guilt at being so helpless to save Edward plagued her. She became at times grim and unsmiling. There were times when she turned away from Rodrigo, giving vent to a flood of tears as she huddled beneath the blankets on her lonely side of the bed. She suddenly seemed to feel guilty that she was hiding herself away.

Rodrigo kept a careful eye on her, fearing she might do something rash. He watched as she marked out the days on the calendar, tried to comfort her when she jumped at the sound of rifle fire beneath the window. He watched as the fragile happiness they had shared was threatened by what was happening around them.

Angelica seemed to punishing herself for what she viewed as cowardice on her part. Though they had no reason to argue, they fought over the silliest things such as taking too much of the blanket or a wrong word spoken. It was as if their confinement, far from being a haven now, was as much a prison as Santa Anna's jail had been. Even Margaro's good-natured bantering was met with frowns, and in the end he decided to remain silent when she was around.

"She acts as if I were the one putting her gringo brother up against the wall," Rodrigo confided to Margaro as they sat in Margaro's room playing chess. "One would imagine this brother of hers had been a saint!"

"Saint or demon, he shares her blood. Would you not feel likewise, amigo, were Luisa in such danger?" Margaro strategically placed his bishop. "Ah, you had best watch out."

"Luisa is an entirely different matter. She is gentle and kind. She has never harmed anyone. How can you speak their names in the same breath?" Rodrigo moved his knight.

"Would you love Luisa any the less were she Satan incarnate? Were she as evil as this Edward Howe, would that make it any easier for you to know she was going to die? And what of Luisa? Did she love you any the less knowing there was a price on your head? When you held the gringos captive, did she still not have a soft spot in her heart for you? We have all done some evil in this life, Rodrigo. It seems to me that when all is said and done there is much good and bad done on both sides." Moving diagonally, Margaro captured three of Rodrigo's pawns, adding the white chess pieces to a growing number he had collected. "Rodrigo, your mind is most definitely *not* on this game."

"How could it be?" Rodrigo was short of temper. Just when he and Angelica had been so content this matter of her brother's capture had happened. He hated to see her so unhappy, especially when there was nothing that could be done. "I think what is tearing her up inside is not knowing what is going on. We are isolated from the city's gossip. Were it not for Father Diego's bits and pieces of information we would be lost." He rested his chin on his hands. "Will Santa Anna really shoot her brother?"

"It is difficult to say. It could have been a trap. That is a thought I have toyed with. What better way to flush a bird out of hiding than to threaten one of its own? Eh? What if Edward were being used as bait? What if he had not angered Santa Anna at all but was merely cooperating in a game?" Margaro studied the chessboard, tugging at his mustache. "Maybe they are trying to make us do something foolish."

"Like leave this sanctuary to make a daring rescue?" Rodrigo had to admit that it had crossed his mind. If saving that bastard of a brother would make Angelica smile again, he would have done it were it possible. "Could they really think I would be such a fool?"

"Not you but her. If she fell into their hands again they

391

know you would follow. If you want to ensnare the ram what better way than to lure the ewe?''

Rodrigo slapped his hand against his thigh. *"Dios!* You are right. Why hadn't I thought of that?''

"You are too blinded by love." Margaro shrugged his shoulders apologetically. "Checkmate!"

Rodrigo scanned the chessboard but had to admit, "You won. I am trapped, amigo, just as surely as I am here. I have to admit that I am glad the game is over. I don't like to leave Angelica alone for too long. Besides, I regret what I said to her before I left.''

"And that was?''

"We argued about her brother again. I tried to make her see reason, that what will be will be. She was talking crazily, saying that she should go to him and make her peace with him before he died. I told her the only way she would be able to manage that was to become an angel, to walk through Santa Anna's prison walls. When I left she was looking out the window as if she wished that she could fly . . .'' Rodrigo's eyes met Margaro's. "She wouldn't . . .?''

"Women do strange things. They are overly emotional and not rational like we are . . .''

In sudden apprehension they both started for the door, tipping the chessboard over in their haste and scattering the chess pieces all over the stone floor. Pushing through the doorway at the same time they ran to her room, hoping to find her still standing by the window, but instead found her gone.

"I should never have left her . . .'' Rodrigo searched through her belongings and found that her cloak was missing. *"Dios!* She has left.'' Tomorrow morning was the scheduled day for Edward's execution. He remembered her saying over and over again that time was running out for her brother.

"She could be in the chapel, in the kitchen, the refectory, or walking the parapet.''

Hopefully, they made a thorough search of all four places, even seeking out Father Diego, thinking she might be in the priest's company. But she had disappeared.

"I must go after her . . ." Rodrigo strode down the long, echoing corridor towards the front door.

"No! Then there will be two of you in danger. Even if she is caught by Santa Anna she will not be killed. You, amigo, are another matter. Besides, I think she will come to her senses long before she gets very far. She will turn back and come running into your arms . . ."

"And if she does not?"

"*Then* we go after her."

"It might be too late by then. I cannot take that chance, Margaro. I love her. If I have to bring her back kicking and screaming, I will. If I have to sit on her, tie her up until tomorrow is shadowed in sunset, I will do it. Her brother is not worth her little finger. Somehow I will make her see that, before we come to tragedy."

"Let me go. I can use one of my disguises and slip through the crowds. The beggar again, eh? A padre? A nun?" Margaro blocked Rodrigo's way but he stubbornly pushed him aside. "Don't do this, Rodrigo. You are being, as the *americanos* say, "hasty." She will come back and find you gone and then I will have to talk sense into *her* head." He mumbled angrily beneath his breath. "All right, then, amigo, get yourself killed. I wash my hands of the matter." He started to turn away but changed his mind. Grabbing Rodrigo by the shirt, he held him immobile. "I will hold you back, amigo, if I must. *Caramba.* You are *obstinado*, Rodrigo Delgado O'Hara. Your Irish stubbornness is going to get you killed. Think."

"I *am* thinking. I cannot live without her . . ." Both men gave a gasp of surprise as Angelica pushed through the door. Flinging herself into Rodrigo's arms, she collapsed in a flood of tears. "*Querida,* don't. There is

393

nothing either you or I could do for him. I'm . . . I'm sorry I said what I said."

"No. You were right. I wanted to think of Edward the way he used to be when we were children, but he had changed. I . . . I was going to do something utterly stupid, but as I walked along I saw your face and knew I couldn't take a chance on losing you. I came back. Forgive me for being so . . ."

"There is nothing to forgive . . ." A sudden sound of thunder exploded. Looking through the open doorway they could see the red glow of fire, the accompanying smoke. *"Dios!* What is going on?"

"The *americanos*. It looks as if they are here at last. Come."

Margaro led the way up the stairs to the parapet that ran around the bell tower. The sound of the bell nearly deafened them as they looked out towards Chapultepec, known simply as "the castle." It was as much a shrine as a fortress to the Mexicans. Here, over three hundred years before, the Aztec emperor Montezuma lolled beside splashing fountains. Here the Spanish conquistador Cortés came with his gold-hungry soldiers to destroy the Indian civilization that had built it. The Mexicans had restored it and made it the home of the National Military Academy where young cadets, some of them mere boys, drilled in their gray uniforms. Now it was in danger.

Against the black velvet backdrop of the night the shells exploded, screaming through the quiet of the night. Smoke hovered like an ominous cloud. Margaro, Angelica, and Rodrigo watched with great sadness as the battle raged. In the end, the castle fell in just over an hour. A town crier shouted out the news. By morning, a tidal wave of Americans flowed into the fort, and from the parapet Angelica could see the Stars and Stripes rippling out against the morning sky. Angelica couldn't help but wonder if this was an end or a beginning.

Chapter Forty-Nine

Mexico City was in a state of panic. Watching from the parapet, Angelica could see the citizens milling about and felt sorry for them. They had reason to be afraid. Emboldened after the surrender of Chapultepec, the Americans were marching, following the same route of Hernando Cortés, the sixteenth-century Spanish conqueror of the Aztecs.

"Oh, Rodrigo, I can't blame them for being fearful. I am too, a little . . . though I have hope that the Americans will show mercy. Perhaps now there will be an end to all of this."

"Father Diego says the Mexican Army has fled the city in small groups and that Santa Anna has fled too. That means we are free once again, *querida*. That we can walk about if we want to. Santa Anna is a threat to us no longer."

Mexico City fell quickly that morning. Americans swarmed up the two causeways to the capital and wasted no time in battering down the gates. By noon they had driven through the Belán gate into the city. The soldiers were a sorry, tattered, bedraggled group. Angelica could see from the frowns etched on their faces that the fighting had not been easy for them.

That afternoon the city lapsed into anarchy. From her perch of safety high above the rooftop of the church near the bell tower Angélica watched as people crowded the streets or clamored for safety on flat rooftops. There was weeping and cries of fright. Toward nightfall a surprisingly savage counterattack drove the invaders back to the gate. Then, just as suddenly as it had begun, the resistance ceased. The war was really over, at least for the soldiers, that is.

Hoping to find Jesse and Luisa, Rodrigo and Angélica left the confines of the church grounds to mingle with the citizens of Mexico City. What they found was total pandemonium. The cobbled streets and alleyways were filling with the frantic crowds.

"The *americanos* are pushing their way back into the city!" an old man shouted.

A steady stream of refugees was moving towards the outskirts of the city to make their escape, their faces showing anger as well as sadness. There were barefooted women with babies strapped to their backs, old men and women dragging behind them all their wordly possessions. Rodrigo and Angélica dodged the wagons and carts, trying to maneuver themselves through the throng and to where the inn was. Rodrigo held Angélica protectively, watching as scores of Americans were being beaten or stoned in the streets by hate-filled youths and young men. Only then did Rodrigo realize the full import of the danger. Like a tidal wave, violence was being unleashed on those who in no way were to blame for what was happening. A mob, he thought. Separately these people might be peaceful, together they were a shouting, bloodthirsty group of animals, intent on shedding blood.

"There is one. Look at her hair. She is not one of us."

"Remember Chapultepec!"

Just in time, Rodrigo hurled himself in the path of a whirling sting of stones. Only by darting quickly to the left was he able to keep Angelica from having her skull crushed.

"Back to the church!" He tugged at Angelica's hand, but the crowd surged towards them, blocking any escape. The only way open was the inn and so they proceeded in that direction. It was as if they had stepped into hell. They were swallowed by the crowd. Adding to the tumult were the looters. They were all over the city like vermin, ransacking stalls and shops along the streets.

"Vultures!" Rodrigo swore between clenched teeth. "Men who make a profit off other people's woes." Picking up a large wooden stick, using it as a club, he chased several such looters away. "It is the worst of all evil, when men prey on their own poor. The rich, *sí*, the poor *no*." He shrugged. "Even *bandidos* have some code of honor, *querida*."

They were pushed and shoved, forced to stand and watch the procession which now rode into the city in triumph. The Americans hardly looked the part of conquerors as they rode through the cobbled streets. One general wore only one shoe as he walked at the head of his ragged, bloodstained troops. The streets of the city were silent, all of the people lining the curbs staring at the men who had so thoroughly beaten Mexico's great army. In the great square the Americans formed orderly ranks in front of the National Palace and raised the American flag over the city. The soldiers looked tired, haggard, thin. Few of them were smiling, most looked relieved that it was finally over.

A roll of kettle drums and resounding toots of brass announced a band of dragoons, riding with drawn swords. Cheers were heard a few blocks away. The American general, Winifield Scott, had decided to make a grand entrance. Astride a heavy bay charger, wearing a full dress uniform complete with gold epaulettes and white plumed helmet, he led a victory march down the streets and into the Grand Plaza. His gold decorations and buttons were a gleaming contrast to the blue of his uniform and his white plumes billowed in the breeze. His army's bands broke into "Yankee Doodle" and "Hail, Columbia," songs Angelica knew well, and she felt a surge of pride flow over her. Pride mixed with sympathy for those whose city had been taken. War was a terrible thing and all she could hope was that some good would come from the tragedy. That, above all things, was her prayer as she stood watching.

Suddenly Angelica felt Rodrigo stiffen, his hand clasp hers with such pressure that she winced in pain.

"*Madre de Dios!* Garcia!"

Angelica followed the line of his vision and saw the swarthy *bandido* standing only a few feet away from them. "I would bet that he is up to no good."

As they both watched, the bandit was inching his way closer and closer to where the American general had reined in and was acknowledging his troops. They greeted him with cheers that drowned out the sound of the drums and trumpets and Angelica's warning shout. With knife poised he lunged, and it was in that moment that Rodrigo acted instinctively. Throwing himself at Garcia he grappled with the weapon as the two former comrades rolled over and over on the hard, rocky ground. "To kill an unarmed man, even a gringo, is treacherous, Garcia. You will be the cause of a bloodletting such as has never been seen before. Give me that knife."

"*Bastardo!* Has slipping between the thighs of a gringa woman made a gringo-lover out of you? He is an enemy. *Idiota*, why do you fight me. Let me kill him!" Kicking out with his foot, Garcia caught Rodrigo in the groin. "Then I will kill you as well."

Angelica held her breath, horror stricken as Garcia raised his knife again, this time towards Rodrigo's chest. "Rodrigo, look out!" He rolled away just in time.

"You gringo pig! Traitor to your own!"

398

"I am no traitor, but you are a savage and a killer who will instigate more bloodshed with your hatred." Rising to a crouching position, Rodrigo shook his head, trying to rebound from the pain that lashed through him. The crowd was staring in fascinated wonder as the two men renewed their fury at each other. Only the intervention of the soldiers kept the two men from killing each other. "What do we have here, men? This one don't look none like a Mex. Not with them blue eyes."

"I am half Mexican and proud of it." Rodrigo looked the soldier in the eye, daring him to say one word to anger him. Instead the soldier smiled.

"Whatever you are, you sure as hell saved the general's life." He nodded his head in Garcia's direction. "Take that one away." Turning back towards Rodrigo, he asked, "You a soldier? Hell, you look more like a bandit with them clothes you're wearing."

"He's not a bandit!" Angelica's voice was lost in the rumble of a deep, booming voice as General Scott, having regained his poise, rode nearer.

"Quite a fracas, Rawlings. Care to tell us what it's all about?" His piercing eyes appraised Rodrigo in curiosity. "This man trying to kill me?"

"He *saved* your life, General. This Mex here had a knife and was going to slice you up a bit." The soldier nudged Garcia with the toe of his boot. "We've had a bit of trouble with some of them. Guerrilla fighter no doubt. Bastards just won't give up even if ole Santa Anna did. Been continuing their raids. Guess he thought if he killed you they'd have a better chance at getting their country back."

"Might very well have been true." He pulled himself up tall in his saddle. "I don't mean to appear to be bragging, but I have accomplished quite a feat, soldier. I've taken Mexico. Just might get me to the White House."

Looking down at Rodrigo, he tipped his cocked hat in gratitude and rode off. In another moment he was

399

enjoying a show of respect from his men, a grand, sweeping saber salute. Rodrigo and Angelica watched as he walked up the stairs of the National Palace of Mexico and disappeared inside.

"Thanks again." With a stiff nod of his head, the soldier renewed his strutting march down the street, following after his general.

Coming to Angelica's side, Rodrigo embraced her. "It is a very strange thing that I did, saving that man who I did not even know. He is by all that is holy just as much my enemy as Garcia. Why then did I interfere?"

"Because you are brave and bold and very, very wise. You were right in what you said. Had Garcia killed him there would have been a riot. Soldiers against civilians. The streets would have run red with blood. You saved more than just one man, my love, and I am very proud of you." There in front of a thousand eyes, she kissed him. Rodrigo stood with her clasped against him for a long, long while, savoring the taste of her lips.

"Mmm, I could come to like experiencing your gratitude." He pulled her body closer, until there was not even an inch that separated them. "Shall we do that again?"

Suddenly embarrassed by all the staring eyes, Angelica pushed away. "I think while it is quiet and the crowd has quieted down we should hurry to the inn."

Putting her hand through the crook of his arm, she guided him across the street and around the block to the inn. Pulling his hat low on his forehead, Rodrigo followed her inside. They were up the stairs just in time to avoid another melee, one right outside the inn's front door. A group of Californians tangled brutally with a band of American sympathizers. Shouts and the sound of rocks striking the door, the noise of broken glass accompanied Rodrigo's muffled curse.

"I'll show you the way." Angelica led him to the room

he and Luisa had once shared and knocked on the door.

"Who's there?" Luisa's voice.

"Open up, Luisa, it's Angelica."

"Angelica?" The door was flung open and Angelica wept up in Luisa's fond embrace. "I was so afraid . . ." Luisa gasped out as she saw Rodrigo, crying and laughing all at the same time. "Rodrigo! Rodrigo! Oh, dear brother, thought I'd never see you again. The last we heard Angelica was in Santa Anna's clutches and you were playing the part of a guerrilla in order to keep her safe. I have been so worried. So worried. There have been so many killed, so much confusion." She stepped back, blushing as Rodrigo's eyes roamed over the swell of her stomach. "Jesse and I are going to make of you an uncle. I hope you will be pleased." Her contrite expression revealed her need for his acceptance and blessing. She couldn't help but remember that her brother had violently opposed her marriage.

"Very pleased." Rodrigo's gaze sought out his red-haired brother-in-law as he held out his hand. "Much bad blood has passed between us, we have been on opposite sides, yet it is time to call a truce. You have taken care of my little sister these past months, amigo, and for that I am grateful."

"I love her very much." Jesse put his arm around his wife, smiling down into her eyes. "Perhaps loving her as we do, we can both tolerate each other. It's worth a try." Taking Rodrigo's profferred hand in a firm grasp, he grinned.

"Edward . . . ? What have you heard of him? Did he . . . did he . . . ?"

"Did I what, sister dear?"

Angelica's head whipped around at the sound of his voice, thankful that he was still alive. Her elation soon disappeared as she saw the upraised pistol he held in his hand. "Edward, no! Please! What are you doing?"

"Just a little insurance, Angie dear, that I can make a place of prominence among the winners of the war. Santa Anna was in such a hurry that he forgot his haste to execute me. The Americans freed me. For that I'm very grateful. Taking them the most notorious bandit in the region will be just a token . . ."

"No! You can't . . . you wouldn't." Her eyes were cold. "I mourned for you, I nearly gave up my own happiness to try and save your life. I wanted to come to you in prison, heal the anger between us. Now I wish Santa Anna had shot you."

"Well, he didn't." Edward gestured to three American soldiers who came up behind him. "This man is a bandit and a thief. His name is known throughout all of California as a murderer. Your general ought to be gratified to have him in his custody. I understand he was a guerrilla fighter. General Scott will no doubt reward us." He gave Rodrigo a shove. "Take him away."

Angelica watched helplessly for the second time as her brother ruthlessly and heartlessly destroyed her happiness.

Chapter Fifty

Angelica anxiously paced up and down the hallway of the National Palace, cursing her brother with every breath she took. It had been hours since Edward and the soldiers had taken Rodrigo away and though she had followed, had begged to see him, she had been denied. Visions of Rodrigo's fate danced before her eyes and she closed her eyes trying to chase them away. It was said that the Americans took great pride in hanging bandits. That was what one of the Texas Rangers who stood guard outside the palace had said. Dear God, she couldn't let that happen. Rodrigo had hoped that the Americans would be more merciful than the Mexicans or Californians. She had thought so too. Had they both been wrong?

Two soldiers were whispering together, winking at her and trying to get her attention. Turning her back, Angelica made it obvious that she held little interest in the two men. And yet . . . Seeing them gave her a sudden inspiration. General Scott. Perhaps he was the answer. Hadn't Rodrigo saved his life today? Surely then he would show some kind of mercy.

"I have to see General Scott immediately!"

"Have to see the general?" The young soldier laughed. "Have to wait in line then. Hell of a lot of people want to see him." He playfully tugged at a strand of her hair. "'Course, now if you were real friendly like I might be willin' to use my influence." He strutted about like a rooster. "I'm not without my influence."

"Please. I have no time to waste. It's a matter of life and death. My life." Without Rodrigo, she knew for all intents and purposes her life would be over.

"Your life?"

"Yes, my life." Angelica squared her shoulders and took a deep breath, taking a dangerous risk. "If you do not take me to see General Scott I will go on a hunger strike." She had heard of soldiers and sailors doing such a thing and their reasons had been far less desperate than hers. "I will do it on the very steps of the National Palace."

The two soldiers guffawed, certain they could call her bluff. "Well then, little lady, you had best get started 'cause you sure as hell ain't gonna see General Scott. Not while he's trying to get a peace settlement worked out."

"He'd have our heads on a silver platter for sure." The younger of the two soldiers walked around her slowly, eyeing her up and down. "Be a pity to let that pretty little body waste away. But if you were nice to me . . . really, really nice, I might . . ."

"No. I would never betray my husband that way." Angelica tried to keep her hand from shaking as she crossed herself. Dear God, give her strength. Could she do it? Would it really matter if she did? She had to think that it would. The Americans could hardly afford for the news to get out that one of their own had taken such a desperate step. They were trying to work out a peace treaty with the Mexicans, surely such a determined action would get the general's attention. If not, was she fully prepared to go through with it? Yes, her heart answered, she was. It was perhaps Rodrigo's only chance. There would be no escape this time and even if there was, it was time they had a chance for a normal life, one without constant running

404

and hiding. She knew that, above all, was what Rodrigo wanted too. A chance for a life together.

"Now you just go on out of here then. Buy yourself a pretty little dress." The young soldier jabbed the other in the ribs. "Ole Andrews and I know where you could get one real cheap." They broke out in gales of laughter, alluding to the fact that some of the soldiers had gone on a rampage, looting several of the market stalls. "Give you a good price."

Angelica eyed him coldly. "You call my husband a bandit? I call you and your kind thieves. You make me ashamed of my heritage. The people of Mexico City are not your enemies. Most of them are poor, as much victims of Santa Anna as you are. And yet you steal from them." Though they angrily turned their backs on her, at least she had the satisfaction of having stilled their laughter. Moving towards the door, she brushed off the muddied stone step so she could sit down and have at least a small measure of comfort as the hours dragged by.

Soldiers marched up and down the steps, some staring, some swearing, others threatening to drag her away, but not one of them tempted fate by creating a scene. Night came and Angelica tried to ignore her hunger and thirst, huddling up in a tight ball on the steps in an effort to get some sleep. She was awakened by the sound of hammering. Right in the center of the plaza a scaffold was being erected, a grim reminder of what would happen to Rodrigo if she was not successful.

Poor Margaro, she thought. His life was in danger as well. She wondered if he had heard any news about what had happened to his friend, or if he was still waiting patiently at the church expecting them to come back. Oh how she wished they'd never left the security of the adobe walls, but perhaps it would only have been a matter of time anyway. She and Rodrigo could not have spent their lives living under Father Diego's protection. Perhaps this day was meant to be.

The soldiers seemed proud of the scaffold. Many talked about the "example" it would set for all the "Mexes" who might get ideas. She heard there were mobs of disbanded Mexican soldiers and guerrilla fighters running loose in the city, fighting the occupying American troops from rooftops and from street corners. The thought of Rodrigo's life being taken in retribution for these acts made her shudder. Except for that one moment when he had gone with Santa Anna, he had been neutral in the war, as if his mixed heritage had not allowed him to take sides. Perhaps when all was said and done he was not as filled with anger and resentment as he once had been. She wanted to hope that her love had changed him.

"Gonna be a necktie party for someone," she heard a soldier say, and in horrified silence had looked in the direction of his pointing finger. She heard the grisly story of what had happened to a group of American deserters who had formed a battalion to fight on the side of the Mexican Army. Thirty of the captured soldiers had been forced to watch the fighting at Chapultepec with nooses tied around their necks as they hung from a gigantic scaffold erected on a nearby hill. The men were hung at the very moment of American victory, as soon as the Stars and Stripes had been put in place at the top of the castle.

"Dear God!" Would Rodrigo receive mercy when they had not even granted it to their own? She dared not even contemplate the matter. Willing herself to remain calm, she passed the time in remembering the blessed moments she and Rodrigo had had together. A lifetime of happiness for her in such a short span of time and yet she would not want to relive one moment, not even the weeks spent in the camp. She had found courage then and she would find it now.

Thunder rent the heavens, giving threat of a storm. "For God's sake, you're carrying out this threat of yours a bit too far." The young soldier wiped his sleeve across his freckled face as he looked down at her. "It's gonna rain. You'll get all wet. Don't want to see no woman catch a chill." He reached out to help her up but Angelica shook her head. "You are one stubborn woman!"

"I love my husband very much. Please, if I could only talk with General Scott, his life might be spared. That's all I'm asking, a chance to talk with him."

"That's all?" The soldier sighed. "And I suppose you really will sit out here in rain and lightning, starve yourself to death, and make us all look like horses' behinds if you don't get your way?" As she shood her head, he whistled in admiration. "That husband of your must be one hell of a good man to have earned such love and loyalty. At first I thought this was all a humorous game, but it's not very funny to me now." He sat down beside her. "I watched over you last night to make sure you didn't come to no harm. You see, I'm not such a bad sort after all."

"No, I don't think you are. I've learned that there's a little good in everyone."

"There sure as hell is a lot of good in you. Wish I'd seen you first." He winked at her. "Do you think I might have had a chance?"

Angelica's mouth turned up in a smile. "We'll never know, will we?"

The soldier grabbed her hand. "Come on. I may be running laps across the plaza for the next week for doing this, but somehow I can't do anything else. You've won my respect, ma'am." He pulled her to her feet. "I'll take you to the general."

Angelica was weak and a bit dizzy, but her elation at winning an audience with the general gave her the strength to follow the soldier up the steps and through the large double doors. He led her down the hallway, knocking at the thick wooden door they came to. A loud booming voice told them to come in.

"This better be important." Looking up from a stack of

407

papers, the general seemed more than a little irritated. "Well, what is it?"

"A . . . a woman to see you, sir."

"I can see that she's a woman, Sergeant. If this is some fal-dee-rawl matter I'll skin you both." He eyed Angelica up and down as if trying to remember her.

Angelica pushed her way inside, walking boldly up to his desk. "My husband is imprisoned in your soldiers' quarters. I'm asking you, no, begging you, for his release." At his astounded look she continued. "I'll come right to the point. Yesterday, when you were in the parade, a man tried to kill you. My husband saved your life by forcibly taking the knife from his hands. Now my husband is being held in your custody. Is that how you show your gratitude, sir?"

"What?" He stood up, sending the papers flying in a flurry about the room. "Andrews, what is the meaning of this?"

"He's a bandit, sir. An American fella had him arrested and brought here to us, but I . . . I think you ought to listen to her." His voice lowered to a whisper. "She's the one you might have heard rumors about who sat all night on the front steps and . . . well . . . I kinda thought she deserved a chance to be . . ."

"You thought?" In frustration he raked his stubby fingers through his brown hair. "We make the decisions here, soldier." He nodded to Angelica. "Well . . ."

Taking a deep breath, Angelica related the story as quickly as she could. She told about her brother's part in bringing guns and ammunition into Mexico, about his ruthless attack on the bandit camp. "He doesn't like Mexicans but he thought they were going to win so he sided with the Californians against his own. When he saw that he was wrong he changed sides without even blinking an eye. And it is upon the word of such a man that my husband now awaits justice."

"And is your husband a bandit?" General Winfield

408

Scott's expression was stern."

"Yes."

"And a guerrilla fighter?"

"He was blackmailed into going with General Santa Anna to save me. I was being held captive and might have been harmed had he not done as he was told. But his heart was never in this war. Rodrigo is of mixed ancestry, Mexican and Irish-American. I think he has long been involved in his own private war. A war within himself, but . . . but if such a brave man's loyalty was won he could be a great asset to you. I have heard about justice all my life and have been proud of coming to California from the United States. Now I'm asking you to give Rodrigo justice. We have been married for two years and in all that time he has never reverted back to being a bandit . . . and . . . and wasn't the death of his people at the hands of my brother punishment enough for any wrong he might have done up until then? It was a lie that took him from his rightful home and took away his wealth. He might never have been a bandit if he had received mercy and justice then."

Before the general could answer she told the story of Rodrigo's betrayal at a neighbor's hands, how a lie had been told to send him to prison so that it was possible to steal his lands. All through the story Winfield Scott remained silent, so silent that Angelica feared that her plea had failed.

"Have this Rodrigo Delgado O'Hara brought to me," he said at last. "I will hear from his own mouth just what has really happened."

In a very short time his order had been obeyed. Angelica ran to Rodrigo's arms, burrowing herself against him. Poised like the figures in a tableaux they faced the general together as Rodrigo related a similar story to what Angelica had already said.

"And were you pardoned would you promise to swear allegiance to the United States? To give me your word that you will . . . uh . . . forswear your banditing?"

"I would." Rodrigo reached up and took Angelica's fingers in his, bending to kiss the palm of her hand. When he looked up, his eyes glowed with a burning emotion. "I want to give my wife the world. Up to now I have given her very little except heartache and grief. I would give her the world, or at least a small hacienda." Rodrigo thought with a smile that he had not promised he would not make use of the gold he already held. At the church Margaro was protecting the large chest of gold coins that had once belonged to Santa Anna. Surely this American general would not mind.

"In California?"

"To live there is my greatest desire and I think it is also Angelica's wish." His fingers closed around her hand.

"Hmm." Rubbing his chin with his fingers, the general tapped his foot as he contemplated the matter. "You did keep that guerrilla scoundrel from stabbing me. That says something for you, my good man. Yes indeed it does. And with this matter coming to a close, I suppose a show of mercy might not be a bad idea." His voice lowered conspiratorially. "We'll just omit the matter of your saving my life, if you don't mind. My image and all that." He affected a pompous stance. "Been a lot of talk about my being a hero. I might even be President one day. They said I couldn't do it. Thought I would fail. Proclaimed this invasion would be a disaster. Well, I showed them. Now even the Duke of Wellington is chanting about my remarkable feat in this defeat of Mexico. Ah yes, perhaps I can afford to be merciful." He motioned to the young soldier. "Let this man go free . . . and . . . and, soldier."

"Yes, sir?"

"There's a ship in the harbor at Veracruz, the USS *Natchez*. I don't suppose it would hurt to give these two safe passage back to San Diego, do you?"

The young soldier was smiling. "Definitely not, sir."

410

Epilogue

Santa Barbara, Summer 1850

Angelica O'Hara stood on the veranda, shading her face against the sun's glaring rays as she watched the figure on horseback galloping over the crest of the hill. Her small two-year-old daughter was at her side, her auburn curls pressed against her mother's pink calico skirts. She was a beautiful child with all of Rodrigo's fire and temperament. A "daddy's girl" in every sense of the word, Angelica thought with a smile. More than a handful at times.

"Yes, it's Daddy, coming back from Aunt Luisa's and Uncle Jesse's place. If you're a good girl I'll just bet you he'll give you a piece of fudge your auntie has made," she said to the child who tugged at her skirts.

The last two years had been turbulent but happy. The happiest days of her life. Rodrigo's *rancho* had been regained through a miracle that Angelica could only attribute to God. Surely He did work in a wondrous way.

After arriving back in Santa Barbara, Angelica and Rodrigo had visited the Mission only to learn that a priest in a bordering town had been present at a dying man's bedside. The man had made a startling confession, duly witnessed by the man's family and the old Indian healer

411

and their friend Najalayogua. In the confession the man had admitted bearing false witness against Rodrigo for the sole purpose of obtaining his property. In truth, the death Rodrigo had been accused of had been an accident. Now with Margaro as his foreman, Rodrigo had reclaimed his lands and was making them prosper. All had been put to right, and Rodrigo had granted Jesse and Luisa a large tract of the land for their own hacienda.

For some of their neighbors things had not gone quite as well. All too often the Spanish land grants which had been recognized for so many years were ignored by the Americans streaming into California. Only last year with the discovery of gold droves of people flocked across the country to California in hopes of finding wealth. The United States government had been concerned but so far nothing could be done about the situation. Several prominent families who had been in the territory for generations had been evicted from their homes, starting a new generation of *bandido* gangs. The fact that Angelica and Jesse were Americans was perhaps the one factor that had assured the O'Haras their land.

As for the war, the Treaty of Guadaloupe Hidalgo had been signed February 1848, ceding Texas with the Rio Grande as the boundary between the United States and Mexico as well as New Mexico, California, and the rest of the western territories. President Polk had withstood the many demands for the annexation of all Mexico, and the American army of occupation returned home leaving Mexico to the Mexicans. As for Santa Anna, he had gone into exile again, claiming it was not the last time he would lead Mexico. He promised to be back again. Rodrigo believed that the people would take him back, though Angelica doubted it. Surely he had proved himself a coward to his people? It was puzzling, but then politics always was, she supposed.

And what of Edward? That was the most ironic of all. In

412

trying to harm Rodrigo and secure his well-being within the American-occupied California, Edward had sealed his own doom. He had boasted of being Santa Anna's right-hand man once too often and far too loudly. Evidence had been found against him, proving his sale of arms to the enemy. He had been branded on the cheek with a small "T" for traitor and sentenced to three years in an American prison.

"Ah, my two señoritas . . ." Sliding from his horse, Rodrigo gathered his wife and daughter into his arms, interrupting Angelica's musings. Together they walked up the veranda steps holding hands. "The *vaqueros* were breaking some wild horses. This Jesse just might not be so bad. A fine horseman." Wiping the dust from his boots, he stepped inside, only then taking a letter out of his pocket. "This came for you. It was delivered to Jesse and Luisa's hacienda by mistake. I think it is from your brother."

"Edward?" Could Angelica ever find it in her heart to forgive him? Her throat tightened as her eyes locked with Rodrigo's. "No, I will not read it. Not now. I have some special news for you that I hope will bring you joy. Later. I'll read it later. I don't want to spoil this moment." Taking his hand, she placed it on her stomach, letting him feel the fruit of her love for him. "There is going to be a brother for out little Elena." Suddenly feeling shy, she blushed.

"A son?" He couldn't disguise his pleasure. "Or a daughter perhaps?"

"I sense it, know somehow that this baby is going to be a *boy*." She laughed. "I think you deserve some competition. You have gotten much too sure of yourself in the last few months . . ."

"Oh . . . have I?" Suddenly his lips were on hers and she felt his arms go around her. A flame rose within her soul to answer the flame that burned in him. His eyes were filled with love, twinkling with amusement. "Too sure of

413

myself, am I?" Laughing, he traced the path of her blush with his lips.

"But I don't mind. I wouldn't want it any other way. I *am* yours, Rodrigo . . ." Her kisses showed him just how true that statement was. She belonged to him for now and all their tomorrows.

<u>FREE</u> Preview Each Month and $ave

Zebra has made arrangements for you to preview 4 brand new HEARTFIRE novels each month...FREE for 10 days. You'll get them as soon as they are published. If you are not delighted with any of them, just return them with no questions asked. But if you decide these are everything we said they are, you'll pay just $3.25 each— a total of $13.00 (a $15.00 value). **That's a $2.00 saving each month off the regular price.** Plus there is NO shipping or handling charge. These are delivered right to your door absolutely free! There is no obligation and there is no minimum number of books to buy.

TO GET YOUR FIRST MONTH'S PREVIEW...
Mail the Coupon Below!